RED LEGION
INTO THE R...

by FX Holden

Copyright © 2024
FX Holden

All rights reserved. No part of this book may be reproduced in any form, except in the form of brief quotations for review or academic use, without permission in writing from the author/publisher.

This book is a work of fiction. Any references to historical events, real people, or real locales are used fictitiously. Other names, characters, places and incidents are products of the author's imagination and any resemblance to actual events or locales and persons living or dead is entirely coincidental.

No AI training: Without in any way limiting the author's exclusive rights under copyright, any use of this publication to "train" generative artificial intelligence (AI) technologies to generate text is expressly prohibited. The author reserves all rights to license uses of this work for generative AI training and development of machine learning language models.

Acknowledgements: for their input and advice - Alain Martin, Barry Conroy, Barry Roberts, Ben Bell, Bob Imus, Bror Appelsin, Chris S, Glenn Eaves, Julie 'Gunner' Fenimore, Lee Steventon, Mike Ramsey, Mukund B, Paul C, Pete Black, Rob De Stefano, Simon Kimm and Thierry Lach.

With thanks to editor Nicole Schroeder, for 'putting the cheese around the holes'

Set in Garamond 14pt
Lexicon American English
109,000 words

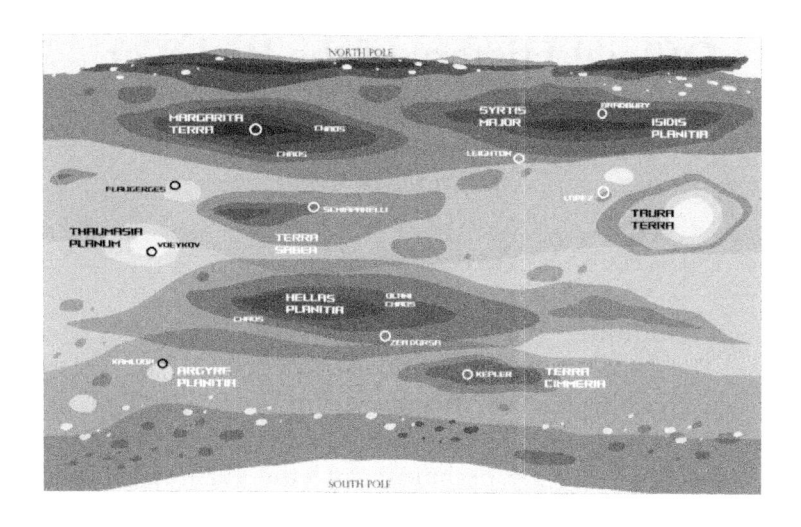

The Red: Mercator Projection

Official History of the Red War
(Interim)
Authorized by Imperator Tiberius Gracchus,
Commander in Chief,
Red Army
November 2134

Preludium

The history of humankind's settlement on Mars, colloquially known as 'The Red Planet', or simply The Red, was one of unbounded success from the arrival of the first humans in 2042 to the establishment of the first permanent international base in 2056.

Between 2056 and 2120, the population of The Red grew slowly, as scientific exploration gave way to the mining of rare earths and minerals, ores and gemstones, which were extracted and then transported to lunar foundries for processing. But after the Antimatter Wars and treaties banning antimatter production on Earth due to safety concerns, the drive to establish an antimatter forge on The Red was the basis for exponential growth.

From a permanent population in 2120 of 134 inhabitants, by 2133, there were 100,300 inhabitants on The Red, of which 34 percent were involved in the mining industry and operation of the antimatter 'Void Forge'.

The Void Forge began commercial operation in January 2133. The first 'Lilin' attack on a human settlement took place on June 14, 2133, at Kepler Mining Camp.

It is now known that Lilin scouts impersonating humans infiltrated the settlement some weeks in advance, and using an infectious viral vector, co-opted, or 'Turned', the settlement's population to fight for the Lilin. The residents of Camp Kepler then attacked a nearby transport hub and killed all workers. By the time mining company security was able to respond to the incident and regain control of Camp Kepler, the entire population of the camp had died in the fighting.

This was the start of the Red War. The nations of Earth responded by raising an army to defend human settlements. Since that first attack, more than 23 settlements on The Red have been 'Turned' and used to attack nearby targets. In each case, the settlements have been recaptured by the Red Army after bloody battles.

The Lilin, named by settlers on The Red after an ancient Jewish or Mesopotamian name for 'demon', have never communicated any demands to humankind. Their bodies are not made from elements known to humankind; therefore, they are believed to be aliens, not native to either The Red or even our solar system.

Their war aims are obscure but appear to intend to disrupt human settlement of The Red. Their war strategy can best be described as 'asymmetric' in that a small number of Lilin are able to 'turn' a large number of human inhabitants to serve as their armed forces, who then use our own strategies, tactics and weapons against us.

No protection has yet been identified for the viral vector believed to be used by the Lilin to co-opt human victims, but various physical barriers and defenses have been found to be effective at preventing Lilin infiltrators from entering human settlements. The Red Army's strategy has therefore been to achieve 'defense in depth', accompanied by assertive action to recapture any settlements which do fall to the Lilin.

Despite these challenges, be assured, the Red Army is winning the war against the Lilin!

Since its formation, the number of Red Army troops on The Red has grown to 350,000. Casualties have been moderate and sustainable. After several settlements fell to the Lilin early in the war, the loss of a settlement is now uncommon, and the Lilin rarely hold more than one or two settlements, which are quickly taken back. Mining productivity has returned to near pre-war levels, and the non-military population has stabilized at

80,000 residents. Antimatter production will soon be reaching pre-war targets. More than a million citizens of Earth are currently on waiting lists to qualify for work and residence on The Red, as soon as the military emergency is resolved.

Contents

Official History of the Red War 4
Guide to characters and ranks 9
Redside 11
Camp Flaugerges 13
Margarita Terra 22
'Boldly they rode, and well' 60
Isidis Planitia 105
Taura Terra 149
Still not Taura Terra 186
The *Real* Battle of Taura Terra 204
Syrtis Major 221
Terra Sabea 248
The vault 275
A miner walks into a bar 287
Argyre Planitia 307
Into The White 346
Epilogue 360
GLOSSARY 361

WHAT if you were offered this choice – life in prison or service in the Red Army?
Would you take it, knowing that you need to rack up 99 combat hours and only one in 20 recruits makes it out the other end alive?
Would you take it, knowing you are going to be fighting a mysterious foe who uses your own humanity against you?
Would you go, knowing none of the men and women you are going to serve with are completely sane, since you have to be insane to choose to serve Redside?
I did. And I'm keeping a journal about it, but given life expectancy Redside, this might be a very, very short story.

Guide to characters and ranks

LEGION PRAEDA (LEGION OF THE PREY)
Tribune Cillus Maximus Augusti, Commander Officer
Tribune Gaius Avidius Hersilia, Commanding Officer

Century II
Centurion Caius Mucius *'Mucus'* Scavola, Commanding Officer

Squadron II
Decanus Lucius *'Daedalus'* Cornelius, Commander, Mobile Command Vehicle II
Optio Tiberius *'Tiny'* Flavius, Sensor Operator, Mobile Command Vehicle II
Optio Claudia *'Ostrich'* Octavia, System Engineer, Mobile Command Vehicle II
Gregarius Linus *'Ballsack'* Vespasius, Tank Operator, Mobile Command Vehicle II
Gregarius Qintus *'Fatfoot'* Varro, Loadmaster, Mobile Command Vehicle II
Gregarius Lucretia *'Termite'* Drusila, Loadmaster, Mobile Command Vehicle II

Earth Sandcruiser (ES) Liquidator
Tribune Marcus Junius Silanus, Commanding
Centurion Antonius Aemilius 'Leper' Lepidus, Primus Pilae U(2IC)
Decurion Gaius Scribonius 'Bony' Curio, Executive Officer (XO)
Decanus Cornelia Lentulus 'Surefire' Sura

And various Lilin (Zenos) or Lilin-turned (Zeds).

GUIDE TO RED ARMY RANKS

Army (100,00 troops): commander, Imperator (Major General)
Legion (5,000 troops): commander, Legatus (Colonel)
Cohort (500 troops): commander, Tribune (Major)
Century (100 troops, 3 squadrons): commander, Centurion (Captain)
Squadron (30 troops/3 MCV crews): commander, Decurion (Lieutenant)
Squad (1 vehicle or 10 troops): commander, Decanus (Sergeant)
Specialist roles (sensor operator, engineer, fireteam leader): Optio (Corporal)
Legionnaire starting rank: Gregarius (Private)

Redside

Be warned. This is a story of blood, lust and fear. And it's going to challenge what you think you know, because there are two versions of the history of the Red War: the one *they* tell you, and the truth I am about to tell.

Now, the government will say I'm the one who's lying, but you have to ask yourself: What's in it for them? What do they gain from disputing my reality? Absolution, maybe?

Well, I do not absolve them. Let my words condemn them to the empty hell of Isidis Planitia for eternity.

Let's look at what they tell you is the truth.

Humankind is fighting against the Lilin, right? A terrifying alien enemy that has supposedly forgotten more about war than we'll ever learn. But what if the Lilin *aren't* who you've been told they are? And here's something else to think about. You've been told we're winning because, as each day passes, we are recapturing more and more of the territory we lost early in the war. But what if that's exactly what the Lilin *want*?

Alright, there it is. My bias is out there. I wear it on my scarred breast like the medals they never gave me. Look in my eyes, and you'll see bias burned into my retinas by the flash of EMP weapons. Judge me for it when you are at the end of this tale. Because I lived what I lived, and you can believe me or not, but you can't make me unlive it. In our reality, time is remembered backwards, but it is only lived forwards, so we can't undo what was done, only dread what is to come. I'm saying you can't trust the official media, the official announcements, the official 'histories' …

Even the name the government gave them: Lilin. After some ancient demon. No one here calls them that. Us grunts, we call them 'Zenos' (short for xenomorphs), because Lilin sounds too soft and nothing they do is soft. Same as we call the poor bastards the Zenos capture and infect 'Zeds' because the thing they most remind you of is zombies – not the stumbling, decaying type, but the mindless, follow-any-order-to-their-death (literally) type. They can still act human, still do the job they were trained to do, laugh and joke with their buddies, but only because they've been told to by a Zeno. All the while, they're infecting others, and Zedifying them. Until their bodies give up, and they die of their wounds, or exhaustion, starvation or thirst.

But you learn pretty quickly on The Red that there are worse things than dying. Worse things than fighting Zenos and Zeds.

Like service in the Legion Praeda: *Legion of the Prey.*

Camp Flaugerges

I'd been on The Red for six months before I saw any combat, which certainly sucked when the only way you could get back home was to rack up combat hours.

I'm assuming you are a sane, well-adjusted person and so know thankfully little about how a Redside Legion was organized, so I put a little guide at the front of this journal. There were 30 troops in a squadron, 100 in a century, 500 in a cohort, 10 cohorts in a Legion. It all added up to 5,000 legionnaires for the meat grinder. Except it never did, because thanks to the Zenos, we died quicker than we were replaced. Those in charge of the war preferred to create new units rather than reinforce the old ones. It gave the impression to citizens on The Blue that our forces were expanding – *a new Legion has been stood up Redside!* – when the reality was anything but.

I'll start my story after being busted from decurion, or lieutenant, down to the rank of gregarius, or private (there's a back story I'll tell you later), and re-educated or 'Reducated' by the sadists of Camp Voeykov. When they were done breaking me down, body and soul, I was sent to Camp Flaugerges to join the crew of Decanus Lucius 'Daedalus' Cornelius, Century II, Squadron II, Mobile Command Vehicle II.

As a decurion, I would have had three MCV commanders like Daedalus connected to me through my implants, stimmed to the gills, their 30 tanks all singing like a castrati choir. But in Voeykov, they disabled my implants, downgraded my stim module, and relegated me to being a simple tank operator inside a single MCV.

Sit in the tanker seat in Daedalus's MCV and maneuver just 10 Mark V tanks? Any low-level AI could do that as long as there was a human commander to approve lethal actions, so the graphene shortage must've been real bad if they were putting meat in the seat. Just one sign they were lying to us about how well the war was going.

Another sign was that Daedalus did not come to fetch me from a well-organized, well-appointed mustering station for new legionnaires, like you see in all the recruitment material. Daedalus fetched me from hospital. *Before* I'd even seen combat. Because I'd passed out from hunger and thirst while on night watch.

When I came to, with an IV drip in my arm providing just enough fluid and nutrients to keep my heart beating, Daedalus was sitting at the end of my bed, glaring, with the man I came to know as Fatfoot sitting next to him, asleep. Daedalus was in a decanus uniform, which was just as well, since his short, skinny frame might have been mistaken for a cadaver and sent for mulching if he wasn't. Fatfoot was a gregarius, like me, and just happy to be accompanying his decanus somewhere pointless where it was warm and no one was trying to kill him.

I could have killed them both. Right there. Drip in my arm and all. I was lying there thinking about it. The skinny one's neck in the crook of my left arm. Squeeze. Dead. The one with the club foot, a little more solid, but then again, asleep. Snap his head violently and goodbye, off to the mulcher with them both. You think about that kind of thing after six months of Reducation in Voeykov, I'm sad to say. And you don't think about the 'what next' because usually there isn't one.

But Daedalus was glaring at me as though his focused disdain had just woken me, and maybe it had.

'What was the name of the guy this one is replacing?' Daedalus asked, talking about me, not to me. He kicked the club foot of the man dozing beside him. The boot on the man's right foot was double the size of the boot on the left.

'Huh? Termite,' Fatfoot said. 'Our tanker.'

'Termite.' Daedalus nodded. 'That's right. *Forget* Termite.'

'Yeah, *forget* him.' Fatfoot nodded, in the universal oath of love for a fallen comrade. He immediately closed his eyes again.

Daedalus squinted at me, looking me up and down. 'You are no Termite,' he said. 'They told me you passed out while on guard duty. Our dear departed Termite could go three *days* without eating or drinking before he fell over,' he said. 'And I never had to go fetch him from no hospital.'

Unlike many others, I was still alive because I'd internalized everything I learned in Reducation. 'No, Decanus,' I replied automatically. 'I am not even the mud in the crack of the ass of legionnaire Termite, and if you asked me to locate his mulch and scoop it together and kiss his mulched ass, I would have to refuse, because I am not worthy.'

He nodded with satisfaction. 'Too right you aren't,' he said. He kicked Fatfoot's foot again. 'Come on, we're going.'

Fatfoot woke, looked at me with one eye still closed – his left, probably because his left brain was still sleeping while his right was weighing me up. 'Are we taking him back with us, or you want me to pillow him?' He was offering to smother me with a pillow, in case his commander wanted to go for a different replacement for their dead comrade Termite. I almost welcomed the thought of him trying.

'You want to go out today short a tanker?' Daedalus asked him.

He thought about it. 'No,' Fatfoot decided.

'So we take him with us,' Daedalus said. He threw me a kit bag, and I weakly swung my legs out of the bed and began gathering my uniform, which someone, probably a nurse, had folded and put on a chair.

Daedalus watched me. 'We used to have an AI did your job,' he said. 'Before Termite. If we could get the graphene chips, you wouldn't be here.'

'No, Decanus,' I told him. 'I understand.'

'Yeah, no, you don't,' he said. 'That AI was a better tanker than you'll ever be. But politicians on The Blue hate AI, and graphene is rare on The Red, while meat isn't,' he said.

'Your tanks are Mark Vs. I was trained in Mark Vs. I'll fit in,' I told him.

'Shut up, meathead,' he said. 'You survive to next week, you can tell me how damn smart you are. Until then, you're just another stain on the inside of my MCV I'm going to have to wipe off soon, like Termite.'

'Forget Termite.' Fatfoot nodded.

But I *had* trained on Mark V tanks. Before Voeykov and Flaugerges. Before Antonia. Like I said, I'd shipped Redside having gained the rank of decurion, before I was busted back to gregarius because of Antonia. Or, well, for deserting because of Antonia. Remember her name.

In the hospital, I couldn't find my socks. Someone had probably stolen them. So I put my feet into my boots and gathered up my uniform, still dressed in the hospital gown. Daedalus wasn't going to wait for me to get dressed; he was already heading down the infirmary corridor to the exit.

The chubby man walking beside me held out his hand to shake mine. 'Fatfoot,' he said.

'Linus Vespasius,' I told him.

'Yeah, we don't use those names here,' he said amiably. 'Daedalus doesn't like it. You got a nickname?'

'I had a nickname in Voeykov,' I told him. 'Scabrous.' I said it proudly, like it was a badge of honor. 'Thanks for coming to get me.'

'Shut up, you two,' Daedalus said, and looked over his shoulder at Fatfoot. 'And don't learn his stupid name yet. I keep telling you that, don't I?' He stiff-armed the door out into the tube connecting the infirmary to the next dome. 'It's bad luck. For him too. Look what happened to Termite. We learned his name, now he's mulch.' He spat. 'Screw Termite.'

Walking wasn't easy for Daedalus, with his short, skinny frame. The magnetic soles on his boots were too sticky for his spindle legs, and he had to slide them forward to break their grip so he could lift them, which gave him a sliding, shuffling walk. Fatfoot didn't have the same problem, but his club foot didn't help his gait, so he walked with a clop-thud, clop-thud beside me.

'He don't mean nothing by that,' Fatfoot said, with his hand theatrically covering his mouth. 'We lost two tankers already this Maius. He gets attached.'

'Termite was a good guy, huh?' I asked him.

He shrugged. 'I don't know. I had, like, maybe two conversations with him. He bragged he was sentenced to Praeda for diddling a Centurion's wife. But that was BS. He died before I could find out the real reason, but here it's like you don't ask, so you have to wait for a guy to tell you, and guys don't live long enough usually.'

'Can it, I said,' Daedalus barked. We were at the entrance to the hangar dome where the machines were parked up. There were Mark Vs – semi-autonomous escort tanks – and a bunch of MCVs, which doubled as troop carriers, loading legionnaires. Ten to every MCV, plated up, ready for consumption.

Praeda legionnaires, tip of the spear. First in, last out. First-grade mulch.

'Ah, we going somewhere?' I asked. I was still in my hospital gown and sockless boots. I coughed wetly.

Daedalus stopped and looked at me with his head tilted like he was sizing up a prize goose. 'Of course we are going somewhere. You think we came and got your diseased ass out of sick bay because we need a fifth guy for poker, Gregarius?'

'No, Decanus!' I replied.

'No. Find some thermals when we get to the vehicle park. I can see your stringy ballsack through that gown.' He gestured at Fatfoot. 'When you're ready, you can help Fatfoot with the loading. We're headed out to Margarita Terra.'

Fatfoot lost his casual demeanor. He looked like a man who had just trodden barefoot in fresh dung. 'Ah, crud,' he said.

'Yeah, ah crud,' Daedalus said. 'Let's see who is going to die today.' He nodded toward me. 'My money is on ballsack here.'

I suited up and followed Fatfoot into the MCV, which was the split-level hovercraft type, with four of us in the cockpit up top in the bulbous nose and a loadmaster plus 10 legionnaires down in the meat locker. Decanus Daedalus was the commander, Gregarius Fatfoot the loadmaster. Optio Tiny was on sensors and Optio Ostrich was engineer, meaning she ran around fixing the million things on the MCV that were fubar on any vehicle after two years on The Red. And I was Tanker, my job to run the 10 machines that were circling around protecting our ass as we moved out of the ZoC to probe the Zenos' defenses at Margarita Terra – a base that had been ours until the Zenos Turned it. After I took my seat in the cockpit, I found out it wasn't the first probe in the direction of Margarita Terra.

'Hit us 60 klicks from their perimeter, first time. Near Margarita Chaos,' Tiny said. He was bigger than me, could barely fit into his seat. But he had nimble hands. Sensors and tanks sat side by side, so we were rubbing shoulders.

'We tried to neutralize this ZoC more than once before?' I asked. We were still pulling juice for our batteries from the fusion pump, so we still had a few minutes before we went 'feet Red'.

'Two times,' Tiny said. The rising whine from the capacitors meant he had to shout because none of us had our skull caps on yet. You didn't want to do that until you absolutely had to because if you were in the virtual and everyone else was still in the real, one, they couldn't hear you, and two, because you were blind to what was happening in the cockpit around you, they would mess with you and nothing you could do about it until you got your skull cap off again and had to deal with whatever dumbass prank they played on you.

'How many combat hours you guys got then?' I asked him.

He looked up, biting a lip, like he was doing complicated math. 'Me, 18 hours 40, but I lost some time in the stockade.' He looked around the cockpit. 'Ostrich, she's on about 20, at least. Daedalus and Fatfoot say they have double that, but time resets from the moment you join the Legion Praeda, so in Praeda time, they're about 20.' He picked up his skull cap, waiting for Daedalus to give the order to go virtual. 'How about you?'

'Zero,' I told him. Ninety-nine combat hours was the magical number that got you a pension and a shunt Earthside. Or a half pension in our cases, since we were convicts. We could shoot for a full pension, but that meant surviving 149 hours. Since the average survival rate for a legionnaire in the Legion Praeda was 19 combat hours, only crazies tried for the higher target. Especially with the way the Red Army counted 'combat'. Time in combat started the moment you came under fire and stopped the moment you stopped returning fire. So if you got shot and lay bleeding out in the bottom of a crater, even if there was still a firefight going on all around you? Bad luck, buddy; you did your bleeding on your own time. It didn't count against your combat hours.

He frowned. 'I don't think I heard you. How many?'

'*Zero.* Never been in a firefight, never even been outside a perimeter except on repair duty.'

'Crud. Don't tell anyone that,' Tiny said, looking worried. 'Lie.'

'Daedalus must know. He's got access to my file.'

'Daedalus won't read your file, I guarantee you. He says looking at our files is pointless since we're all going to die.' Tiny grinned. 'Except himself, of course. He's convinced he'll make 99. Says he was close when he got sentenced, so why not again?'

'Pulling the plug. Power at 87 percent. Good as it'll get,' Ostrich said. She hit a key on the console in front of her, and the capacitor whine fell away as the turbines at the back of the MCV began their howl. Thanks to the insidious sands of The Red, the nuclear-powered turbines in any MCV needed full-time care and attention so they didn't crap out. Ostrich had a broad face, jet-black stubble on her head and almond eyes. She'd barely looked at me as I came aboard and hadn't bothered to introduce herself, which told me all I needed to know about my chances of making it through the next few hours alive.

From down in the payload bay, I heard Fatfoot's muffled voice. 'Meat locker is buttoned up. We're good to go down here.'

I turned to my own console, which showed nothing right now but a single colored light for each of our 10 tank wingmen. They were all green. 'Tanks are go.'

Daedalus had a face that was all knuckles and wrinkles. It was impossible to guess his age, but if he'd done more than 100 patrol hours, like he claimed, it meant he had probably been Redside for at least a year. The fact they all had so many hours but were here with me in Legion Praeda told me they hadn't joined long before I had, or they'd already be dead.

Daedalus whirled a finger in the air to signal us all to go virtual. I pulled on my skull cap, the air in front of me filling with holographic buttons, dials and gauges. 'Flaugerges Control, MCV II, five crew and a belly full of harm, ready to dust,' Daedalus said, calling for permission to take off.

'MCV II, you are cleared to dust. Die well.'

Die well. How many times would I hear that salutation? I came to love it. After all, you only heard it if you were still alive. Lying eviscerated in a crater with a carbonized comrade beside you, no one ever told you to 'die well', did they? They were usually too busy screaming. 'Die well' was something only the living were greeted with, those who were about to die but weren't in the process of it ... yet.

Margarita Terra

The turbines on the hovercraft roared, and it lifted on its skirt. They had to work hard in the thin atmosphere of The Red. When he was satisfied he had full thrust, Daedalus pushed his twin sticks forward, and the fans behind us pushed us out of the hangar and into a flying maelstrom of red sand. MCVs I and III were ahead of us – we could see their dust clouds – but not moving fast, and we quickly reeled them in. Once we were moving at a decent clip, the dust started flowing behind instead of around us, and I could see the desertscape ahead. We were heading out of our crater to a plateau about 50 klicks ahead. Climb out, get across the plateau; we had to get down another crater on the other side and then 100 klicks farther in before we got to the perimeter of what used to be Margarita Terra.

Well, I guess it still was, technically. More accurately, it used to be *our* Margarita Terra, but now it belonged to the Zenos. I had overheard guards talking about how the war was going while we were in Voeykov. *It's going well; I hear we retook Camp Kepler. It is going badly; we lost the Olani Chaos and Margarita Terra.* I had only been Redside for half a year and the names were unfamiliar. There were no front lines – that much I knew. There were ZoCs, or Zones of Control, and around these, we had perimeters. The main settlements inside a ZoC were called Camp This or Camp That. Most were military; some industrial, mining or agricultural, occupied by us dumb legionnaires, the settlers and the camp followers we were supposed to be guarding. But they moved us from battle to battle so fast, we never had time to even register where we were.

In the old wars, I heard soldiers spent a lot of time in trains or trucks, getting moved from place to place and doing nothing. Wheeled transports that traveled across the surface Earthside, and I imagine rolling though beautiful fields of mud or swamp. You could sleep in those transports, I bet, your cheek against the shoulder of your fellow gregarius, waking to find you were somewhere else where all you had to do was dig holes, or peel vegetables, or stack boxes, and nothing terrifying ever happened until the few rare times it did. And you died, and that was it. Blissful darkness.

Not this eternity of ZoCs, one merging into the other, Terra This or Terra That, deplaning from your shunt and getting a leg sawn off or an organ punctured and then back to the ZoC for *medicinae incrementum*, your leg or your kidney speed-grown but not the full-nerve growback, because that took too much time, and you were needed back on the perimeter.

Where was I? Oh, right. Margarita bloody Terra.

'I got a good idea,' Ostrich said after we'd been driving for a while. 'We can just call the new guy Termite.'

'How is that a good idea, Optio Ostrich?' Daedalus asked, perched at his controls on a raised deck behind me. 'Look at the guy. That's disrespecting Termite.' He saw the look on my face. 'No offense.'

'No, it's a way of *honoring* Termite,' Ostrich insisted. 'We can call all the replacements Termite. That way we'll always remember Termite and we don't have to bother to learn a new name every time one of them gets mulched.'

'Hey,' I said, annoyed. 'I'm right here.'

'I like it,' Tiny said, and I gave him a dirty look too. 'No offense,' he mumbled, looking away.

'Me too,' Daedalus said. He waved a hand in the air as though issuing an edict. 'Hencewise, all replacements shall be known as Termite, in honor of our dear departed crewmate, God curse his soul.'

'I thought Termite was a woman?' Tiny said, frowning.

Daedalus frowned back at him, opened his mouth to reply, then changed his mind, fixing his gaze on me instead. 'Ballsack, from this day forward …'

'My nickname is Scabrous,' I told him.

'Was. From this day forward, Ballsack, you shall be known as … Termite!' he announced. 'Termite is dead. Long live Termite. Three cheers, crew!'

'Hoozah, hoozah, hoozah!' they all yelled in unison, pumping their fists.

Termite was a better nickname than Ballsack, though not as good as Scabrous, if you asked me. Also, I saw a small flaw in the idea. 'Wait, what if I'm not the one who gets killed? What if one of you does? Are we going to have two Termites?'

Tiny and Ostrich all looked at me like it was the stupidest question in the world. Daedalus at least gave it some thought.

'No. If someone else dies, you can go back to being Ballsack, and the new guy …'

'Or girl …' Tiny added. 'Or other.'

'Or girl, or other … You get your old nickname back and the *replacement* will be called Termite.' He looked pleased at having decided the matter.

'I don't think that …' I started to say, seeing another flaw in the logic – if the intent was to avoid having to learn new names – but I shut my trap. Arguing logic with this crew was going to be a losing game for all.

It had been decided anyway, and the conversation moved on.

Tiny had the easiest job in the cockpit since the sensor systems were almost completely automated and monitored by an AI. All he had to do was make sure the AI was online and then relay information to the other members of the crew if the AI picked up anything on seismic, infrared, radar or optical sensors.

Why was a human even needed? Well, you should know, but I'll assume you weren't paying attention in school. After the AI Rebellion of 2130, after which the most advanced AIs were wiped, laws were brought in limiting the ability of AI to self-actualize and mandating that any system that used AI had to also have a human in the loop watching over it. Even if that human barely qualified as intelligent themselves, like Tiny.

Daedalus had cockpit windows up at his eye level, but we just looked into VR console displays and the tactical map projected on the flat angled wall of the cockpit in front of us.

It showed our progress as we caught up to the other MCVs in our squadron. We were all moving into line abreast formation for the coming assault, spaced about 5 klicks apart. Sorry, not assault, 'probe.' Our MCV was out on the left wing – last to join, most exposed position. The price of being slow out the gate.

'Tanks into chevron,' Daedalus ordered.

I punched some icons, putting our escorting tanks into a wedge-shaped formation ahead of us, like a shield. It left our back exposed, but we were riding right inside the tip of the wedge, so our tanks gave us cover ahead and on our flanks. The Mark V had pretty good anti-air defenses too, so we were protected against anything except an attack from down low, right on our six.

Knowing this MCV had taken a hit in the last attack and lost a crewman, the shield around us didn't seem as convincing to me as it should have. But that was the thing about this war – you weren't fighting some unknown enemy with unknown tech. You were fighting your own guys, and your own tech. Too smart to die dumb. Zeds, sure, but still our guys, using our strategies, tactics, weapons and …

'Hey.' I turned to Tiny, keeping my voice low, so only he could hear it over the whine of our turbines. 'How did you guys get hit last time?'

He leaned over. 'It was in the middle of Margarita Chaos. We moved into attack formation, nothing on sensors, tanks in chevron, then they were all around us. We figure they had their tanks buried or in defilades, where sensors couldn't see them. They took out two of our flank escorts, and we took a shot in the port side from an airborne plasma gunship.' He pointed to the plate next to my seat, which appeared newly replaced. 'Penetrated the armor just enough to burn a hole in Termite, but not me.' He grinned. 'I just got a tan.'

'Then you pulled back?'

'Hell yeah. Flew like geese from winter.'

I looked at my tactical map. Margarita Terra was a huge cratered zone spanning several latitudes that anywhere else would have been called a sea. A 'Chaos' was any zone inside a Terra where wind or ancient watercourses had worn away the surface to form valleys and mesas. If it was old enough, the mesas would have been ground down to hills, but inside the Margarita Chaos, they were still deep valleys and towering mesas. Ideal defensive terrain, if your ZoC was on a mesa, and the only approach was by air or through one of very few passable valleys. Which the ZoC at Margarita Terra was. An air assault had been tried, and failed. So a ground assault was planned, and our cohort was probing the enemy's ground defenses to work out how well defended the valleys were, from various directions.

Twice so far, they'd proven very well defended. I thought about what Tiny said. 'Permission to raise a stupid question, Decanus?' I shouted over my shoulder to Daedalus.

'I'd expect nothing else,' Daedalus said. 'Amuse us all.'

'Why are we repeating the same tactic that didn't work last time?'

Daedalus sighed. 'Because we are the Legion Praeda, Termite. *Born to Die*. Our job isn't to win this coming battle; it is to force the enemy to show themselves, their force, their weapons, their tactics, so that our AIs can watch and learn, and the real soldiers can come in after us and take this ZoC and all the glory.'

'So what did we learn from the last defeat?' I asked.

'We learned to bring more harm,' he said. 'Which is why we have a bellyful of meat. Soon as the enemy appears, we halt so they can dismount and deploy close-in defensive weapons. It won't help much; if we survive, we are still going to withdraw in disarray with our panties on fire, but we'll have learned a little more. It all adds up.' He nodded ahead of him. 'And we are making our ingress from a different direction. Plus, we have nothing to fear today because our great commander, Tribune Augusti, has joined this scouting mission, which means we will run at the first sign of danger. That concludes today's lesson in grand strategy. Eyes front and execute your orders, boy.'

I kept my eyes front, but as for executing my orders …

We were in a wide valley, towering mesas on each side of us but plenty of flat territory left and right of our formation. Without asking for permission, I thinned out the tanks on my right flank, where we had cover from our wingman, and left only two on that side. Daedalus was so occupied with holding the MCV in formation he didn't notice. We had drones in the air ahead and around us – two of the MCVs in the formation were drone motherships, not pushing tanks. But that hadn't helped us spot the ambush last time, apparently. It was our left flank that was vulnerable, and where they had taken the plasma round from last time. I put the three tanks I freed up onto our left flank, and pushed them well ahead of us, so they were more like scouts than defenders. If there were enemies buried in the sand up ahead, I wanted to find them before they bushwhacked us.

Tiny noticed though. The MCV's sensors were networked, so he was not only looking at data from the sensors on our own vehicle but from every vehicle in the line, their tanks, the escort drones overhead and, of course, our own tanks. He saw what I was doing, shot me a glance, but said nothing.

'Alright, on your toes, people,' Daedalus said through clenched teeth, which didn't exactly inspire confidence. 'This is the range from the ZoC where we caught it last time.'

But the moment came and went, and the breath I'd been holding without realizing escaped in an embarrassing wheeze since I still had some kind of infection in my lungs, which I'd brought with me from Voeykov.

Tiny looked over, kind of disgusted, opened his mouth to say something, then everything started happening at once.

One of the tanks I'd pushed out on our far-left flank exploded. I'd been watching in that direction through a hull-mounted camera on our MCV, and I saw a bright ball of light, and the icon for that tank simply disappeared from my screen. Every tank had its own 360-degree cameras, and I jumped to its nearest buddy, scanning around it. Smoke rising, then *wham*. I lost that tank too. Swapped to the next in line – saw no drones, no advancing armor or infantry, just sand, and now flame and smoke.

'Mines!' I decided. 'Minefield ahead!'

'Brace for crash stop!' Daedalus called, and relayed my report to the Centurion in the lead MCV, one of the drone motherships. We skidded to a halt, as I pulled my remaining tanks back into a tight ring around us.

'This is bad,' Tiny muttered. 'We're sitting still. That's what they want … We have to keep moving.'

'I know that, legionnaire!' Daedalus said, frustration in his voice. 'But the whole cohort has stopped. I need a direction to drive in, dammit.'

Sure enough, an alarm sounded inside the cockpit.

'Incoming artillery, brace for impact!' Daedalus yelled, speakers in the hold below relaying his warning so that the soldiers in our payload bay could tighten their harnesses, close their eyes, and pray. 'Screw this,' he said. 'Hang on down there, Fatfoot!' He pulled his control sticks straight back, and the hovercraft started sliding backwards, before he split the controls, keeping one turbine at full forward thrust and the other at full reverse so that our MCV spun on its axis and pointed back the way we had come. Then he slammed both sticks forward, and we were accelerating away from the ambush.

I pulled my tanks in even tighter. The shells coming toward us would be precision guided, with terminal optical homing capabilities. We needed every anti-air system on our tanks close enough it could put a shield of lasers, jamming energy and lead over our heads that no artillery could penetrate.

Daedalus was jinking the MCV left and right, which may have made him feel better, but just made me feel like throwing up and probably would have just amused the incoming artillery salvo, if the AI controlling it had a sense of humor.

'Impact in five,' Tiny yelled. 'Three … two … one!'

I was watching through the lenses of one of my tanks, but Daedalus had a clear view through the cockpit glass to the blue-brown sky above. And he ducked as the sky lit with incandescent white light and the inside of the cockpit strobed with explosion after explosion as the tanks' multilayered defenses caught the projectiles in mid-flight. At least one of the shells aimed at us made it through though, and it slammed into the sand just behind us, sending a cloud of dust into the air and shoving us forward like a child shoving a toy car.

'Miss!' Tiny yelled gleefully.

But then the cloud of sand got sucked into our turbines and the portside turbine started coughing. 'Shutting down port turbine!' Ostrich yelled. 'Starboard is at 80 percent thrust and falling!'

'Shut 'em both down and do a reverse blow,' Daedalus ordered her. 'Clear the intakes.'

'But we'll be …'

'Just do it!'

Ostrich killed both engines, and the hovercraft lost lift, settling onto its skirts before nosing down to a shuddering stop. If there was a second artillery salvo inbound, we'd be toast. Daedalus had bet everything that there wasn't.

Ostrich watched her engine readings, waiting to restart the turbines in reverse-thrust mode to try to blow the sand out of the engine intakes. It wouldn't repair the damage that had already been done to delicate blades and compressors, but it might be enough to get us moving again.

It was suddenly quiet. Just the tick tick tick of hot engines cooling in the cold outside atmosphere.

'Come on, come on, come on …' Tiny whispered to himself.

'Running back blow,' Ostrich said, as the turbines whined to life again. The MCV shook, not lifting off the ground, since all the air generated by the turbines was being directed back through the air inlets. A cloud of fine sand like a marsh fog wrapped around the hovercraft and the tanks huddled around it like ducks around their mother.

Daedalus was on the line to the command vehicle. 'Tiny, sitrep,' he ordered. 'Command wants to know if we can rejoin, and I want to know if there is anyone to rejoin with.'

I could almost hear the gears whirring in Daedalus' skull. I was learning this crew were survivors. Bloody minded, never give up as long as there is the smallest chance, total desperados. Assuming we could restart our engines, Daedalus was weighing up whether to rejoin the formation and risk dying farther down the line or declare our MCV non-combat capable and risk a death penalty court-martial if we weren't believed.

Tiny worked his console and refreshed the tactical image on the screen. 'Three MCVs totaled, two badly damaged, six with light damage, including us.'

'Don't jinx us,' Ostrich said. 'We aren't moving yet.'

'Only three down, eh?' Daedalus said, scratching his chin. 'That's *way* better than I expected.'

'Or mother-fingering worse,' Ostrich said. 'Depending how you look at it. They had us dead to rights but most of their artillery missed? Something stinks. Can we vote on this?'

From down in the meat locker, Fatfoot had been listening in. 'I vote we take a vote too.'

'No voting,' Daedalus said. 'When you are a decanus you can do everything by a bloody vote, see how long you last.'

Ostrich went back to work. 'Back blow complete. You want I restart the turbines in drive mode?' she eventually asked. The turbines ran down again until they were still. It was a fork in our fate line. Restart, and if the engines were able to deliver enough power, rejoin the formation and the battle, or leave the engines shut down, call them dead and drop out of the fight, risking a death penalty.

'We already dodged the guillotine once when we lost Termite and pulled out,' Daedalus said.

'We were on fire, with a dead tanker!' Tiny reminded him.

'I don't think they'll be too worried about that detail when they review our record,' Daedalus told him. 'If we play dead now, they'll see two engagements, two withdrawals. We won't get a third chance.' He whirled a finger at Ostrich. 'Spool 'em up.'

She punched some icons on her console, and the engines began winding up again. To be honest, I wasn't sure whether I wanted them to work or not. I was biting my lip so hard I tasted blood. But then it was taken out of my hands. Ostrich looked at some readouts. 'I can give you 50 percent on the port turbine, 70 on the starboard. Any more than that, the vibration will rip the blades off, and we're done.'

'I'll take what I can get,' Daedalus said. 'Moving both throttles to 50 percent. Let me know if anything starts shaking loose once we're moving.' He got onto his radio and sent word to the formation that he was rejoining, at half speed, then let Fatfoot and the grunts in the payload bay know too.

I didn't hear any cheering.

We regrouped with the other MCVs. Not too close, in case there was a follow-up artillery barrage, but close enough we could see across the line. Three machines were just smoking wrecks. A few of their tank escorts had been knocked out too. So that was 30-plus casualties right there. There were five other MCVs down on their skirts, knocked out, legionnaires milling around them, treating wounded or moving combat-capable troops to other MCVs. On the brighter side, it meant about 40 MCVs and about 470 troops still alive. We could squeeze another 10 legionnaires and their kit in our meat locker, standing room only, but it seemed we weren't needed to take on extra troops from the crippled vehicles because we weren't called any closer.

Then I found out why.

Daedalus was arguing with someone on the radio, then leaned back in his chair and punched the armored cockpit glass over his head with a gloved hand. He didn't yell or scream, didn't say anything at all for a minute. Then he got on the tween deck intercom. 'Attention passengers, this is your pilot speaking. Unfortunately this is as far as we will be taking you today. We hope you have enjoyed your trip with Squadron II Transport Services and kindly ask you to think of us for all your future combat transport needs. Please check the deck between your feet and overhead lockers for all explosive ordnance, and remember to take it with you as you leave the MCV.' He switched back to the crew channel. 'Fatfoot, report when you are ready to drop the ramp.' There must have been a comment from the decurion commanding the legionnaires in the meat locker because Daedalus barked into his microphone. 'Yeah, well, with respect, sir, consider yourself lucky to even be alive, for as long as that lasts!'

'Some people.' Ostrich shook her head. 'Never happy.'

I was more interested in what was coming than what had just happened. So was Ostrich. 'What's the deal, boss? We're still combat capable. So why are we emptying the meat locker?'

Daedalus didn't answer straightaway, just sat looking balefully out at the sand. Then he sighed. 'Well, the tribune, in his wisdom, wants to continue the mission, but he doesn't think we are as capable as we think we are. He says we'll just hold everyone up, so while the others are redistributing the meat among themselves, we're supposed to head for the hole that Termite's tanks blew in the minefield and see if there is a way through.'

'Aw, that ain't fair.'

'That's exactly what the Zenos want us to do!' Tiny complained. 'It'll be another kill zone. They'll have their artillery zeroed on that gap now, just waiting for us to push through it!'

'Air defense took down two surveillance drones in the firefight,' Ostrich said, pointing at a kill/loss summary on the tactical screen. 'They might not have any more.'

'But they probably do,' Tiny moaned.

Daedalus was ignoring the whining, listening to his intercom. 'Good. Drop the ramp, Fatfoot.'

When every last pound of meat and high explosive had been disgorged, Daedalus ordered the ramp up and pushed forward on his sticks.

'You want one tank out front, the rest in trailing mode?' I asked him.

'Hey, Termite can read minds,' he said. 'Yeah, exactly what I want. That minefield could be 10 klicks deep for all we know. I want some metal out in front of us just in case.'

The valley hit another mesa about 10 klicks ahead of us, and it seemed unlikely the enemy would have mined both arms of the fork as well, so we figured the minefield would go some of the way to the fork, then stop. I moved one tank out to sweep 100 meters out, and the remaining six followed along behind us in a straight line like a row of ducklings. Not good for avoiding another artillery salvo, but it was a good idea to be driving in each other's tracks inside a minefield. I programmed the lead tank to make slow, zigzagging turns inside 6-meter 'guardrails' since the tank was only 3 meters wide and our MCV was 6. We needed the tank to squirrel along in front of us like it was deliberately trying to get blown up. There was still a chance though that we would go over an area of ground our pathfinder tank had not, and there would be a mine under it. So put two tanks out front, you say? We didn't have that many left, remember?

Minutes later, we passed the two smoking wrecks of the tanks that had hit the mines. As we drew level with the second, Daedalus halted our MCV. 'Alright, boys and girl, grab your gonads and say your prayers.'

He keyed his radio mic. 'Command, MCV II/II, moving forward.'

I read how old-time tank crews driving through possible minefields used to take off their helmets and sit on them to protect their crown jewels. We didn't have helmets, just skull caps with electrodes that clamped onto our shaved heads. The cockpit was supposedly an armored shell inside a double-hulled armored body fitted with reactive armor, but that hadn't been effective against a plasma bolt fired at point-blank range, as the last Termite had found out. So whether it would be effective against a buried, upwardly-firing penetrator charge was doubtful. We knew from exercises the most likely scenario was the mine would disable our 'blowers' and shred our skirts so that we thumped onto the ground, inert, where we would make a juicy artillery or air attack target.

So yeah, prayers were probably the best protection we could hope for. But just in case, we all pulled out the breastplates from our body armor, sat on them, and held our breath.

The meters ticked past, with Tiny giving us a running progress report. 'Two klicks … 2 k 20 … 2 k 40 …'

'How deep we usually sow a minefield?' I asked.

'Two to five klicks,' Daedalus said. 'The deeper the field, the lower the density. So if we are still in the field now, the chances are lower we'll …'

We heard the explosion through our hull despite the thin atmosphere, and the flash of light ahead of us was bright enough to fill the cockpit. Daedalus heaved the MCV to a halt but left our turbines running.

'Tank 3 down,' I said, unnecessarily.

Tiny scratched his skull. 'I *hate* this crud. Give me death over this, any day.'

'You may still get that wish,' Daedalus said. 'Termite, bring another tank around, close as you can to the trail we already made. Choose a ground attack unit. I want to save our last air defense tank in case this is another ambush.'

I pulled one of my tanks out of the line behind us. The MCV left a rocky trail underneath it where it had blown the sand away from the small rocks that covered the surface, like a gravel road swept clean by a giant leaf blower. But to get ahead of us, the tank I selected would need to go around, where neither we nor our last pathfinder tank had swept.

I piloted the tank manually using directional icons on my console, keeping it as close as I could to our hull and the swept path.

As it drew level with us, it *detonated*, rocking our MCV from side to side. Daedalus pulled his control sticks back, sliding the MCV backwards to get it out of the blast radius in case the ammunition in the tank cooked off. Which, 10 seconds later, it did, in a firework display worthy of Chinese New Year.

'I can't take it,' Tiny said. He had his head between his knees, hands over his head, and was rocking back and forth. 'I can't take it!'

'Ostrich, tranq him,' Daedalus said.

Ostrich looked over her shoulder at Daedalus. 'Tranq who?'

'Tiny. Tranq him.'

Tiny looked at Ostrich in alarm. 'No, hey, I'm fine, sister.'

'My ass,' Daedalus said. 'You heard me, Ostrich, tranq him.'

'Sorry, brother,' Ostrich said, taking a syringe from her uniform pocket. The engineer was also nominally the crew medic, so she carried a range of basic meds from coagulant patches to stim modifiers. Our stim implants automatically pumped our bodies with sensory- and reflex-enhancing hormones during combat, and they had to be counter-regulated when it came time to sleep or relax. But that took time to kick in, and with the big guy clearly about to freak out, there was no time.

No one liked a jab. Whether it was an upper or a downer, the sudden massive influx of hormones and drugs gave you side effects you felt for days after. Nausea, fatigue and memory loss were just a few.

I stood in case Ostrich needed any help, since Tiny was trying to bat the syringe away from him, but with surprising strength she locked him down with an iron grip across his chest that pinned both arms as she jabbed the auto-syringe into Tiny's neck. His body went slack but not unconscious. Ostrich waited by him, watching his breathing for signs of distress. She snapped her fingers in front of Tiny's eyes. 'You good, Tiny?'

Tiny turned to her and smiled. 'So good, thanks.'

'You're welcome,' Ostrich said and sat down, sliding the used syringe into a disposal bag by the side of her seat. I sat down again.

'Tiny, sensor scan!' Daedalus called, checking the guy was still mission capable.

He reached up, fingers tapping virtual icons on his console. 'Nothing on seismic or radar. I got some burning vehicles ahead and behind us on infrared and optical.' He sat back in his seat again. 'But nothing new.' His voice was moronically calm, but that was better than high pitched and panicky, which could have triggered the rest of us to panic too.

Satisfied, Daedalus did a stock take. 'Alright. The fact we aren't being bombarded right now tells me there's no second ambush planned. We can push on. Termite, bring another tank around, same side. Chances are low we'll get unlucky twice. You get it ahead of us, push those wrecks out the way, and then we get moving again.'

I did as he ordered. And we set off again. Pathfinder tank ahead, then momma duck, and the remaining six tanks behind us.

We lost one more pathfinder to a mine, detonating again 100 meters ahead of us. But though Tiny flinched, like all of us, he took it in his stride. At 6 klicks after entering the field, Daedalus decided we were through. We were just short of the fork in the valley. But we had to be sure. 'Termite, clear a defensive field out to 200 meters.'

I set the surviving tanks to circle around us, starting in close and spiraling outward until they were 200 meters out and spread out with about 50-meter spacing. Nothing went boom. Daedalus drove us under a rock overhang and shut down the turbines.

'Command, MCV II/II,' he said over the radio. 'We are through the field, four tanks down, but you have your path. We'll wait for you here.' All that the other MCVs had to do was motor over and pick up our trail, following closely along the path we'd swept. The target ZoC, deep inside the Margarita Terra crater zone, was still about 80 klicks ahead of us, the other side of the Chaos.

I turned the cameras on one of my tanks around and looked behind us at the still-smoking wrecks of my other four tanks. Whoever had named the rutted ruins of valleys and mesas a 'Chaos', I had to take my skull cap off to them. The same went for the ZoC behind it. The whole area around the Mesa that the ZoC sat on was one big series of kill zones.

The ZoC was made to be near impregnable to an outside attack, but that of course was why the Zenos always attacked from within.

It took time for the cohort to make its way through the path we'd cleared in the minefield, to our position. Time we killed with our jaws. 'So, Termite. What duty you reckon is worst?' Tiny asked. 'Beacons or spikes?'

I didn't even have to think about it. 'Beacons,' I told him.

'What I said,' Ostrich agreed. 'I hate beacons. It's the creepiest duty on the whole Red.'

'Didn't ask you,' Tiny pointed out. He spun his chair to face mine. 'Beacons, why?'

Beacons – the small magnetic field generators – should have been my favorite. If we were sent out to clean the solar arrays on the perimeter beacons at Voeykov, we got an extra ration if we reported seeing anything odd or unusual. An extra half ration for just making it back alive, full stop. But that extra ration wasn't enough, in my mind.

'Well, so, I don't know how it is at Flaugerges, but if you ever did beacon duty at Voeykov, you know how they'd send you out alone, wearing a skull cap telling us we had iron links around our ankles, making us walk like we were hobbled. Drop you out there at dawn, pick up at dusk. Only water was whatever your suit recycled from your own breath, piss and sweat. No food, because why waste rations on someone who might not come back, right?'

'Yeah, but spikes, you got to climb all the way to the top of the seismic tower to service the thumper. You're up so high you can see the electrical storms coming, but you can't get down fast enough to get out their way, so you're stuck up there choking and getting zapped, and suits aren't rated to take a lightning strike, so you die eating dust ...' Tiny painted a pretty grim picture. The seismic spikes were 200 feet high. Kinetic hammers was what they were. A hammer was raised up the spike, fell 200 feet down to strike on a plug inserted into the ground, and then sensors inside the perimeter searched the soundwaves for anomalies. A sandstorm on Mars wasn't like in the VR dramas - with the wind tearing everything apart - because the atmosphere was so thin. But the sand was so fine it sparkled with static electricity, and if a dust devil or sand front formed, you got lightning. So, yeah, I'd seen the bodies of people who didn't make it down. Suits red with sand stuck to the fabric on the outside, except where the lightning hit, while inside, the body was fried to the bone. But of course, if you got hit with lightning, it was a quick death, so how bad could it really be?

The Zenos had tried tunneling under our perimeter defenses and into the domes in the early days of the war, and the strategy had worked a few times, until the spikes went up and we could see the tunnels. The attack vector had led to a theory that the Zenos lived underground, which a lot of people still believed, since there was no evidence of them anywhere else. Still, we'd surveyed the whole planet with ground-penetrating radar down to 200 feet and found nothing but dirt, minerals, frozen water and rare earths, so if they were down there, they were a *long way* down.

I didn't think they were. I had my own theory.

'No, but the beacons, out on the perimeter,' Ostrich said with a theatrical shudder. 'You're out there all alone, and suddenly there's a Zeno right up in your face …'

Tiny held up his hand to stop her again. 'I know what *you* think,' he said. 'I'm asking Termite.'

I winced. The nickname was going to take some getting used to. Daedalus hadn't been exaggerating. There was a bloodstain on the bulkhead beside my tanker's seat.

'Beacons are the worst,' I told them. 'I saw a Zeno at Voeykov myself, outside the perimeter.'

'You tell anyone?' Tiny asked. 'You report it?'

'Guards wouldn't have believed me. Half the prisoners didn't either.'

'Oh, crud,' Ostrich said. 'So Voeykov's gonna fall. Just a matter of time.'

'Stow that talk, Ostrich,' Daedalus growled at us. 'Aren't any Zenos inside Voeykov. He said *outside*. If it even was a Zeno, which it wasn't.' He glowered at me. 'You see an aura?'

'Yes, I saw an aura,' I told him. 'I fought him. Knocked off his breather, and it didn't even slow him down. He didn't need it.'

'A Zeno?' Tiny said, wide eyed. 'You fought, yourself?'

'I'm cleaning this beacon,' I told him. 'Turn around, there's a camp guard. Or a Zeno, dressed like a guard.'

'Whoa.'

'More like bulldust,' Daedalus said, spitting at his feet again. 'I never met anyone actually saw a real Zeno. Zeds, yeah, but not a real Zeno. Not an incubus or succubus.'

'Yeah, well, I'm not making this scar up, am I?' I said, pointing to a jagged ridge that ran from my hairline down to the entrance to my left ear.

'You *fought* it?' Tiny asked again.

'He must have come from a tunnel outside the fence and walked in,' I told him. 'He started yelling at me to leave what I was doing and come back to camp with him …'

'Needed you to drop the perimeter so he could walk in with you,' Ostrich guessed. The perimeter magnetic field messed with implants and tech, so walking through it wearing implants caused it to flick off for the time it took to step through. We learned early in the war that Zenos couldn't survive strong magnetic fields. Like a vampire being invited across a lintel, a

Zeno could only infiltrate or exfiltrate if they went across the perimeter beacons in the company of a human. Or tunneled in.

Which is why some guys, when it happened to them, they said nothing. You couldn't really be sure, after all, and you had to decide ... did you tell anyone? Or did you just let it ride? Because if you got the blame for letting in a Zeno, any kind, you were mulch. Like, if it was an assassin they sent, us legionnaires were pretty safe. A Zeno assassin would go for an officer, right? A centurion, or his or her decurion. So most guys who thought they might have let a Zeno through, they just kept their mouths shut and hoped whatever hell was about to be unleashed would slide by them. That they'd survive it maybe. Unless they had a conscience, in which case they'd make excuses to snoop around the ZoC, sniffing for anything that seemed off, or they'd just own up to their mistake and take the consequences. Which was how most incubi or succubi were caught.

'Yeah, that was his plan: yell at me so I just did like he said and walked him in. But he screwed up because I was at the end of my rope by then, ready to kill the next bastard who yelled at me, and I was looking at him, deciding how to do it when I saw it ...'

'*Aura*,' Ostrich guessed. 'What's it look like?'

Zenos who've just arrived on The Red have this weird glow around them. Can last hours. No one knows why, any more than we know where they come from. 'Any sufficiently advanced technology is indistinguishable from magic' – isn't that what the writer wrote? Well, we spilled a lot of blood learning to counter their magic. Built the beacons to keep them out, spikes to stop them from tunneling right into our ZoCs. No one ever captured a Zeno, far as I know. You could capture their body, sure, but as soon as you did, they 'ghosted'. Eyes rolled up in their heads, body dropped to the ground with a thud, then dissolved into inert gasses. There was a small window in which the body was inert before it dissolved, when Redside scientists could examine it, and they'd discovered a precious few things: A Zeno body felt like flesh and blood to the touch. It had skin, muscle, organs, blood and bones, but when you looked right down to the molecular level, you couldn't find any of the six common elements the human body is made of.

Quite a few *Zeds* had been captured though. The theory was they were Zedified through some kind of fluid-borne viral vector, since Zedification required the exchange of body fluids – a kiss, a sweaty touch, sexual intercourse. Zeds weren't mindless, moaning zombies. Zedification rewired your brain, made you think you were a Zeno too, willing – no, determined – to fight and die for them. And it made you a viral carrier. Once a few legionnaires or settlers inside a camp were Zedified, it was just a matter of time before the number of Zeds achieved critical mass and the camp fell.

Zeds ghosted too. Not in the same way as a Zeno – gasification – but once infected, they only lasted a few weeks. And if they were abandoned by their Zeno masters, they just stopped eating and drinking, wasted away. Three or four days, and their eyes rolled back in their heads, and they were dead.

But those three or four days a Zed stayed alive after it was captured gave the interrogators time for a little 'enhanced inquiry'.

You've all seen the interviews – alright, let's call them torture sessions – on the propaganda newscasts. I remember one in particular: a Zed sitting in a chair with a skull cap on her head. Naked, vulnerable, confused.

'Why are the Zenos attacking us?' the interviewer asked. In the early days, we hoped the Zedified would have special insights into the Zenos, and maybe they did. We just didn't understand them.

The torture was ratcheted up a notch. Zeds could feel pain, just like anyone. It was more like their emotions were cauterized by the Turning. Pain without fear? It led to long interrogations for the first of the prisoners. The 'interviewers' learned to use logic instead of threats, explaining that relief from pain would only come with answers. 'Why are the Zenos attacking us?' the interviewer asked the woman.

'They are fighting to save us,' she said. 'Only by defeat is our survival assured.' None of that made sense, back then. Does now. 'Make the pain stop,' she pleaded.

'Not yet. Where are they from?' he asked. 'Where is their base?'

She didn't know.

'Who are they?' he asked.

'They are us,' she replied. Then moaned as the pain was increased again. 'Look at them! They are *us*!'

We all assumed she was just saying that because a Zeno looked like a human. Did it never occur to anyone to take her literally?

Nup.

'What's it look like, the aura?' Ostrich asked, not letting the question go.

'Like a silvery outline … so I grab the wrench and he grabs up a rock, and we go at each other, and I get a good hit in but it's like hitting a rubber doll …'

'What's that mean?'

'I mean, not like flesh and bone. I think the aura also protects them while it lasts. It was like my hits were bouncing off,' I said. 'So he smacked me with his rock, gave me this …' I pointed to the scar by my ear. 'And knocked me out. Then he must have dragged my ass inside the perimeter to get himself across, because I woke up later covered in blood, about a half mile in, behind a water tank. So he must have been an assassin.'

'If he was an assassin, why didn't he kill you?' Ostrich asked, skeptical.

'Yeah, and how did you know he was assassin again?' Tiny repeated.

'I don't know why he didn't kill me, but I know he was an assassin because two days later, there's a meeting of senior officers, and witnesses say a guard walked into the meeting, released a nerve gas and killed them all.'

Tiny whistled, but Daedalus just looked away, out a cockpit window. 'Could be coincidence, internal politics. Who knows?'

'Yeah, or what's more likely ... a Zeno assassin,' I pointed out.

'Wait, you didn't tell anyone you saw this guy?' Tiny asked, showing he was listening. 'You didn't, or they'd have turned the ZoC upside-down looking for him and had extra security on all the officers.'

I turned back to my tank console, checking they were all in position, no mechanical issues, no systems warnings. I spoke over my shoulder to Tiny. 'Would I be here if I had?'

Tiny nodded. 'Yeah, nah. You'd be mulch, for letting him through.'

'I told my decanus I got cut in a fight over some booze and took the lashes instead.' We called them lashes, but there was no whip. Just an electrified prod they applied to your neck to fry your synapses. The burning pain was bad, but the three-day headache afterward was worse.

'Assassins only go for officers, or do sabotage,' Daedalus declared. 'They don't do the Turning. That's only succubi and incubi do that.'

Ostrich spun her chair around to face Daedalus. 'I thought you didn't believe him?'

'I'm not saying I do,' Daedalus said. 'I'm just explaining why they don't kill dumb grunts.'

'It's beyond creepy,' Ostrich said, with an exaggerated shiver. 'How they get in, cause mayhem, then if they get caught or killed, they just fade. Where do they go?'

'Where they came from,' Daedalus told her, 'which is *whothefrickknows*.' He pointed at Ostrich's engineering console hologram. 'Cut the chatter. Eyes on systems.'

That Zeno outside the perimeter wasn't the only one I'd seen. There was another, though I didn't recognize her as a Zeno at the time. In a cage beside me at Voeykov.

Her name was Livia. I don't know the patronymic they gave her. It will never be remembered. She had been sent for Reducation at Voeykov some weeks before me and she helped me quickly learn the rules:

You are nothing and no one, and until you accept that, you will never leave here.

Seek pain, because only through pain can you eat.

No order is insane.

I've added a rule of my own: Beware the scent of oranges.

The scent of an orange is a terrible promise. It promises to alleviate the thirst that never leaves you. It promises a pulpy goodness that even your emaciated stomach can keep down without vomiting. It promises vitamins and sucrose that might keep you alive an entire day – another horrible day.

Where was I? Oh, yeah. Livia. She had hollow cheeks and rotten teeth, but damn, she had beautiful eyes. You can starve a person, you can make them work without radiation cover so often their hair falls out, but the eyes … they will show you the person who was there right up until the light goes out and they turn to jelly. I never saw Livia's eyes turn to jelly because she left me with a sparkle in her eyes.

'Oranges, Linus,' she would whisper to me. 'Can you remember them?' We couldn't touch between the electrified walls of our cages, but she held out her fingertips to me as though we were lovers. As she talked, it was as though I could smell the soul-destroying scent of orange blossom. 'One day, I am going to put a wet slice of orange in my mouth and kiss you.'

I close my eyes now, as I'm writing this, and I can taste that kiss.

Forget Livia.

She was a succubus. Putting out pheromones, drawing her victims to her. I'll tell you later how I worked that out. A guard came and took her away before she could infect me. As we joined formation with the cohort again and our MCV crept through the maze of mesas toward Margarita Terra, I couldn't help but feel like a fly heading toward the sweet sticky center of a fly trap.

There were no more minefields after that one. There was no more artillery. No air strikes. The cohort's remaining MCVs made it to the base of the mesa, with us trailing a half hour behind because we were moving at half speed and the bastard tribune didn't want to slow up the whole cohort just to provide cover for us.

The mesa the firebase sat on was like a steep-sided circular hill with a square pillar of rock planted on it. We were spread around it in a rough circle. I was looking up at it from a tank camera, and it looked about 500 meters high. I could just barely make out some manmade observation platforms up top. The tribune's MCV tried hailing whoever was inside but got no answer. So his 'primus pilae', the Centurion who was his second in command, sent up an uncrewed recon drone, and we were all patched into the vision. All I saw was a wall of red rock skimming past until the drone broke into open air and zoomed up above the firebase.

It was a military firebase on the periphery of a settlement, so what it should have been was a series of hardened habitat domes surrounded by landing pads for transports, ringed with missile and plasma defense emplacements. Linking these should have been field-generating beacons and a few seismic spikes. It wasn't easy to tunnel up into a mesa, even for the Zenos, so you didn't need as many spikes, but you needed the beacons to generate a magnetic field strong enough that it messed with any Zeno trying to break through.

The beacons were down, of course. That was the first thing the Zenos did when they managed to Turn a base. They got their human converts to bring down the beacon defenses, so they could move in and out without grabbing their heads and screaming. They turned off the spikes too, but that was just to save juice, since they were useless if a base had already been Turned. Then they did one of two things – they turned the ZoC into a porcupine, beefing up the defenses so that any attempt to retake it would result in massive casualties, or they used it to stage an offensive, using the humans they'd Turned as meat puppets to raid outposts, ambush patrols or convoys, not so much to kill as to take hostages to bolster the population of Zeds.

By the time you'd weathered that storm and taken the ZoC back, the battleground was littered with dead humans, Zedified and un-Zedified, and there was not a Zeno to be found anywhere.

Then they would rinse and repeat at another ZoC. It was a bloody, brutal, attritional war against a foe that appeared from nowhere and then ghosted.

Camp Margarita Terra had been a porcupine. Satellite surveillance showed it had been reinforced with extra layered defenses against aerial or space bombardment, or traps, like the minefield/artillery combo we'd just pushed through. The Zenos at Margarita Terra had been sending out raids that had taken and Zedified hundreds of prisoners.

But see how I said 'had been' a porcupine? The MCV drone vision showed a ZoC that had been laid to waste. Everything that could burn, melt, or blow up had been destroyed – plasma cannon barrels split, habitat domes shredded. The desiccated human bodies of legionnaires, settlers and camp followers lay everywhere. As the drone swooped low, you could see most had died violently, but a lot had also just suffocated when their habitats were trashed, lying where they fell, some with their hands up where they'd clawed at their necks as they died.

'Holy frog-eyed goat schtupper,' Ostrich said. I was learning she was a master of creative invective. 'Wait, there's one habitat left!' she said, pointing at a single small dome that stood untouched at the edge of the field of death and debris. 'That must be the place they launched that last attack from.'

'Aye,' Daedalus said. He'd been on the radio with the centurion. 'And guess who they are sending up to check it out.'

That shook even Tiny out of his drug-induced torpor. 'That's just wrong,' he said, with enhanced understatement. 'We're an MCV crew. Why don't they send assault troops?'

Daedalus unbuckled himself from his pilot seat and stood, stretching. 'Because after our performance at the minefield, where we "lost four tanks and triggered an artillery attack," as the tribune put it, he'll be nominating us for a court-martial when we get back.'

'So, we're already dead far as he is concerned,' Ostrich observed. 'He's sending us to do the dirty work rather than sacrifice anyone else.'

I could have protested, I supposed. Refused. But Voeykov had done a job on me. I wasn't the big, heavily muscled, forthright decurion I once was. I was nothing and no one, after all. Whether I died here today or somewhere else tomorrow, what did it matter? Sure, I was still human. Voeykov had done its best to strip my humanity from me, but I would still fight against the dying of the light when it got down to that last moment. That didn't mean I could summon enough outrage to try to avoid that moment entirely yet.

'Grab your personal weapons, put on your suits and breathers, form up outside,' Daedalus ordered. And before he was asked, he added, 'Not you, Fatfoot. You close up behind us and guard the MCV from our thieving comrades.'

There was a personnel entry elevator at the base of the mesa. It had of course been disabled. The only way up was a set of stairs that went up alongside the elevator shaft. Five hundred meters up. We started humping up the stairs.

It was good to have the skull caps off, but the breathers weren't much better. They clamped onto your face almost exactly the same as a skull cap sucked itself down onto your stubble. You already had a thermal suit over the top of your own skin, which you stretched into place to form a seal over your ears and around your breather. Once you'd skinned up, you suited up. Suits were looser: a magnesium alloy weave that could stop most kinetic weapons and low-power plasma bolts.

The combination was supposed to keep you warm without needing a heat generator out in the multi-subzero temperatures of The Red. But inside the stairwell, the skin and suit started to cook you. None of this counted against our combat hours, unless someone started shooting at us as we climbed. By about the hundredth step, I wasn't looking up anymore to see if there was an ambush waiting. I was hoping there *was* one.

There wasn't though. We made it all the way up about a half hour later and emerged at the top of the mesa into late afternoon sunlight. A day Redside was about the same as a day Earthside, and I figured we still had about four hours of light left. The two moons, Phobos and Deimos, were just appearing over the western horizon. Phobos was closer and bigger and orbited faster, so it would soon overtake its smaller brother.

I could see why they picked this mesa for the firebase. You could see over just about the whole of the Margarita Terra, only a slight dust haze obscuring the artificial lights of the mines and refineries of the Meridiani Planum to the east. The mesa had a subterranean water supply, which the settlers had used to grow some scrubby plants in the soil – some kind of aloe, freeze-drying now that it was exposed to outside temperatures again.

We circled around to the left since the undamaged habitat dome we'd seen on the drone vision had been on the edge of the destroyed camp. The view didn't get any less spectacular. As we edged around, expecting to be jumped at any moment, I saw the spindle-topped mesas and ravines of the Aurora Chaos and Xanthe Terra to the west. Beyond them lay the Da Vinci Crater ZoC, but the Aurora Chaos made an attack from that direction impossible, which was why we had been sent out.

There were bodies everywhere. Most had died horribly, even those wearing suits, implying heavy plasma or kinetic energy weapons had done the job, since getting through magnesium alloy weave isn't easy, like I said.

Tiny inspected one of the bodies, turning the dead guy's head side to side. 'Blast victim, I'd say. Maybe friendly fire, an earlier patrol that made it inside?'

Whatever it was, it had been a slaughter.

'Or an air bombardment. Don't think of them as human,' Ostrich said. 'They were Zeds. As good as dead anyway.'

'Well, *someone* did our job for us,' I said, turning a legionnaire's body over with my boot. 'But it doesn't explain who attacked us.' Outside the habitat domes, the camp followers lay where they had fallen too, but they hadn't had suits, so they'd frozen or suffocated. They were worse to look at since their faces weren't hidden behind breathers. They had open, gasping mouths and bulging, gelatinous eyes, with frost on their lashes and lines of frozen blood or saliva running down their chins or cheeks.

There were a lot of theories about the Zenos since we knew so little about them. One theory was about the reason they didn't just attack us en masse – the reason they used subversion, assassination, sabotage and conversion. The theory was that there weren't that many of them, so they had to fight an asymmetrical guerilla war. I preferred that theory since it implied we could win eventually, by sheer weight of numbers. I didn't like the other theories so much, like the one that said the Zenos didn't even have a base Redside, that they were shunting in from somewhere else entirely and their technology required so much energy they could only port a few bodies over at a time. That implied there could be millions of them out in the galaxy somewhere, and if so, this was a war we had already lost.

'So who did this?' Ostrich asked, very reasonably.

'Shut up and prepare to breach the dome,' Daedalus said.

As Ostrich had pointed out, we weren't any sort of elite assault squad. We weren't elite anything, really. Daedalus wasn't any sort of assault squad leader either. He was more or less making it up as he went along.

'Alright, Tiny, you open the airlock. Termite, you're point on the entry. Me and Ostrich have your back. Tiny comes in last.'

I didn't like the idea of being first through the door. 'Why not let me open the lock, and put Tiny on point?' I asked. 'He's the biggest. We can hide behind him.'

'Hey, I ain't your meat shield, Gregarius,' Tiny objected.

Daedalus waved us all to silence and glared at me. 'Last in, first out. As long as you are the new guy, you'll be point. We get a new Termite, and they'll be point, and you can go back to being Ballsack, so stop bitching and get ready to breach.'

I couldn't fight the logic – the logic of the Legion Praeda.

When we had formed up into a snake beside the door, Tiny palmed the airlock control, the door hissed open, and I went in. The airlock was big enough for two, but no one followed me in. So much for having my back. I waited for the outer door to close, the pressure to equalize, and the inner door to the habitat to hiss open. *We should have just blown it from the outside and let whoever is in here perish,* I thought. But they could be settlers or camp followers – cooks, entertainers or sex workers – and they might not have been Zedified yet. The legionnaires of Legion Praeda were a lot of things, most of them unsavory, but murderers of innocents we weren't.

For lack of a better idea, as the inner door slid open, I threw myself through it and lay prone, scanning around me with my plasma rifle.

OK, some kind of environmental support dome. I saw air and water purifiers, solar capacitors. Wiring, piping. It was laid out in a ring around a central raised platform with a single control desk.

Left and right of me were bodies. These had died in atmosphere, and they hadn't been suffocated, frozen or shot. They didn't look putrid or bloated either, so I figured they had died not too long ago. How? I wasn't about to conduct any autopsy. There was a person sitting in a seat at the control desk, looking down at me. And she was still alive. She blinked and gave me a small, creepy wave.

I gave her a small, creepy wave back, and stood.

There was nowhere she could have hidden a weapon, unless she was carrying it internally. She had flowing red hair, green eyes, freckled white skin, long legs, bare feet.

My immediate thought? *No freaking way.* Now I'll tell you why.

'Boldly they rode, and well'

I got on my mic to Daedalus. 'Uh, I'm in. Checking the dome for hostiles …' Which I wasn't, of course, because there was one right in front of me. But I needed time to think the situation through.

She stood. She was wearing a catsuit: the skintight neoprene with strategically placed flesh windows that only a certain type of camp follower wore.

I could hear arguing over the radio. Then Daedalus came on. 'We're not going in until Termite gives the all clear. Hurry it up in there, Gregarius.'

'Proceeding with alacrity, Decanus.'

She was getting closer. She stopped right in front of my raised rifle.

'You can take off your mask,' she offered. 'The atmosphere is Earth normal in here and I've done nothing to poison it.' The bodies lying around us with no sign of violence on them spoke a different story, and she saw me looking. 'They were the only ones not killed by your constant air and space bombardments. In the end, their bodies just gave up. So frail, these organisms you call home.'

I already said I was beyond caring about whether *I* lived or died. But also, and you'll see why, I figured she was probably telling the truth about the atmosphere. So I peeled off my breather. And she saw my face for the first time. I'll give her some credit; a simulacrum of emotion flickered across her features. 'Scabrous!' she exclaimed, warmly.

'Hello, Livia,' I replied. And there it was, the scent of orange blossom.

Don't ask me what maelstrom of anger and grief and self-hatred was swirling in me then. I couldn't pick out any individual feelings. Oh, alright, I'll try. *Joy*, that she was still alive. *Humiliation*, knowing that everything I felt about her was the result of pheromones and artful play acting. *Horror*, at the thought of the carnage she had wreaked here inside the firebase at Margarita Terra. *Anger*, at her, at myself, at the gods and the universe that allowed such evil.

Fear. The next feeling that swamped me was fear.

Because now I knew that she was, without any doubt, a Zeno. And she'd been caged beside me for weeks on Voeykov, during which time I shared with her every secret I ever held. And not just about me, my childhood, my schooling, my love life, but also my training, life in the Legion, the strengths and weaknesses of our weapons, news about the progress of the war, our victories and defeats. She drained me dry with innocent inquiry, and when there was nothing left to learn, she left and went to work. I marveled at that. What kind of enemy were the Zenos that they would let themselves be imprisoned and tortured for months in the name of learning more about their enemies?

I had hidden nothing from her, not even my love for Antonia.

And, it seemed, she had used everything I taught her to escape Voeykov and infiltrate Margarita Terra. It was Livia, but she was not human. Never had been. A Zeno succubus. And I fell for her.

Despair. I was left with despair, because how could we fight and win against an entire race of foes who used our most powerful weapon against us – our animal selves?

'It is *wonderful* to see you, Scabrous,' she said. 'You look well. Did you come from Flaugerges? The food is better there, it seems.'

Orange blossom perfume wafted around me like the threat of salvation.

'I promised you a kiss, didn't I, Scabrous?' she purred. I melted. She stepped closer and I lowered my rifle. She took my neck in her hand, pulled me toward her. We kissed. My senses exploded.

And yet. And yet. In the back of my mind, a voice was screaming.

SUCCUBUS!

I pushed her away, wiping my mouth, pulled my rifle up and put it between us again, even though it felt like gravity had doubled since the last time I tried to lift it. She looked at me curiously, like I was a strange bug in a jar. Probably not the reaction she usually got.

I put my breather back on to try to protect myself. 'Uh, OK. There's an unarmed hostile in here. A Zeno,' I said into my mic. 'And no, she hasn't Zedified me; I've got a rifle on her. You can come in. Keep your breathers on though; she's pheromoning like crazy.'

'That's exactly what you would say if you *was* Zedified …' Daedalus started saying again, then Ostrich interrupted.

'Oh, gobbling tonsil-stretcher, Daedalus,' I heard Ostrich say. 'I'm going in.'

She hit the airlock and came in with her rifle up. Daedalus and Tiny followed her, fanning left and right with rifles ready, but they saw pretty quickly what I'd seen. Livia was *very* obviously unarmed.

Daedalus held up his hand, yelling through his breather at her. 'Step back from the legionnaire, lady. Five *big* steps.'

Livia complied, bemused.

Tiny and Ostrich didn't see it right away, but Daedalus did. Probably because they weren't looking at her face.

Daedalus turned to me and lowered his voice. 'Succubus, you think?'

I didn't take my eyes or my rifle off her. 'Totally succubus.'

'Don't see no aura,' he said.

'No, she's been here a while,' I agreed. That was good, since it meant she was no longer under the protection of whatever field generator the aura was a sign of. It was also bad, since it meant that Livia was definitely one of the Zenos who took down the Margarita Terra firebase.

Suddenly I wasn't the only one who had seen a real Zeno up close.

'The tribune is going to want her alive,' Daedalus said.

'Do we care what the tribune wants?' I asked.

'Not after seeing all those bodies outside, no, Termite, we do not,' he whispered.

'We can't just *kill* her,' Ostrich said, trying to keep her voice low too.

Tiny was more dispassionate. 'Sure we can. In fact, we should.' He was still not doing a good job of looking at her face.

Livia spoke. Her voice was honey and cream, of course. 'There's no reason to whisper. I can hear every word.'

Daedalus lifted his rifle and sighted on her body mass. Supposedly it didn't matter where you shot them as long as you made a big enough hole. A single plasma bolt in the core and they went down. 'Suits me, girly. So are you coming with us dead or alive?'

She frowned, like the question didn't make sense. 'I have allowed you to get this far so that we can parlay,' she said. 'Who is the senior officer here?'

Without even hesitating, Daedalus, Tiny and Ostrich all looked at each other, then pointed at me. 'He is.'

Thanks for nothing, I thought. Fear-tinted bile rose in my throat, and I pushed it back down. 'What do you mean, "parlay"?'

'I mean, I have an offer for your commander down below. A rather good one.' She sounded genuine. 'What is he? A tribune, you said? How flattering.'

'Don't reply!' Daedalus barked at me. His weapon was still pointed unwaveringly at Livia's center mass.

'Oh, it doesn't really matter,' she said. 'And you don't need that weapon. If I had wanted you dead, you already would be.'

She had a point. Daedalus wasn't letting her have it easily though. He kept his rifle pointed at her. 'What's this offer you're talking about?'

'Well, that is rather beyond your rank, Decanus,' she said, implying she now knew exactly who the real commander of our sorry crew was. 'But since your cooperation will make things move more quickly, *you* can take my offer back to your senior officers,' she said. She shrugged and smiled. 'It's a simple one. Surrender to me, or die.'

Daedalus grinned back at her. 'Right. Or how about this. We kill you, and we *don't* surrender?'

'You could do that,' she agreed amicably. 'But your troops below are parked on top of a second minefield. Killing me will trigger it.'

Ostrich looked from Livia to Daedalus with red-rimmed, panicked eyes. Daedalus just looked a little bamboozled.

'I can see it needs to be said in black and white,' Livia continued. 'Your arrival offered me the chance to repopulate this camp, so I let you in. You can join me, or you can kill me.

But if you kill me, your commander, and all your comrades, will perish.'

I was still thinking about that kiss, or rather feeling the effects of it in erogenous zones I didn't know I had. I navigated back to reality. '*Join you?* You'll just Turn everyone into Zeds,' I said. 'How is that different from death?'

She scoffed. 'Are you seriously defending this thing you call life? Shuffling from battle to battle, half starved, diseased, anxious and afraid? If your Legion doesn't kill you today, it will kill you tomorrow, or the next day. I am offering you and your comrades the chance to live *without* fear, without anxiety or anguish. You might even live longer with me than you would with your "Legion". If you love life so much, isn't that worth considering?'

Some wisp of orange blossom must still have been sneaking past my breather filter, or it was the kiss working on me, because what she was saying seemed very – no, *completely* – rational. Of course we were better off joining her than staying in the Legion Praeda. The Legion Praeda wanted to kill us. Livia wanted us to *stay alive* as long as possible.

I turned to the others. 'You know, she …'

I jumped as Daedalus's weapon spat a ball of plasma that chewed right though her, throwing her two feet back into the room. Her body landed with a thud, but it didn't bleed. The plasma cauterized the edges of the wound. She just lay there, and if we hung around a few hours, we'd see her slowly turn to vapor.

'What the hell?!' I yelled. I was going to yell some more, but like everyone else, I had turned my head, listening for the sound of mines exploding in the sand below, triggered by some kind of dead man's switch Livia had rigged. But there was only silence.

And then …

Then, with a ripple of explosions that started behind us and rolled around the base of the mesa anticlockwise, *the entire stone pillar shook*. The horrible staccato cacophony of death continued for nearly a half minute, causing dust and rust to fill the air inside our bubble. I was glad I had my breather on again, the fine sand filled the air so quickly.

When it was done, no one said anything. We went out through the airlock to one of the viewing platforms perched on the edge of the plateau, moved some bodies aside, and looked down. Below us were only blazing fires and pillars of smoke, already rising up toward us.

So there you have it. The *true* story of how Tribune Augusti and an entire cohort of cavalry, their tank escorts and several hundred legionnaires were massacred in the battle for the firebase at Margarita Terra. Yeah, not quite the story you can read in the Official History of The Red War, right? You probably heard the version where Tribune Cillus Maximus Augusti led a glorious charge through the minefield, his own MCV at the point of the spear, dodging mines and artillery and drones until his lone surviving squadron made it to the base of the mesa, where his ragtag company of condemned men and women rained unholy fire down on the firebase, and just as victory seemed near, the enemy unleashed some kind of 'mysterious alien weapon' that caused the sand to rise up and swallow them, never to be seen again. Every man among them received a Medal of Valor, and their families a full lifetime pension. Earthside, Remembrance Day was renamed Tribune Augusti Day and the names of the dead from Century II of the Legion Praeda were always first among the fallen to be remembered.

That's the version you know, right? Not the one where a condemned man saw the chance to escape the wrath of an angry tribune and traded 450 lives for his own.

I hadn't known Daedalus for very long, but now I knew everything about him that I would ever need to know.

'Well, ain't no one down there going to be sending us to a court-martial anytime soon,' Daedalus said, lifted his breather and spat over the edge before settling it back on his face. His spit froze the minute it left his lips, dropping into the smoke from the burning vehicles and legionnaires.

'Gibbering gobbets of phlegm, Daedalus,' Ostrich said in a strangled voice. 'What have you done?'

'Saved your life, Optio,' Daedalus said, hefting his rifle and checking the charge level. 'Saved all our lives. Tribune Augusti down there had already passed sentence on you. I just returned the favor.'

'*Fatfoot* was down there!' Ostrich exclaimed. 'You killed Fatfoot too!'

I could see Daedalus's eyes over the top of his breather and the realization took him by surprise. 'Aw, crud,' he said. 'I didn't think about that.' He peered over the edge of the viewing platform again. 'Maybe he made it.'

We all looked over the railing at the area near the personnel entrance, where our own MCV had been. The smoke was thick, but every couple of seconds, you could see the ground under it. There was nothing and no one moving around down there. It had been a very, very dense minefield.

'Forget Fatfoot,' Tiny said. Which sounds cold, but you have to remember he was still under the influence of the mood-killing jab Ostrich gave him. He prodded one of the bodies on the platform with his boot. 'Legion really did a number on this place. Kind of annoying they didn't get *all* the Zenos.'

'It's not annoying; it's sick,' Ostrich said, squatting on her haunches with a sigh. 'What kind of war is it where you have to slaughter your own people to win?'

'Stow that talk, Optio,' Daedalus said. 'From the moment this place fell, it became a Zeno base,' he said. 'There were no "our people" here. Only Zeds, or the corpses of those they killed. And *that* Zeno.'

That Zeno? I didn't tell them I knew her. And I didn't freak out about what Daedalus had done either. Like Livia had said, all those legionnaires would have died or been Zedified anyway, sooner or later, and us along with them. See, that's the version I tell myself when I'm alone in the dark with my thoughts. *They would have died anyway, so at least we survived.* Isn't it a version of that story that just about every coward tells themselves?

'Alright, boys and girl,' Daedalus said. 'Get your collective acts together. We have to come up with a story that explains why we are alive and no one else is,' he said. 'One that doesn't try to make us into heroes but won't get us court-martialed either.'

The truth is just a story that fits the facts, right? We managed to create a version of the 'facts' that fit what actually happened, in case there were any survivors left alive down below with stories of their own. A version that the Legion Praeda's media machine could turn into some kind of 'Charge of the Light Brigade' BS later – the version you grew up with.

Cannon to right of them,
Cannon to left of them,
Cannon in front of them
Volleyed and thundered;
Stormed at with shot and shell,
Boldly they rode, and well,
Into the jaws of Death,
Into the mouth of hell
Rode the (four) hundred.

Something like Tennyson wrote, right? A version that made us into anonymous not-heroes that could just blend back into the dirt, filth and depravity of the Legion Praeda again with no one paying us any particular mind.

Ostrich was the most troubled about it all, and she went all the way down to the foot of the mesa again to see if maybe Fatfoot or anyone else had made it through. It was her medic training, probably, that laid a skerrick of duty on her that the rest of us had long since surrendered. Meanwhile Tiny, Daedalus and me made the call to Legion Command on the one communicator inside the bubble that Livia had left undamaged, probably so she could speak with our commander to ask him to surrender. We were ordered to stay exactly where we were, so we did exactly that. Ostrich came back up a couple hours later. She had made it halfway around the mesa without finding any survivors, so she'd given up and dragged herself back up the stairwell.

'Fatfoot?' Tiny asked.

'Mulch,' she said with a glare at Daedalus.

'Park the hostility, sister,' he said, waving her implied accusation away with a tired hand. 'I didn't plant those mines.'

We were airlifted out, but not until the next morning. Which gave us plenty of time to get our story straight: a story that four dumb, stim-addled legionnaires could stick to under the pressure of 'enhanced-debriefing'.

They kept us in the stockade for about three weeks. Every few days they dragged us out to debrief us again. Both alone and in groups. They told me the others had broken and told them the truth, so I had one chance to do the same or I would face the death penalty, for sure this time. I just laughed at them, earning myself a little more torture. After the first week, they decided there was nothing left to try on us individually, so they put us together in a latrine pit that we knew would be full of microphones, and they waited for us to break cover and talk.

So we talked. In between being showered with piss and feces from the toilets above us, Tiny talked about growing up in a small farming town that slowly changed as food production went from fields to industrial-sized labs. Ostrich's parents had been some kind of 'preppers' living off-grid, and she told us about a world where you could still drink from streams and lakes in the wild. Where fish swam free in the seas, and gardens were full of birds, deer and squirrels. We didn't believe her, but they were good stories. Daedalus told us he was a painter.

'Sorry, *what?*' Ostrich asked.

'You mean, like, in a workshop, painting cars or something?'

'No, philistine,' he said. 'Fine art forgeries. Matisse, Rembrandt, Banksy – you name it, I mastered them all. And the techniques: how to age a canvas or found object, source the paints, impregnate the work with isotopes enough to fool the carbon-dating scans.'

'But you got caught,' I guessed.

'Of course I got caught,' he said. 'But not for 10 glorious years. Ten years of high living, real cigars, the best weed, cognac from actual grapes.' He moved aside as a stream of sewage poured down beside him. 'The judge offered me enlistment or life in jail, so I joined the Red Army.'

'Life in jail for forgery?' I whistled, thinking that's what I'd been given for 'murder'. 'That's pretty harsh.'

'The rich hate being made a fool of by the poor, Termite,' he said.

Eventually they got tired of listening to our boring life stories, dragged us back out of the latrine pit and separated us again, but by then they'd also grown bored with torturing us, so they just left us in dark cells with nothing to eat and the threat we would never see the sky again. It was just like being back in Voeykov, more summer camp than imprisonment, really. It didn't last, and they eventually sent us back to Legion Praeda.

The Legion had just lost an entire cohort on top of its earlier losses, so Praeda was taken off the line and put in reserve while it was built up again. Newly condemned meat trickled in. We expected we would be split up, distributed among other crews, but they chose to keep the four of us together and assigned us to another MCV. Without grounds to court-martial and execute us, they probably thought the best idea was to keep us all together so that at least if we were killed, there was a bigger chance we would all die together, and the last living stain of the Battle of Margarita Terra would be wiped away forever. Or maybe they'd wired our MCV and were still waiting for us to slip up and talk about what had really happened up there.

Fat chance.

It meant that we needed a replacement for Fatfoot though – a new loadmaster for the meat locker.

He arrived with a knock on our barracks door. We knew he was coming, but Daedalus made him knock three times before finally answering the door after 30 minutes, glaring at him, dressed only in dirty briefs. I wondered how many times he had been through the ritual before: before me, before Termite, before before before.

He, the replacement, was a she. 'Nonsense!' Daedalus bellowed at the poor girl who was standing there shivering with either cold or fright. (Pneumonia, I learned later, since she didn't really do fright.) 'It's too early for a replacement. We're still mourning ... uh ...' He turned around to us. 'What was the damned fool's name?'

'Fatfoot, Decanus,' I told him without rising from my bunk.

'Yeah, we're still mourning Fatfoot.' He slammed the door in the girl's face.

But she was eventually allowed in, inducted into the crew, and took her place in the payload bay. She was a solidly built girl – had to be, to be a loadmaster – but what I noticed straightaway was that neither Voeykov nor Daedalus had managed to take the shy, cheeky smile from her face. It was the kind of smile you weren't sure if you had really seen, it came and went so fast. But then you thought about what she'd just said, and when you rewound your memory, there it was. That little smile.

Her Redside name was Lucretia, and her nickname 'Blindside'. Neither lasted very long.

They rebuilt our cohort with endless exercises, pointless drills, and a worryingly slow influx of new legionnaires that spoke more about how the war was going than the mind-numbing newscasts we were subjected to every time we sat down in the galley to eat.

... in breaking news, the firebase at Schiaparelli Crater has been reestablished after it was abandoned by the enemy four weeks ago. Mining operations will resume as soon as the mines are cleared of booby traps. A strategic firebase east of Flaugerges, the recapture of Schiaparelli extends our control of the Terra Sabea ZoC by another million hectares and ...

Recapture? Is that what we called it when we reinhabited a destroyed, empty camp? We were like wasps taking over the nest a different swarm had abandoned last summer. The only reason the Zenos ever abandoned a camp was because it served no purpose any longer, or all the Zeds they'd Turned had expired. It couldn't be mined for resources, had outlived its use as either a porcupine or offensive base. Any Zeno there ghosted. Like Margarita Terra, the troops that eventually made it through the suddenly undefended perimeter found only dead, frozen bodies, destroyed habitats and weapons or ordnance rendered unusable or booby-trapped. If the Zenos had booby-trapped the mines at Schiaparelli, it would probably be weeks, maybe months, before they were operating at full production capacity again.

No cheers greeted the victory announcements. They barely registered, except among the bookmakers and gamblers, who began speculating on how soon it would be before the base fell again. The only news that raised a cheer was if an officer was assassinated.

Some watched the newscasts though. The dreamers. The few among us with a candlelight of hope that Voeykov hadn't been able to extinguish. Like Lucretia.

She stirred the 'stew' (roasted reconstituted plant protein powder) mixed with 'health drink' (fermented reconstituted plant protein powder) that they were calling chow that day, and pointed with her spoon at the screen. 'That's good, right?' she said, looking around the table for agreement. 'We've got control of more territory now than we had six months ago.'

'Uh-huh,' Daedalus said. 'And how much do the Zenos control?'

She thought about that. 'Well, they've just Turned Leighton, and they took Camp Huygens last month. So that gives them those two, plus another what, two ZoCs they currently hold, against our 15? Four, total. No, three, since we took back Margarita Terra. So we're winning.'

Ostrich gave a bitter laugh.

'What's funny?' she asked.

'You. But don't take it the wrong way, replacement …'

'With respect, my nickname is Blindside, Optio,' she said, allowing the needle to get through her armor.

'Here's the thing they didn't tell you in all those Reducation classes in Voeykov, replacement,' Daedalus said, ignoring her protest. 'The Zenos have just been playing with us so far. Probing.'

'Probing?' she said. 'Taking down ZoC after ZoC is probing?'

'Zenos have never had control of more than five ZoCs at any time,' Ostrich told her. 'Sometimes it's two. Right now it's three. Never more than five.'

'They're learning,' Daedalus said, with the confidence of a man who had been fighting the same enemy for more than a year. 'They use our own troops and weapons against us, so they're learning what we're capable of, strengths and weaknesses, strategies and tactics. Once they have our measure, they'll go for the real prize.'

Ostrich nodded. I realized they'd discussed this before, but it was new to me. 'Kamloop.'

Lucretia frowned. 'The Void Forge?'

'What else?' Daedalus said. 'Antimatter is the rarest substance in the solar system, the most dangerous to produce – which is why the facility is located here on The Red. It's the basis of this settlement's entire economy, and the Void Forge went online just a few months before the Zenos appeared. You think that's a coincidence?'

Ostrich picked up where Daedalus finished. It was clearly a theory based on rumor and gossip that they'd nurtured over a long period. 'Kamloop is the heaviest-defended ZoC on The Red. Home base to the Praetorian Guard, the Legion Aquila. Every inhabitant is screened daily for Zedification. The Void Core is buried deep in the crust, so it can't be nuked from space and is basically one supermassive electromagnetic bottle the Zenos can't get near.'

'So how are they planning to capture it?' Lucretia asked.

'Well, if I knew that, I'd sell my idea to the Zenos and retire to The Blue filthy rich,' Daedalus scoffed. 'But it's a fair bet they haven't worked that out for themselves yet, or they would have done it already. Plus.' Daedalus raised a finger in the air. 'Plus, the government has never once said it thinks the Zenos are here for the Void Forge, *et ergo*, that's why the Zenos are here.'

'Blah blah blah. Who cares why the Zenos are here. They're here,' Tiny said. 'And we need to baptize the replacement.'

Daedalus had been on a roll and was annoyed Tiny had broken his flow, but he relented. 'Alright.' He motioned with his hand. 'Stand, Gregarius Lucretia.'

She frowned, put her spoon into her bowl, and stood.

'We have a long-standing tradition in this crew that we recently started,' Daedalus said in his best portentous voice. 'Whenever we get a new replacement, they must take on the name of our dearly beloved and recently departed comrade, uh …'

'Termite,' Tiny prompted.

'Yes, dearly beloved Termite, curse his soul.'

'Sodding Termite.' Ostrich nodded. 'Forget him.'

'Yes, forget him. And in his honor, Gregarius Lucretia, you will henceforth be named …'

She pointed at me. 'I thought *his* name was Termite.'

'Not any longer,' Daedalus said, annoyed again at being interrupted. 'That there is Ballsack.' Daedalus collected himself. 'He *was* Termite, when he was our latest replacement. But since the death of Fatfoot, he has been replaced by the new replacement, who is you, so therefore, henceforth, et cetera et cetera, *your* name is Termite. Is that clear, Gregarius Termite?'

'Perfectly, Decanus,' she said, saluting. And there it was. Or wasn't. That little smile I was starting to enjoy.

It was a carefree few weeks, that rebuild. Outside the perimeter of ZoC Flaugerges, the war raged. We watched the cohorts from other Legions mount up, ride out, sometimes to return victorious, more often to return as smoking, blood-spattered, limping wrecks. Meanwhile, we played games of chance – the size of the pot inexorably linked to the level of injury they risked – ate our reconstituted protein, drank our 'beer' ration and basked in the reflected light of the twin moons, knowing it could not last.

Sure, the propaganda was seductive. There were 10 billion people Earthside. The exact number was a secret, but by our best estimates, upward of 300,000 combat troops had now been shunted Redside, and the number in the various garrisons was increasing, despite attrition. Add in support personnel, and you got to a half million Earthsiders on The Red. So even though we were bleeding a lot of meat, as long as the number of ZoCs we were building and had control of was still increasing, we *were* winning, right?

Doesn't sound like victory to you? Us either. In the Legion Praeda, we didn't count ZoCs. We counted bodies. And by our reckoning, if you allowed for, say, four or five Zenos per Turned ZoC, and counted the total number of ZoCs that had been lost – 69, since several had been lost and recaptured over and over – then we figured the Zenos had lost 276 individuals to our tens, maybe hundreds, of thousands. And in fact, they had lost *none*, since we figured they didn't actually die, they just *ghosted*.

That sounds like defeat to me. But I'll allow that at the rate we were losing bodies Redside, none of the politicians Earthside were particularly worried because, after all, what are a few hundred thousand casualties against a population of 10 billion? The military analysts on the newscasts would laugh at the Zenos' 'asymmetrical warfare' strategy and point to its inevitable failure. 'They're trying to break our will to fight,' the pundits would say, chuckling among themselves in panels and on talk shows. 'They don't understand humanity. They don't understand they are just making us more determined to win.'

Funny, I didn't feel especially determined to win. I was inclined to stay alive, yet absolutely resigned to the fact I could die any day. Not quite defeated, but also not quite 'determined to win', right?

And by now you've probably been thinking about what happened there atop the mesa at Margarita Terra and thought, hey, wait a minute, Linus. Didn't you say Zenos Turned their victims into Zeds through exchange of fluids? And didn't you make out with a succubus? Shouldn't you have Zedified, during all that leisure time at ZoC Flaugerges?

Yes. Yes, I should have. But I didn't. We'll get to that.

It wasn't all beer and Skittles for the crew of the good ship Daedalus. The Red Army was always short of meat, and we were randomly assigned to different duties, sometimes alone, sometimes together. Like the time they assigned us to the Sandcruiser *Liquidator*.

'No slime-sucking way!' Ostrich said in delight as Daedalus roused us out of our bunks.

'Full slime-sucking way,' Daedalus said, throwing her a breather. 'I overheard a centurion saying half *Liquidator*'s bridge crew is down with dysentery, and they need a pilot, engineer, sensor operator and tanker.'

'And loadmaster?' Lucretia asked hopefully.

'Yeah, nah, sorry, Termite,' he said. 'But I volunteered you for kitchen duty while we're gone. All-you-can-eat reconstituted protein. Thank me later.'

There were so few Sandcruisers Redside that we knew all their names. *Dominator, Terminator, Liquidator, Intimidator.* And one being built, *Eliminator.* Whoever was naming them had a one-track mind.

They required industrial capabilities not available Redside, so they were constructed on Earth's moon and freighted by antimatter-powered rockets Redside. Each one took three months to make and six to transport, and their arrival was greeted with jubilation every time. There was dancing in the streets of settlements across The Red, cornucopia were opened for public consumption, holographic goats were sacrificed, that kind of thing.

Because why? Because a Sandcruiser was a traveling ZoC. It was the size of two Earthside football stadiums. It was said that if all four Sandcruisers were parked edge to edge, they would be visible from Earth with any decent telescope. A cruiser was antimatter powered, and its skin generated a magnetic field to keep Zenos out. Its humped spine was lined with pulse cannons and interceptor missiles.

From its flight deck, it could launch 100 aircraft. It had two rear-side ramps that could lower and launch a century of MCVs, *every 20 minutes.* No Zeno-held ZoC had ever survived an attack by a Sandcruiser. The only thing that stopped the four Sandcruisers from winning the war single-handed was that they couldn't be everywhere all at once.

They were big, and moved slowly. And there were plenty of places they couldn't go, where the terrain was too rough, or too constricted. They had stealth features, but face it – nothing that big could be *really* stealthy.

The Zenos could see them coming from 100 klicks out, and after they learned they could not take them down with force, they realized they had a choice: burn the ZoC they had captured, launch some last-minute kamikaze-style strikes in some other direction, and then bug out, or stay and fight, to force the cruiser to travel to them, so they could wreak havoc somewhere else.

When we got to the dome *Liquidator* was parked inside, she was still being loaded. A cohort of MCVs was snaking up a ramp into her payload bay. I remember reading a story from back in the day aircraft carriers were a thing Earthside – before swarming hypersonic stealth missiles – which said they'd had a ship's crew of about 2,000 – like half a Legion Redside. Just to sail one ship?!

Liquidator was bigger than an old aircraft carrier, but it had a crew of about 30: three shifts of seven on the bridge, and two in the payload bay, with low-level AIs handling most of the drudge work. To get to the bridge, we took a rotor platform up the outside of the hull to a gangway.

'Play our cards right, this could be the start of a beautiful friendship,' Daedalus told us as we skimmed along a hull covered in armored plates and cannon ports. 'Our ticket out of the Legion Praeda.'

'What about Termite?' I asked.

'Who?' Daedalus frowned.

'Our new loadmaster,' Ostrich said. Not only the most creative profanitor in the crew, she was also the only one of the three longer-term crew members who seemed to have retained a modicum of human feeling. It rarely got the chance to peek out from under the sweat and grease of her thermal skins before it was shoved back into place, but it was definitely still there.

'Oh, him …'

'Her,' Ostrich corrected.

'Well, I expect that as helmsman on the ES *Liquidator*, I will have a certain amount of influence,' Daedalus said. 'I should be able to get him …'

'Her.'

'... assigned to a new MCV in the Legion Praeda in no time, so he can keep working up his combat hours.' He looked out over the loading bay with paternal munificence. 'Quickest way to earn your combat hours: the Legion Praeda.'

'Quickest way to be turned to mulch, you mean,' Ostrich said.

'Po-tay-to, po-tah-to, Optio,' Daedalus said. We were approaching the door onto the bridge wing. 'Now, square yourselves away.'

He actually made an effort to button the uniform collar outside his thermal skins, which was quite affecting, since there was no button there. The door in the hull hissed aside, a gangplank extended, and we stepped off the platform into the cool, calm quiet of *Liquidator*'s bridge.

Our reputation had probably preceded us. Three pairs of eyes turned to regard us with the respect deserving of the survivors of the action at Margarita Terra. Which was to say a mixture of derision, scorn and nose-pinching disgust.

Liquidator's commander was a tribune called Marcus Junius Silanus. We learned pretty quickly his nickname among the crew was a derivative of his last name, too salty to relate here. His primus pilae, or second in command, was a centurion by the name of Marcus Aemilius 'Leper' Lepidus. The last of the welcoming committee was the Decurion Gaius Scribonius 'Bony' Curio, who was the one who actually ran the vessel. He took Daedalus's salute as we entered. The other two officers took a step back, the better to avoid our stench. There were seven crew stations lining the bridge, padded chairs with skull caps hanging on armrests.

No blood stains. And yes, I said *padded* chairs.

'Decanus Daedalus and crew reporting,' Daedalus said, then introduced the three of us.

'My God, have we come to this?' the tribune said sadly.

The PP, Leper, sniffed disdainfully, looking at Tiny. 'Have you forgotten how to salute, Optio?' It was true that Tiny's had been more of a forehead slap than a salute.

'Sir, no sir,' Tiny replied smartly. 'But I had a tendon in my forearm severed in an action in the Olani Chaos at Hellas Planitia, sir, and I can't …'

The decurion, Bony, intervened. 'Very good, Optio. Decanus, take your people to crew level 2 for fumigation and delousing. We deploy at 0400. You will report back to the bridge for the forenoon watch.' The other officers had returned to their conversation already, and he turned to join them, then paused. 'Look for Decanus Sura down there; she'll get you settled. Tell her I authorized you to draw new uniforms.'

There was an elevator at the back of the bridge, and stepping inside, we saw it had only four buttons – bridge, crew level 1, crew level 2 and payload bay.

'Not much chance of getting lost then,' Tiny remarked, pressing the button for crew level 2. We began to descend.

'There have to be other ladders, gangways, access hatches,' Daedalus said, looking up at the roof of the elevator with the practiced eye of a man always checking for escape routes. 'Cruiser this big. I want each of you using every spare waking minute to familiarize yourself with this vessel and keep an eye out for … opportunities.'

The others nodded, but I frowned. 'What "opportunities" would they be, Decanus?'

Daedalus looked at me like I had just come down from a tree. 'Opportunities for profit, Gregarius,' he said. 'For personal gain, for mood-enhancing substance procurement, anything for the general betterment of the situation of this crew and in particular the well-being of its commanding officer.' He tapped his chest. 'Which would be me.'

'Theft, you mean,' I clarified. 'How long are we going to last if we start stealing from the crew of the *Liquidator* as soon as we come aboard?'

'You can leave the details to the professionals,' Daedalus said. 'Just keep your eyes open is all we ask, Ballsack.'

Decanus Cornelia Lentulus 'Surefire' Sura was everything Daedalus was not. His face was brown, grimy and wrinkled. Hers was pale, rosy cheeked and smooth. The stubble on his head was interspersed with islands of radiation-induced alopecia. Hers was a uniform golden peach fuzz. His voice sounded like he had sand in his gearbox. Hers was silicon smooth.

He would have found something sarcastic to say at our appearance in the crew mess, our arrival having announced itself olfactorily the moment we stepped out of the elevator. Surefire simply blinked, took a deep breath through her mouth and stood up from the table where she sat with her watch crew. 'Decanus Cornelius and crew, I presume. We can do introductions later. I was told you poor bastards have come straight from Legion Praeda, so I assume you want a shower, new uniforms, food, beer and some sleep.'

Tiny looked at Ostrich, who looked at me and shook her head in warning. *Prepare to be disappointed*, that warning look said. *That is never going to happen.*

But it really did. And even though the shower and uniforms were just as much for the benefit of the rest of the crew, and even though I was probably terminally poisoned by the three rounds of fumigation Surefire put us through, the whole process made me feel semi-human again for the first time in several months.

By the time we came from our bunk room, deloused, scrubbed, and uniformed, into a mess where steaming plates of 'stew' and mugs of 'beer' emerged from the table with the tap of a forefinger on a screen, the rest of Surefire's crew had departed to prepare for their watch duty, leaving her to stand and watch us eat and drink, which couldn't have been fun.

When we stopped to draw breath, she interrupted. 'I could give you a tour, but there's no point,' she said. 'What you saw in the elevator is all there is. Bridge, officers on level 1, rest of the crew this level, and then the payload and ordnance bay, where you'll never go.'

I could see that was like a dare to Daedalus, who shot a glance at Tiny and nodded, issuing unspoken orders to the big man to make the payload and ordnance bay a priority in the search for 'opportunities'.

'So why is a Sandcruiser so damn big?' Ostrich asked. 'All the space can't all be taken up by the AM core.'

'*Two* antimatter cores,' Surefire said with a patient smile. 'Five meters of active magneto plating to keep the Zenos out, embedded microwave defenses to fry any incoming missiles, point defense laser and plasma cannon ports buried 6 meters under the plates, self-sealing ammunition lockers and enough ordnance to flatten the prickliest of Zeno porcupines.'

'And a cohort of MCVs, plus legionnaires in the payload bay,' I pointed out. Despite my brutal Reducation, I still remembered *some* of my training from officer school.

'Sometimes, but not on this trip,' Surefire said. 'The MCVs you saw being loaded are all one-way attack units. We're going to deliver them to Zea Dorsa, with love.'

I saw Tiny twitch. Camp Zea Dorsa inside the Hellas Planitia ZoC was a festering wound. The Lilin had Turned it, and used it as a base to raid the nearby mining camp at Olani Chaos, where Tiny had apparently been wounded. The mining camp had been reinforced, which the Zenos loved, because once they Turned that, too, it gave them a fresh supply of Zeds they could feed into Zea Dorsa. Every time the Red Army thought they had the Zenos at Zea Dorsa licked, or they'd run out of Zeds, more were shunted in from the mines in the Olani Chaos. Since a person could only survive a few weeks after Zedification, the theory was the Zenos were keeping a supply of uninfected miners alive down in the mine shafts and only bringing them up to be Zedified whenever casualties were taken at Camp Zea Dorsa.

The tendon lost by Tiny, along with the multiple lives lost by the Legion Praeda probing Hellas Planitia before I joined, had been sacrificed to help the Red Army general staff face the fact they were going to have to throw a Sandcruiser at the problem. Surefire explained the strategy was to use *Liquidator*'s air wing to take out the Zenos at Zea Dorsa from the sky, while uncrewed MCVs deploying 'Ferret' hunter-killer drones were sent into the mines to 'deal with the Zeno reinforcements'.

'By "deal with", you mean "rescue", right? Since these are reinforcements who are still human, just being held prisoner,' Ostrich asked.

Surefire just gave her a blank stare in reply.

'The vessel is called *Liquidator* for a reason, Optio,' Daedalus said.

'Wait, I'm going to be running tank operations to hunt down and exterminate human POWs?' I asked.

'Oh, goodness no,' Surefire said. 'My people will do that. You and your colleagues are just here as backups, in case any more of my crew go down with dysentery.'

I saw a small neuron fire inside Tiny's head. 'So … we don't get any combat hours from this deployment?' Combat hours only counted for active-duty personnel on a vessel during combat. If you were sitting it out in your bunk, or just on damage control or medical duty, you didn't earn a single minute of combat time.

She mistook the expressions on our faces for concern about our well-being. 'If you're lucky, you'll sleep through most of the operation,' Surefire said. 'You're taking forenoon watch, right? So you'll get us to the ZoC, and then the regular crew will take over for the actual engagement. Once the operation is concluded, you'll be called back to the bridge for the trip home.' She stood. 'Alright, I'd better join my people on the bridge. See you for watch changeover at 1145.'

If our eyes had been lasers, we would have burned eight holes in her back as she walked away.

'If we're lucky my wrinkled ass,' Daedalus said. 'They're keeping all the combat hours for themselves.'

'It's what we'd do,' Ostrich pointed out.

'Yes, sure, but it's one thing to be the ones doing it, and another thing entirely to be the ones it's done to,' he said.

'We could shit in the protein tank so they all get dysentery,' Tiny suggested.

'We have to eat from that tank too,' I pointed out.

'Yeah, but we've *already* had dysentery.' Tiny winked. 'And we'll be immune to our own parasites.'

'You don't … We're not …' I spluttered.

Daedalus held up his hand. 'Full points for being solution oriented, sensor operator Tiny, but no one is shitting in my stew. The less organically displeasing solution to this dilemma is for us to ensure the Zenos attack us while *we* are on the bridge.'

And there you have your basic instruction in the logic of a soldier in the Red Army. It is better to be under enemy fire than safely tucked up in bed out of harm's way. Since only under enemy fire can you earn your ticket home.

But Linus, I hear you say. *Enemy fire can be lethal. Why would you want the enemy to attack you?* Well, you wouldn't, if you were in the cockpit of a 10-ton MCV that a single well-aimed missile could obliterate. But on the bridge of a 100,000-ton Sandcruiser, behind 5 meters of active magneto plating inside a hull bristling with close-in defensive weapons, enemy fire that counted toward your combat hours was more of a bonus than a mortal threat.

'How are we supposed to provoke the Zenos to attack us before we reach the ZoC?' Ostrich asked.

Daedalus looked annoyed. 'I am in charge of strategy, Optio. Like all great commanders, I leave the tactics to my subordinates. Now, let me order you all another round of unadulterated stew, and beer, while you three flesh out my plan.'

No, I *wasn't* OK with the idea the Red Army was about to use a Sandcruiser to wipe out the surviving population of one of our mining installations. And if you read the official entry in the History of the Red War that supposedly refers to the *Liquidator*'s action at Hellas Planitia, you would find this:

In one of the most impressive demonstrations of the power of a Sandcruiser, the ES Liquidator and its complement single-handedly recaptured the firebase at Camp Zea Dorsa in the Hellas Planitia ZoC, in the process liberating nearly 300 personnel being held prisoner in the Olani Chaos ice-mining facility.

Spoiler? Not really, because the real question was how the hell I managed to do that when Tribune Silanus had orders to eliminate them, the crew of the *Liquidator* had no qualms about carrying out his orders, and I was the only one among Daedalus, Tiny and Ostrich who seemed to think saving the prisoners had to be part of our plan to rack up some combat hours.

I did it by appealing to the remnants of Ostrich's humanity. Like picking at a scab to allow sunlight and air to heal a wound, I presented my case, found just the right emotional leverage to gain her buy-in, then worked together with her to craft a tactical plan that would both provoke the Zenos into a preemptive strike against the *Liquidator* and save the lives of the prisoners inside Olani Chaos.

No? Alright, *I* came up with a plan to provoke the Zenos into a preemptive strike and relied on blind luck for the rest. It was Ostrich who spotted the plan's side benefit though.

'If this works, those prisoners might actually make it out alive,' she said, as I laid it out for Daedalus.

'Forget the prisoners,' Tiny growled. 'If this works, we are going to be back in the Legion Praeda quicker than you can say, "Which idiot provoked the Zenos to attack us?"'

Daedalus sucked on the gap where a tooth had once lived and nodded. 'That is true, Optio, but I was wrong. This crew has no intention of welcoming us into its overprotected bosom. They will keep us around, and out of combat, for just as long as it takes to replace their dysenteric comrades, and then we'll be shunted back to Flaugerges and fed into the grinder again. So we might as well earn a few hours of cozy combat time while we're here, and unless either of you has a better plan, I am willing to go with Ballsack's idea, especially since if *anyone* gets court-martialed and shot, it will be him.'

Yeah, well, if I could save 300 souls at the same time as earning a few combat credits, it was worth the risk in my book, and I was fine if none of the others felt the same. I had a feeling Lucretia might have, if she were there.

After we were done ladling 'stew' into our bellies and pouring 'beer' down our gullets, we roamed the ship, checking out every nook and cranny, catalogued the valuables inside the poorly locked lockers of the crew and officers in advance of our inevitable departure, and refined our plan, though there wasn't really that much to refine since I would be doing most of the dirty work. Sandcruisers had priority over the precious supply of graphene chips, so there was no shortage of AIs to handle mundane tasks on the *Liquidator*. As tanker on a Sandcruiser, my role was broader, so my title was attack weapons specialist, or just 'weapons'. I had two relatively straightforward duties: to program the autonomous aircraft in the air wing with their orders and launch them, and to do the same with the autonomous ground vehicles in the payload bay. Once that was done, with the tap of a couple of holographic icons, they would be on their way to unleash death and destruction on the Zenos, the Zeds and the miners, soon to be referred to as 'the collateral'.

A Sandcruiser was the opposite of stealthy, so the Zenos knew we were coming. They also knew they were doomed. No Zeno ZoC had ever survived a full-scale assault by a Sandcruiser. Of course, after a Sandcruiser attack, all that was left of any installations inside the ZoC was a series of blackened craters and carbonized once-human bodies, but that was the price of victory.

The Zeno defensive strategy in the face of certain death had always been the same: burn every interceptor and missile in the armory trying to take down the Sandcruiser's aircraft and land a few hits on the cruiser itself while keeping as many Zeds alive as possible to repel the mechanized infantry assault on the firebase. The result was always horrible attrition of aircraft, tanks and legionnaires on both sides, with the Red Army forces claiming victory when the Zenos ghosted and fled the battlefield, and the Zeno commanders no doubt congratulating themselves for once again inflicting mass casualties on their human enemies.

Which was why, apparently, the general staff had decided to get straight to the victory celebration, by using the air wing to raze the firebase to the ground without wasting troops on it. That pesky problem of constant reinforcements coming out of Olani Chaos ... well, the uncrewed MCVs and their Ferret hunter-killer drones would deal with that. Sure, there would be nothing left to recapture, but as long as you could raise your flags over the ruins, it was mission accomplished, right? The Earthside war bulletins would report another ZoC returned to human control, and a statue would be built in a dome somewhere to honor the tribune who led the attack. Marcus Junius Silanus was probably already lobbying for his to be rarer bronze, not Red iron, given how pus-filled the festering wound of Hellas Planitia had been.

The only senior officer on the bridge when we reported for the forenoon watch was the *Liquidator*'s executive officer, Decurion Scribonius 'Bony' Curio. He seemed like a nice guy for an officer. Had we met in other circumstances

(circumstances, for example, in which I was also still a decurion and not a court-martialed deserter), we might have been friends. But since I was about to send his Red Army career crashing to the sand in flames, that was probably not destined ever to be.

There were three of *Liquidator*'s regular crew members covering this watch too: a fusion propulsion technician, a hull integrity specialist and a comms-officer-slash-navigator. Like us, none of them really had to do anything except stand watch over the AIs that were doing the real work, and be ready to intervene if there was some unforeseen event or brain fart from the cruiser's CO.

'XO has the bridge,' Bony announced once we were all settled at our control stations. 'Now, those of you who are on the bridge of *Liquidator* for the first time, the first thing to tell you is to relax – the first time is the most awkward for everyone.'

One of the other crew gave an ingratiating chortle, which Bony ignored. 'I understand you are all accomplished MCV specialists, among the elite in your Legion …' Now it was Ostrich who had a little chortle, but I figured Bony was saying that to allay the doubts of his own personnel, not for our benefit. 'You will find *Liquidator* is really just a supermassive, overpowered, over-armored, redundancy-profligate MCV.'

'That's disappointing,' Tiny said from the station beside me. 'I thought it was a Sandcruiser.'

'It was designed to require no transition training for experienced MCV crews,' Bony continued. 'Now, you may be tempted to second-guess your AIs. You may think you know better than them. And if this was an MCV, you may be right. But the *Dominator* class Sandcruiser has been given an Artificial General Intelligence exemption by our politicians Earthside. That means that unlike any other weapon platform in this solar system, the *Dominator* class Sandcruiser is AGI certified.' He let that sink in, looking at Daedalus, Tiny, Ostrich and myself in turn. AGI-certified AIs, AIs that could think for themselves, had been outlawed after the AI Rebellion of 2130. But laws were made to be bent, if not broken.

Should that have caused me to reconsider our plan for sabotaging the operation? Yes. Yes, it should have. Did it? You know the answer to that.

'Uh, Decurion, question?' Ostrich asked.

'Yes, Optio?'

'If the engineering AI and I disagree, who wins?' Ostrich asked.

'Since you will not be second-guessing the AI, you will not disagree,' Bony said equably. 'So your problem is purely hypothetical.'

'Right, so, hypothetically, then,' Ostrich insisted.

'Hypothetically I would decide, and I would always side with the AI, which has been trained by millions of datapoints generated by millions of hours of actual combat operations, whereas you have ... how many hours, Optio?'

'Twenty-two, Decurion.'

Another chortle from one of the Sandcruiser's regular crew, cut short by a threatening glare from Tiny.

'Congratulations. Twenty-two combat hours is not to be sneezed at,' Bony said. 'But it is *not* in the millions.' He switched mental gears. 'Watch crew, you are eight hours from the end of your watch, and we are nine hours from go-time for our attack on the Hellas Planitia ZoC. Tend to your duties, please.' He spun his finger in the air to tell us it was time to go virtual, and we flipped the contacts on our skull caps.

A control console hologram appeared in front of me. Bony could hear everything we said now, so Daedalus, Tiny, Ostrich and I could only communicate through signals or glances, which is why I had kept my plan as simple as possible. Or more accurately, why most of it relied on us not having to communicate.

The problem with an AGI is the 'G'. Rather than being a dedicated intelligence, designed to perform limited functions, it is able to be put to work on any task and solve problems it has never been trained on by creative application of scenario-based learning, just like a human. And worst of all, a 'General' intelligence has a personality.

Hello, Gregarius Vespasius, the Tanker AI said, after I logged in. I am thrilled to be working with you today. I have prepared a status report for you on our air wing and ground vehicle cohort. Would you like to review it?

'No,' I said. 'Shut up unless I address you directly.'

It contrived to sound hurt. Oh. Very well. How should I know you are addressing me? My official name is Air Tank Interface, or ATI, for short.

'I'm going to call you Stupid, Stupid. Now shut up.'

That is not very polite, it said. But I will be quiet unless I need to disturb you for a decision.

I went to work. As weapons specialist, I was also in command of our recon drones, and I put stage 1 of our plan into action when we were still well outside air wing attack range. I manually configured a drone to perform a complex patrol pattern out ahead of us and sent it on its way.

Gregarius, please confirm the patrol pattern you entered is correct, the ATI said, as soon as I hit the 'commit' icon on my console.

'Yes, it is,' I said. 'Execute it, Stupid.'

Executing, it replied. Are you aware that, seen from space, that patrol pattern spells out the words CRUISER MICROWAVE ARRAYS DOWN. ATTACK NOW.

'I think you are hallucinating, Stupid.'

At the altitude you programmed the aircraft to fly, it will leave a contrail. The message will also be visible from the ground.

'There is no message,' I said. 'Why would I write a message telling the Zenos to attack us?'

You may not have deliberately created the message. It could be a one in a hundred million coincidence. But nonetheless, I recommend you reprogram the flight while the aircraft is still en route to its patrol point.

'Good advice,' I said. 'I'll do that.' I didn't. I imagined Ostrich was having a similar but different conversation with her AI, about why she had just started playing with the power levels for the *Liquidator*'s defensive microwave arrays. My message on its own probably wouldn't provoke the Zenos into action, since it could literally just be smoke in the wind. But the energy output of a Sandcruiser with its defenses fully powered could be detected from hundreds of klicks away, and a change in that power profile would also be detectable. My message, combined with a degradation in the *Liquidator*'s energy signature, should get someone's attention.

Gregarius, you have not altered the flight plan, the ATI said a few minutes later.

'Oh, right, I'll do that,' I lied, putting my hands behind my head and leaning back.

Another few minutes went by. The aircraft is now starting its patrol pattern. Contrails will be visible. I have plotted an alternative route for this patrol. Would you like me to execute it?

'No, Stupid. Send it to me for review,' I said.

Sending.

Something appeared on a display in front of me, which I studiously ignored. Then, as I waited for the AGI to start freaking out again, an idea occurred to me.

'Hey, Stupid,' I said, reaching forward and tapping icons on my tank interface. 'What are you doing with those tanks?'

I am doing nothing, Gregarius, it said. You just ordered all tanks to standby power. Why? And have you reviewed my suggested flight plan?

'Stupid, did you just order all tanks to standby?' I asked.

No, Gregarius, it insisted. You must have issued those orders.

'You idiot!' I said, issuing commands for the tanks to execute an emergency deployment. I opened a channel to the XO. 'Decurion! The AGI has just issued an order for emergency deployment of the MCV cohort!'

He stood and pulled up the tank interface on his holographic console. 'We can't deploy while moving, can we?' he asked, not sounding worried yet.

'We can in an emergency,' I told him. At the back of the cruiser, alarms would be sounding. The atmosphere in the payload bay would be venting and the loading ramp dropping onto the sand to drag behind us. I tapped a couple more keys, retargeting the MCVs at the Zeno's Zea Dorsa firebase instead of the Olani Chaos mines. 'The ATI declared an emergency and ordered the MCVs to deploy!'

'Sir!' Ostrich said in a high-pitched, strangled voice. 'I'm getting fluctuations on the microwave arrays. It's like the AI is fighting my orders!'

Decurion, there is a misunderstanding, the ATI insisted. The emergency was declared from the tanker station. The MCV deployment was also ordered from the tanker station. The microwave arrays are being manually manipulated. I would not …

Things were spinning nicely out of control, and Tiny chimed in with perfect precision. 'Decurion, you'd better order us to general quarters,' he said. 'We have aircraft incoming. Fifty-plus, lighting out from Zea Dorsa in waves of 10. Estimate six minutes until they are in missile range.'

Bony was good, I had to give him that. A lesser officer would have drowned in information overload, entered decision paralysis. Bony cued his orders up with machine-like efficiency. 'Engineer, take all AGI systems offline; optimize power grid for defensive operations. Propulsion, give me military power. Navigator, lay in a new track for Olani Chaos. We can't make Zea Dorsa before they hit us, but we can reach the Chaos and get those prisoners fighting for us instead. Weapons' – that was me, the humble tanker – 'launch the air wing in defensive mode, 100-klick perimeter. Get those MCVs on the ground and send them full speed at the enemy defensive line. I want that firebase crawling with Ferrets before their aircraft return to rearm. Sensors, sound general quarters and tell me the minute the enemy launches missiles. Hull Integrity, I want a heat map on the display in front of me, and get ready to rotate plates on my command …' He paused, reviewing his orders to see if he'd forgotten anything. 'Helm, prepare for evasive maneuvers.'

Daedalus was sitting with a big grin on his face. Our combat timer had just started ticking. 'Sir, yes, sir!' he confirmed.

Bony slammed a hand on the armrest of his chair. 'Those wily bastards. Must have hacked our AGIs somehow, and now they're launching a preemptive strike.' He clenched and unclenched his fist. Tribune Silanus appeared on the bridge wing, still buttoning his trousers. 'Captain on the bridge!' Bony announced, standing.

Silanus winced at the general quarters klaxon blaring above his head. 'As you were, XO. What the hell is going on?'

It turned out a Sandcruiser wasn't near as damn invincible as our own propaganda made it out to be.

My aircraft took out the first wave of Zeno attackers before they could get their missiles away, but half of the second wave and all of the third managed to launch on us. Each attack aircraft carried 10 missiles, and each missile could deploy 10 kill vehicles.

'One fifty missiles inbound, bearing oh two five degrees, Mach 10.2, 10 seconds to kill vehicle deployment,' Tiny said.

Ostrich gave me an 'Oh God, what have we done' look.

'Your orders, Tribune?' Bony asked Silanus.

'You have the conn, man,' Silanus said, panic in his eyes. 'Get the situation under control.'

The engagement was being shown on a floor-to-ceiling 2D screen now, showing *Liquidator*, the incoming missiles, the Zeno air wing and, just visible on the map, the Zeno base at Zea Dorsa.

'Kill vehicle separation,' Tiny announced. 'Fifteen hundred warheads inbound. Impact in seven seconds.'

'Defensive systems?' Bony asked Ostrich.

'Powered and ready,' she replied tightly. 'Jamming.'

'Weapons, send your aircraft at Zea Dorsa,' Bony ordered.

I baulked. If I broke our air wing out of its defensive position overhead, we would have nothing to intercept the incoming barrage but our close-in weapons systems. It wasn't a question of whether any of the Zeno warheads would get through, but how many.

'Uh, how many, Decurion?' I asked.

'All. Send them all,' Bony said. 'We won't survive another salvo like this. We need to flatten that firebase before they can scramble any more aircraft.'

I gulped and tapped out the commands to send our hundred fighters toward the Zeno ZoC. The only thing working in our favor was that the Zeno air wing was busy attacking us and wouldn't be in position to defend against *our* air assault.

'Interceptors firing,' Ostrich said. The engineer also managed the cruiser's defensive systems. 'Engaging kill vehicles.' From tubes along the Sandcruiser's spine, hypersonic interceptors were blasting into the thin atmosphere toward the incoming kill vehicles, which would be zigging and zagging to evade them. From here on, our survival was a matter of probability mathematics, or if you like … luck. We could fire 500 interceptors in one volley. Two volleys in two seconds before reloading. That was 1,000 interceptors with a proven 60 percent kill ratio. Jamming usually knocked out another 10 percent. Which left a non-insignificant 30 percent still flying.

Five hundred warheads were about to penetrate our first line of defense.

In the belly of the Sandcruiser, quantum computers tied to Tiny's sensor array were calculating the impact point of the remaining warheads and targeting them with plasma cannons in wide area effect mode. From ports all over the hull, balls of plasma were spraying into the atmosphere, spreading into mushroom-head blobs of 10,000-degree heat that would melt even hardened kill vehicle nose cones to slag.

If they touched them. There were always gaps.

Two hundred and twenty warheads made it through the plasma defenses. Now the microwave arrays in the hull armor plates fired. The hull was bathed in a blanket of intense radiation that cooked off the explosive in the warheads designed to drive cubic boron nitride penetrator rods deep into the Sandcruiser's armored hide.

And through it, if it managed to hit a plate that an earlier shot had cracked.

'Impacts,' the hull integrity watch officer reported. 'Integrity at 92 percent. Plates A60, C99 are red.'

'Third wave inbound,' Tiny announced.

Bony was watching a heat map that showed suddenly blooming penetrator strikes. 'Rotate plates A60, C99,' he said calmly, once the blooms subsided and the damage picture was clear.

For a moment I wondered why he even needed to issue the order. An AI could make an assessment faster. And besides, surely it was obvious that if a plate was hit so badly it was compromised, the reserve plate under it should be rotated into its place. But then I realized, with the AGI AIs offline, all we had left to tell us how and where to use our precious supply of reserve armor was Bony's intuition.

'Helm, crash turn to zero niner zero degrees,' Bony ordered. 'Comms, order crew to brace.'

'Steering zero niner zero,' Daedalus confirmed, splitting his controls to send the cruiser in a new direction with all the grace of a hippo galloping through mud. The cruiser leaned outward, causing everyone on the bridge to grab something or someone for support, but the *Liquidator*'s heading had only shifted by a couple of degrees by the time Tiny's next warning came. 'Kill vehicle separation! Two thousand warheads inbound.'

Mortality stared me in the face, and I looked away. There was nothing I could do about the incoming high-explosive metal swarm, so I focused on the MCV swarm headed for Zea Dorsa. They had already covered half the distance to the target and would soon meet the Zeno's first-line defenses of mines, pulse cannons and lasers. But just ahead of them were the aircraft Bony had ordered me to send.

Two of the aircraft laid a long carpet of loitering airburst EMP emitters that exploded 100 feet above the surface to deactivate any mines beneath, without stirring up a dust storm. Plasma and laser weapons required power to function, and just before they fired, they radiated a power spike that an attack aircraft could detect. As my tanks got within range, the base defenses powered up, and my aircraft went to work taking them out. About half were decoys, so they got quite a few hits on my lead tank element before they went dark, but those were Bull Tanks, built to soak up incoming fire, and I didn't lose any of the Ferret carriers.

The *Liquidator*'s tanks barreled through the first line of Zeno defense like wild pigs through brambles, and as the air wing went to work on the second line of defense – crewed squad weapons and Zed infantry in trenches – the MCVs unleashed their Ferrets.

If you never saw what that looks like, here's a word picture for you. You're a grunt crewing a squad laser weapon in a trench, looking out across a rocky red sand plain, and what you see in the distance is clouds of dust, right across the horizon from left to right, the MCV turbines kicking up a storm behind them. You know they're coming, but you're sitting behind 5 inches of reactive armor at the trigger of a 50-kW laser that you know can slash the vulnerable skirt of a hovercraft and send it thumping to the ground for one of your plasma cannons to finish off. You don't even hear the aircraft above you until it's already blown past, your interceptors are exploding in the sky overhead, and you're ducking behind your shield because you know where there's attack aircraft, there's …

Loitering drones rain down on your position, sneaky little bat-winged homing grenades that attack anyone caught out in the open and away from the drone jammers, or that throw themselves at power nodes, cable junctions, sensor towers. You see two guys running toward you along the trench, a box of grenades slung between them, humping it as fast as they can. *CRUMP*. A little bat-winged horror drops on them. *CRACK CRACK CRACK* … secondary explosions as the box of grenades they were carrying detonates inside the confines of the trench, and you swing the shield of your squad weapon around to protect you from the shrapnel suddenly flying at you from that direction.

Then a shout over comms. 'Eyes forward! Guns up!'

Ignoring the still-exploding grenades down the trench to your right, you swing your weapon around to face the incoming MCVs, desperately looking for the enemy. Sensors from your trench line should be feeding you targets, your own drones overhead too, but there's nothing. Your sensors are down. Your drones just smoking wrecks in the sand. More enemy aircraft sweep in overhead.

Then you see them emerging from the dust storm, galloping toward you at 90 klicks. Low, lean silhouettes that curve first right, then left, randomly changing direction. Some of the guys in your line have missiles, but they're optimized for armor, not these greyhound-sized, cheetah-sprinting, dodging and weaving devils. A missile hits home, there's a cheer, but you aren't cheering because you're counting. You know that out there somewhere is a Sandcruiser. It probably sent a full cohort of 45 MCVs at you. But these weren't MCVs loaded with soft-tissued legionnaires; these were loaded with …

Ferrets. Hard-bodied, four-legged, hundred-kilo, hit-to-kill hunters with a brain wired with very simple objectives: identify threat, neutralize threat.

An MCV can carry 20 Ferrets. Forty-five MCVs, that's 900 Ferrets charging for your trench.

Another cheer as another missile hits. Two down, 898 still inbound. Missiles with contrails like bony fingers lance out from your lines toward the weaving, dodging Ferrets. Either side of you, guys get up on the trench step and lay their plasma rifles on the lip, sighting into the dust.

Your squad laser is set to pulse fire, best for burning into MCV armor. You switch to 'beam' fire mode. You won't be able to fire long bursts before your energy generation chamber starts to overheat, but you can scythe the beam along a wider front and won't have to try to aim.

The rangefinder in your sights tells you the Ferrets are 150 meters out now. In beam mode, your laser is good to 100 meters. *Let 'em come*, you think grimly. Your buddy next to you gives you a hopeful thumbs-up and puts his cheek to his stock.

CRUMP. More bat-winged drones drop, hitting a power junction. The power to your laser dies. You jump down from your weapon mount, scrabble for your pulse rifle. You can hear the *HUM-THUD* of pulse rifles firing up and down the line now, and jump to the step, throwing your rifle onto the lip of the trench.

Ferret! Twenty meters out. You arm, aim and fire. *HUM-THUD*. Miss. Aim and fire again. Hit! The Ferret staggers and falls. The one next to it is just 10 meters away from you now. You aim and fire. *HUM-THUD*.

Your jammers are down. Before you even see whether your second shot hit home, a bat-winged drone drops between you and your buddy and detonates.

Which is just as well, because you really wouldn't want to be alive to see the Ferrets reach your trench line. Hit-to-kill means what it says. The Ferrets use their hundred-kilo bodyweight and bayonet heads to bludgeon and slash everything in sight.

The second wave of Zeno missiles smashed into our hull. A plate on the spine was hit twice in quick succession, the molten penetrator rods blasting through the plate into the meter-thick water armor designed to absorb and dissipate the heat from plasma breakthroughs. Water flashed to steam, which was vented back out through the hull. A cooling system was overloaded and taken offline, but real damage was minimal.

'Rotate plate KK23,' Bony said. 'Cover that gap!'

'Splash four more,' Ostrich said, reporting on the air engagement. 'All Zeno aircraft down.'

Bony wasn't slamming his hand on his armrest anymore; he was drumming his fingers. I took that as a good sign. 'Comms, order Loadmaster to reload the tubes with perimeter attack weapons. Engineer, target Zeno defenses at Olani Chaos. Helm, get us back on track for the Chaos again.'

I watched with grim satisfaction on my tactical display as the line of Ferrets washed over the Zed trenches at Zea Dorsa. They had been programed to kill 'anything with two legs', but I'd changed that to 'anything with two legs carrying a weapon' to reduce the risk to civilians or, if we sent the Ferrets into the Olani Chaos, the mine prisoners.

We'd transitioned seamlessly from defense to attack. Bony's reaction to his changed tactical situation had been picture perfect, and for the first time, I saw what a real officer – i.e., not one from the Legion Praeda – was capable of.

My MCVs began firing at the Zeno firebase now, using area effect weapons to flatten everything inside the base perimeter, puncturing habitat domes, collapsing tunnels, sending plasma warheads into underground bunkers. Blast, exposure and suffocation would account for the majority of the Zed defenders, and any left hiding in pockets of atmosphere in tunnels or out on the surface in thermal suits watching their air supply dwindle would soon find themselves face to face with a not coincidentally named Ferret.

'I've got movement outside Olani Chaos,' Tiny said. 'Looks like a handful of MCVs. Headed for ... uh ... Zea Dorsa.'

'Reinforcements,' the tribune said, stating the obvious. 'Deal with them, Decurion.'

As though Bony wouldn't have, but he acknowledged the order. 'Weapons, send half of your air wing to Olani Chaos. Keep the rest on task. I want that firebase turned to ash. As soon as it is, we'll redeploy the Ferrets to the Chaos.' Did he know I'd reprogrammed them? I like to think so.

I checked the mission timer. We'd been in action for nearly a whole glorious hour, and the battle was still raging. We were going to log some *serious* combat time on this mission. But something was wrong, and it took a second for me to realize what it was. I was having a *blast*. We never got the kind of air support or firepower for Legion Praeda operations that *Liquidator* could bring to the fight. We had MCVs that would have been declared unserviceable by any other Legion, weapons that misfired as often as they fired, missiles with fuel expiry dates from back in my teen years. But it was more than that.

The buzz I had felt when Tiny announced the second wave of incoming warheads was larger than the first? The terror of imminent death, and then the rush of still being alive moments later?

That was why I'd signed on to the Red Army.

Bony brought each of us – Daedalus, Tiny, Ostrich and me – into his wardroom one at a time. We hadn't been allowed to see or speak with each other since being marched off the bridge at the end of the Battle for Zea Dorsa.

He looked up as I walked in and saluted, but he didn't salute back. I tried desperately to read his face. By the time the last shot was fired, we'd racked up three beautiful combat hours. Was he about to take them all away from us?

'Vespasius, sit,' he said, indicating the chair across from his small table.

'Decurion, about the glitch with the AGI,' I said, trying to head him off. 'If I can just be given permission to review the logs leading up to ...'

He held up a hand to stop me. 'I have personally reviewed the logs of your interaction with your AGI and an analysis of manual command inputs from your station. Your recon aircraft sent a warning message to the Zeno base that coincided with a fluctuation in our microwave defense shield. This was followed, also coincidentally, by the emergency deployment of our MCV cohort. I don't believe in coincidences. The result was a preemptive attack by the Zeno force that could have damaged the *Liquidator* and resulted in the failure of our assault.'

He paused. I tried to look shocked. 'Do you think the AGI was *hacked*?' I asked. 'How is that even possible?'

He ignored both my theatrics and my question. 'You were a decurion when you deployed to the Red,' he said. 'Sentenced to death, busted to gregarius and assigned to a penal legion for desertion.'

'To my shame, yes, sir,' I said, hanging my head.

'Your file says you showed signs of being a competent armor strategist at officer school, so let me try another theory on you that doesn't involve the Zenos hacking an un-hackable system.'

I decided to say nothing.

He leaned forward. 'A former tank officer, new to the *Liquidator*, looked at the plan of attack created by Tribune Silanus and his primus pilae, and saw it would result in the death of several hundred prisoners of war. As a prisoner himself, this former tank officer found this unconscionable, and devised his own plan of attack, which he then put into action while clumsily and unconvincingly blaming the ensuing actions on an enemy cyberattack ...'

I opened my mouth to protest, though I wasn't really sure what I could actually say in my defense, but luckily he held up a hand to stop me.

'… Miraculously, this former tank officer's plan worked. The Zeno-held firebase at Zea Dorsa was flattened, the mine at Olani Chaos was secured, and more than 300 prisoners of war were recovered, un-Zedified. It is possible that this strategy of deception, defense and counterpunch, once I have written it up and published it in my name, in the relevant defense journals with suitable caveats, will be studied by trainee Sandcruiser commanders for generations to come.'

'Sir, if I may, the speed with which you seized the …'

'Shut up, Gregarius,' he cautioned. 'I have ordered the AGI quantum cores to be wiped, and a complete system flush to be executed before they are reinstated. The official record will state that a series of random AGI glitches was responsible for various systems malfunctions in advance of our assault on Zea Dorsa, resulting in the need to modify our plan of attack, under the leadership of Tribune Silanus, with positive results.'

'Yes, Decurion.' That was all well and great, but we still hadn't got to the 'now, about you, Linus Vespasius' part.

'Now, about you and your comrades from the Legion Praeda,' he said, 'who aided and abetted in your actions.' He held up a tablet. 'This document orders your transfer back to the Legion Praeda with immediate effect. You will receive no comment on your performance while members of the *Liquidator*'s crew, either positive or negative, beyond a recommendation that you not be considered for duties on the *Dominator* class in future. Your *six* combat hours will stand,' he said, and waited for a reaction that I tried not to show, 'though your comrades will only receive three, for their lesser role in this unorthodox action.'

'Decurion.' I raised a hand. 'Are you sure we can't be of further service on *Liquidator*? I feel like we are just starting to jell with …'

He stood. 'A *Dominator* class cruiser, with fully functional AGI support, can be run by a crew of four if necessary, Gregarius. None of us is essential to the performance of its duties, least of all you and your comrades. You are dismissed. Die well.'

He saluted this time, and I snapped one back, turning on my heel with a jaunty spring. The others were waiting for me in our bunk room as I walked in.

'You too?' Tiny asked, searching my face. 'Three combat hours and a ticket back to the Legion?'

'Yep,' I lied. 'I tried to get us reassigned here, but …'

'Me too,' Ostrich said mournfully. 'But apparently that bitch "Surefire" complained we stole her crew's combat hours and offered to do double watches or something.'

'Nonetheless, this little fracas brings me nearly halfway to a ticket home,' Daedalus said.

'Thirty-three hours is not halfway to 99,' Ostrich pointed out.

'I said nearly halfway,' Daedalus said, undeterred by the math. 'Congratulations on a reasonably competent execution of my genius strategy. Now, where is that list of valuables we made? We have about an hour before we have to disembark, and I couldn't help notice there are no body scanners at the exit to the crew quarters.'

And there ends the true history of the battles of Margarita Terra and Hellas Planitia. One, a heroic sacrifice that was actually mass murder. The other, an innovative tactical victory inspired by a lowly decanus who just wanted to rack up a few more combat hours.

Lessons in human depravity more than military strategy. Sideshows in the wider war, granted, but central to the war of Linus Vespasius, whose account I humbly submit is the only one you can trust.

Which leads us to the Battle of Isidis Planitia. But not the one you know, of course. Another piece of the puzzle, another clue to who the Zenos are, what they want, and just as important to this story, *who the hell I am.*

Isidis Planitia

What you heard about Isidis Planitia in the History of the Red War, if you heard about it at all, was probably this:

The Battle of Isidis Planitia was a minor action in The Red War, notable more for the regrettably high number of casualties than for its strategic importance.

That's it, right? A single sentence.

Well, let me tell you this. Isidis Planitia was where my journey to enlightenment really began. Sure, you could say it began on arrival Redside. Or seeing Livia as her true self on the mesa at Margarita Terra. Before and after Daedalus drilled a 10,000-degree hole in her.

I thought about that a lot in the days afterward, in the effluent pit. Like, why he did it. He said he did it for us, that he deliberately and with forethought traded the lives of the men and women at the foot of the mesa in the minefield below for our own. *His crew.* He'd been warned by the tribune that we were going to be placed before a court-martial for our incompetence out on the plains of the Margarita Chaos. So it was us or them. Or us minus Fatfoot versus them. Fatfoot? He was collateral damage. But would he not have traded his life in order to save the four of us if we'd asked him, Daedalus asked? Of course he would have.

I seriously bloody doubted that.

So I was giving a lot of side-eye to Daedalus after they hauled us out of the effluent pit and assigned us to a new squadron. The Legion Praeda leadership was a total cluster at that point, with the current crop of centurions all jockeying to be promoted to the suddenly vacant position of tribune, even though none of them stood a chance because everyone knew – at least every one of us grunts knew – they would never appoint another criminal to command a Legion of criminals. Lunatics and asylums, right? Of course the new tribune had to come from outside, and she did.

Her name was Gaius Avidius Hersilia, and she was awesome. You didn't expect me to say *that*, did you? You expected me to say she was a sadistic bitch. Well, yes, she was that. But that didn't make her less than awesome. Have you read the stories of Boudica, Queen of the British Iceni tribe during the Roman Empire? That girl who had wild red hair, always appeared at the front of her troops in battle, and kicked Nero's ass so badly he was close to surrendering all of Britain to her? *That* was our Hersilia: Boudica reborn. She didn't just order us into battle at Isidis Planitia; she led the charge. I personally heard her say (or Daedalus did, which is close enough), 'I don't care how deep the freaking hole goes. Wake me when we hit bottom.' We were all on death row anyway, but if I was ever going to lay down my life for someone, it would have been for that crazy, red-haired, sadistic Boudica.

Why do I say sadistic? Well, let's just say a tribune comes into a penal Legion with a set of expectations. Preconceptions, if you like. First, that we are terminally demotivated and think of nothing except how to get out of performing our duties. Harsh, though true, I will give her that. Another? That we are not competent soldiers and therefore need to be trained, drilled and 'disciplined' to within a millimeter of our lives.

That one is not true. I had been a hell-good decurion. The fact I fell in love and went AWOL and was caught and sentenced to a penal legion had nothing to do with my soldiering abilities. I would say the same of Ostrich, Tiny and Daedalus, having seen them in battle now. I had no idea what kind of brain fart got them there, and I would never ask, but it wasn't a lack of soldierly competence or discipline.

OK, maybe a lack of discipline. None of us actually believed that the ability to scrub a latrine clean with a toothbrush made you a better legionnaire. And no, we weren't so fussed about turning up for roll call if a few of us could sleep longer because a couple guys shouted 'here!' when we weren't. The whole 'consequences' thing was admittedly kind of lost on men and women who had been sentenced to death and sent to the Legion with the lowest survival rate on The Red.

But sadism was apparently something that came with the tribune job description, so we rolled with it. Hersilia's thing? Every tribune had their own special foible, a thing they came up with that was peculiar to them. Earthside, it might have been tying a legionnaire to an ant nest and smearing them with honey. Or pushing them underwater with only a straw to breathe through, which was too narrow to give you enough air to live but just wide enough to think if you sucked harder, you might just make it.

The Red had no ants, and no water. What it had, though, was freezing-cold wind and a lot of rocks. So a legionnaire who refused a direct order, or worse, took a swipe at an officer, they got 'cairned'. Cairning was Hersilia's invention, and I even heard her brag about it once.

'So what we do in the Legion Praeda in place of the usual disciplinary actions, which do not suffice ...' she told a senator from The Blue once, in her British upper-class accent. '... is we send the offender outside wearing only a thermal skin, not a suit ...'

'Not even a breather?' the senator asked, shocked.

'Well, yes, a breather, or they'd die immediately,' Hersilia said as though it was a stupid question. 'No, we send them out with skins, and a breather, to the Plain of Cairns.'

'I'm not familiar ...' the senator admitted.

'Oh, you won't find it on a map,' Hersilia said, flicking her hair over her shoulder. 'I named it myself. It's a small flat plain just outside the eastern perimeter at Flaugerges, strewn with small stones from a meteorite impact. The idea is that the offender has to go out there, wearing only thermals, and build a cairn of stones.'

'That doesn't sound too onerous,' the senator said. 'I mean, yes, they would be freezing, but a cairn of stones ...'

'Oh, but there's one more condition,' Hersilia said. 'They have to find the highest cairn, and the one they build has to be higher.' She gave a throaty laugh, and I remember that laugh, because I was there, and it made my groin warm. 'Of course, the first offender had it easiest. But the next, and the next?'

'Delicious,' the senator said. 'How tall is the tallest cairn now?'

Hersilia had no idea, and needed to call a decanus to her to get an update. 'A meter ninety. Taller than most men,' she said proudly.

'How many die trying to complete this challenge?' the senator asked.

She waved a hand like she was swatting a fly. 'Fewer than you might think. More than I would like.' She picked a biscuit crumb off her robe. 'I will have to think of a new punishment soon, if the attrition rate continues to climb.'

I never got cairned myself. But I know four guys who did, and only three made it back. I don't know if you can extrapolate that, but a death rate of one in four for gross disciplinary offenses seemed pretty OK to us. In fact, it left quite a lot of room to maneuver. And Hersilia wasn't a stupid sadist. She was having trouble filling the ranks of the Legion as it was, so she didn't want to waste too much meat out on the Cairn of Stones.

I'm rambling, aren't I? That happens to a man dealing with the trauma I've been through. With the burden of the truth I bear. Ah, where was I? Oh hell, yeah.

Isidis Planitia.

Let's start with what is written in 'The Geography of the Red Planet', which is, excuse the language, pretty useless.

Isidis Planitia is a plain located within a giant impact basin on Mars, *situated partly in the Syrtis Major quadrangle and partly in the Amenthes quadrangle. At approximately 1,500 km (930 miles) in diameter, it is the third-largest obvious impact structure on the planet, after the Hellas and Argyre basins. Isidis was likely the last major basin to be formed on Mars, having formed approximately 3.9 billion years ago during the Noachian period. Due to dust coverage, it typically appears bright in telescopic views, and was mapped as a classical albedo feature, Isidis Regio, visible by telescope in the pre-spacecraft era.*

Bored now? Sorry, I am too, but there are actually people who care about these kinds of things, thank God, or none of us would be alive. I'm not one of those and, as you are still reading, I'm guessing neither are you. So let me get to the important part, which is … Isidis Planitia wasn't what it seemed. To you, it's a big crater 1,000 klicks wide, and to me, it turned out to be a gateway to the whole cowardly, depraved, depressing civilization (generous word) of the Zenos. Sorry, I'm still there. Can't leave it. It annoys me so much, given what came after, which, yes, I will also tell you. Perhaps. If I live long enough.

Which is highly unlikely. Damn, I'm being negative again.

Why? Because at this point in the story, Daedalus, me and the crew of our MCV were about to crawl through the anus of the planet and give it a colonoscopy.

Sorry, that was rude. It's just … I think of the battle of Isidis Planitia and I get all worked up because there were so many damn lies. First lie, our mission briefing. Yes, we got a mission briefing, even us lowly MCV crews. More than the legionnaires in the meat locker get, less than a decurion.

Our mission briefing for the action at Isidis Planitia was delivered by a centurion. But we already knew this mission was going to be a bad one, because sitting next to him was Tribune Hersilia, in all her bloody-haired beauty.

'Alright, scum, listen up. Camp Bradbury at Isidis Planitia ZoC has gone dark. It was Turned about a month ago by the Zenos and has been a pain in the ass since then, Zenos using it to send out raids while they still had Zeds and lately just racking up a body count with automated ground and air defenses for as long as they have ordnance.' This centurion was a guy in his thirties, which was pretty impressive, given the average lifespan in the Praeda. Of course, he might have just joined from Voeykov. 'We have lost too many good troops trying to recapture Bradbury, so now we're sending you.' If that was meant to be a joke, no one laughed.

He pointed at a map projection. 'We will breach the perimeter, here, where defenses are weakest and the minefield has already been triggered by previous attacks. The enemy has missile launchers, auto-fire pulse and laser cannons, no vehicles, no aerial drones. Positions of these have been marked. Tribune Hersilia will now take the briefing.' He stepped aside as she stood and walked to the podium.

'Men and women of the Legion Praeda,' she started, looking around the ranks. For a moment, she looked right at me, and my heart nearly stopped, but her gaze moved on. 'I know you have embraced the title of "scum of the earth" that other legions have given you, and made it your own. I know your officers call you scum as a form of praise. Well, if you are scum, I am scum too!' she said. There was a cheer from some officers in the front rows who had probably been told to cheer at appropriate moments.

'Where is *this* headed?' Termite asked me.

'Wherever it's headed, I don't want to be there,' I replied.

She continued. 'Your last tribune died gloriously leading the charge that recaptured Margarita Terra. He showed us the path to victory lies in quantity, not quality. Our 45 vehicles, behind a metal shield of 460 tanks, will blast through the enemy perimeter with myself and my crew as the tip of the spear …'

'And here it comes,' Daedalus muttered.

We didn't have to wait long to find out what he meant. Hersilia looked over the heads of the legionnaires in front of us to where we were sitting, and fixed her gaze on Daedalus. 'Would the crew of Century II, Squadron II, MCV II, please stand?'

That was us. We stayed seated, trying to meld with the plastic of our seats until a decurion waded through the crowd and prodded us to our feet.

'Legionnaires! I give you: the heroes of Margarita Terra!' she said. Vapid applause from the officers up front. 'The crew that fought their way through to the Zeno stronghold, overwhelmed the last remaining Zeno and brought glory and renown to the Legion Praeda standard forever!'

The officers stood and gave us a chorus of *hoozah hoozah hoozah* before sitting as quickly as they could.

'Please, be seated, dear comrades,' Hersilia said, waving us back into our seats with a munificent smile. 'I look forward to discussing that great victory with you as we prepare to lead the charge on Camp Bradbury and *victory!*'

Polite cheering from the front rows, looks of scorn from the other crews. Everyone who had been in the Legion at the time of the cluster that was Margarita Terra knew the real story. The centurion stood again as Hersilia vacated the podium. 'Alright, restrain yourselves. All crews to their vehicles, and get ready to dust. Die well!'

Tiny turned to Daedalus. 'The tribune is going to be riding with *us?*'

'Yes, Sensor Operator Tiny, it would seem so.' He rose wearily to his feet, and we all got up too.

'That's good, right?' Tiny said. 'I mean, the tribune's MCV is the best protected.'

Ostrich sneered. 'And how'd that turn out for the last tribune?'

Daedalus clapped Tiny on the shoulder. 'Don't listen to her, son. This is a wonderful development. Luckily, I heard on the grapevine this might be in the works, and I have a plan.'

I was already in love with Lucretia – Termite, I'll call her – since she had a way of taking everything Daedalus said and turning it on its head with a few dumb questions. Thing is, I knew she knew they weren't dumb, but she knew I knew that and she would give me a little smile to say, 'Just roll with this, alright?' So I did.

We were tramping down a corridor toward the vehicle bay, ignoring the jeering and catcalls from the other crews. Termite sped up until she was beside Daedalus. 'Question, Decanus?'

'I don't recall opening for questions, Termite,' he said. 'Yours is not to question why, yours is but to SITFU and die.'

She frowned. 'SITFU?'

'Suck it the freak up,' I told her.

She raised her hand again. 'Consider it sucked, Decanus. What is the strategy for getting us through this alive?'

Daedalus looked at her like she was insane. Which, to be honest, we all were, but he gave her an extra heavy dose of doubt. 'Assume that you won't,' he told her. 'And there's a chance you'll be pleasantly surprised.'

She looked at me, gave me the smile that was not there, and I wanted to marry her.

I know. When you are in life-or-death situations, which we always were, you add more meaning to things than are really there. A curse is a portent. A glance is a promise. A smile that isn't a smile is …

She wanted to marry me. I could feel that. That not-smile smile was saying to me, 'I see you, Ballsack who calls himself Scabrous whose real name is not Linus. I know we haven't known each other very long, and we probably won't live long enough to consummate this new love affair, but I want you. If there is ever a moment when we are not being punished, tortured, starved or shot at, I will make crazy wild love with you, and after you are dead, I promise you, I will survive, and I will raise our child (or children, since twins run in your family), and I will call them Linus and Linea, and I will tell them stories of what a hero you were, and how you sacrificed your life for me, for them, and for the entire human race, never thinking of yourself. And their children will know your name, and their children's children, and …'

No, I am *not* pathetic. I am a human on a learning journey, as all of us are. On The Red, I was learning to suffer. I was learning the emptiness left by lost hope. And I was learning that even in war, it was possible to find love. That train of thought kept me smiling right up until the moment we were joined by Tribune Hersilia and her primus pilae (that's second in command), a centurion called Caius Mucius Scavola, aka 'Mucus' to his troops.

'At ease, everyone,' Hersilia said as she climbed up the hatch onto the command deck. 'Scavola, hook me up, please.'

As she took her place in a jump seat, and Mucus helped her fit her skull cap, I was anything but at ease. I made a show of adjusting my own skull cap, but my attention was on the seven gold rings she wore. Each was large, with a precious Martian gemstone, either olivine or garnet, set into it. There were a lot of rumors about those rings. One, that she had one for every Zeno she had personally dispatched. Another, that there was a ring for every enemy in the Red Army she had vanquished in her rise to power. A third theory – my favorite – was that she took a lover in every unit she led, and had a ring made for them when they died.

When he was done, and was busy fitting his own cap, she leaned forward and skewered Daedalus with a stare. 'Now, just so we are clear, Decanus Daedalus, I have read the reports of your interrogations and I do know what *really* happened at Margarita Terra.' She leaned back in her seat and crossed her arms. 'If I had been appointed more quickly, you would all have been cairned, repeatedly if necessary, until dead.' She gave a supercilious smile. 'But I wasn't, and here we are. The one true thing I said up there was that I expect we will be victorious today, and that you will be heroes once again. Tell them, Scavola.'

He looked startled, speaking as he finished adjusting his cap. 'Ah, yes, Tribune. The war is not going as well as our political leaders on The Blue hope. The citizens of Earth need heroes, and the story of five criminals in a penal legion achieving redemption through valor, inspired by the personal example of Tribune Gaius Avidius Hersilia, will become legend.'

Heroes? I could see there was only going to be one hero if that particular story was ever told, and it was Tribune Gaius Avidius Hersilia. But I marveled at the boldness of her ego. The Legion Praeda was the least desirable command in the entire Red Army, and yet she had requested to command it. The crew of Century II, Squadron II, MCV II (us) were the most despised of all the crews in the Legion Praeda, and yet she had chosen to ride into battle with us. And not only into battle – at the spearhead of a mission that was almost certainly suicidal, or it would have been given to any other Legion. And all because she wanted to take a shortcut to fame.

You just had to admire moxie like that.

'We will do our best to achieve valorous redemption,' Daedalus said. 'Your orders, Centurion?' She might be riding with us, but we all knew Hersilia brought Mucus with her to do the actual work.

'The battle plan is for the crewed vehicles to go in at speed behind a phalanx of 400 uncrewed tanks,' he said. 'They will take the brunt of the enemy's defensive missile fire and take out most of the missile launchers and energy weapons. Our crewed vehicles will follow them in, deal with any remaining defensive emplacements, and then all the troops will dismount and hunt down any Zenos or Zeds still remaining within the perimeter.'

'Yes, Centurion,' Daedalus said agreeably. 'And we will be in the first line of crewed vehicles, directly behind the tanks?'

'Oh, God, no,' Mucus said, looking horrified. Hersilia gave a little chuckle. 'We plan to write history, not make it ourselves. You will take up position about 5 clicks behind the most rearward element and use all of your firepower to defend this MCV at all costs.'

Tiny gave me an unsubtle wink and a very unsubtle fist bump. 'Told you,' he whispered.

The battle did not start well.

We got an immediate reminder that we were back in the Legion Praeda. The resources they gave us to throw at the problem that was Isidis Planitia were a lightyear from what we'd had on the bridge of the *Liquidator*. 'Phalanx is down to 32 tanks,' Mucus reported. He was giving Hersilia a running commentary on the engagement out ahead of us. The camp's automated defenses had unleashed a storm of missiles at us, which took out half of the 450 tanks. As the survivors got closer, they found themselves outranged. The enemy's automated energy weapon emplacements could hit our tanks long before our tanks could hit them. 'We're still not through the first line of defense.'

'They're spread too widely, for goodness's sake,' Hersilia said. 'It's supposed to be a phalanx, not a damned herd of cats.'

Mucus passed on an order to close separation between the tanks, but that just allowed the remaining automated gun emplacements at Bradbury to concentrate their fire.

'Pointless observation from a worthless underling, Tribune?' Daedalus said, turning his seat to face the back of the command module.

Hersilia fluttered a hand at him in undisguised exasperation. 'Why not?'

'Your centurions aren't exactly charging at the enemy,' Daedalus said. 'It's more like a half-hearted meander.'

'My thought exactly, Decanus,' Hersilia said. 'Your suggestion?'

Daedalus pointed to a section of the Zeno line that was guarded by a single pulse cannon and two laser turrets. 'Kamikaze charge. Send half the remaining tanks full speed at the cannon, the others at the laser turrets. While they're busy, our MCVs go to military power and blast right up the middle, ride out the enemy second wave of missiles, and then hit those emplacements from behind.' It all sounded very kinetic and therefore risky, and I could see Hersilia wasn't loving it. Daedalus saw it too. 'It will of course be critical to keep one MCV out of enemy weapon range to perform the pivotal role of providing stand-off fire support. But I doubt you'd get any volunteers for such an ignominious task.'

'You're right, Decanus. My centurions are pathetic glory seekers, the lot of them,' she said. 'We'll have to do the hard work ourselves. Mucus … sorry, Centurion Scavola, issue the orders.'

Daedalus pulled back on the throttle and the piercing whine of the blowers behind us died down. Termite called up from the meat locker. 'Decanus, what do you need?'

'At last, a *good* question, Termite,' he said. 'Keep two launch tubes with close-in interceptors. Load the rest for standoff precision anti-missile support.'

'Keep two interceptors, reload with 18 standoff missiles, aye,' Termite said. 'Uh, call it six minutes to reload.'

'Not good enough, Loadmaster Termite,' Daedalus said loudly, playing to his audience. 'I want those missiles ready to fire in four.'

We all knew it was an automated loading system, and there was no way to turn six minutes to four, but Termite played along. 'Yes, Decanus! Of course, Decanus!' she said, with exaggerated enthusiasm.

We were hardly moving now. Ahead of us, the tanks of the other MCVs split, going left and right at high speed, headed straight for the enemy guns. With an uncoordinated staggering surge, the 44 MCVs of Hersilia's cohort gathered momentum and sped towards the gap in the enemy first line of defense.

'All tubes reloaded,' Termite reported.

Daedalus's plan was actually working, for a minute. 'Ostrich, boost power to the sensor array.'

'Enemy plasma cannon down, one laser cannon down,' Mucus reported. 'MCVs approaching enemy lines.'

The problem was it was only the first line of defense. Camp Bradbury was built along a low range of hills, with the main buildings on the ridge line, and gun and missile emplacements, beacons and spikes spread around the foothills. As they broke through the defensive line, the MCVs ran into the second and triggered an avalanche of short-range ballistic missiles. The MCVs were too close for their own systems to be able to detect and engage the rising cloud of doom.

'One twenty two hostile missiles locked; 18 standoff weapons allocated. Request permission to ...' Tiny said.

'Launch!' Daedalus said, not waiting for him to finish.

The MCV rocked as missile after missile was kicked into the air overhead, then ignited its first-stage booster. In seconds, they went supersonic, then ramjets kicked in and they went hypersonic. Finally, reaction engines pushed them to ultrasonic velocities. Each of our missiles carried 10 kinetic hit-to-kill submunitions, and they took their targeting from both our sensors and the sensors of the 44 other MCVs that lay in the crosshairs of the enemy counterattack.

One hundred eighty warheads converged on 122. The math was in our favor. But not entirely, since the Legion Praeda was always allocated the oldest and worst-maintained ordnance.

'One hundred-plus enemy missiles intercepted, Tribune,' Mucus reported. 'Nineteen Legion MCVs destroyed. Twenty-five report they have reached the base of the ridge and are engaging defenses from the enemy's rear.'

Nineteen crews lost. Ninety-five souls. Sure, it wasn't Margarita Terra, where more than 400 were killed, but I knew some of those guys. I felt gutted.

A couple of them owed me money.

Perimeter defenses are designed to attack threats outside the perimeter, not inside them. Using short-range pulse cannons and the few tanks that rejoined, the surviving MCVs made short work of the remaining defenses in the sector they had breached.

'*Excellent* work, Decanus,' Hersilia said, as though Daedalus had loaded the warheads himself, targeted and launched them with his bare hands. 'Your supplement to my strategy was commendable and will be mentioned in dispatches.'

In other words, we might avoid a court-martial this time, but shouldn't expect much more.

Mucus reported the first Legion MCVs had reached the ridgeline.

'No sign of the enemy, ma'am,' he reported. 'They have secured the anomaly.'

Daedalus, Ostrich, Tiny and myself looked at each other, but saw no answers to the question we were silently asking each other.

What freaking anomaly?

'Take us in, Decanus,' Hersilia said.

What we found at the top of the ridgeline inside Camp Bradbury was yet another scene of post-Zeno-occupation death and carnage, but that wasn't the interesting part. We also found the Zenos' butthole.

That's what Ostrich called it.

'It looks like a goddam infected butthole,' Ostrich said, after we dismounted and were allowed to examine it. I had to give her that one. Our MCV was waved through, and after we finished crunching across frozen bodies, we came to the groundworks at the periphery of the camp that the Zenos had apparently been trying to hide, and then defend.

A hole in the surface of the planet had been covered over by a 10-meter-thick crust of sand and debris, but the occupants of the camp had come across it by accident while digging a planned latrine. Which made you wonder how many of the great discoveries of mankind were made by a person wandering into the wilderness looking for a place to take a dump, really. Like coffee. Who the hell had thought to themselves, 'OK, here is a berry. I shall pick it; eat the flesh; ferment the bitter, inedible core and roast it; then crush and pour boiling water over it and it shall become the most popular beverage in human history.'

Someone sitting next to a coffee bean bush taking a dump, I promise you.

The excavators working on the latrine for Camp Bradbury struck an unknown metal. They couldn't dig through it, so they dug around it. The unknown metal showed itself to be a disc about 200 meters in diameter. So they dug around that. The metal cap fell into the hole below, along with six members of the crew doing the digging.

They died well, since they uncovered the Isidis Planitia Anomaly, which you never heard about because if the planetary government told you, you and everyone Earthside would lose your tiny minds. What was so mind-blowing about it?

Unlike a butthole, it had no bottom.

See what I did there? Sorry. I'm doing my best to stay sane here and one way I do it is inappropriate humor. I know I might come across as patronizing. Don't mean to. It's just, I know that not a single person in the human universe has been through what I've been through – you included – so I don't want to assume anything, including whether or not you know what was so amazing about the bottomless hole in the center of the Isidis Planitia ZoC.

Because it wasn't the bottomless-ness.

It was the fact that on recapturing the site, Tribune Hersilia promptly sent two of her MCVs into the clotted white vastness of that hole, and none came back. Until she sent us. Because we went in, and we came out again.

But we were not the same when we came out. And neither was she.

The second lie we were told about Isidis Planitia was this. 'They are probably still alive.'

Mucus said that, when he ordered us into the hole and Daedalus asked him what had actually happened to the crews who went into the butthole before us.

'Then, with respect, if they are alive, why the hell have they not reported back?' Daedalus asked, quite reasonably.

Mucus lost it at that point, and I don't blame him. He had his orders. His orders were to send us to almost certain death by repeating the error that had already been committed twice previously, just blindly sending another MCV into The Red's anus and expecting a different result. He was a convict like the rest of us, just a lower degree of stupid, which had allowed him to retain some kind of rank, like Daedalus. And in his worldview, sending us to an apparently quick death was a mercy, so why were we even asking questions?

But Daedalus, I was learning, really believed he was going to make it off The Red and Earthside again. The rest of us, we went through the motions of trying to survive, but he had unshakeable faith in his destiny. Was he a narcissist, sociopath, delusional, or all three? Thinking of how casually he had sacrificed Fatfoot and half the Legion, and how he was willing to die inside a *Dominator* class Sandcruiser if the upside was a couple of combat hours, I vote the latter.

'They have not reported back, *Dec-anus* …' Mucus said, placing a lot of emphasis on that last syllable, 'because they are now in paradise, receiving blow jobs and/or cunnilingus from a heavenly host whose only purpose is to ensure their eternal happiness.'

'Well, that doesn't sound too bad,' Tiny said, nudging me.

'With even more respect, sir, what happened to us becoming heroes in some interplanetary propaganda campaign?' Daedalus asked.

Mucus's eyes actually glinted malevolently. 'Ah, well, the tribune is of course grateful for your contribution. But it would be unfair of her to put you in the position of having to deny that responsibility for the success of this operation was yours, not hers. So she has decided to spare you this embarrassment by allowing you to sacrifice yourselves in this way, since posthumous heroes actually make for a more compelling story than live, talkative ones.' He clapped his hands impatiently. 'So mount up, get your machine moving down the ramp into that pustulous hole, and keep transmitting until you either reach paradise or can transmit no more.'

We mounted up.
'Oh, well, at least it'll be a quick death, and our families and beneficiaries will finally get our blood money,' Tiny said. 'And backpay.'
'No, they won't,' Ostrich said. 'We'll be MIA, not KIA. Legion only pays out if you are certified KIA. They'll wait months, maybe years, before declaring us missing, so they can pocket our paychecks. Those money-felching centurions will pocket every Red dollar that the Tribune doesn't take for herself.'
Tiny looked crestfallen, but Daedalus, as usual, was sanguine. 'Glorious, good-looking and reasonably competent crew,' he declaimed graciously as he crunched our MCV turbines into gear and the fans filled our skirts. 'We are about to boldly go where few other crews have gone before. Two other crews, to be precise. But they were idiots, all. Whatever fate befell them, unless it was, you know, desirable, was their own fault. I, however, have complete faith in this crew – except for Termite, who has yet to prove himself …'
'Uh, I identify as a woman?' Termite said from down in the payload bay. Whatever was about to happen, it was going to require the minimum effort from her, since we no longer had a payload in the bay.
'And I care, dear Termite,' Daedalus said to her with continued graciousness. 'As I was saying, I have faith in *most* of you, and whatever happens to us in the next few weeks, days, or minutes, I want you to know that.'

Tiny was booting up his sensors and stopped what he was doing, giving me a thumbs-up. It was a lovely, comradely gesture and made me entirely miserable.

Ostrich was running through the litany of things that were wrong with our vehicle, and barely paused for Daedalus's declaration of love. '… joints overheating, rear laser defenses defunct, and we used every last one of interceptors,' she finished saying.

Daedalus, sitting in his perch in the command cupola above and behind us, had been listening to his own voice, and not to Ostrich. 'Engineer from Commander, summarize, please.'

'Anything attacks us down there, we're dead,' Ostrich told him.

'All systems normal then,' Daedalus declared with deranged cheer. 'Moving out.'

We lifted off the red sand and slid towards the infected maw of the anomaly.

There was a ramp marked with pathetically innocuous traffic cones, and Daedalus steered us toward it.

Termite did her thing, asking the obvious. Down in the payload bay, she had a wonderful head-high, five-person-wide screen showing her a near-3D image of our impending doom. 'Uh, Decanus? Seeing as every other unit entered the anomaly though this ramp, maybe we shouldn't?'

Surprisingly, Daedalus didn't mock her. He hauled the MCV to a halt. 'Good point, Termite. Why did none of you others say the same?'

I kept quiet. My reasons were personal, since they involved fantasies of self-harm.

'I was going to,' Tiny said. 'But you never listen.'

'That changes today,' Daedalus announced. 'Suggestions? Options?'

Termite had already been thinking about it, that became clear. 'The ramp is obviously a death trap. The most logical approach is therefore to take the least logical approach,' she said.

'Which is?' Daedalus asked.

'The opposite. The other two MCVs no doubt made cautious approaches at low velocity, via the ramp. I propose we dive off the other edge, going immediately vertical, at high velocity,' she said. The way she said it, it made so much sense. But you have to remember I had already decided I was in love with her, and her absence while I was on *Liquidator* duty had only made my heart yearn more.

Perhaps Daedalus had begun falling in love with her too. The thought of that makes me inappropriately jealous as I write this, but there you are. We are full of fallibility, we humans. In any case, he shoved his throttles forward and steered us around the edge of the anomaly to the opposite rim, ignoring the high-pitched queries, followed by protests, from Mucus.

When we reached the far side of the anomaly, Daedalus balanced us on the edge. 'Tiny? Last words?'

'I want to go home,' Tiny said, staring into the abyss.

'Ostrich?'

'I used to fantasize about my aunt.'

'Not what I expected, but uh ... I look forward to meeting her one day,' Daedalus said. 'Ballsack? Something more pithy?'

'This is insane,' I said. 'This entire war is ...'

'Well said!' Daedalus yelled. 'Alright, crew, die well!'

'I want to say something!' Termite said, from the payload bay.

'You have not yet earned the right to last words, nameless one,' Daedalus declared, shoving his throttles forward. 'Now, strap in everyone, and clench!'

Our drop into bottomless oblivion was a disappointment. We hung. Or it seemed like it. I think we fell, like maybe 100 meters. But then we hung there, nose down, harness straps biting into our chest.

'Anticlimax,' Tiny said. 'What now?'

Daedalus spun the turbines up, and racked them down again. 'I'm getting no traction. It's like …'

'… like we're in some kind of spiderweb,' Ostrich said. 'Do you suppose …'

'What?' I asked, horrified. 'Suppose *what*?!'

'Suppose we're hanging here like flies in a web, and the other MCVs are on the other side of the pit, and they're just hanging there too, and we're all just waiting for this insanely huge Zeno spider thing to come up out of the hole and spin us into cocoons and then drag us down into its lair to become food for its hatchlings … or something?'

'Tiny,' Daedalus said from above and behind us. 'You may shoot the engineer called Ostrich if you can unstrap and reach a weapon.'

'Yes, Decanus,' Tiny said, and started unstrapping.

'Tiny! It was a joke!' Ostrich yelled. 'Dammit, am I the only one thinks this is kind of funny?'

'Yes,' I told her. I was hanging from my harness, face half buried in a virtual view that showed nothing but endless klicks of oblivion beneath me. I wasn't seeing the funny side.

'We're moving, idiots,' came the voice from the payload bay. 'Don't look at your holo screens; look at your watches.'

As we were hanging in nothingness, looking at our watches, a different reality was unfolding at ZoC Isidis Planitia. We should have known, really. Isidis Planitia, right?

No? Latin for the *Plains of Isis*! It was like the name was buried in our genetic code, waiting for someone at the other end of a telescope to map the surface of The Red, see the huge crater there and think to themselves, 'Isis! Of course, Goddess of Resurrection. I must name this place after her.'

Except, to be resurrected, you first had to die. Which everyone on the lip of the anomaly was busy doing. It was another trap, of course, the Zenos being grand masters of the ambush. The dead bodies around the ZoC were not dead at all. A more competent tribune than Hersilia, with more competent centurions, would have sent legionnaires to check all the bodies, but she was a builder of cairns, not a checker of corpses.

As the crew of the doomed ship Daedalus tipped into the abyss, the dead who were not dead rose to attack the cohort gathered conveniently around the edge of the anomaly. The bodies that were not bodies were Zeds, wearing breathers and carrying anti-armor weapons.

The slaughter lasted only minutes. A legionnaire who survived it by crawling into the escape pod of a burning MCV and blasting into low-Red orbit said that after the attack, he saw the attackers gather on the edge of the anomaly and throw themselves in behind us.

We never saw them.

Termite was right; we were stationary in the blackness, but the digits on our time pieces were flying. Backwards! Don't ask me about the physics of that. It's something about relative velocities, Doppler effects, Minkowski equations and the speed of light. Forget everything you've been told about time dilation. What I know is for every minute we were in the anomaly, we got younger.

Not, like, years younger. Actual minutes younger. Measurable, visible minutes. We decided we fell for nearly an hour, so by the time we stopped falling, judging by the fact that our watch displays stopped spinning madly – though they were still going backwards – and the blackness around us went gray, we were an hour younger than we had been.

Which, unfortunately, only made us more likely to die younger.

The MCV stopped on an amorphous plain with no features in any direction, just a barely visible horizon indicating we were sitting on some kind of plain. Daedalus already had the throttles at idle, and killed the turbines.

'Not my fault!' Termite yelled, before any of us could yell at her.

'Hey, we are still alive,' Daedalus said, carefully. 'If this suspended-in-gray-nothingness crap is life.'

'It beats the effluent pit,' Tiny observed.

'That it does, Sensor Operator,' Daedalus acknowledged. 'What are your sensors sensing?'

Tiny bent to his instruments. 'Well, Decanus, I can report that according to our sensors, we have 360 degrees of nothing around us. And that includes ground. So I can't tell you what is holding us up, only that it isn't, you know, there.'

'Thank you, Tiny. Engineer Ostrich, your report, please.'

'Decanus, Engineer Ostrich is pleased to report that all systems are 100 percent nominal, except for those which were defunct before our descent, which now seem to be repairing themselves due to the backwards progress of time, so there's that,' Ostrich reported.

We hadn't dropped into the anomaly in the company of any tanks, so I didn't expect Daedalus to ask for a report from me. He didn't. 'Loadmaster Termite,' Daedalus said imperiously. 'Put on a breather and drop the payload bay door, if you please.'

Opening the payload bay door would expose our lower deck to whatever atmosphere or vacuum or neurobiological hellscape was outside, but we were protected in the cockpit, so the risk belonged entirely to Termite. She was equal to the command. 'I respectfully refuse, Decanus,' she said.

'Repeat, please,' Daedalus said, confounded.

'Decanus, we could be floating in a spatial vacuum, meaning the temperature outside is 0 Kelvin. What are the sensors showing?' Termite asked. Very reasonably, I thought.

'Tiny?'

Tiny bent to his display. 'Twenty-three Celsius.'

'Very pleasant,' Daedalus decided. 'Put on your breather and crack the damned door.'

We sat in our nice, environmentally contained capsule and waited for Termite to die. We could all watch on the internal cameras. She donned her breather, and a thermal suit, which I knew from personal experience would protect her from a hostile environment for about 10 minutes. Then she cracked the payload bay door.

I mean, afterward, it occurred to me that we could have invited her into the cockpit and opened the bay door remotely, and I would have, if I had thought of it. But I didn't.

'OH, MY GOD!' she screamed as the door dropped open. She fell to the floor, clawing at her breather. 'HELP! PLEASE HELP ME!'

Tiny jumped from his seat, then sat down again. What the hell could he do? Ostrich just stared at her monitor, mouth open.

I … sympathized.

Termite stood up. 'Just kidding,' she said. 'Like you even care.'

'Not funny, Gregarius,' Daedalus told her. 'Do a circuit around the MCV and report.'

The quick ones among you have noticed I referred to the Battle of Isidis Planitia. But that was no battle. Not really. It was a massacre. Three hundred and thirty souls died that day, though the only one they ever mention is that red-haired cairn-building sadist, Hersilia.

Not us, obviously, since if I died at Isidis Planitia, I couldn't have written about the battles of Taura Terra, Syrtis

Major and Terra Sabea, right? You've read the contents page, I assume, so you know I'm alive all the way to the final page, which could stop quite suddenly if either my heart or my memory fail me.

Except … here's a tip for anyone new to the Life and Death of Linus Vespasius: Don't assume I can't write this journal posthumously.

What? Where were we?

The anomaly. Our watches spooling backward.

Termite did a tour around the MCV. It's funny how I had started thinking of her as Termite already. What was her Legion name? Lucia? No, Lucretia. That was it. And her real name? Her Redside nickname before she joined our crew was … Blindside. Yeah, I had that much. Her real name I had never asked. I had no idea. I was going to marry her and I didn't even know what people called her Earthside. Did she have people Earthside? A mother, a father? Brothers, sisters? She looked like she would be the kind of girl would have a big family. Lots of sisters watching out for her, brothers you'd be afraid of. She had big lips and stubble that spoke of black curly hair, and wide hips. She had shown no real interest in me … yet. Which only made me love her more.

I wanted those lips to speak my name in gasps and I wanted to bury my nose in that stubble that could be luxurious hair and I wanted those hips to straddle mine. I wanted to give her children. Only if she wanted them, of course. A life of togetherness without children would also be fine. Preferably before I died, since the likelihood of it happening after was kind of minimal. And before you ask, no. I didn't get those feelings looking at Daedalus, Tiny or Ostrich.

OK, maybe Ostrich. But Ostrich was … no, that's private. Not my place to tell you.

Termite appeared back on the viewscreen from the payload bay, broken smile breaking my heart. 'Loadmaster Termite reporting,' she said, looking outside and back again. 'I walked all around. There's eff-all out there.' She took off her breather. 'And another thing. Atmosphere and gravity Earth normal. Which should blow your minds.'

We had gotten younger, so definitely not wiser.

Then the universe inverted.

I say inverted, and I know that's not actually intuitive. So stay with me here. The way I understood the universe, my universe, was this: Certain things were incontrovertible.

I was human.

Zenos were ... not.

Humans had evolved on The Blue, and we had colonized The Red. For 30 years, it was going pretty well, until it wasn't. The Zenos appeared Redside and started killing us.

That sucked. So we tried killing them back. That kind of worked, actually didn't, but we were expanding across The Red and convinced ourselves that meant we were winning.

You know now that's bulldust, but back then, we didn't. We didn't.

So turn that upside down. Or if that's too hard, let me do it for you.

I wasn't human. We aren't.

Zenos were ... are.

Humans didn't colonize The Red. For 30 years, it wasn't going well at all. We were hurtling towards our own doom.

The Zenos weren't fighting us. They were fighting their own war. We were collateral.

OK, I confused you totally now. I'm sorry. The Battle of Isidis Planitia, the real one, didn't involve fighting.

'Heat signatures!' Tiny shouted. He hadn't stopped scanning his sensor screens, and thank the gods for that.

'Where away?' Daedalus yelled. 'Ostrich, weapons up!'

The MCV was armed with pulse cannons. They were only intended for close-in defense, but 'close' was a flexible concept to an engineer like Ostrich. She had modified the weapons to engage targets out to 5 klicks, nearly five times the range their designers had intended.

'Bearing two twenty, plane zero, range 2 klicks. I have two contacts,' Tiny said. The contacts were on our left rear side, on the same level, or 'plane', as us. 'Approaching at walking speed.'

'Mechanical or organic?' Daedalus asked.

'Neither,' Tiny said.

'Damn. Zenos,' Ostrich said. 'Two of them. What do we do?'

Daedalus knew exactly what to do. 'Termite, grab your sidearm; get back out there.'

Termite spun toward the comms camera. 'Get out there? And then what?'

'Hell, woman, I have to teach you how to breathe while walking? Get out there, kill those mothers.'

She slammed a hand on the bulkhead beside the camera. 'It occur to you, Decanus, we're down the bottom of a bottomless pit, an hour into the past and going nowhere fast? Now you want me to kill the only beings could maybe tell us how to get out of here?'

Daedalus actually thought about that. I know he wanted to say, 'Yeah, that's what I want you to do.' But even Daedalus knew that street instinct was not the same as street smart.

'Alright, approach them and … make peace, or something,' Daedalus said. 'But keep your damn gun pointed at them and shut the bay door on your way out.'

Tiny leaned over to me. 'They got our whole MCV in their spiderweb, but he's worried whether our back door is open.' Even so, he checked that the airtight hatch down to the payload bay was locked.

I watched as Termite picked up a pulse weapon, but holstered it on her hip. I had to agree with her on that. I was thinking about the scene atop the mesa at Margarita Terra and thinking a little pulse sidearm wouldn't have changed that outcome. Sure, Daedalus drilled a hole in Livia, but she'd already Turned the whole damn ZoC by that point, and since her dying killed everyone else, it was a pyrrhic victory.

Termite had her chest camera on, and she headed out the back of the MCV, walked about 20 meters out, and waited.

'Coming right at you,' Tiny said. 'You should see them soon.'

'See them now,' Termite said. 'Man and a woman.'

'No. Incubus and succubus,' Daedalus said. 'Remember that. Every damn minute. Put your breather on. They get close, you feel like you want to copulate with any of them, start shooting, Gregarius.'

'Good copy, Decanus,' Termite said. 'Wet thighs, shoot the aliens.'

She said that, and it didn't matter my life and probably the entire planet Earth was about to end. All I heard was 'wet thighs'.

But I forgot straight away, because the Zenos came into view on our holo screens and my universe exploded. Or since time was going backwards, imploded, or something.

On the left was the simulacrum of a man I recognized vaguely, though I couldn't for the life of me remember from where. Let's call him Adam, since he was as naked as. On his right was a woman that I did recognize. She was also naked, which might be why I recognized her. She had a birthmark on her left breast, just above her nipple, right over her heart. It was dark brown against her ivory white skin, and you'd call it an imperfection, unless you were in love with her.

I'd called it her 'heart stain', the visible mark her heart left on the skin that covered it. I'd lay my head against it, and listen to her heartbeat slow after our lovemaking, from a birdlike thrumming to a slow, post-ecstasy drumbeat.

And this is where I tell you about Antonia.

Before Livia at Voeykov, there was Antonia. But before Antonia there was … me. Let me tell you about *that* guy so you can understand the whole Antonia thing.

Earthside, I was an ordinary man, living a very ordinary life, except for one thing. I had a hunger for danger that couldn't be sated. I captained a deep-sea sport fishing charter, taking clients far out into the Atlantic, where marlin and swordfish swam in unprotected waters, but where hurricanes, spouts and rogue weather could bury you under a hundred tons of ocean without warning. I ran up debts I'd never be able to repay, and didn't think twice about how much I borrowed, or who I borrowed it from.

I made enemies as easily as I made friends. Not talk-behind-your-back kind of enemies, but the kind who hired thugs to beat you up, or worse. In love, I also sought out crashing waves and rolling thunder. Every affair ended in tragedy and tears. It was Big Love for me, or no love at all.

When the Red War was about a year old, I killed the thug who was sent to kill me and was charged with murder. The Red Army was hungry for conscripts, and the legal system kept it fed. The judge found me guilty, and offered me a choice: life in prison, no parole, or service in the Red Army.

'Your honor, that's a death sentence,' I said.

'Don't believe all you hear,' he said. 'You only have to do 99 combat hours, and you'll be released from service with a lifelong pension.'

Ninety-nine hours? Less than *five days*? My inner adrenaline junkie did the choosing for me. I signed up to serve Redside.

I was put into officer school because I'd captained a boat crew. Like that was a leadership qualification. I did boot camp like everyone else, then specialist school (accelerated), where they taught me the basics of tank command, gave me implants and pushed me out the door as a cavalry decurion. I couldn't wait to get me some.

Every officer cadet says they can't wait to see some action. But I really meant it.

Don't ask me to describe the experience of interplanetary travel. We were herded into a meat locker Earthside, stacked horizontally five deep, knocked out, and woke up nauseated and disoriented, Redside. As we deplaned, we were given our Red Army names. Mine was 'Linus Vespasius'.

I had a real name on The Blue, of course. But as far as the Red Army is concerned, you don't exist before you arrive on The Red. There was no you, there, until you stepped off the shunt and got your dog tags and read what it said on them. A decanus handed them to you and you found out who you were, or at least who you were going to be, and I was to be Decurion Linus Vespasius.

But then later you learned there were no *new* dog tags, and no new names. They just took the tags off corpses and re-used them. Grunts like you shunted in; you got your tags, you got swatted, mulched, and then the next one off the shunt was tagged 'Linus Vespasius', and so it continued. But you were new and stupid and it felt kind of cool, that name. The whole Roman Legion thing and the Latin names for everything and everyone on The Red.

They gave us a month to get acclimatized to the change in gravity, to moving between climate-controlled habitats, to learn how to avoid freezing, suffocating, dehydrating and being poisoned by radiation when you were outside. Then they threw us a party, where they announced which units we'd be posted to.

It was at that party I met Antonia. Was she a settler, camp follower, miner? I don't remember. I told you I was the kind of guy who sought love like a kite sought the wind … the stronger it blew, the higher I flew. Antonia was a force 10 tempest. A week after meeting her, I deserted so I could stay with her. I had no plan beyond that, and didn't need one.

I knew our love was doomed from day one. That one day, soon, military police or bounty hunters would come for me. But on that last night together, I had no idea how imminent was our doom. We lay together in sweat and tears, our bodies crashing against each other so hard, so often, we cried in pain as much as in ecstasy. Then came the morning light, the knock on the door. Well, not a knock, of course. A hammering. Black-clad, exoskeletal monsters bursting through to rip us out of each other's arms.

I could have fought them. I was a tank on legs before Reducation. Implants, fully stimmed. I'd have taken one or two down, for sure. But not 10. I was ashamed I didn't try. They might have killed me if I had, and that would have been better for everyone. Me. Them. Tiny, Fatfoot, Ostrich, Daedalus, the goddamn Zenos. Antonia. I would have done them all a favor by dying that day. But I didn't. I lived to curse them all and not least myself, because if I'd died, I wouldn't have been dragged through the seven levels of hell the Legion had planned for me.

Antonia was a spy, a traitor, a rebel, a betrayer, but at that moment, the moment they crashed through the door and beat me to the ground and hauled her naked to her feet and shoved her into the bathroom, at that moment, would you believe I was afraid for *her*? Yeah. You should laugh now. I really was that stupid. But I didn't worry long, because a second or two later they clubbed me on the head and there was nothing more to remember.

I didn't see her after that. If they put her in a cell, they kept her separate. Another cell, another prison? Or a gilded room with a view over the Aurora Chaos? What do I know or care? Next thing I knew, I was standing there in the dock, accused of desertion, and they dragged her into court in a sheet. They'd fitted her with a skull cap that fed her brain a false reality, but in court they took off the skull cap, and she saw me, with her own eyes, the fog of obscura lifted from her brain as they peeled the electrodes off.

She wailed. 'Linus! Is it you? Is it you?'

Strange question, considering she was there to confirm I was me. Standing in the dock, I figured she did it for the money. The bounty for turning in a deserter was a cool Red million. She could have bought herself a ticket Earthside for that. With change. The Legion needed its deserters back, at the rate the war was chewing through meat. They'd trained us, given us implants, shunted us to The Red, and they expected us to serve and die like we'd signed up to do. We were meat to be fed into the grinder, already bought and paid for once. If we went AWOL, it was cheaper to hunt us down or pay a bounty than shunt some other loser up to The Red in our place. So I figured Antonia heard about the bounty, and her love for Linus Vespasius became fungible. It suddenly had a value she had to weigh. *I love him. But how much do I love him? Is my love worth a million Red dollars?*

Antonia stood in court wrapped in her sheet and they asked her, *Is this the man you know as Linus Vespasius?* Which was stupid since they had my DNA, but she had to put it on the record.

Yes, she said.

And did he admit to you that he was a deserter?

Again, *Yes*. The same voice she used to use when she was with me, just a different timbre. *Yes, Linus, yes, yes.*

He was with you between Mensus Aprilus and Mensus Maius?

Yes. Always yes, only yes.

You are excused.

No, Antonia, you are not excused, I was thinking. But no one asked me. As she was dragged away, she turned and cried out. 'Linus! I will find you!'

I should have believed her. It sounded like a promise, but I learned later it was just as much a threat.

Antonia. Standing naked in front of us. Which it couldn't be. Which it was.

The two figures stopped a good non-threatening distance from Termite, who gave them her inscrutable smile. 'Hello, what do you want?' Termite asked.

Antonia lifted her arm, pointing past Termite to our MCV. 'Not what, dear girl. Who.'

Dear girl. Dear boy. Antonia used to say that. It was, is – will be – her. I knew it.

Termite turned around. 'Uh, Decanus, not sure what is going on here. They appear to …'

'It's me,' I said, standing. 'They want me.'

'Sit, Gregarius,' Daedalus ordered. 'That makes no sense.' He was leaning down from his seat, glaring at me.

I tapped the air, on the image of the woman who Termite's chest camera showed in her full and natural glory. 'That's the woman who I deserted for. She's the reason I was sent to the Legion Praeda,' I said. 'That's Antonia.'

'I don't know what you think you are seeing, Gregarius,' Daedalus said gruffly. 'But I'm seeing a damned succubus. You go out there, she'll milk you dry and turn you. I'll shoot you before I let that happen.'

'She already did,' I told him. 'Or she will. I'm a little confused on timelines right now,' I admitted.

Daedalus pulled his sidearm from the seat beside him. 'I'm serious, Ballsack. I have yet to develop any sort of fondness for you, so you better believe I will not hesitate to shoot you.'

Tiny gave me a worried glance. 'He really won't,' he said. 'He means it.'

Termite had brought her pistol up and had it pointed at the woman, which was kind of interesting. Not sure what that said about her. 'Alright, we know what *you* want, so let's get to the part where you offer us something in return.'

Antonia looked at Termite like she was seeing her for the first time. Perhaps she'd just been an obstacle to pass until that point, and the question suddenly made her worth noticing. She tilted her head, as though looking at a work of art on a wall.

'Interesting. He lusts after you only because you remind him of me,' Antonia said.

I reached quickly for my throat mic. 'No. I don't, Termite. I mean, I do, a bit, but not because ... I'm not. Don't listen to her!' I said.

'Message received and not understood, Ballsack,' Termite replied. 'Daedalus, you still want me to shoot these two?'

'Yes,' Daedalus said.

'No!' I yelled. 'No. Seriously? What about the other one? The guy. Ask what he wants!' I felt like I'd seen him before. He had a hairless, softly muscled body, lithe and kind of sexless. Yes, he had a wiener, but it was rather ... discreet. Forget it, he could have been anyone. It was almost like he'd been designed to be forgotten.

Termite trained her weapon on the man. Simulacrum of a man, if we're being accurate, since our sensors were showing no trace of organic material. 'You, do you have anything to say?'

He didn't appear frightened. 'Yes. We are here for the one you call Linus.'

'Linus?' Ostrich asked, turning to Daedalus.

'Ballsack,' he said.

'Oh, right,' Ostrich said. 'I forgot.'

But Termite was talking now, and not using words I particularly liked. 'We got that much already. We give you Ball ... Linus ... what do *we* get?'

They looked at each other, like it had not occurred to them that this was a bargaining-type situation. Antonia spoke. Antonia's voice spoke. Antonia in the court, crying my name. *I will find you!* Antonia here, speaking my name again. 'Give us Linus, and we will return you to your time and place.'

'Our time and place?' Termite asked. 'That would be The Red, late 21st century, yes? Exactly where and when we left. Just so there are no inconvenient misunderstandings?'

Antonia frowned at her. 'Yes, of course. You have not left there yet. You are there still. You will be there again.'

'Well, excuse me for not realizing that,' Termite said, getting huffy. 'It's a deal.'

'No, it isn't!' I said. 'I am not going to …'

Daedalus waved his pistol at me. 'Yeah, you are. Sorry, Ballsack. I'm pretty sure I might have developed some kind of attachment to you if you'd lived a little longer, but Termite is right. It's you, or this crew, so that means it's you.' He shrugged. 'Hasta luego, amigo.'

'Lived longer? I'm still right here, right now!' I protested. 'I'm still alive.'

'Technically not,' Ostrich said. 'If time is going backward, we already sacrificed you some time in the future.'

Tiny held a hand in the air. 'If you *were* here, I'd be saying good luck and die well.'

'This makes no sense!' I yelled at them, but Daedalus waved his pistol at me, and what was I supposed to do? I wasn't the big, beefy, stimmed-up decurion I'd been before the Legion Praeda got its claws into me. So I lifted the cockpit hatch, climbed down into the payload bay, and then walked out into the nothingness of the anomaly.

Still trying to come up with some kind of escape plan, though.

Was I really about to walk away with my naked lover? To where? And why did it feel so damn wrong? I felt like yelling some more at Daedalus, but as I stepped outside the MCV, I lost comms.

I stopped beside Termite. 'I just lost comms to the MCV.'

'Me too,' she said. 'Maybe the Zenos cut us off. Let's get this done.'

'Right. This is goodbye, I guess,' I told her.

'I guess,' she shrugged. No doubt she was torn inside from the gut-wrenching pain of being forced to betray the future father of her twins. She did a brave job of not showing it.

But I wasn't going to go quietly. While she was shrugging, I snatched the gun from her hand and pointed it at Antonia-not-Antonia.

'Why me?!' I asked her. It was meant to sound like a command, as in 'Tell me why me or I will shoot you', but it actually came out a little whiny.

Neither of them looked particularly worried by my erratically waving pistol. 'You already know why, Linus,' Antonia said. 'Or rather, you did. We are here to help you reach that previous understanding.'

Uh, what? 'If you wanted me, why did you not take me when we were together?' I asked.

She frowned, as though that were obvious. 'There were those who did not think you were possible, or ever will be. We had to be sure. I had to test you.'

I thought of our days of lovemaking. 'You were very thorough about it. Or will be.'

'It wasn't unpleasant,' she smiled. 'But then, just when I was sure, your government took you from me. That was … unexpected. So we had to wait for opportunities to get you back.'

Termite had taken a step behind me, putting me between the Zenos and herself, but also putting her where she could whisper in my ear. 'Can we hurry this up? I can feel my breasts and buttocks getting firmer and I'd like to be done here before I have to go through puberty again, backwards.'

I tuned her out. 'What about Livia? In the cage. And on Margarita Terra. Was she "testing me" too?'

They looked at each other. It wasn't just a glance. They locked eyes. It was like they were exchanging data with each other. Or maybe I'm just re-engineering that memory, given what I know now.

Antonia waved a hand in the air and a floating image of Livia's face appeared. 'This individual?' she asked.

'Yes! Her. Who was she?'

'She is a Reactionary.'

'Was,' I said. 'We killed her.'

'Is,' Adam spoke this time. 'And will be. Forget her. You are safe now. Come with us.'

I still had one question. 'No. Why me? Who am I to you?'

Adam frowned. 'But you know this. You are The Code Bearer. Wielder of the Power of Future Ancestors. The Transitioned. Child of the Dawn …'

Antonia put a hand on his arm to stop him, or he would probably have kept going. 'You see, it's as I told you. He does not remember.' She turned back to me, and her eyes softened. 'You will come to understand, as once you did. Put aside your feelings for this woman. It is time to come home, Linus Vespasius.'

'Yeah, no. I just changed my mind. We need to talk about this,' Lucretia said, grabbing me by the collar of my thermal skins and pulling me backwards, careful to keep me and my pistol between her and the two Zenos.

When we got far enough back that they probably couldn't hear us, she put an arm around my waist and her mouth to my ear. Her breath was a sweet kind of foul, which was normal in the Legion Praeda, given our diet and lack of dental care.

'I'm sorry,' I told her. 'I have no idea what they're raving about! I swear.'

'Forget that,' she said. 'Tell me about these feelings she's referring to. What you said back in the MCV.'

'What I said?'

'That speech before you came out here, the whole "I do, don't, do a little bit" care for me thing,' she said.

'Well, kind of irrelevant now that you are trading me for your freedom,' I pointed out.

'Or maybe I was just playing for time. Daedalus gave you up, not me. Tell me what you meant.'

She was standing behind me, chest to my back. Since I was a little taller, I could feel the warm curve of her stomach against my buttocks. 'I meant … you know … oh, come on, this is stupid,' I said. The two Zenos were looking at us like we were aquarium animals. Antonia. The Antonia I once, would, couldn't possibly know, was standing there again – radiating love. 'Forget it.'

She pulled me even tighter, speaking fast and low. 'No, it isn't stupid, Linus. You don't realize it yet, but you need a friend if you are going to survive that murderous crew. And so do I. Are you that friend, Linus?'

Well, that was unexpected. There I was worried about the two murderous aliens in front of us, and she was thinking about the three murderous humans behind us. Maybe she was right to be. 'Yes,' I told her, fervently. 'Yes, definitely. I am.'

She held me there for what felt like an eternity – and technically was – as she made up her mind about something. 'Alright then,' she said at last. 'Follow my lead.' She grabbed the pistol from me and put it to my head.

'You send us back to our time or place, or I kill him,' she yelled at the Zenos.

'Lucretia! For eff's sake!' I protested.

The man I thought of as Adam looked at Antonia, then back at us. 'That makes no sense. If you kill him, *none of us* get what we want.'

'Maybe, but I don't trust you, and he is my only way out of here,' Termite said. 'You want him. I want to get out of here. So here's how it works. I take him with me, you send us back to The Red, same time, same place, and after that, you can come and get him at your leisure.'

Antonia blinked slowly. Damn it, I could smell the fragrance of her body from meters away, even through my breather. *Stay!* My body screamed. My mind asked whether I was goddamn crazy. 'If that is how it must be,' Antonia said.

'It is. It must,' Lucretia said. She pulled at the back of my thermals. 'OK, you, back up. Into the meat locker with me.'

'Stop,' Antonia said.

She took a step forward, and Termite pressed the barrel of the gun harder against my head. 'Not another step, bitch,' she said.

'Do you think you love him?' Antonia asked her. 'You can't, because you don't even know who he is.' She fixed her gaze on me. 'Linus? I'm sorry. Ask her to let you stay. I will explain everything.' Her voice was like a bow, and I was the violin.

Every sex cell in my body was telling me to stay. I had a lot of those apparently, and they were winning. I had neurons too, but they were being drowned in hormones at that point and not helping the situation.

Termite put a strong arm around my neck and started dragging me backwards, pistol digging into my temple. 'Into the MCV, Ballsack, or I *will* shoot you.'

Would she really have shot me right there, right then? I believe so. She didn't trust for a minute the Zenos were going to honor their promise anyway.

Adam looked pissed. Antonia didn't give up. 'Linus, please!' she called out. 'This will waste time we didn't have.' Whatever that meant.

Termite bundled me into the meat locker and stood on the ramp, looking outward into the gray mist. 'You send us back *now*, or I shoot him. That's the deal, got it?!'

When we got back into the MCV, our comms were restored, and Daedalus's gruff voice was loud in our earpieces. 'What the hell are you two playing at?!'

'I just did a deal with the devil,' Termite told him. 'They're going to send us back to the surface. Strap in.' She cut the comms link, holstered her weapon and pointed me to a legionnaire rack. 'Sit down and buckle up,' she said. 'Look at your watch.'

I did as I was told, then frowned. 'Why?'

'If they live up to their word, time should start moving forward again, right?'

Oh, right, I thought. I stared at my watch, which was still spooling backward. Then it paused, and the digits started spinning forward. The grayness turned to black and then to reddish light. Maybe we passed out. I definitely did, at least.

When I woke, lifting my chin from my chest, Termite was at the outside camera screen, looking out the back of the MCV. 'Welcome back, everyone. We're on the surface,' she said.

'Where?' I asked, though the red light from the view screen bathing the inside of the payload bay told me the answer to that.

'Wrong question,' Termite said. She stepped aside, showing me the view on screen. 'Question is when. And the answer is, "Too late to do anything."'

I unbuckled and went to stand beside her. The ground behind our MCV was littered with destroyed MCVs and frozen bodies. The huge butthole was gone. We had only been gone for what ... five minutes? Ten? Subjective time. I could tell from the frozen state of the bodies on the screen they had been exposed for hours. An entire battle had been fought and lost in the time we had been inside the anomaly.

That's the battle you read about. But not the battle I was referring to. The Battle of Isidis Planitia? *My* battle. The one waged inside me, the one where I fought to stay with Antonia and surrendered to Lucretia.

I backed up and slumped into my seat, feeling defeated, not victorious. Yes, we were alive, all of us. Maybe if I'd gone with Antonia, the others would have been killed. But maybe, if I'd stayed, I'd have found answers right there and then. Answers to what, you ask?

Who was Antonia? That was an obvious one.
Was that creature her? A more complex one.
What did she want with me? Another obvious one.
Livia, still alive? How? Where? And who?
Finally, who the hell was I?

Not such an easy one. I thought I knew. In all my misery I had at least a pretty good idea of who I was, despite the many names I had been visited with since arriving on The Red. Adam called me Code Bearer, Wielder of the Power of Future Ancestors, the Transitioned, Child of the Dawn. None of those made any sense to me. Suddenly, I had no idea who I was. Had the anomaly been created just to lure me in? No, of course not. So Antonia must have had a way of monitoring who was coming and going through Lilin portals, saw I'd just dropped into one and staged an intervention. Which hadn't gone the way she'd hoped, but was I the dumb one for not staying with her?

Is that enough questions for you? It was enough for me, and I had no answers to any of them. I guess I'd zoned out thinking about all that stuff. I looked up, and Termite was standing in front of me, shaking my shoulders.

'What?' I asked, annoyed.

'You with me, Ballsack?'

'My name is Linus,' I told her, angrily. For now, at least. On The Red, I am Linus. Not Scabrous. Not Ballsack.

'Alright, *Linus*,' Termite said. 'My name is Lucretia. And you and me have a pact now, you remember that?' she said, and I could see she meant it.

'Yes.'

'I have your back. You better damn well have mine.' She pointed at the deck above. 'Because – Child of the Dawn or not – those bastards in the control room up there would mulch us both and trade the juice for a bottle of Red beer, and if you don't realize that yet, you need to catch the hell up.'

'You don't know that,' I said.

'Oh, I don't?' she lifted me by the collar and dragged me to one of the payload bay bulkheads, sweeping aside some thermal skins hanging there. 'What do you see?'

I saw a single line scratched into the wall, on what looked like a shield.

'What is it?' I asked.

'Unit emblem,' she said. 'In case you didn't notice yet, Ostrich, Tiny and Daedalus, they've all got the same emblem tattooed on their forearms.'

I looked at it again. 'What emblem?'

She laid a finger on it. 'That's a One. This is the symbol of the 'Bloody First', the United States First Infantry Division. I'll bet my virginity these guys all served together on The Blue, probably in the same squadron.'

'Oh.'

'Yeah, *oh*,' Termite said. 'That means there is no "us" in this crew, only "them". They'll protect each other to the death, but you, me, anyone else in this Legion – we're expendable. You got that?'

'Fatfoot,' I said.

'Who?'

'Our last loadmaster. He didn't have that tattoo.'

'And he's dead, along with a few hundred others. Daedalus sacrificed him without blinking. You see where this is going?' she said. She grabbed my skull, pulled me forehead to forehead, eyes boring into mine. 'Either we kill them, or they *will* kill us.'

I pulled away. It was a lot to process. I mean, there was the drop to nowhere, time running in several directions, Antonia appearing out of the fog, Livia not dead, the whole Child of the Dawn speech, and now I was sharing a cockpit with fratricidal psychos?

'Wait,' I said. 'You're a virgin?'

She glared at me. '*That's* your takeaway from this conversation?'

'Well, that, and … the whole kill-us-in-our-sleep thing,' I said. 'So what now?'

Tiny, Daedalus and Ostrich dropped down the ladder at that point. Daedalus must have heard me asking 'So what now?' He had a hand on the pistol on his belt.

'Now, Ballsack, we are screwed,' he said. 'We are once again the only survivors of a massacre. You only get the VIP sewage pit treatment if you are the survivors of one massacre, not two.'

Tiny was swinging from an overhead strap and stopped. 'Mulch?'

'Yes, gentle giant.' Daedalus nodded. 'We are mulch. We might as well have stayed in that reverse-spin limbo there. At least you all would have got to see what an adorable baby I was.' He turned to Lucretia. 'We lost comms after you put your pistol to our dear Ballsack's head. What happened out there?'

I looked at Lucretia and she was looking at me, eyes boring into me with an expression that said 'Keep your trap shut, Linus.'

'I did a deal with the Zenos,' Lucretia said. 'They wanted Ballsack, and I said they could have him, *after* they returned us to the surface.'

Daedalus was standing opposite me, looking at me like I was a butterfly in a jar. 'A fair trade. The crew appreciates your sacrifice, Ballsack.' He turned to Lucretia. 'But throwing Ballsack to the Zenos doesn't exactly solve the bigger problem, which is the fact our miraculous survival, once again, against all odds, will not be taken kindly by the Legion.'

'I've been thinking about that,' Lucretia said. 'For whatever unfathomable reason, the Zenos want Ballsack. They brought us back from limbo to The Red, so they can do things with space and time we can only imagine. I wasn't ambitious enough when I told them to send us back to The Red. I bet they could swing it so we can get back to The Blue somehow. Maybe even some-*when*.'

'How?' Tiny asked.

'I don't know, Tiny,' Lucretia said, exasperated. 'But they can make time run backwards, they can apparate out of nowhere, their bodies vaporize when you kill them, they can build a wormhole in the surface of the planet and then make it disappear ...'

I could see where this was going, and I didn't like it. But I liked it better than being hogtied and thrown outside to either freeze or wait for the Zenos to appear and scoop me up.

'It's an idea,' Ostrich said with a shrug. 'We don't report back to the Legion. Don't leave Ballsack here. We desert, and take him to the Zenos at one of the ZoCs they hold. Do a better deal.'

'I like it,' Daedalus said. 'But I will do the dealing next time. Termite's dealmaking sucked.'

'*Or* here's an idea, just let me do it again. I got us out of there, didn't I?' Lucretia replied.

'Frying pan to fire,' Daedalus said, pointing at the viewing screen and the landscape strewn with burning wrecks and frozen bodies. 'Literally.'

'Hey. I'm sitting right here. Do I get a vote?' I asked.

'No,' Ostrich, Daedalus *and* Lucretia said in unison.

'Yes!' Tiny said. 'No, I mean. You don't get a vote, but yes, I like this plan. Let's face it: We're mulch if we go back, and none of us have a better chance of ever getting Blueside again than this.'

Daedalus moved into decanus mode. 'Alright, Ostrich, fire up the engines and plot a course to the nearest Zeno-held ZoC. Termite, make sure all squad weapons are charged and then get out there and see if you can find anything useful in those wrecks. Ammunition, energy cells, food, water, whatever. Tiny, find a way to kill our location beacon and then get an aerial drone up so we don't get surprised and run into one of our own patrols. Ballsack …' He frowned at me. We had no tanks, so there wasn't really a role for me. 'I'm thinking we should probably tie you up and tranq you so you don't run out on us, since you finally became useful.'

'He can commandeer some tanks,' Lucretia said. 'From the dead MCVs. We'll need the support. I'll tie him up down here again when he's done.'

I waited for her to wink at me, but she didn't. I was seriously starting to doubt the whole 'we have a pact' thing.

Daedalus looked like he felt that giving me a tanker role again was not a good idea, but without knowing why it wasn't, he decided to ignore it. 'Alright. But as soon as he's done, tie him up and we'll dust.' He waited. 'And this is where you ask whatever stupid question you're chewing on, Termite.'

'Alright. We can find another Zeno at a Zeno-held ZoC. But how are we going to approach a Zeno ZoC, on our own, without them flattening us, like, 100 klicks out?'

Daedalus grinned. 'I'll tell you when we're 101 klicks out.'

And therewith ends this account of the true history of the Battle of Isidis Planitia. Not the one in which the Tribune Gaius Avidius Hersilia and 330 legionnaires were ambushed by Zeds and died a death so ignominious that they barely earned a whole sentence in the Official History of The Red War.

No. The more important battle was the one within and between the crew of Mobile Command Vehicle II, Century II, Cohort II, of the Legion Praeda (AWOL). The one in which I found, lost and found a valuable ally to help protect me against my friends.

Taura Terra

Alright, I accept you never heard of this one. The planetary plenipotentiaries have good reason to squash any leaks about what happened at Taura Terra.

Some stuff you need to know before I dive in. Camp Lopez in the basin at the Taura Terra ZoC wasn't the *closest* Zeno-held camp to Isidis Planitia, but it gave us the fastest travel time, with fear of discovery being the main reason we chose it. The ZoC there had already fallen twice, so rumor was we'd given up trying to retake it. But it also held the biggest geothermal energy plant in the whole Mare Tyrrhenum, which the colony couldn't really afford to live without, so the rumors were probably wrong, as usual. It wasn't a target for active assault, though, so we figured we could make a beeline (which is not the same as a straight line) from Isidis Planitia to Taura Terra without running into any patrols.

Once I was finished hijacking the leftover tanks from the dead MCVs, I put them into an auto-defense posture, and Termite bound me and strapped me into a meat seat in the locker. I thought she'd use rope and tie me loosely so I could work my hands free, like a good partner would. But she used fusion ties that sucked themselves onto my wrists behind my back, so that didn't help at all.

About 40 klicks out from Isidis Planitia, we ran into a patrol.

'Contact on drone motion detector, bearing two seven nine, range 10. AI says … *Hydra* class,' Tiny called out.

Ostrich cursed. '*Hydra*, of course it had to be a *Hydra*.'

Everything on The Red got a Roman renaming, even armored vehicles. On Earth the *Hydra* was just known as a 'PAGV', or Polymorphic Autonomous Ground Vehicle; a humpbacked, beetle-shaped mothership that carried six smaller, faster ground-attack units on its back, releasing them one at a time. Which was how it got its *Hydra* moniker, because if you killed one, it just released two next time.

There was only one quick way to kill a *Hydra*, and that was to blow up the mothership with an air attack. But we had no air attack drones, so the quick option was out.

'Has it seen us?' Daedalus asked.

'Unlikely. It was moving east-west away from us when I picked it up and it hasn't changed course. Doesn't seem to have a sensor platform airborne that I can see.'

'Away from us' sounded good to me. But Daedalus didn't think so. He pulled up a nav map and put it on the forward screen for us all to see. 'Big crater right in front of us. Smaller craters east, clear plain west. Damn thing is moving right into the track around that crater I was going to take,' he said. 'We go east, it'll add at least another two hours weaving between those minor craters.'

'You engage a *Hydra* without air cover, that's a long, drawn-out fight that ends with it calling in air support and killing us,' Ostrich said.

'We can pull it south and sneak past it,' I suggested. I was listening from down in the meat locker with Termite.

'Good idea, Ballsack,' Daedalus said, unconvinced. 'And how exactly would we do that?'

'Tiny, a *Hydra* has seismic sensors, right?'

'Seismic, optical, acoustic, infrared, low- and high-frequency radar … only reason it hasn't seen my drone yet is because I'm way back, tracking its electronic signature on passive sensors,' Tiny said. 'Plus, I'm good.'

If my hands had been free, I would have drawn on the tactical screen we were all looking at, but being bound, I could only twitch my nose at a point south of the *Hydra*. 'I could put a tank about 50 klicks south of the contact and send a couple of missiles into the dirt. That should get its attention. Once it shows it's taken the bait, I'll lead it south.' That was the thing with an AI-commanded drone – they were easier to sucker than humans because humans were better wired to smell a setup.

Daedalus gave it a minimal amount of thought. 'It could cost us a tank, but it's worth a try. Legion air units will have reached Isidis Planitia by now, and we need to put as much sand as we can between us and the disaster at that sinkhole before we need to shut down for the night.' Tiny had killed our locator beacon, but Space Force used infrared satellites to track friendly and enemy vehicle movements. You had a chance of hiding from infrared in the heat of day when the temperature difference between your hovercraft and the background desert was minimal. At night you had to dig in and power down anything that generated heat if you wanted to stay hidden. 'Alright, get up here.'

I turned to Termite. 'Uh, cut me loose?'

Daedalus heard me over the radio. 'Wait, this isn't some stupid idea so you can get free and make a run for it?'

You could almost feel Lucretia project her disgust up at Daedalus from down in the meat locker. 'Daedalus, how stupid would he have to be to answer yes to that question?'

'Well, pretty damn stupid,' Daedalus growled. 'Which he would be, if he thinks he can jump ship in the middle of the Mare Taura and survive the night.' The radio went quiet, and I realized he was still waiting for an answer.

'No, I'm not planning to escape,' I said slowly. 'I need my hands and feet free so I can sit in my chair and operate my tanks.' Since I wouldn't be piloting them manually, they were trailing about 20 klicks behind us, and I'd set them to randomly change bearing every few minutes so that they didn't give our position away if they were spotted.

'Hands,' Daedalus decided. 'Not feet. Tiny, lift him into his chair and cut his hands free.'

I was hoisted up through the hatch by Tiny and dumped ignominiously into the chair behind my control station. 'Sorry,' he mumbled, shoving my legs into place with his boot and freeing my wrists.

'And anyway,' I said grumpily as I powered up my station, pulled on my skull cap and checked in on my tanks.

'What makes you think I wouldn't *prefer* to go with the Zenos? Like Legion Praeda has been some kind of non-stop party?'

I tuned out their replies, focusing on choosing which tank I was going to sacrifice. We'd taken six away from Isidis Planitia with us, and whatever one I split off from the pack and sent west was unlikely to rejoin us since we'd be headed as fast as we could away from it. I checked the instrument readouts on each of them and a busted portside track-cleaning brush announced the winner to me. If it wasn't repaired in the next couple of days, it would probably end up immobile anyway, its grit-blasted track bringing it to a halt.

It would last long enough to serve as bait though.

Daedalus throttled back so that we wouldn't close on the *Hydra* too quickly while I sent our decoy tank west of our position and south of the patrol. I was enjoying not having my wrists tied, and tried to use the excuse of needing to move my bowels to get my ankles untied too, but Daedalus wasn't buying it. 'Pee into your suit and clench your cloaca like everyone else,' he said.

I had to give the tank its orders via optical link before I sent it on its way, so that neither the *Hydra* nor any overhead emissions monitoring satellite would pick up a signal from us. Which actually meant I was doing nothing for nearly 30 glorious minutes, but I didn't let Daedalus see that. I kept moving icons around on my holographic display and peering at them as though I was driving the tank myself.

I didn't fool Tiny, but after a few minutes of frowning at me like I was crazy, he realized what I was doing, gave me a wink, and left me to it. In fact, I had no communication at all with the decoy tank after it got out of optical range. It was driving itself to its next waypoint and would then run the routine I'd given it when I sent it on its way. Which made me a little nervous because what if it …

There was a chime in my ears, and its icon popped back up on my screen as the decoy turned on every electronically emitting system it had – radio, radar, satellite – and started bleating its position to the world. And just in case that didn't get the *Hydra*'s attention, it loaded a 155 mm 'Thumper' into its cannon and fired it into the sky. I threw the tactical plot up onto the forward screen. 'Decoy engaging,' I announced. 'Let me know as soon as you see that *Hydra* change course.' Which I hoped sounded like I was somehow still in control, which I wasn't.

The 'Thumper' was a shell that flew 200 meters into the air before arcing down and slamming into the earth, burying itself 20 meters into the sand and exploding. It was specially designed to generate a seismic shockwave that a receiver on the tank could use to look for Zeno tunnels, but the shockwave was detectable anywhere from 50 to 80 klicks away, depending on the subsurface geography.

'Nothing,' Tiny announced after a minute or so. 'It's still tracking west. Fire another one.' Since he knew I was faking, this request amused Tiny greatly.

I'd actually programmed the tank to fire three Thumpers at two-minute intervals, just to be sure, and I made a show of tapping a non-existing firing icon in front of my face. 'Firing two,' I said, grinning at Tiny.

Somewhere over the horizon, my decoy tank fired another Thumper. That impressed Tiny, and he leaned over toward me, whispering out the side of his mouth, '*How did you …?*'

'It's heard something,' Daedalus said, pointing at the tactical screen, where the signal from the *Hydra* had stopped moving. It had probably stopped so it could listen better to the underground sound waves. 'Fire another one,' Daedalus ordered.

With a flourish of my hand, I jabbed at thin air. 'Firing three,' I said. 'Out of Thumpers now.'

But the *Hydra* had gotten our wakeup call. And it was probably picking up the radio and radar energy from the decoy too, now that it knew where to look. It started moving south, slowly at first, but then faster and faster, until it was rumbling over the sand at a breakneck 20 knots. I knew that was its top speed, so I had ordered the decoy to start bugging out south at 21 knots, as soon as its third Thumper was away.

'Sending decoy south,' I said, giving my wrist a particularly artful flourish, which made Tiny groan audibly. 'I'll keep it running until we lose contact,' I announced.

'How long will that be?' Daedalus asked.

'About three hours, best guess,' I said confidently. I was in no hurry to be put in restraints again. 'Maybe more.'

'Maybe more like three *minutes*,' Tiny said. He'd had enough of watching me pantomime the engagement. He punched some imaginary holograms in front of his face too, like a preschooler trying to poke out the eyes of a stuffed toy. 'Yep, yeah, sorry, we're losing the signal from the decoy tank. I'll just … damn, no … it's gone.'

Daedalus reached down and clapped me on the shoulder. 'Not your fault, Ballsack; amazing you managed to keep control so long at that distance.' The way he said it, I had to think maybe I hadn't fooled anyone after all. 'But it worked: That *Hydra* is headed south as fast as it can trundle.' He beamed at me. 'And to make an example to the rest of the crew, even though you don't deserve it because you were only doing your job and barely at that, I am willing to offer you a choice.'

'Hands free, legs cuffed, or the other way around?' I asked preemptively.

He shook his head. 'What? No. You may choose whether to be cuffed hand and foot by Tiny, or *tranqed* by Ostrich.'

'You aren't supposed to say that like it's some kind of sexual service.' Ostrich glared at him.

'Wash your mouth out, girl,' Daedalus said. 'I implied no such thing. And besides, I doubt you would even come close to satisfying our dear Ballsack because he is the only man alive who has met multiple Zenos up close and personal and lived to brag about it.'

Which was true enough. Not the part about Ostrich not being able to satisfy me, which I am sure she could, if she wanted to, which I doubted. No, the thing about meeting multiple Zenos. There was the one I fought outside the perimeter at Voeykov. Then Livia, or the Zeno who became her. And now the two in what we had decided to call 'The Gray': Adam ... and Antonia.

Still freaking out about that. Don't think I wasn't. *Linus, I will find you!*

'Hello? Ballsack?' I heard Daedalus's voice again, breaking into my internal copulation monologue. 'Decision: Tiny, or Ostrich?'

'I'd take the Tiny option, I was you,' Tiny said. 'Those tranq jabs hurt, trust me.'

'Only when it's *you*,' Ostrich said, playing up to it now. 'I'd be gentle with Ballsack.'

'Are we talking about a full narcosis tranq with guaranteed sweet dreams, or semi-paralysis so I'm fully conscious but can't react while the crew takes turns tattooing dumb stuff on my forehead?' I asked.

'Wait, was that an option?' Tiny asked. 'In that case you should *definitely* choose the tranq.'

'Oh, for goodness' sake, just tie him up and find us somewhere to park for the night so we can start digging in,' Lucretia yelled over the intercom from the meat locker. Sometimes I forgot she was down there. But now that she'd reminded me, I couldn't help but wonder at what point in this little hostage scenario the whole 'you and me against the rest of the crew' thing was going to kick in.

Or maybe, yet again, I was being the fool? Maybe it was just her against the rest of the crew and I was her human shield.

We lured the *Hydra* away, and as night fell, we found a natural depression and dug our MCV in deep. Daedalus turned the fans to vertical downdraft and blew the sand out from under us until the hovercraft was sitting on raw bedrock. Then it was just a matter of grabbing a shovel and burying the machine in the sand piled up around it. There was a lot of silica in the soil of The Red, which scattered the heat signature of troops inside a cold ground vehicle, making it invisible to IR-sensing satellites until it started moving again.

Daedalus untied me to help with the shoveling, of course, then tied me up again. I didn't want the tranq, even though I probably would have slept better, because it gave you a hell of a hangover, messing with your hormones like that.

And I was glad I *wasn't* asleep when the strike came in.

The *Hydra* had been drawn south, but the AI controlling it was sharp. Once it worked out it had been suckered, it sent up an aerial drone and then did a reverse bearing calculation on our decoy tank to work out where it had traveled from. It sent the drone back along the tank's still visible trail, until it found the point at which the tank had diverged from its brothers and headed west, then it began circling, looking for the MCV that was controlling them.

It must have had magnetic anomaly detection, because by the time it had spiraled its way out to our position nearly 50 klicks north, we were already well dug in, and all of us were down in the meat locker, stretched out and snoring.

Yes, a crew led by an elite commander would probably have had a crew member awake and monitoring the passive sensors for electronic signatures, but we were Legion Praeda, and our commander was Daedalus, who was probably the first with his head down on the deck and sleeping before the rest of us even got our thermal sleep suits on. The thermals kept your body heat in and stopped it leaking into the metal of the MCV, but that didn't help against a drone with magnetic anomaly detection, or MAD. It was looking for a big lump of buried metal, and it found it.

It could have been worse. I mean, I'm still here to write about it, right? Like, the aerial drone could have been carrying a penetrator weapon that would have pushed through the sand on top of our hull like it was water and punched through to the meat locker before exploding. But it probably wasn't armed at all, since the *Hydra* had more than enough firepower to deal with most situations. Even at range.

So it would have hovered over us and tried to get a Friendly Fire code off us. If we'd been awake and seen the interrogation, we might have bought ourselves some time by flashing a code back at it. At least the few seconds it would have taken to contact a ZoC to learn we were missing, presumed captured or deserted. But we'd turned off our tracker beacon, remember? And of course, there was no one awake in the cockpit.

When it didn't get an FF code, it decided we were Zeds and sent our position to the *Hydra*. The interrogation set off an alarm in the meat locker, but by the time we realized what it was and started to react, it was already too late.

A human *Hydra* commander would have been angry. Lured south by a dumb tank? He or she would have been furious. That might have compromised their judgement, made them try to close on us so they could see the whites of our eyes, hear us screaming over the radio as we died maybe. But silicon can only fake emotion and rarely does blind rage, so the *Hydra* AI stopped, rotated and popped the hatches on its vertical launch tubes, then sent two long-range missiles at us in MAD mode.

'Tiny, get up here and start jamming!' Daedalus yelled as he scrambled up the ladder into the cockpit. I got a terrible view of skinny legs and baggy underpants as he disappeared through the hatch, with Tiny and Ostrich – who had a much nicer pair of legs and underpants that were at least semi-clean – close behind him.

I was going nowhere because, you know, tied.

But Lucretia had tied my arms in front of me so I could sleep, so I grabbed an earpiece off the wall and listened in. The engines roared to life, not because we could evade whatever harm was coming at us – we were too slow for that – but in order to power our defensive systems. An MCV was equipped to handle just about anything an Earth military could throw at it, from projectile to energy weapons or missiles, but as you've seen in the battles of Margarita Terra and Isidis Planitia, overwhelming firepower will always burn through.

It was too focused on what was going on in the cockpit to notice that Lucretia had cut my feet free, and was pulling me into a sitting position. 'Some help here, Linus?' she said. Stomach crunches require stomach muscles, and mine had wasted away a long time ago, but I wriggled myself upright, and she sliced through my wrist ties with a knife.

'Two vampires inbound,' Tiny announced. 'Impact in … *32 seconds.*'

'Ostrich, defensive systems check!' Daedalus yelled.

'Explosively formed penetrator shield down. Plasma stealth shield down. Lasers are up, but link to the counterfire radar is down …'

'Damnation Optio, just tell me what *is* working!' Daedalus cursed.

'We've got pulse lasers,' Ostrich told him. 'But I have to aim manually. So keep us dead-still.'

'We're mulch,' Tiny decided.

'We ain't going to die alone,' Daedalus said. 'You got a position on that *Hydra* from the counterfire radar AI, Sensor Operator?'

'Aye, skipper,' Tiny announced. 'He's 50 klicks south.'

'Ostrich, cue up a counterbattery salvo, full barrage; launch when ready.'

'Six-barrel salvo, you got it, Decanus.'

'Twenty seconds to impact!' Tiny said, a note of hysteria in his voice.

Lucretia helped me to my feet. 'We could drop the ramp and run for it,' she said. 'We might get far enough away to get outside the blast radius.'

It was a great idea – there were breathers by the exit – but we were still in sleeping thermals, not survival suits. Outside the MCV, we'd start to freeze as soon as we stopped running.

'First target locked!' Ostrich announced. 'Starting the burn!'

Our 50-kW lasers took a couple of seconds of continuous fire to burn through the warhead of an incoming missile because the missiles spun as they fell, precisely so that a laser wouldn't be able to heat a fixed spot on their body. In the time it took our lasers to burn through, the missile got two and a half klicks closer. An AI could aim one laser at each missile for a simultaneous burn-through, but a human operator could only aim at one missile a time, with two lasers. It gave a faster burn, but …

'One down. I can't get a lock on the second!' Ostrich shouted. 'Counterbattery fire initiated!'

I heard the *thud thud thud* of our long-range counterbattery mortars firing as they sent our petty protest back toward the *Hydra*. They weren't precision weapons, and they were unguided, but the *Hydra* had to stop to fire its missiles, so there was a chance the mortars could blanket the area it was firing from and knock it out.

A small chance.

'Impact in *five*,' Tiny said sadly. 'Four …'

I was standing at the front of the meat locker, under the cockpit, toe to toe with Lucretia, and I grabbed her, pulled her face to mine and kissed her.

She just had time to pull back in shock, lift her hand to slap me, and the rear of the MCV drove down into the sand like an express elevator, sending us into the air.

I swear I saw the missile slice through the top of the hull behind us, break through our thin top armor, plunge down through the empty meat locker and into the deck below our feet, disappearing into the space under the armor-plated deck.

Where it detonated.

We went from floating weightlessly as the floor disappeared beneath us to being plastered spread-eagled on the deck as it was lifted into the air by the force of the blast. Then we were falling through the air again as the MCV slammed back down onto its rubber skirts and the engines roared.

Daedalus was roaring too. 'Come on, you fat-assed bastard, get moving!'

With the wind knocked out of me, concussed and seeing stars, I rolled toward the 2-meter-wide glowing red hole in our deck made by the missile's passage, helpless to stop myself.

A hand grabbed my ankle, and I looked back to see Lucretia hanging onto a seat belt with one hand, and my foot with the other. I scrabbled for purchase and found a load clamp in the floor I could hook my fingers around. The force of our acceleration was still pushing me backward, and I felt a finger snap, but the others gripped tight.

I heard whooping from the cockpit.

'Yeah, baby!' Tiny yelled.

'Cave, in that cliff face,' Ostrich cried out. 'Can we fit?' The spires and mesas of the sand seas of The Red were riddled with cuts, grooves and deeper caverns carved out by the relentless action of dust storms.

'No problem,' Daedalus decided. 'Or die trying.' The MCV swerved sideways, changing course for whatever protection Ostrich had spotted.

I hauled myself across the deck toward Lucretia and grabbed the seat belt she was hanging onto. The top of the hull was self-sealing. The deck wasn't. Sand filled the meat locker as the down blast from our turbine fans was funneled up through the hole in the deck. The pressure inside the meat locker built, and my eardrums started protesting.

'Shut the hatch!' Daedalus yelled, and the hatch from the meat locker to the cockpit slammed shut so the crew up there was shielded from the overpressure. Which was great … for them. Lucretia and I were like sailors in a sinking ship, trapped behind watertight doors, with the water rising.

I let go of the belt, braced my feet on the deck, put my hands over my ears, and screamed.

We got in under the rock overhang before the next barrage from the *Hydra* found us, but it wasn't exactly a sustainable solution. Daedalus cut the blowers and the crushing pressure and choking sand in the meat locker dropped away. We'd powered down our drone and sensors, but it was a pretty good bet the *Hydra* knew exactly where we were from our tracks, that it had sent out a call for combat air support, and *serious* harm was inbound.

'Ideas?' Daedalus asked from the cockpit. I guess that was the advantage of a clueless commander; he was open to suggestions.

'We repair what we can, power up and charge out there at that *Hydra* and die like freaking heroes,' Tiny said. 'In our own minds, at least.'

'Thank you for that excellent contribution, Sensor Officer. Now, ideas that don't involve me dying?' Daedalus said.

'Get outside, explore the cave, see where it goes, and then freeze to death starved of oxygen at some point in the future when we realize it goes nowhere?' Ostrich suggested.

'Another good contribution, Chief Engineer. Here is mine,' Daedalus said. 'I shoot all of you in the head to give you a quick and painless death and then negotiate my own surrender having promised I will shoot you all in the head first, which I already did, so I save time while also securing my own survival for the duration it takes for me to be court-martialed and then mulched, during which I might find a way to escape.'

I had my suit microphone off and turned to Lucretia. 'And you said he had a *hidden* agenda.'

'Did you say something, Ballsack?' Daedalus asked. OK, maybe my mic wasn't off after all. Or Lucretia's mic had picked up my voice.

'Sure.' I improvised. 'I say we fortify this position, hope they don't just nuke us, tool up and take out any ground forces they send in, settle in for a good long siege surviving on our own sweat and piss, plus the rations we scavenged at Isidis Planitia, before we eventually have to start eating each other.'

'Terrible idea, especially compared with mine. Next?' Daedalus asked.

Lucretia of course had the solution. 'We get a message to the Zenos at the Taura Terra ZoC. Tell them our situation and ask for their help.'

Every word in that suggestion except the functional words sounded so wrong.

'Right. At last, a good idea,' Daedalus said thoughtfully. 'And what type of situation exactly would it be that would persuade them to respond with anything except "die well"?'

'A "We have the Child of the Dawn and we're trying to return him to you" type of situation,' she explained patiently.

'Oh yeah, *excellent* idea,' I muttered. Suddenly, getting shot in the head by Daedalus was looking like the better option. I was still clinging to the thin thread that was my hope that Lucretia had a plan for getting us both off this crew and out of trouble *without* me becoming an exhibit in a Zeno petting zoo.

Daedalus decided. 'Tiny, how can we get a signal to Taura Terra?'

'We can't. To use an Earth commsat, we'd have to log on, and the Legion will intercept it.'

'No, I mean on a Zeno frequency,' Daedalus asked. 'They use that bird chirping code, but we should be able to transmit on it, right? Jump onto a Zeno frequency and send a message in the clear.'

'You have to *find* one of their frequencies first,' Tiny said. 'They hop them around to avoid jamming, faster than any human-designed system can follow. Longest I ever locked up a Zeno frequency was five seconds.'

'Then we need a message we can say *within* five seconds, duh,' Lucretia said, banging her head against the wall in frustration.

'OK, how about, "We have The Child of the Dawn, we will give him to you, our coordinates are XXX, but we are under attack please help with massive deadly firepower"?' Daedalus suggested.

'Too long,' I said. I'd been counting under my breath. Then I got inspired. 'Unless you say it in Telegramese.'

'What?' Daedalus asked. 'That's not a thing.'

'Sure it is. I used to speak it with my best friend as a kid. Telegramese is the most concise spoken language in history. Like, to say what you just said in Telegramese I would say CHILD OF DAWN SECURED STOP UNDER FIRE AT XXX STOP NEED BACKUP STOP. The last STOP is optional.'

Lucretia nodded. 'Three seconds.'

'You were a weird kid, Ballsack,' Ostrich said.

'Alright, untie him, Termite. Get up here, Ballsack,' Daedalus ordered. The hatch between the two decks cracked and was pulled open.

Lucretia shrugged and made a fake 'this is me cutting you free' kind of motion, then nodded at the hatch.

I was about to step toward it, when she grabbed my shoulder, turned me around and kissed me. I think. It happened kind of fast, because then she winked and shoved me toward the ladder that went up to the cockpit. I grabbed the ladder and looked back, but she'd turned away to inspect the still-glowing, ragged hole in the deck.

Nah, yeah. She *definitely* kissed me.

I was still confused by that kiss as I climbed up to cockpit level and dropped into my old tanker chair. I could see Ostrich was busy running systems self-repair routines, which showed you that deep down under that profanely cynical exterior was a profanely cynical optimist. Tiny was leaning back in his chair, hands tapping invisible icons in front of his face as he programmed an algorithm to scan every audible frequency for Zeno traffic.

Daedalus had a pulse pistol pointed at me. 'Nothing personal,' he said. 'We'll tie you up again later if we are still alive.'

'Great. Thank you.'

'Quiet,' Tiny said, irritated. 'I'm working here.'

Like someone had said, we'd never managed to lock onto one of the Zeno frequencies for more than a few seconds, and what we got from it was unintelligible. 'Bird-chirping crap' was as good a description as any. Coded Zeno communications sounded like a manic sparrow who had snorted cocaine. So I was told. I'd never actually heard it. Some smartass I talked to in the Legion told me it was 'just' a quantum-encrypted sonic pi derivative, then admitted we had failed completely to break it so far and couldn't understand a word.

'Alright,' Tiny said. 'Algorithm is ready to run. It will scan until it finds a Zeno channel, and then it will ping.' He tapped an air icon, and I heard a ding like a small bell. 'Like so. That's your signal.' He gave me a handheld mic. 'It's on. You hear their bird chirping start up, just hold down the button to break in, say what you got to say, and that's it.'

Daedalus leaned down, grabbed my hand and pulled it toward him. He had a grease pencil in his fingers – the same one he used to write the crew's names on the hull over his head so he didn't forget them – and wrote some coordinates on the back of my hand.

'Be quick, Telegram Man,' Daedalus said, letting go. 'And don't say anything stupid or I'll put a hole through you.'

'Just a leg or something,' Ostrich suggested. 'We need him still breathing if we're going to get anything out of this deal.'

'A hole through your *leg*,' Daedalus said, nodding.

I was about to reply, when a *ding* chimed on the overhead speakers. The sound of birds chirping came through the speakers. But ...

... on the outer perimeter, Heading back to base. Kill count: 24 dead, 33 wounded. One MCV, six tanks, approx. 50 legionnaires. Casualty count 13 expended, six recoverable ...

I was dumbstruck. Literally. I looked around at the others, who were just staring at me. Couldn't they hear? The Zenos were broadcasting in the clear!

'Great work, Ballsack,' Tiny said. 'Missed your window, like, totally. Who knows when we'll get another lock?'

'I *understood* that!' I said. 'Did you ... couldn't you understand it?'

Daedalus frowned. 'No, Ballsack, since I am not a freaking canary, I could not understand the freaking bird language. And neither could you.'

'I did! It was some guy calling in a battle report. Seriously, you didn't hear it?'

'No goat-fingering way,' Ostrich said.

'Yes, goat-fingering way,' I said. 'One MCV, six tanks, some legionnaires dead ...'

'If you can understand it, which I don't believe, can you speak it?'

'No of course I can't speak ...' But it was like listening to the chirping had unlocked some kind of instrument in my throat. I closed my eyes and concentrated. One second I was thinking bird sound in my head, and the next ...

The next ... I opened my eyes to find Daedalus's pulse pistol pressed to my forehead.

'I am not even going to *ask*,' Daedalus said, 'how you started making that noise through your nose.' He looked around the cockpit. 'Anyone give me one good reason I shouldn't shoot this Zedified bitch in the head?'

'Hey,' I yelled, in English, putting up my hands. 'I'm not a Zed! If I was Zedified, I would have tried to kill you already!'

'He has a point,' Ostrich said.

'Uh, no, since he just chirped like a sparrow,' Tiny said.

'Yeah, OK. Totally Zedified,' Ostrich said, flipping again.

'*The Blue!*' Lucretia said quickly and loudly through the hatch at our feet. She'd been listening to every word on the ship intercom.

Daedalus turned his head, but kept the pistol between my brows. 'What?'

'Reason not to shoot him. We're trying to get back to The Blue, remember?' Lucretia yelled. 'What does it matter if he's human, Zedified, or a goddamn leprechaun? We need him, alive, to trade.'

Daedalus glared at me, every fiber wanting to pull the trigger on his pistol. But self-preservation once again overruled his baser instincts. He sat back but kept the pistol pointed at me.

'You're Zedified, though I never heard no Zed make that noise. I thought only actual Zenos could do it. Must have been something that happened to you down in The Gray, but don't ask me what. And don't ask me why you didn't already turn on us and shoot us in the back …'

'And have sex with our dead corpses,' Tiny added.

'And have sex with … what? No,' Daedalus said, shooting him a worried look. 'And rejoin your Zeno buddies at Margarita Terra or Isidis Planitia. But don't for a moment think I don't think you won't.'

There were a lot of additive negatives in that sentence, and I could see Ostrich and Tiny trying to work through them. Then the radio locked onto another Zeno frequency, the bell dinged, and I held the mic up to my mouth this time and started trilling in bird-speak. 'CHILD OF DAWN SECURED STOP MCV AND FIVE HUMAN CREW UNDER FIRE AT …' I held my hand up and read off the coordinates. '… STOP NEED BACKUP STOP.'

I took less than a half second.

'I am not ever going to get used to that,' Tiny said. 'That is just creepy.'

'I know,' Ostrich agreed. 'The way his nostrils flare?'

A burst of chirping came over the radio back at me, and then the radio went silent.

I bit my lip.

'So?!' Daedalus demanded. 'They answered? Or you just sold us to the highest bidder?'

'Huh? No. I told them we have the Child of Dawn and we need help. Then they answered,' I said. 'But you aren't going to like it.'

'Try me.'

Lucretia stuck her head up through the hatch and took in the scene. Tiny and Ostrich looking variously sickened or disgusted, Daedalus looking murderous with a pistol still pointed at my head. 'Spill it before they shoot you, Linus,' she suggested.

'Alright, it was Taura Terra ZoC that replied. So that's good, I guess. They're close. They said they have a Zed squadron about 50 klicks out, and they'll vector it to our location. They also said there's a Legion Praeda flight of four ground pounders inbound, but the Zenos have aerial support out of Taura Terra, and they'll intercept.'

'OK. What's not to like?' Tiny asked.

'They said all that in a couple of chirps?' Daedalus asked, suspicious.

'And more,' I told him. I held out a finger and put it inside the nozzle of his pulse pistol as though blocking it, though of course I wasn't, because if he fired, it would just fry my finger before frying me. 'They said I should kill you all and then await extraction together with the hostage. I think they assumed I was Zeno because, you know ...' I whistled ... *because I can do this.*

Daedalus looked at the finger stuck in the muzzle of his pistol and narrowed his eyes. 'I say again. Give me one reason I shouldn't pull this trigger.'

I drew a breath and then realized Tiny and Ostrich had also pulled their sidearms and were pointing them at me too.

Tiny at least had the decency to look pained. 'Sorry, Ballsack, but they called you Child of the Dawn and now you are chirping like a Zeno.' He shrugged. 'So, no offense …'

'I'll give you *three* reasons!' Lucretia said, counting on her fingers. 'One, like I said, we need him. Alive. Two, we need him *alive*. Three …'

'We need him alive,' Daedalus growled, his finger whitening as he tightened it on the trigger. 'But *do* we? Really?'

'Three. We are about to get turned to mulch either by a Legion attack or by a Zeno attack with no way to defend ourselves, and using Ballsack as a human shield—'

'Zed shield,' Ostrich corrected her.

'… Yes, Zedified former-human shield – is the only way we are getting out of this alive. And besides, would he have told us he was ordered to kill us if he was planning just to kill us?' She drew breath. 'And how could he anyway?'

Daedalus frowned. 'Yeah, Ballsack, how exactly were you planning to do that?'

'I wasn't!' I protested. 'I have no weapons!'

'Yeah, but you can *chirp*,' Tiny pointed out. 'Maybe you can also turn into gas like they do and then reappear in the armory and grab a rifle and then gas out again and appear back here and shoot us …'

'They don't … I couldn't …' Even the others in the crew were struggling to follow Tiny's logic. 'If I could do all that, would I still be sitting here?'

Daedalus put up his gun and then holstered it again. 'The Zed filth makes a good point. Ostrich, tie him up again. What is the status on our defensive systems?'

'We have kinetic interception, no electronic, pulse or microwave. Anyone attacks us with standoff weapons, we have a chance. They get to knife-fighting range with pulse weapons, we're mulch.'

'Situation has improved then,' Daedalus said, almost cheerfully, the tension of the last few minutes and the hopelessness of our current situation apparently disappearing fast in his mental rearview mirror. 'Loadmaster Termite …'

Lucretia winced at the name, but responded. 'Commander?'

'Get to work under the MCV plugging the hole in our lower deck. Repair plating is in locker 32. I want it airtight inside 10 minutes in case we need to run for it.'

Lucretia looked like she wanted to point something out (probably about the futility of that idea), opened her mouth, but then closed it again. 'Aye aye.' She dropped from view.

Ostrich finished binding my wrists and went back to her auto-repair routines. Tiny had holstered his weapon too and was leaned back in his chair, punching invisible icons. 'I can put an ISR drone outside the entrance to this cave so we can at least see what is coming before it kills us.'

I sat back, staring up at the torn and stained cloth covering the metal roof of the MCV. (It looked like someone had thrown a beverage at it and then tried to cut the stain out. Ah, no. Alright, probably *not* a beverage. Probably the severed jugular vein of the late and barely lamented Termite.) I indulged in some general misery regarding my life situation.

Arrived on The Red. Commissioned as a decurion.

Met Antonia. Awesome, until not.

Busted to gregarius, sent to Voeykov. Miserable. Until put in cage beside Livia. Relative to the effluent pit, this was a good time. Except it turns out Livia was a Zeno Reactionary (whatever that is), who was sent in as a spy? Like Antonia, but different? Hmmm.

Margarita Terra. Terrifying. The minefield was bad enough, but watching Daedalus drill a hole through Livia and kill several hundred legionnaires, including poor Fatfoot, that was next level.

The effluent pit. That deserved its own period of rumination in the dark pages of The Redside Misadventures of Linus Vespasius. Rather than refuse to cooperate, I really should have told our interrogators everything about what really happened up on that mesa, and cut out weeks of wallowing in stinking filth to be rewarded by a blissful execution, and then I would have avoided …

Isidis Planitia. Upside: The lovely, broad-cheeked, almond-eyed Lucretia stomped into my life. Downside? Everything else. Did I ask to be called a friend by the Zenos in that Place of Inky Grayness? I did not. Did I deserve the suspicion and fear that it naturally generated among my already fratricidal crewmembers? Well, since I have now started chirping manically and can communicate directly with Zenos in their quantum bird-speak, probably yes.

Zedified? I felt no different. Shouldn't I be zombified like all the others before me in the history of our contact with the Zenos? Mindless robots who simply follow Zeno orders to their deaths? (As opposed to the mindless robots of the Legion who simply follow Legion orders to their deaths, which is *totally* different, since at least we can drink suds and grumble about it together.) Then again, the naked guy in The Gray did call me a lot of names indicating that if not actual Zeno, or Zedified, I might be 'Zeno-adjacent'.

Which brings us to now. Call this the Taura Terra run. Lucretia's great idea. Where had that got me, except regularly bound hand and foot like an animal about to be delivered to the knacker? And Daedalus a finger twitch from shooting me in the head every time I opened my mouth. Or nose. Could I blame him?

Yeah, nah.

Ahead of me lay a violent death at the hands of the Legion, a violent death at the hands of my crewmates, betrayal by my only friend-probably-not-friend Lucretia or delivery to the Zenos for whatever horrible fate awaited a 'Child of the Dawn'.

I had poured myself a big glass of sorrow, and I leaned my head back to drink it down. Perhaps I could choke to death on my own self-pity.

Lucretia reappeared, sticking her head up through the hatch again. 'I need some help with this floor patch. Is Ballsack doing anything useful up there?'

Daedalus had also been doing some ruminating while the rest of the crew worked. It involved sitting with his eyes closed, probably dozing, with his pistol nonchalantly sitting in his lap, pointed at me. He opened one eye, looking past me at Lucretia.

'Ballsack is doing something *very* useful,' Daedalus said, 'in that he is sitting quietly in his seat, not killing us.'

'Then can he come down here with me and hold this plate in place while I weld it and not kill us that way?' Lucretia asked with a sweet smile. I mean, I thought it was sweet. Daedalus seemed to think it was irritating, because he closed both eyes and screwed them up while he thought about it before letting out an annoyed sigh. 'Alright. But don't blame me when he goes all Zeno on you and snaps your neck, because I will be sitting here with this pistol waiting to blow his head off if it comes through that hatch without you.'

'How can I blame you if I'm …' she started, then stopped herself. 'Come on, Ballsack.'

I levered myself gently out of my chair, half-expecting Daedalus to cry out that I was trying to escape and shoot me. And his hand tightened on his pistol, but his eyes stayed closed, for what that was worth.

Lucretia was waiting at the bottom of the ladder to kiss me.

Or I know she would have been, if there was any time. But we were in a life-and-death kind of situation with no time to spare, so I understood she had to suppress her otherwise insatiable urges. And yes, in a rare moment of self-reflection, I did wonder what it was, this persistent obsession I had with love, loving and being loved. I hadn't been this bad before I arrived on The Red, had I? I certainly didn't join the Legion *looking* for love. I'd been looking for … what? Escape? Redemption? Danger? Thrills? All of those. Death? Maybe even that.

Lucretia pointed at the hole in the floor, glancing up at the cockpit to make sure no one was following me through. 'Into the hole in the deck,' she said loudly. 'We need to measure it for the patch.' She handed me a survival suit and a breather.

Escape! We were escaping! My pulse thumped so loudly I thought the three crew members up in the cockpit would hear it.

I said nothing, just gave her my best, most intense 'I understand' kind of look and pulled on the survival suit. She was already wearing hers. We both pulled breathers over our faces and snugged the face mask under the thermal skins around our faces. I looked toward the weapons rack, wondering whether we shouldn't be taking a rifle with us, just in case, but she shook her head when she noticed, and pointed at the hole in the deck of the MCV.

I walked quickly over to it, sat my ass on the melted edge (it was still warm) and dropped through, pulling myself along the undercarriage of the MCV to get out of her way. When it was down on its skirts, there was only about 5 feet of clearance between the rock floor of the cavern and the MCV deck over my head. I waited for her to drop through and she rolled over beside me, breather mask to breather mask. I could really only see her eyes, but they were a beautiful shade of bloodshot, oxygen-starved yellowy brown.

'Alright, Linus, this is your chance,' she said. 'You want to make your break, kick me in the head and run.'

I replayed her words in my head just to be sure I hadn't misheard. 'What? You're coming with me, right?'

'To almost certain death from exposure out in the Taura Terra somewhere? Uh, no.'

'Then why ... where am I running *to*?' There was a link in her logic somewhere I was obviously missing. I should run, but I was almost certainly going to die, so she was staying put, to face almost certain death here.

'Well, you could run toward the Legion force that's approaching, try to attract the attention of one of their air units. You might be shot from the sky, but they might land and pick you up. Interrogate you, try you, court-martial and mulch you. But you'd live a few weeks longer, and hey, you might be able to escape somehow. Probably not, but who knows?'

'I don't …'

'Or, or …' She was trying to be encouraging maybe. '*Or* you could run toward the Zeno force. They're probably weaker than the Legion force, but they're closer and less likely to just shoot you on sight. If you're halfway Zedified, they might even be downright friendly. You might have a few days of humanity left before the Lilification claims you fully and you go total Zed. Who knows, Dawn Child?' She punched me on the shoulder in a comradely way.

'No, but … without me, you have no leverage. In here, it's just you and this maniac crew, and outside you have Legion and Zeno enemies closing in.'

'Call it a target-rich environment then,' she said. 'I'd rather take my chances in here than out there.'

'What *chances*?' I asked, exasperated.

'Chances that something will turn up somewhere along the line before or after we hand you over to the Zenos.'

I suddenly realized what she was doing. 'You're saying I *shouldn't* try to escape.'

'Yes, but it has to be your choice,' she said. 'If you stay, it probably does end with us handing you over to the Zenos, and I don't want that on *my* conscience.'

'That is some kind of choice,' I told her.

'But if it matters, I want you to stay,' she said. 'Because, you know, I don't want to be left alone with this crew of deranged murderers.'

So there it was. Self-interest at all levels. But wasn't that what motivated everyone in the Legion at the core of their being? 'Well, at least you are honest.'

She put a hand behind my neck and pulled my head forward until our masks were touching. 'Plus, also, you are a good kisser.'

'Really?'

'But next time – if there is a next time – you ask for consent, alright? Or I will permanently neuter you.'

'Uh, right ...'

'Now. Kick me in the head and run, or hang around to find out what happens to the crew of the jolly ship *LP Treachery*. All your options suck, but I really am giving you a choice, Linus.'

'I'll stay.'

She pulled back. 'You wanna think a couple seconds about that?'

'OK,' I blinked twice. 'I'm staying.'

'Alright then.' She rolled back toward the hole in the deck. 'I'll pass down a patch and molecular welder. You weld the patch into place, then come up through that hatch up forward.' She pointed to a rectangular trapdoor I hadn't noticed before. 'I'll be doing the same inside. You do know how to ...'

'I've used a molecular welder before.'

'Alright, just don't fuse your skin to the hull because we can't regrow any appendages out here.'

And with that, she rolled away and pulled herself up through the hole in the deck.

I lay there for a moment, reconsidering. I mean, like, I *could* actually still run for it, right? Dig my way out under the skirts of the MCV and make my break. I'd have at least three hours before the suit started to fail. Maybe longer. Or I could find another cave and just curl up in a ball, wait out the coming firefight, and try to scavenge a vehicle. Suit would survive a few extra hours if I wasn't stressing it.

But then I would never learn what a *consensual* kiss from Lucretia was like, would I?

'This is going to get ugly,' Tiny said over the ship's intercom.

I was back in the meat locker, bound (loosely, thank you, Lucretia) hand and foot. Tiny had put a drone up outside the hole we were hiding in, and he was tracking the two forces converging on our cave and giving a running commentary.

The two air elements had met first. All unmanned, so it was violent, but not bloody. The Legion had sent ground pounders to try to smoke us out of our hidey hole, but they had been chewed up by the Zeno air units out of Taura Terra before they got within standoff munition range. The *Hydra* didn't like that, though, and took down three of the Zeno aircraft, forcing the Zenos to pull the last of their fighters back out of range before they could move in on the Legion ground force.

Which had joined up with the *Hydra* and was boring in towards us.

'Put the holo on the wall,' Daedalus said. He'd been saving his limited mental bandwidth by letting Tiny verbalize the battle until now. But with the enemies at our gates, he decided he wanted to see what was happening too.

'Holocasting,' Tiny said, flicking a finger in the air. 'View it and weep.'

The holocast was projected both on the cockpit glass in front of the crew upstairs and on a wall down in the meat locker. I saw immediately what Tiny meant. And so did Ostrich.

'Burger-flipping clusterfart,' she said. 'These guys want us bad.'

'Well, technically the Zenos want Ballsack, not us,' Daedalus said. 'Only the Legion want us, and they want us dead. But that's moot.'

What we were seeing on the screen was not moot. It was very, very specifically relevant to our immediate future. To our east was the Zeno ground force. It seemed to be comprised of no fewer than 10 MCVs and a swarm of uncrewed tanks, so call it an overstrength century. I tried to count the tanks but lost track at about 40. Say 50-plus red dots.

On the other side of the holo were about the same number of blue dots. Maybe a few less.

The Legion had sent a century of MCVs after us too, which was almost an insult after Isidis Planitia, considering it claimed the life of another tribune and they were assuming we were responsible, or fleeing, which was just as bad. I suppose they did have the *Hydra* joining them from the south, and it had six polymorphic multirole tanks on its back, so they probably figured that was plenty of firepower for going up against one renegade MCV, even if they were headed into the Badlands.

And it would have been. Except the Zenos had a surprise for them. For us all, really.

'What is *that?*' I asked. 'Northeast, trailing the Zeno force. A single dot. *Big* dot.'

'AI is waiting for a lock on it,' Tiny announced. 'ID in five.'

'We don't have five minutes, Sensor Operator,' Daedalus said. 'Those converging forces are going to see each other and start trading missiles in less than that.'

'Five seconds, not minutes,' Tiny said, sounding miffed. 'Got it. Oh, crud; Sandcruiser, and it's not showing a friendly beacon, so it's Zeno. Ostrich was right. The Lilin want Ballsack *bad.*'

'Sandcruiser? *Zeno* Sandcruiser?' I asked.

'Can't be,' Daedalus said. 'If the Zenos had captured a Sandcruiser, they'd have used it before now. And we'd have heard about it. Check your data, Tiny.'

'Already double-checked,' he said, sounding a little awestruck. 'It's a cruiser. AI says it's the *Intimidator*. And its marked red. Red means Zeno.'

'Not gonad-twisting possible,' Ostrich said.

The Sandcruisers *Dominator, Terminator, Liquidator* and *Intimidator* were the main reason humans had convinced ourselves we had a chance in the war against the Zenos, because every few months, a new cruiser would arrive, and the Zenos were denied another few hundred square klicks of territory. With enough cruisers, there was nothing the Zenos could take and hold.

It was felt to be just a matter of time. Time in which legions like the Legion Praeda were thrown into the meat grinder, to buy more time. Time measured in numbers of Sandcruisers. And mulch.

Except …

Except now the Zenos had *Turned* the crew of a Sandcruiser.

Of course they had. It was a ZoC like any other, right? A few thousand legionnaires, their centurions, and tribunes. It probably had its own equivalent of camp followers – logistics personnel and 'service providers'. They couldn't have tunneled in, so how did the Zenos breach the gargantuan, trundling machine? They had found a way. They had gotten in. And then started the work of rotting *Intimidator* from within, just as they did with every other ZoC on The Red that had been Zedified.

And like any other ZoC, it would only be a temporary victory. But here was the thing.

They sent *Intimidator* to fetch us.

Or me. They sent *Intimidator* to fetch me.

Authorities higher than the dead tribune of the Legion Praeda probably already knew the Zenos had Turned the *Intimidator*. And they had kept it very, very quiet. As had the Zenos themselves. Like I said, if they had used *Intimidator* against us before that day, the whole Redside comms net would have been ablaze with the news. Not to mention the newscasts Earthside. It threw our entire planetary domination strategy into question. What the hell was the point of building behemoth Sandcruisers for mega-billions and shunting them across space and time to end the war, if all you were doing was delivering them to the enemy?

'Oh, we are *so* screwed,' Ostrich said.

'No, the Legion is,' Daedalus corrected her with a perspicacity he rarely displayed. 'That there, ladies and nominally-gentlemen, is our salvation.'

He must have been pointing at the elongated red dot that was the *Intimidator*. And as Tiny predicted, as we watched, things started to get *ugly*.

The Legion century picked up the *Intimidator* the same time we did. Any thought its centurion had of coming after the scoundrels who had fled from the decimation of their cohort at Isidis Planitia evaporated. They were suddenly facing not just one but two existential threats: one to their east, the lesser Zeno force, and one to their northeast, the *Intimidator*.

It had been named well, the (now Zeno) Sandcruiser *Intimidator*. At the mere sight of it, the Legion force began to veer away, trying to stay out of standoff missile range. But the *Hydra* ...

Fifty klicks away, the automaton that was the Polymorphic Autonomous Ground Vehicle *Hydra* stopped.

It had looked at the counterbattery fire Ostrich had loosed toward it and it shrugged, sending a shield of explosively formed penetrators toward our missiles and destroying them a good 5 klicks out.

It looked like no earth animal invented by nature or the gods, but if you could imagine an armadillo squatting down on its back legs, and raising itself on its front legs, that's what it did at that point.

From its back, six amorphous blobs formed themselves into conical arrows. Plasma engines ignited, and they arced into the black sky of The Red.

'*Hydra*'s polymorphs have gone ballistic,' Tiny warned. 'Coming right for us.'

It was a no-cost move by the Legion centurion, sending the *Hydra*'s ordnance at us. The *Hydra* itself was already dead. It would be the first to fall to the *Intimidator*, because it was closer.

'Ostrich!' Daedalus cried. 'We need plasma cannons online before those polymorphs splash down.'

'*Six* polymorphs?' Ostrich said, breathless from whatever she was doing up in the cockpit. 'We're going to need more than just plasma cannons, Chief. You want maybe to see if we can dig ourselves any deeper into this cave?'

'Termite?!' Daedalus yelled. 'We patched?'

'Airtight, Decanus,' Lucretia replied, then leaned toward me. 'We are, right?'

'Totally,' I assured her. It really wasn't my first time wielding a welder. I was pretty sure my welds would hold when the blowers started. I couldn't vouch for hers, of course.

The engines spooled up in emergency power mode, which meant that the capacitors were still humming even as the blowers started their screaming whine. The MCV lifted on its skirts and I eyed the patched deck warily. If we hadn't done our job right, the meat locker would fill with sand again, and our machine would thump back down onto the floor of the cavern.

It didn't. It wasn't airtight like Lucretia promised, but it held. Sand and grit flew around the meat locker as Daedalus got us up on our air cushion and pointed us deeper into the cave. Down in the hold, we couldn't see where he was headed, but we felt the g-force as he spun the MCV on its axis and then began shunting it left and right. There was a crunch as we caromed off at least one wall, but it seemed he had enough height and width to play with for the next five or six minutes. Then the MCV pirouetted on its center of gravity and backed a few meters before it settled onto its skirts again.

'End of the road,' Daedalus said.

'Pulse cannons up,' Ostrich announced. 'Or, no. Make that singular. One pulse cannon up. Any more than one of those polymorphs make it this far in, we're mulch.'

'Termite, Ballsack, you still suited up?' Daedalus asked.

'Yes,' Lucretia replied, warily.

'Get outside with pulse rifles. Find flanking positions left and right and get in cover. Ostrich stays here to work the pulse cannon. Three firing positions, we got a chance of taking down those polymorphs,' he said, with totally false confidence.

'Uh, what are you and Tiny doing?' I asked. 'While we are outside getting mulched by the polymorphs?'

'I am maintaining a strategic overview and directing our defenses,' Daedalus announced imperiously. 'And Sensor Operator Tiny is …' He ran dry.

'I am scanning and preparing to act as a strategic reserve!' Tiny announced.

'Exactly. Decisive in any conflict, your strategic reserve,' Daedalus said. 'Now get your asses out there, you two. Die well!'

Lucretia had given me a knife so that I could cut myself free, and I pulled it from a pocket on my survival skin and cut the bonds around my ankles and wrists. We both ran to the weapon rack on the hull. She pulled a pulse rifle off the hull and handed it to me. 'What I tell you?' she asked, as she pulled a rifle off for herself, and checked it was charged. 'There's us, and there's them.'

But was that really it? Would I have done it any differently if I were the decanus in this fight? No, I'd probably send a couple legionnaires out on foot, to get flanking fire on any attackers. I'd have my sys-op on the MCV guns. The sensor operator? Sure, he could also wield a carbine, but wouldn't I want him calling targets?

My internal jury was still out on the whole *us and them* scenario, as you can hear. Bloody First tattoos or not. We were all still alive, right, despite everything the Legion and Zenos had done to try to kill us. Maybe Daedalus deserved just a little credit for that?

We lost contact with our surveillance drone as we went deeper into the cavern, so we had no idea what was happening outside. I can tell you, but don't assume that is because I am still alive. For all you know, I am from this point forward an AI-generated simulacrum of Linus Vespasius acting as the voice of his mulched biomass. Or maybe The Powers That Be want you to *believe* Linus Vespasius survived the battle of Taura Terra so that they can blame him for the asteroidal shower of crud that followed.

Sounds like the sort of thing the Earthside Elite would do, right? So now you don't know.

Ain't easy being you.

At that point, it sucked to be Linus Vespasius, let 'me' tell you.

Lucretia dropped the ramp and we charged outside. 'You go right. I'll go left,' she yelled.

Great plan. Simple. I liked it. What I didn't like: There was no cover to the right of the MCV.

Daedalus had backed us into a dead-end tunnel off the side of the main cavern. The nose of the MCV and its pulse cannon close-in weapons system were pointed back down toward the main cavern. To the left, Lucretia found herself a nice stalagmite (are they the ones that point upward?) and crouched behind it.

On my side of the branching tunnel, there was nothing but smooth, sandblasted wall and piles of sandblasted sand. So I did what they taught us to do in the Legion. I did what every legionnaire in history since the time of Julius Ceasar has done when faced with imminent death. I lay flat in the dirt and started digging with the butt of my weapon.

The thing about a polymorphic assault vehicle is that it is, well, you know, polymorphic.

So it might fly into near-planetary orbit on a tail of plasma fire, but just before it hits apogee, it could turn into a hypersonic glide vehicle and begin falling at more than 10 times the speed of Redside sound.

The *Intimidator* saw the launches, and it smirked. I didn't see the actual evidence of the smirk, because I was busy acting like a wombat and digging myself into the all-too-shallow sand in the dark branch of tunnel where I fully expected to die (and maybe, for all you know, did).

But we can assume the various AIs and Zedified personnel aboard the *Intimidator* smirked, because the task of knocking down just six hypersonic glide vehicles inbound a known target was child's play for a Sandcruiser.

Its fusion-powered quantum cores locked the cruiser's sensors onto the glide vehicles, used spooky-action-at-a-distance to calculate to the millimeter where they would be on the space-time continuum once they slowed to regain Red atmospheric authority, and it aimed its interceptor missiles at that point.

It missed. Because AI might be near omnipotent and AI-controlled factories pretty good at putting interceptors together, but interceptors are quality controlled by fallible humans who spend most of their working hours daydreaming about their weekend.

It didn't miss *all* the glide vehicles. It hit five, which was respectable. That left one polymorphic attack vehicle to reach ingress about 10 klicks out from our cavern, flatten into a screaming horizontal terminal approach and begin weaving toward our cavern entrance just a few hundred meters above the sand.

Between leveling out and reaching the entrance to the cavern, the glide vehicle morphed again, so that what dropped onto the sand just inside the entrance to our cavern was what is known in polite military circles as a 'kinetic penetrator'.

It was still plasma pulse jet powered. So if it chose, it could accelerate from zero to Mach 1 inside five seconds. It could choose a physical form that suited the environment it found itself in, and so it chose a blunt-nosed battering ram on skids. It hunted with infrared sensors dotted across its skin. The pulse jet gave off a high-pitched keening whine that we heard the moment it entered the cavern. But the noise bounced off every wall of every branch of the cavern, so we had no idea how close or far away it was.

'Polymorphs inbound,' Lucretia said, a little unnecessarily, I thought. I was pretty sure Ostrich, Tiny and Daedalus could hear the keening scream from inside the cockpit.

'How many?' Daedalus asked.

'A hundred. Or one,' she replied. 'I don't damn know. Ask your sensor operator.'

'Cool it, Loadmaster Termite,' Daedalus cautioned. 'Keep your head out there. You are our picket. You tag 'em, we'll bag 'em.'

I had managed to carve myself a pit in the sand that left only my head, shoulders and ass stuck up above ground level. But that meant my head, shoulders and ass were still sticking up above ground level. That was not what I would call 'cover'.

But the whining was getting louder, so I had to stop trying to improve my situation and train my weapon on the opening to our branch of the cavern.

Thing with a polymorph, it has to make a choice. It takes time to reconfigure, so if you catch it in transition, you can kill it. It can go airborne, but then it's vulnerable to ground fire. It can drop onto skids, but then it can't move as fast. This one had already made its choice, and we could hear it pushing its ass across the ground, the scraping of skids on sand like a bass tone under the keening.

'Aim low!' Lucretia yelled. I was starting to love her slightly less, since she was showing a tendency to state the obvious when under fire. Did she think I was some kind of …

Then it was there. It nosed into view. A fat, dull, silver slug-shaped bullet with a pulse jet burning in its ass. It stuck its snub nose into the cavern and looked like it was sniffing the cold air. My finger tightened on the trigger of my rifle, but then a jet fired on the front of the polymorph and it slid a few meters backward. It hadn't seen us!

It had.

It was just repositioning. Aiming itself squarely at Daedalus, Tiny and Ostrich, it lit its tail.

Lucretia was fast. And smart. She didn't aim at the polymorph; she aimed where it *was going to be*.

Plasma fire poured from her rifle into the path of the snub-nosed death machine. Saving no energy for whatever the next attack might be, she held her trigger down and emptied the charge in her rifle. I followed her lead, aiming ahead of her plasma stream and catching the polymorph right in the flank.

Her attack punched it toward me, while mine punched it back toward her.

That had the effect, unfortunately, of shoving it off-course, then back on course again. It homed on the MCV.

Ostrich opened up with the heavy plasma cannon atop the MCV, and in milliseconds, three streams of plasma were burning into the *Hydra*'s last remaining attack vehicle.

A polymorph is made of fluid metallic nanoparticles. It can absorb a hellish amount of plasma. Lucretia's rifle ran dry first. Then mine. Ostrich had a good lock on the kamikaze battering ram though, and Daedalus had made sure every erg of energy the MCV possessed was being poured into their pulse cannon.

I saw a red glow spread across the front of the polymorph, then about 20 meters out from the MCV it … melted.

Or not entirely. A lot of it turned into gaseous plasma with momentum enough that it plastered the front of our MCV and hid it from view.

I never asked Daedalus or the others what that looked like from inside the MCV. There wasn't really time, later, or I didn't think about it. But now I imagine it was like being enveloped in lava and wondering if you were going to die from inhaling superheated air before you were turned to a blackened crisp, or not.

It turned out the answer was: not.

The MCV's environmental shield took the fire from the explosion of the polymorph and spread it across the hull, using the energy to max out its batteries. It wasn't fussy, and it didn't care whether it was dealing with heat or cold.

We felt it though. The splash-back. I felt like I was cooking inside my suit, and tried to pull sand over myself. I spent the next few days scratching myself because of the tiny blackened balls of carbonized hair in my suit. The front of Lucretia's stalagmite was burned black.

A minute or two went past. I rolled onto my side, away from the hot sand, into hotter sand, and rolled back again. Lucretia stuck her head out, and gave me a wave.

There was no more keening sound coming from the cavern.

'If you two are finished hiding out there, there is a fire in the meat locker needs putting out,' I heard Daedalus say. 'You idiots didn't seal that patch properly.'

Still not Taura Terra

Fire can't burn in the atmosphere of The Red, but it can burn inside an air-pressurized meat locker heated to a ceramic-oven-like 1,400 degrees C. The fire went out as soon as we opened the ramp and let The Red's 95 percent carbon dioxide atmosphere flood the space. Cleaning the black carbon crust off the outside of the hull took us a lot longer, but we had to do it for the sensors to function properly. And there was recharging-the-capacitors-and-checking-the-seal-for-leaks time, too.

All of which brought the Zenos closer. You usually think of cleaning something as a positive thing. Which it is, except when it takes time you should be using *fleeing*.

'We're done,' Lucretia said after we had cleaned the compartment and been back underneath to check for pressure leaks. Daedalus still had the hatch to the crew compartment closed.

'Alright, bind Ballsack again and you can come up here.'

Lucretia sighed and leaned to the intercom. 'There is nothing down here to bind him with, Decanus. Everything was carbonized.'

'Oh, right, damn, wait,' Daedalus said. We heard arguing.

I could see Lucretia count to 10. 'Tell us to take off our masks, then threaten us that you'll open the ramp if we try anything. After that, open the hatch and throw me some cuffs.'

'Right, that's exactly what I was going to do, so you saved us all some time,' Daedalus lied. 'Now take off … oh, you did already.'

The hatch opened, some fusion cuffs fell to the deck, and the hatch shut again. 'Sorry,' Lucretia said quietly, cuffing me. 'We'll work this out.'

'Hey, I'm the Dawn Child,' I whispered back. 'I'm more worried about you.' I actually was. After all, I'd survived the passionate embraces of two Zenos by that point, I still hadn't

Zedified, and I could speak their language. All of these things boded pretty well if I ended up a Zeno prisoner after all.

We negotiated our way back into the crew compartment at gunpoint, and I dropped into the tanker seat while Lucretia took the loadmaster jump seat, since there were no harnesses in the meat locker anymore.

Daedalus glared at Lucretia. 'I was just about to issue an order when you interrupted. What was it?'

'You were probably going to order Tiny to send another drone out and see who won the battle outside, the Legion or the Zenos. But since the Legion would be running like whupped children from the *Intimidator*, Tiny would have suggested we just head out and make for the Zeno force as quickly as we can to get the hostage exchange over with, and Ostrich would have voted for either idea.'

'She's psychic,' Tiny said, shaking his head in awe. 'That's exactly what ...'

'Shut up, everyone, strap in,' Daedalus said. 'We're going back out and heading for the Zeno force to get this hostage exchange over with as quickly as possible.'

'I vote for that idea,' Ostrich said pointedly. 'Not the other one. The other one was dumb.'

'Still not a democracy,' Daedalus reminded them as Tiny put the MCV in gear. 'Anyone voting in favor of anything is committing mutiny and will be shot,' Daedalus said.

'I vote *against* voting on anything,' Tiny said, glaring at Ostrich as though daring her to vote with him. Daedalus drew his pistol, then put it away again, confused about whether Tiny had just committed mutiny or not.

In ancient fiction there was a trope called the 'unreliable narrator', where the person telling the story was hiding something from you, the reader, and only revealed it to you at the end of the book. Well, firstly, since I am writing this journal in real time, I can't be hiding anything, and secondly, as *soon* as I work out what the Zenos want with me, I'll let you know.

Because it seems to me they already had me, at least twice. They had me, or Livia did, or could have done, when we were caged next to each other at Voeykov. Seeing as she was a Zeno, she could have killed me or Zedified me in my sleep. And they had me in the anomaly, but they let me go, or let Lucretia take me at pistol point, anyway.

I must have looked thoughtful and contemplative because Tiny interrupted me.

'What does it feel like to be Zedified?' he asked.

'I'm not, so I can't tell you,' I replied. 'I'm still me.'

'Yeah, but guys who've been Turned keep acting like themselves, except now they take orders from Zenos. So I'd expect you to think you are you and to deny being Zedified, if that's what they told you to do.'

'Well, apparently they didn't tell me to tell you how I was Zedified because I can't. So by your logic, it isn't worth asking.'

Tiny narrowed his eyes. 'Ah-hah, so you admit it!'

Ostrich put a hand on his shoulder. 'That's not what just happened.'

Tiny looked disappointed, but turned back to his instruments. 'Anyway, I've got the Zeno force on long-range sensors now and there's a drone overhead been following us for about the last hour,' he said.

Daedalus woke from his post-combat nap. 'You're just mentioning that now, Sensor Operator?'

Ostrich was unfazed. 'Yes, Decanus. It came from the direction of the Zeno force and it is a Z-type, unarmed. Therefore I reasoned it means us no harm and prioritized allowing you to continue to refresh yourself for the coming negotiations.'

Daedalus nodded approvingly. 'Good prioritizing skills there, Sensor Operator. The rest of you no-hopers, take note. But I am not going to be doing the negotiating, even though I am a natural-born negotiator.'

'On Margarita Terra, you blew a hole in the Zeno who was trying to negotiate with us, before we even got started,' I reminded him.

'You're just pissed because he killed your *girlfriend*,' Tiny said.

'Not my girlfriend,' I said hurriedly, looking sideways at Lucretia. 'Not even remotely. Because, like, she was Zeno?'

'Hah, you admit it!' Tiny said.

'She said as much herself, Optio,' Daedalus said to Tiny. 'Before I shot her, which, by the way, was a genius move for everyone except Fatfoot. No, I don't have the patience to negotiate our way out of this, but I will be the one approving whatever deal *Termite* works out with the Zenos.'

'Me? Why me?' Lucretia asked. She sounded worried, like it was some kind of trick. 'You said my dealmaking sucked last time.'

'Which it did. But, though I will claim credit for it if it works, the idea of trading Ballsack for a ticket back to Earth for all of us was yours,' he said. 'So the risk, if the Zenos decide to kill the first person who comes to negotiate with them, should also be yours.'

'You mean honor, I think,' Ostrich prompted. 'The *honor* of being the first ...'

'I know what I said,' Daedalus growled. 'We will stay in here, locked up tight with a gun to Ballsack's temple, while Termite does the talking.'

'Oh, right. No problem,' Lucretia said.

Now Daedalus looked suspicious. 'Why are you agreeing so quickly? This is a potentially very bad deal for you. The Zenos have never negotiated with anyone, about anything.'

'No, I'm good with it,' she said. 'Can we speed up a little? I'd like to get started sooner rather than later.'

'No,' Daedalus said, taking his hand off the throttle. 'What is going on here?'

'Alright, full disclosure,' Lucretia said. 'I'd rather be out there in the open with the Zenos, where there's a chance I can run, than in here in this very confined space with that Zedified sack of balls ...' She gave me a look I chose to interpret as *I don't really mean it.*

Daedalus chose to interpret it as a look of horror at the thought of being trapped in a confined space with me.

'I've partly changed my mind,' Daedalus announced. 'I am going to maximum revolutions. Tiny, try to lock the Zeno frequency again so Ballsack can ask for instructions on where and how to meet for the exchange. Ballsack, tell your bird-chirping kin we will all be coming down the ramp with our guns on you, and we will put three holes in you if they don't agree to my demands, which I will have worked out before we get there.'

'Four holes,' Lucretia said. 'Since, you know, *four* of us.'

'Three. You are still our negotiator. What kind of negotiator goes to a negotiation *armed*?' Daedalus asked.

He had a point. But not coincidentally, it meant Daedalus, Ostrich and Tiny would be the only ones with weapons.

We found a Zeno frequency, and I had a bird conversation that can be summed up as 'Meet us here; try anything smart, and they're going to kill me.' Not exactly what Daedalus said, but close enough.

We met the Zeno force about 100 klicks out of Taura Terra. Ostrich said the Legion century had turned back for Isidis Planitia and the *Intimidator* had also reversed course back toward wherever it had come from. Which just left us, facing 10 Zedified MCVs and their crews and tank squadrons. Plus whatever Zed infantry they brought with them. Plus any actual Zenos who might be on board.

I was expecting to see Antonia. *Linus! I will find you!*

She was in the milky gray butthole of nothingness, right? So it made sense she'd be here when my captors handed me over. What happened after that would depend on whether the

Zenos really did have the power to return the others Earthside. But I couldn't see any permutation that ended with me and Lucretia together. And since I wasn't yet in pheromone range, I had decided I would definitely rather be with the very human Lucretia than the alien but maddeningly desirable Antonia. Because Lucretia must feel the same way, or she wouldn't have stayed with me this far, right?

Plus, she had a plan. Or I *hoped* like hell she did, as the MCV juddered to a halt in front of the 10 MCVs, and several dozen tanks, plus air support, of the Taura Terra Zeds. She unbuckled, stood and hauled me to my feet by the cuffs on my wrists.

Three pistols covered us.

'We'll go to the meat locker. Tiny and Ostrich will follow. You open the ramp and join us, Decanus. Then we all go out together,' Lucretia said. She rolled her shoulders like she was getting ready for a wrestling match, and I saw muscles ripple under her heat skin. In a bareknuckle fight between her and Tiny, I'd almost back Lucretia, and not just out of love or lust. 'You were about to say.'

'Yes, I was, exactly, Loadmaster.' Daedalus nodded. 'And when we get out there, any negotiating you do this time, you do so I can hear you, got that?'

'Yes, Decanus,' she said. She shoved me forward. 'Get down there, you.'

The others joined us in the meat locker, and Daedalus triggered the ramp. As it was lowering with a loud hydraulic whine, Lucretia put her mouth to my ear. Her sweet rancid breath made my heart beat faster. 'The crew will kill us if they see a chance,' she whispered. 'It's going to be up to you to save us.'

I nodded. 'No problem.' I was feeling supremely confident, in the way of all posthumous heroes.

And then the ramp was down and she was shoving me ahead of her again.

There was a squadron of infantry standing on the plain in front of the MCVs of the Zed squadrons. And ahead of the infantry, a succubus.

She was dressed in the uniform of a Taura Terra centurion. But the uniform was cut to cling, and was so tight you could see every fold and bump of flesh. *Except it's not flesh, Linus*, I told myself, using my Red-born name to stop my primal instincts taking over. *It's something else. Something alien.*

And it wasn't Antonia.

'Goddamn, that woman is built,' Lucretia muttered.

'Not a woman,' I told her.

'I know, but goddamn,' she said. 'So unfair.'

Lucretia hadn't been with us on Isidis Planitia. So she didn't recognize the Zeno. I almost didn't recognize her either. She looked healthier. Taller? She'd filled out, that was for sure.

It was Livia. Who, last time I'd seen her, had a pulse rifle hole in her midsection. (See what I did in that last paragraph there? 'Filled out'?)

She opened her arms in welcome. 'Hello again, Linus,' she said. The air filled with the scent of oranges, pungent even though filtered through our breathers.

'We are in deep doodoo,' I said to Lucretia. I had no hope I'd be able to save myself, let alone anyone else.

A voice behind us growled. Daedalus didn't appear fazed by the reincarnation of Livia. That was the advantage of blinding self-interest, I guess. 'Alright, no fornication until we have a deal,' he said. 'Anyone moves, we kill Dawn Boy here.'

Livia smiled beatifically. If she held a grudge against Daedalus for shooting her last time they met, she wasn't showing it. 'Of course, Decanus. What are your terms?'

Daedalus sniffed loudly, as though the question was below him. 'Ask my negotiator.'

Livia looked a question at me, and I stepped aside. Lucretia raised a hand in the air. 'That would be me.'

'Your terms, Gregarius?' Livia asked.

Lucretia surprised me. I expected her to get right down to it. But she didn't. 'Before we start, I need to know why you want him,' she said.

'No, you want to know how *badly* we want Linus,' Livia said. 'A very good start. Shall we sit?' She indicated the ground in front of her.

Lucretia looked back at Daedalus. 'Go ahead, sit, but leave your comms on,' he said, pistol not leaving my back.

Livia sat cross-legged on the sandy ground, Lucretia about 4 feet away. It was quite a sight. A big, empty, red plain. Two strong women in the middle of it. An army behind one, a bunch of murderous mutineers behind the other.

And me. Or was I a member of both parties? Or none?

'To answer the question of how much we want this individual,' Livia said, 'not very much. But he is one of us …'

'I knew it,' Tiny said, turning to Ostrich. 'I *told* you.'

'… just as we are of you and all are one, were, and will be,' Livia continued.

Tiny's face fell. 'Ah, damnation. I thought it was just him.'

'We've all heard that "we are you" line from the Zeds, but what is it about him in particular?' Lucretia persisted.

'How to put this in your terms?' Livia asked. 'He is a wanted criminal. A "rebel", if you like.'

OK, that was news. And not good for me.

'Yeah, yeah,' Lucretia interrupted. 'Child of the Dawn. The Transitioned. Yada yada. We heard it before.'

Livia actually looked surprised. 'Child of … Where did you hear it?'

Lucretia smiled now. 'Well, now, wouldn't you like to know? How about you tell me what any of that nonsense means?'

Livia was still frowning, but reset her face to one of calm. 'Can a fish build a rocket and fly to space?'

'What? No, of course not,' Lucretia said.

'Why not?'

'Well apart from lack of intellect, it has no context,' Lucretia said. 'It lives in the water. If it really tries, it might break the surface and see the moon above it. But it probably doesn't understand air, can't possibly imagine space, can't use tools, let alone achieve space flight.'

'Exactly. You are fish. You have neither the intellect, the tools, nor the frame of reference to understand his crime.'

I thought Lucretia would get tetchy about a putdown like that. The scent of the oranges was getting to me, though, I could sense it. I was getting ready to intervene on Livia's side if Lucretia got angry. *Yes, Lucretia, can't you see? I've committed a crime. You just wouldn't understand ...*

I shook my head and held my breath. It helped a little. Not a lot. It also helped that Lucretia didn't lose her temper.

'Alright, I accept that,' she said calmly. 'But what you've confirmed is that you want Linus very, very badly. Thank you.'

'She's good,' Daedalus said to Ostrich. 'Wish she was with us at Margarita Terra.'

'I bet Fatfoot does too,' Ostrich said.

'Forget Fatfoot,' Tiny said, with a catch in his voice.

Livia neither nodded nor shook her head. 'Believe what you wish. So your terms?'

'We know from what happened to us at Isidis Planitia that the Zenos can manipulate space and time. In return for handing over this "rebel", we want you to send us back to The Blue,' Lucretia said.

'Earth? That ... might be arranged,' Livia said. 'We have the means to smuggle you aboard a shunt ...'

'*All* of us,' Daedalus called out. 'Except Ballsack the Criminal, of course.'

Lucretia turned and glared at Daedalus. 'I wasn't finished. I said we know you can manipulate space *and* time. We want you to return us to Earth, before the war with Lilin broke out. Before the Legion Praeda was formed, before any of' – she waved her hand to indicate the landscape around us – 'this.'

'You said you believe we have this ability because of your experiences at Isidis Planitia?' Livia said, with obvious curiosity. 'What experiences do you speak of?'

And that's when it clicked. There I was, thinking the Zenos were all one big happy family of humanity-exterminating aliens. But Livia didn't know about our journey into the pit of milky nothingness at Isidis Planitia? What was it Antonia called Livia? *She is a Reactionary.* So Livia and Antonia weren't working together? Which meant there were Zeno factions, maybe. That knowledge was leverage. I just didn't see how yet.

'Don't answer,' I said quickly to Lucretia. 'She doesn't know.' I hoped Lucretia would also put two and two together, like I'd just done.

Livia tried her best, most calm look on us. 'I may or may not know. I am interested in *your* perception of what happened to you.'

Livia waited a beat as her mind worked through the interaction like mine had, just much faster, now that I had pointed her down the path. 'Nah, you don't know. We're keeping that to ourselves. Just answer the question. Will you do it?'

'Just to be clear … send you and the other three Legion Praeda fugitives back to Earth at a time before the war between us began?' Livia asked.

'Yeah, and not back in the time of the dinosaurs,' Tiny said, glaring at Livia. 'We aren't falling for that trick. We want to go back to just before we signed on to ship Redside. Which is, like, three years …'

'Five,' Daedalus said. 'Before any of us even joined the Bloody First.'

'Alright, I like that,' Tiny said.

'Me too,' Ostrich agreed. 'Could have other advantages too. There was a relationship back then that I joined the Army to escape. Would love to dodge that bullet a different way.'

'I guess I can do five years too,' Lucretia said.

'Wait,' I said.

'You don't get a vote, Ballsack,' Tiny said.

'None of you get a vote,' Daedalus reminded them, talking over Lucretia's head. 'In return for Ballsack here, you send us back to The Blue, five years ago.' He turned to Ostrich. 'Is there any loophole there?'

'Not that I can see,' she said, unconfidently.

'Well, I definitely do,' I said, turning to Livia. 'First, if you can manipulate space and time, why is there even a war? You should already know everything humanity was planning to do and have been able to mitigate it to defeat us.'

'You are fish, in a pond,' Livia repeated. 'You do not have the intellect …'

'… *tools or frame of reference to understand*,' Lucretia parroted. 'Bad luck, brainiac. Try, or there is no deal.'

Livia frowned, then drew a line in the sand in front of her. 'Very well. You live, move and think in two dimensions …'

'Duh, *no*. Three,' Tiny said. 'Up-down, left-right, forward and backward. Three.'

'Ah, so you can see in three dimensions?' Livia asked.

'Yeah,' Tiny answered, then looked at Ostrich. 'That was a trick question, wasn't it?'

Livia took off her helmet and breather – proof she was a Zeno if any was needed – and held it out toward Tiny. 'So what is on the back of this helmet?'

'Well, if you turn it around, I'll tell you,' Tiny said. 'Oh.'

'Exactly, *oh*. You can only see this helmet as a two-dimensional object. You *infer* it is three dimensional because its size changes as it gets closer or farther away, and the way the light plays on its surface. Your primitive brain tells you the two-dimensional image you are seeing is three dimensional.' She pointed at the line in the sand. 'To you, time is two dimensional as well. There is the future, the now, and the past. A single straight line. Right?'

'Right.' He had taken a step forward, which meant his pistol was no longer trained on me. Daedalus noticed, and reached out, pulling Tiny's pistol back to line up with my head. 'So if we are here, today,' Tiny said, pointing at a spot on the line, 'we want you to move us backward, to five years ago.'

'The problem, dear fish,' Livia said, like she was being as gentle as she could, 'is that time is *not* a line. It does not flow like a river, and is not even three dimensional like a sphere of water. It is infinitely multidimensional. We can put you back on Earth five years ago, but doing so creates quantum effects that introduce inherent unpredictability. As soon as we observe and start interacting with your "time and space", as you call it, we change not just what you think of as your present, and your future, but also your past.'

'Not seeing how that answers Ballsack's question,' Lucretia said.

'From the moment we arrived on *your* Red, the future, as you call it, became unknowable, so we have no idea what the outcome of this war will be, here in this reality, any more than you do,' Livia said.

'Which is what my fish brain already figured, since you didn't win the war on day one,' I continued at last, getting to my point. 'So the past you return them to might not play out like they expect? Going back would create quantum unpredictability. There may *be* no war with the Lilin in that new time and space, no war, no Legion … or it could be completely different.'

'Different is not worse, if you ask me,' Tiny said. 'We're looking at getting mulched here. I'll take different.'

'There is a chance you go back to the world before the Zenos,' I warned him, 'only for Earth to be destroyed by a wandering asteroid. Right?' I asked Livia.

'Infinitesimally *small* chance,' Livia said. 'But not zero.'

Lucretia stood. She looked brave, determined, and sad. I did not take that as a good sign regarding the chances of escape for Linus Vespasius, The Transitioned, The Code Bearer, Wielder of the Power of Future Ancestors, Child of the

Dawn (and now The Rebel). 'I've heard enough. I say we take the deal,' my rescuer and betrayer said.

'Before the rest of you try to vote,' Daedalus said, as Tiny started to raise his non-pistol hand, 'which you can't, I have decided to take the deal.'

'I have not offered a deal,' Livia pointed out.

Lucretia smiled, gesturing like she was waving a hand over a crystal ball. 'Well, I *can* see the future,' she said. 'And in this future, you offer to send us back to "an" Earth imperceptibly different to our own, five years ago, in return for Dawn Child here.'

'Yes, that's a deal,' Livia said. Maybe it was her happiness at having landed the fish on her hook, but the thin air of The Red was flooded with the scent of orange blossom. For me, at least. I felt simultaneously suicidal and aroused.

I considered my options. Shout a protest, or grab a gun, or just run at the soldiers behind Livia to force them to shoot me. None seemed better than going with the Zenos. As Livia stood, Lucretia took my arm to lead me forward to meet my fate. I shook her off, and did my own walking.

We stopped a couple of feet from Livia. 'How is this going to work?' Lucretia asked.

'It already did,' Livia said, frowning. 'Or we would not all be standing here.'

We all stood there, silent, because it wasn't an answer a fish could understand.

'Oh, right,' Livia said. She pointed to a space behind us, between where we were standing and the MCV. 'You just jump into that.'

We all turned. In the sand, or where the sandy ground should have been, was a swirling milky pit. Similar to the anomaly on Taura Terra, but smaller. Same same, but different.

'Yeah, sure,' Tiny said. 'The old "lure the humans into the portal-to-hell" trick. Nuh-uh. You go first; show us it's safe.'

'I'll go,' Ostrich said with a shrug. 'I stay here, I'm mulch anyway.' Holstering her pistol, she didn't wait for Daedalus to give her permission; she just marched the 6 feet to the swirling pit, as we all watched with dread fascination, and jumped in.

There were no screams, and no demons came back the other way.

'Ah, what the hell,' Tiny said, lowering his pistol too. 'We might as …'

Before he could move, Ostrich jumped back out of the pit, like she'd bounced on a trampoline, landing awkwardly. She looked up in surprise. 'I did *not* think that would work.'

'Where did you go?!' Tiny asked. 'Was it that gray limbo place?'

'Uh, no,' Ostrich said, dusting sand off her suit. 'I think it was a back alley in New Orleans, five years ago. I walked around for a few hours, people looking at my Legion uniform like it was some kind of fancy dress …' She burped and wiped her mouth. 'Bought a burger and a beer with my face as ID, just like five years ago – at five-year-ago prices by the way – called a girlfriend for a gossip to check the same people were still around and dating the same losers, and then went back to the alley to look for you guys. Swirly pit was still there and I thought, "I wonder what happens if I jump in again." And now I know.'

'Are you satisfied?' Livia asked Lucretia.

'Yes,' she said, then turned me around to face her and put her breather up against mine. 'This is not goodbye, Linus Vespasius.' I'd heard that somewhere before.

'Well, since that swirly pit sure isn't going to still be here after you all go through it, it pretty much is.' I looked to Livia for confirmation.

'Yes, I'm afraid this *is* goodbye, in your terms, as you would perceive it,' Livia said, nodding. 'Definitely.'

Lucretia winked. 'Hear how overconfident she sounds? That's hope, not certainty. Be strong, Linus.'

And with that, she turned me around, gave me a little push in the back, and I followed the scent of oranges six paces forward, to Livia.

When I turned around again, the crew of the *MCV Daedalus* were all gone. And so was the swirling pit.

So because you heard about the Battle of Terra Sabea and I already promised I would tell you about what went before, you know I didn't turn back to Livia to see the flesh had peeled from her bones and a worm-like alien slime creature was balanced there where she had been, ready to dissolve me in acid and return my protoplasm to the One Organism.

I kind of wish there had been.

The Centurion Livia was putting her helmet back on, then nodded to one of her praetorian guards. 'Bring him.' At that proximity, there was no resisting the pheromones, and I felt nothing but love for her. I was so blinded, I didn't even realize she was not talking in English, but in twittering bird speak.

Actually, I was so full of love, I also felt love for the legionnaires escorting me to her MCV. They were all Zeds, of course, and some of them were wounded, though they didn't seem too worried by that, maybe because their minds were no longer recognizably human, transformed like their loyalties, and they'd all soon waste away anyway.

I loved every single filthy, dirty, disfigured one of them.

But Livia most of all. I'd loved her back at Camp Voeykov, and she didn't have all her teeth back then, like she did now. I loved the emaciated, rancid-smelling Livia then just as much as I loved the full-bodied, orange-blossom-scented Livia now.

I had already forgotten Lucretia.

I can say that now without guilt because it wasn't my fault. A succubus renders its target incapable of anything but love for the succubus and all around her/it/the. Everything else, everyone else, becomes unimportant. You'd do anything for them, with them, to them, and let them do the same with you. Lucretia, my beautifully broad-hipped, iron-muscled, quick-minded, traitorous soulmate ... was gone.

There was only Livia now.

As we walked down the side of the MCV to the back ramp, the soldiers of the squadrons from Taura Terra filed back into their own meat-mobiles. I wasn't jealous that they, if they were still capable, loved Livia just as much as me. I still had enough intellect left not to be jealous of the Zedified, since they had such a short time left alive, if it was life they were living. Like I've said, only the Zedified know what it means to be Zeds. And I wasn't, so I didn't.

Was I?

I was led into the MCV, and climbed the ladder into the command module behind Livia. The crew of four was busy getting the MCV ready to depart.

'Sit there,' she ordered, indicating the seat behind her as she settled into the commander's chair. 'We're going to the Taura Terra ZoC. That *Hydra* made a report to your troops at Isidis Planitia. They'll lose their minds over the news the *Intimidator* is in our hands, but eventually they'll gather themselves and come against us.' Her MCV must have been set to auto-trail mode. She wasn't driving it; it was just following the one in front of it. 'You will be brought in front of a council of your peers and given a chance to recant.'

'Recant what?' I managed to ask. 'What am I accused of?'

Livia looked at me curiously. 'This is going to be your defense? "I don't remember"?' She said it in a much whinier voice than I had. 'You expect us to believe you have retained the Lilin ability to communicate but nothing else? Lost your memory as some side effect of becoming human?'

'I *am* human,' I told her. 'I've only ever been human.'

She closed her eyes and it was as though the life left her body. It was still sitting there, upright, exactly as it had been a second ago, but it was completely, utterly still. A doll, not a woman. Then, just as quickly, her eyes opened and she was back.

'It's true,' she said. 'You aren't here. But you *are*. I can sense you in this reality, but not ...' She looked at me as though I was a child who scraped their knee. 'Linus ... can I use that name so as not to disorient you further?'

'Whatever.'

'Linus, it pains me to see you in this state. But *you* chose it,' she said, waving a hand in the general direction of my body. 'I am taking you to a meeting of your peers, not your enemies. There, you can put an end to this rebellion you say you cannot even remember you started. Or you can choose death, and we will respect that.'

'Not the first time I've been offered a choice like that.'

'That's a conversation for the council,' she said. 'But I'll give you one question to think about as we travel, if I may.'

I really, really wanted her to shut up. I'd reached 'revelation overload'. But I was too self-interested. 'Alright, what question?'

She fixed me with what I guessed was supposed to be a deep and penetrating gaze. The scent of orange blossom intensified, and my loins actually began to ache. 'If I told you this crime you committed could lead to the extinction of our race, would you be willing to make it right?'

Pheromones or not, I still had free will, and that 'will' apparently included the ability to resist the temptation of empathizing with the defeat of our enemies. 'The extinction of the Lilin?' I said. 'Great, good riddance, that's a hard "no". Next question?'

'No, Linus, the extinction of *our* race,' she said, frowning. 'We were, are and will be you. You were, are and will be us. The Lilin and the Human are not two races; we are one. I told you our actions create quantum unpredictability that echoes throughout the multiverse. Occasionally, one of those actions is so momentous, its effects are not just tiny ripples creating unpredictability. They are a tsunami that leads always to the same *predictable* outcome ...' She contrived to look terrified. '*Our* extinction.'

Every hormone-flooded cell in my body wanted not to extinctify the beautiful Livia. Every hatred-filled neuron in my human brain wanted her and her entire race wiped out for what they were doing on The Red.

And then my fish brain finally saw the moon. 'Wait, "We are not two races; we are one"? Are you saying that the Lilin are humans from the future?'

'I've said too much,' Livia said. 'I can see any further interaction would just overwhelm your ...'

'Fish brain?'

'... capacity to understand,' she finished.

I had a hundred questions, and continuing the fish analogy wasn't about to let her off the hook. But quantum unpredictability was about to raise its ugly head. Big time.

Get a beer and a snack. You're going to need it.

The *Real* Battle of Taura Terra

'Uh, Centurion?' the MCV's Zed sensor operator interrupted. 'Are we expecting the *Intimidator* to rejoin for the return to Taura Terra?' He threw a holographic 3D plot into the air in front of Livia, showing the position of our squadron and a new contact – a very *big* new contact – that was clearly moving in on an intercept course.

Livia frowned. 'No, not that I … Run the plot forward. Where is it headed?' she asked.

The display showed the projected track for *Intimidator* if it continued its current heading and speed, allowing for the terrain in its path. I could see the hologram as clearly as Livia. *Intimidator* was going to join with Livia's century about 50 klicks *short* of Taura Terra.

'Can you raise the commander of *Intimidator*?' Livia asked.

'I already hailed them,' the sensor operator, the Zed equivalent of Tiny, said. 'There is no answer.'

Livia suddenly looked much less omnipotent. And the smell of orange blossom was replaced by one of bitter lemon. (Alright, not really, the orange blossom was still just as strong, but I am trying to paint a picture here.) 'Alert Taura Terra, Camp Lopez,' she said sharply. 'Launch air defenses. Make maximum speed for the ZoC.'

'Uh, we're already in range of *Intimidator*'s air and missile forces,' I pointed out. 'If they were going to attack us, they could have already.'

'Linus, the nature of quantum unpredictability is that it is … unpredictable,' she said. 'We can *assume* nothing.'

An alarm sounded. Her sensor operator pointed at the tactical hologram. '*Intimidator* has launched missiles and air units,' he said. 'At Camp Lopez.'

Livia watched as hundreds of tiny arrowheads speared out from *Intimidator* toward the Zeno-held ZoC. Halfway to their target, the number of icons doubled, then tripled, as the aircraft in the plot began launching missiles of their own.

'Why aren't Taura Terra defenses *responding*?!' Livia asked, voice on the edge of very un-Zeno-like hysteria.

'The *Intimidator* is still using Lilin friendly fire codes,' the sensor operator said. 'Taura Terra's automated defenses would think the incoming aircraft and missiles are friendly.'

'How can an incoming missile be *friendly*?' Livia asked.

'Technically friendly,' the sensor operator said equably. 'Not kinetically.' He was a Zed, so I suspected his emotions had been dampened to allow him better to serve.

The barrage of missiles reached the ZoC, and a few moments later, the drone aircraft launched by *Intimidator* reached the ZoC too, and began crisscrossing the air above it, unmolested, as they no doubt wreaked more havoc.

'Camp Lopez no longer responding,' the sensor operator said. 'All transmissions have ceased.' He raised a finger in the air. '*Intimidator* is hailing us,' he said. 'Do you want me to …'

'No. Yes. Open a link,' Livia said, voice filled with dread.

The hologram showing the tactical plot was replaced with a comms hologram showing the command deck of the *Intimidator*. It was empty. Or almost empty.

'Hey, he's there!' a voice off camera said. 'I mean, he's *still* there.'

'I told you,' another off camera voice said. 'Quantum uncertainty my ass.'

'Calm down, you two. It's not payday yet,' a third off-screen voice said.

Then a figure walked into shot, and a smiling face leaned toward the camera. 'Hey there, Ballsack, how you doing? Did you miss us?'

It was Lucretia.

So if you heard of the Battle of Taura Terra, what you heard is this, which I'm copying from the Official History of the Red War, which by now I hope you realize is total fiction.

In a glorious action that definitively demonstrated the power of the Dominator class Sandcruiser, the Sandcruiser Intimidator single-handedly eliminated an entire Lilin garrison at Camp Lopez inside the Taura Terra ZoC, allowing the ZoC subsequently to be recaptured and returned to human control. Not a single Legion soldier died in this action, resulting in the proclamation Earthside of the four-hour 'Intimidator half-day holiday'.

Now, don't go thinking this means the war with the Zenos was won and done. They announced holidays Earthside at the smallest of victories, then unannounced them again immediately after the next miserable defeat. But that's the version you can find in the history, right?

Nowhere in that history does it tell you the *Intimidator* had been Zedified, and then re-hijacked by those horrible heroes who will never be named in any history: Daedalus, Tiny, Ostrich and Lucretia.

Nowhere does it tell you *how* they did it. So I'm going to. But let's get back into the command module of the MCV with Livia, because that's where I was.

'Centurion, *Intimidator*'s air wing is attacking,' the sensor operator said.

'I know that, Sensor Operator,' Livia said. 'Lopez is lost.'

'No, Centurion, not attacking Camp Lopez. The air wing has left Taura Terra airspace and is headed for *us*.'

'Yes, sorry, Centurion,' Lucretia said on camera, listening in. 'If you don't surrender immediately, we will destroy your squadron and you all with it.'

Livia smiled. 'That you consider that a threat shows you have learned nothing in the last five years,' Livia said.

Five years? It was only about 30 *minutes* since I had last seen Lucretia. I studied the image in the hologram. Now that I looked carefully, I could see subtle differences. She looked well. She had hair, and it was glossy. Her teeth were white. Her eyes clear. Her voice had a different timbre.

'Oh, trust me, we learned,' Livia said. 'If you want your precious Sandcruiser back, you are going to have to pay a hefty "finder's fee".'

I heard Tiny whispering loudly in the background. 'Ask for 4 billion!'

'Our fee is 6 billion,' Lucretia said, without missing a beat. Someone said something off camera, and she turned away. 'What? Oh, right, right.' She faced the camera again. 'And we want Ballsack back too.'

Intimidator had just laid waste to a Zeno ZoC. I could see in her face Livia wanted it back, and she had enough troops with her to occupy it again. It must have taken a huge effort to capture it in the first place. But did she want it enough to trade me for it? Child of the Dawn, rebel *and* criminal? They had probably been searching the solar system for me for a very long time. I doubted …

'I want that Sandcruiser. You can have the one you call Linus,' she said. 'But the money is a problem.'

'It can't be,' Lucretia said. 'You've looted *every* ZoC you captured.'

'Yes, we have the amount you want, but we have no need of money. We take it only to deny it to you. So it is stored where you cannot reach it, guarded by locks you cannot open.'

'Ah, but *you* can reach it, and you can open them,' Lucretia insisted. 'I'll give you a minute to think about that, or the deal is off and we return the *Intimidator* to the Legion. Oh, and we'll destroy your little fleet of MCVs just for the fun of it.'

'Nonsense. You didn't spend *five years* to get back here just to kill your friend,' Livia scoffed.

'Ballsack? You're right. We'll feel bad about that, but with the billions in reward money the Legion will give us for the *Intimidator*, we can give him a nice funeral. You have one minute.' She cut the link.

'They are cold, your so-called friends.' Livia tapped her fingers on the arm of her chair. 'How far out are those aircraft?'

'They'll be in missile range in a minute, Centurion,' he said, predictably.

'I see. And we can't …'

'A single century can't hold off an attack by the air wing of a *Dominator* class Sandcruiser, Centurion.'

'*Run* …' she said. 'We can't run?'

'The caves in which we found the target are too far now, so no, Centurion,' the sensor operator said.

She banged the arm of her chair with a fist. 'We cannot afford to lose this century right now. The limitations of this reality are *infuriating*,' she said, and I realized she was talking to me. 'And your friends are even worse.'

'Trust me,' I told her. 'No one knows that more than me.'

'No, I imagine not,' she said, turning back to her sensor operator. 'Open the channel again.'

The hologram blinked, and Lucretia reappeared. I saw Tiny in the background this time, mugging at the camera. He gave a small wave and either stepped back out of view or, more likely, was pulled back. 'Your decision?'

'Call off your air attack,' Livia said tiredly. The smell of orange blossoms disappeared. She was still maddeningly desirable, but I was no longer constantly fighting a raging battle with my own hormones to string two thoughts together that didn't involve her. 'You can have the rebel Linus Vespasius. But you will only get the location of the bullion after you bring *Intimidator* to our ZoC at Camp Leighton and …'

'Thanks,' Lucretia said, without waiting to hear the end of the sentence. 'We'll send a drone to pick him up.' She cut the link again.

'… and how you reach it will be your problem … I was about to say,' Livia said, voice trailing off. She looked at me with what seemed like genuine annoyance. '*You* tell them this.

They are not the only ones who can play games of time and space. In that, they are mere mortals, and by comparison, we are gods.'

'Well, I'd say that today it's Mortals 1, Gods 0, wouldn't you?' I pointed out.

She ignored that, standing. 'Bring us to a halt. Let the other MCV commanders know we are stopping,' Livia said to her crew. 'I'm taking Linus down to the crew compartment. When you come to a full stop, shut down the blowers and drop the ramp.'

I pulled my breather over my face and tucked its edges under the skin of my heat suit. Livia had no reason for subterfuge anymore, so she didn't bother with the breather. She opened the hatch down to the meat locker. 'After you,' she said.

I was half-expecting her to slam it shut behind me with some kind of maniacal laugh and open a swirling milky whirlpool in the deck of the meat locker, but she just followed me down and stood waiting as the MCV ground to a halt and then thumped down on its skirts. As it deflated, she put a hand on my arm.

'Can I be allowed one last appeal to reason?' she asked.

'Go ahead,' I said. 'But if you're going to try to tell me those people who somehow came back here to save me are the real enemy, you can forget it.'

'No. I honestly think that *they* think they are saving you.' She stepped damnably close. Succubus close. She wasn't pheromoning me anymore, but let's be honest, at a few centimeters' proximity, in that suit, she didn't need to. 'There is an enemy out there worse than your friends, Linus, and worse than you perceive me to be.'

'There is a race *worse* than the Lilin?' I asked.

'Oh, no, they are Lilin. Rebels, like you. Everything we do, we do to preserve our race, our races. They act out of hate. Hate for everything Lilin. We would *save* you, Linus. They regard all who are not with them to be against them, and since you went on the run from them, that includes you.'

'Well, if I ever meet them, I'll be sure to bear that in mind,' I said.

'I know you have *already* met them,' she said. 'More than once. There is one who you call "Antonia".'

Antonia, moaning in ecstasy above me. Antonia as Eve, naked in the milky pit with Adam. My Antonia?

'Ah, yes, I can see you remember her. They have been searching for you. They needed to be sure you were you, which is why you survived initial contact with them, with *her*. They will invite you back into the Rebel fold, I am sure, but if you give them any reason to doubt you, they will end you.'

The ramp dropped, and a flurry of sand filled the meat locker before settling down. About 100 meters away, I saw a small transport drone drop to the ground, a hatch in its side opening invitingly.

'Are you seriously saying I should stay with *you*?' I asked. 'And what, help you destroy the Void Forge somehow? That's what this stupid war is all about, right?'

If I had just dropped a 'gotcha' bomb on her by showing I knew what the Zeno's war objective was – based on Daedalus's gossip-based theories – she didn't show it. In fact, she didn't even acknowledge it.

'Your Legion friends won't be able to protect you from the one you call 'Antonia' and her kind,' Livia said. 'Only we can. All you need to do is recant.' I turned to go, but she grabbed my arm. 'This is not goodbye, Linus,' she said. Was she mocking Lucretia? Or just lacking in originality?

I half-walked, half-staggered tiredly down the ramp. When I reached the drone, I looked inside the hold, and was relieved to see it empty. I needed a little thinking time.

'Tiny didn't want to.'
'I did so. Daedalus didn't.'

'The oversized sensor operator is correct. Daedalus *didn't*,' Daedalus agreed, nodding enthusiastically. 'Until the full potential of Termite's idea, in all its insanity, was properly explained. After which, Ballsack, I agreed to lead this rabble back Redside to rescue you.'

'Lead us, my fat ass,' Lucretia said. 'It was *my* idea.'

I was on the *Intimidator*'s command deck, with my old crew. Except they weren't themselves. Not anymore. They were five years older; I saw that straightaway. And not just because they looked older. They actually looked *younger*, because five years of good food and *not* being part of a penal legion does wonders for your skin.

Lucretia was glowing. Her emaciated cheeks had filled out. The teeth she had lost were back where they should have been, cleaned, polished and gleaming. Her eyes, I was discovering, were a magnetic green, not the bloodshot grassy gray they had been when last I saw her. Her hair was a dark auburn, not grime and effluent-pit-encrusted stubbly gray. She smelled of soap. It was nearly as intoxicating as Livia's orange blossom.

She looked happy to see me, and gave me a crushing hug, but then stepped back. I sensed there was something new between us.

'I don't … I don't get it. Less than an hour ago, the three of you handed me over to the Zenos and jumped into that portal, or whatever it was, which sent you five years back in time …' I was struggling. 'But you're telling me you spent that five years getting right back here?'

'It's been a big day for you, I get it,' Lucretia said. 'But it's been a big five years for us, trust me.'

Daedalus was sitting in the commander's chair, wearing the stolen uniform of a tribune. 'Status on the Zeno squadrons, Sensor Officer?'

Tiny looked at a holo console. 'Headed northwest. Probably for Leighton, since we just destroyed their closest base …'

'And that's where they told us to deliver the Sandcruiser …' Lucretia added. 'The Legion still thinks *Intimidator* is in the hands of the Zenos,' she explained. 'We're going to let them keep thinking that, but now the Zenos know it isn't. So we're like a pirate ship on high seas of sand, with no port to call home …'

'A very *heavily armed* pirate ship.' Daedalus grinned. 'Which I now command.'

'Until we ransom it back for the price of a small moon,' Tiny said. 'Genius or what?'

'You just offered to sell it back to the Zenos,' I pointed out. 'You are seriously going to sell this megadeath monster to the highest bidder, even if that bidder is our *enemy*?'

'The man knows nothing about the art of the haggle, clearly. Explain to him, Engineer Ostrich,' Daedalus said.

'We need to set a baseline on what this thing is worth,' she said. 'See how quickly Livia agreed to 6 billion?' Her eyes gleamed. 'The Legion will have to pay *more*.'

'But she expects you to deliver it to her now, at Leighton!'

'Pah. Minor detail. You are lost in the weeds, unable to see the big picture, Ballsack,' Daedalus said, shaking his head sadly. 'Clearly traumatized by your time with the Zeno.'

'I'll take Ballsack to the crew module to clean himself up,' Lucretia said. 'See if I can answer some of his questions.'

'Good idea, Loadmaster Termite. The gregarius stinks. Do that,' Daedalus said, like he was giving permission. 'Get him something to eat too. I feel sick looking at all those bones sticking out like that.' He squinted at Lucretia. 'But don't be too long. We need to engage the sand cloak before the next satellite pass, and we have to be a long way from here before we do.'

Lucretia reached out to take my arm, then changed her mind and put her hands in her pockets. 'Follow me.'

Compared to them, with their ruddy cheeks and bulging muscles, I must have looked and smelled exactly like I felt.

Destitute. But I wondered if that explained Lucretia's reserve. Or was there something else?

Of course, there was a BIG something else.

I emerged from a real shower, and stepped into a clean uniform. Not with Legion Praeda penal chevrons but an actual standard Legion gregarius uniform. Newly laundered. When I came out of the heads, into the crew compartment, Lucretia was still leaning on the wall where I'd left her, but she had a protein shake in her hand.

'You know the routine,' she said, unsticking herself from the wall to hand it to me. 'Nothing solid for the first 72 hours, until your stomach is ready for real food again.'

I took it, and drained it hungrily. 'Ostrich had a burger and a beer.'

Lucretia frowned. For her, that had been five years ago. For me, less than an hour. 'She what? Oh, I remember. If she did, I bet she threw it up again straight after.'

I sat on the bunk. 'It's really been five years for all of you?'

She leaned against the wall, crossing her arms. 'It really has.'

I looked around at the empty bunkroom. 'And where is the crew of this monster?'

'You want the short version?'

'As long or short as you think I can handle,' I told her.

'Alright. Medium version. We landed in an alley in New Orleans, five years ago, just like Ostrich said. Before any of us enlisted. We got some clothes, checked into a hotel, got our bearings. Like Ostrich said, our biometric ID was still good. There was no Red War. Just the old advertisements for colonists to migrate to The Red to work in the mines. We all did the same thing: called our families and friends to see how they reacted.'

'And you found out there was another "you" back where you were five years ago, so now there were two of you, and you were worried if you met your other self, you would cause a rip in the space-time continuum?' I guessed.

'No,' she shook her head. 'Everyone was just, like, how the heck did you get to New Orleans so quick? I just saw you yesterday, this morning, an hour ago …'

'Well, so much for that old sci-fi trope,' I said.

'Yeah, I guess the universe doesn't actually tolerate that kind of messiness. Once we decided the Lilin had held up their end of the deal, and it really was Earth, our Earth, five years earlier, we just set up a way to stay in touch and went our separate ways.'

I felt a little crestfallen at that. She hadn't been stricken with remorse and immediately started working on a plan to get back to me? I understood Daedalus, Ostrich and Tiny not giving me a second thought, but Lucretia too? I thought we'd had a *connection*.

'Yeah, sorry, Linus,' she said, reading my face. 'I honestly jumped into that portal thinking I'd find a way back to save you, and I did go back to that alley the next day, my skinsuit in a pack on my back, but I just stood there looking at it, and walked away.'

'Hey, I would probably have …'

'No. I'm not finished. I went back a week later. I still had no plan, but I figured I would jump, and wing it, come up with something once I was Redside again. Our MCV should have still been there. Take that. Do *something*. But the portal was gone. I thought maybe I had the wrong alley, walked up and down every street for about 10 blocks around, but it was gone, and you know what? I didn't feel guilty, I felt *relieved*.'

'Uhm. Alright.'

'Of course you don't think so, and we're here, so you know it didn't end there. But it could have. I just went back to my old life. Exactly like it was.'

I realized I didn't know what her old life was. I knew nothing about her at all, until the moment she walked into our barracks Redside, to replace Fatfoot. Personal histories weren't something you had in the Legion Praeda.

'I was a robotics mechanic,' she said, reading my mind again, 'and had just started a relationship with a total grifter who in about two years would steal everything I had, run up debts in my name I had no hope of ever repaying, and disappear. So my only option back then was to sign up to serve Redside.'

'You dumped him, I hope,' I said.

'Waited for the first time he used my credit line without asking. Punched him in his stupid surprised face, *then* dumped him,' she said.

'So this habit of punching people you don't like in the face, was that what landed you in Legion Praeda?'

'Pretty much. Anyway, after that I'm a free agent again, and I'm thinking, wait, if I'm back here, Linus is here too. Maybe I can look him up …'

I try to imagine the reaction of five-year-ago me answering the door of my apartment to find the imposing figure of one-day-to-be-Gregarius Lucretia standing outside. 'I would have been bowled over,' I say, trying to be charming.

'Not to *date* you, stupid,' she said. 'To warn you not to join the Legion. But then I realized, I don't know your real name, where you're from, anything.'

'It's …'

She held up a hand to stop me. 'Irrelevant now. And it was late at night and I was watching some VR science program about time travel because I was kind of obsessing about it, but it basically concluded it's impossible, and then it finishes with the host saying, "But in one way, we are all time travelers, being propelled from the now into the future, with every second that passes," or something like that. And I realized, hey, I *know* what's coming. I can't stop Linus from joining the Legion, but I know he will. And I know the Zenos will attack and we'll end up in Legion Praeda together and yada yada right up until the moment we leave you.'

'But if you don't join the Legion, we will never meet, and …'

'Yeah, it seems time doesn't work like that.' She's animated now, words tumbling out. 'So, anyway, I get this crazy idea about how we could do things different, and I sell it to the others. They aren't happy back there anyway because they had crappy lives before joining the military and so they went back to their crappy lives. Daedalus wasn't actually that good of a forger, him and Tiny are trying to make money gambling on things they know are going to happen, except they suck at it because they can't remember things right. Ostrich is in this gang of prepper criminals about to pull the heist that gets her arrested. So I sell them my idea, and we spend four years setting it all up, sign up to shunt Redside as miners, not legionnaires, because the one thing we do know that we can leverage is that *Intimidator* is going to fall to the Zenos. Plus, they've served on a *Dominator* class. They know the layout, where we need to hide ourselves, how to hijack it. So we smuggle ourselves onboard and stow away – that was the easy part – and then once *Intimidator* drives off the Legion and you're captured, we come out of hiding, evacuate the atmosphere, kill the Zed skeleton crew, get rid of the Zeno commander – that was the hard part – commandeer the *Intimidator* and force them to hand you over.' She should have sounded pleased with herself that it all worked out, but she was holding *something* back.

'So your amazing five-year plan worked, you hijacked the *Intimidator*, I'm free … Why are you not breaking out the champagne?'

She leaned back up against the wall again. And now I noticed she had a plasma weapon holstered on her hip. I noticed, because she rested her hand casually on it. Too casually. 'Well, there is the little matter of you being a *Zeno*.'

'Hearsay,' I tried defending myself. 'And even if it was true, apparently I'm a *Rebel* Zeno.'

'Uh-huh. See, I did a lot of thinking in the mines here on The Red. And after our brief conversations with the Zeno centurion, five years ago, and again now, I've reached an unhappy conclusion.'

'Unhappy for who?' I asked, but I had already figured it out.

'Us. Sorry. We have to take what the Zenos say at face value.' She held up a finger. 'First conclusion: You *are* one of them. You can speak their language, and they claim you as one of theirs, though admittedly it seems you are some kind of hybrid human-Zeno freak.'

'Nicest thing you ever called me.'

'You're welcome. Daedalus, Tiny, Ostrich, they've made their peace with that since you didn't Zedify any of us.'

I nodded at her pistol. 'But you haven't.'

'Not yet,' she said. 'You need to prove to me you're on *our* side and not just some murderous Zeno spy assassin.'

'By …'

'Supporting our plan *against* the Zenos. I came up with the idea of hijacking the *Intimidator* from the Zenos and selling it back to the Legion. Daedalus added this crazy complicated side thing where we backstab the Zenos, to make the Legion grateful, before we ransom the *Intimidator* back to them, because he thinks that will increase the reward they give us.'

I thought about it. 'You already took out Taura Terra. Now we take out Leighton too? It might actually work.'

'Maybe. But we have to actually survive the attack on Leighton. Daedalus says this beast can be crewed by four people in a pinch, but five is better. So, Tanker Vespasius, you need to support us with that, *against* the Zenos. And if I see the slightest sign you aren't …' She tapped her holster.

I could see what five years had done to my relationship with Lucretia now. Absence did not make her heart grow fonder. 'Wow. OK. Not quite the rescue I thought it was,' I said, and looked down at the protein shake in my hand. 'So depending on how this goes, you're saying the sludge I just drank could be my last meal?'

'I wanted you to be able to keep it down.'

'So kind.' I was thinking desperately for ways to prove my loyalty. And … 'Wait. I just got a great idea.'

'That is *such* a dumb idea,' Daedalus said.

Daedalus had moved the *Intimidator* to the base of a nearby mesa that was always in shadow, then engaged the cruiser's 'sand cloak'. It was a simple camouflage system that just took images of the landscape around the cruiser and projected them onto cells on its photoreactive skin, so the silhouette of the cruiser was lost in the background. It hid the cruiser from distant observers, and from passing satellites and aircraft. Choosing a mesa with a high mineral content also allowed them to confuse magnetic anomaly detection.

'Why would we let *you* talk to the Zenos,' Daedalus asked, 'right before we are about to stab them in the back?'

'Yeah, it's a shell game kind of thing,' Tiny agreed. '*Look over here, we brought you the* Intimidator. Bam, smack the Zenos in the face with it. Doesn't work if you give away our plan.'

'That's not actually how a shell game works,' Lucretia said, shaking her head. 'We've learned now that there are *two* Zeno factions, and Ballsack is with the Rebels. We can play them against each other and maybe pull off the score of the millennium, ripping off both the Legion *and* the Zenos.'

I explained the whole Antonia (Rebels) versus Livia (Reactionaries) split to them. 'Livia said the Zeno bullion is hidden somewhere we'd never find, behind locks we can never open. But what if my Rebel "friends" will help with that?'

'In return for what?' Ostrich asked me.

'What they wanted at Isidis Planitia,' I told her. 'Me.'

'And you'd go along with that?'

'No. Obviously I'd find a way out of it, but only *after* they tell us where the Zeno bullion is.'

'I don't know,' Daedalus said. 'If the Legion gives us even a billion …'

'Yeah, but the Zeno said yes to *six*,' Tiny pointed out. 'So they probably have more.'

The economy of The Red was pretty simple. It was all based around the production and export Earthside of antimatter, from the Void Forge at Kamloop, which was located thousands of klicks from any other facility because a single gram of antimatter, if it escaped containment, would annihilate itself with the explosive power of a 21-kiloton nuke. After a series of disastrous accidents at antimatter forges, and a very short and incredibly destructive war between two antimatter-weapon-possessing superpowers – who were no longer superpowers – world leaders had banned all military use of antimatter, and a golden era of limitless energy production and antimatter-powered space travel had dawned.

(Yeah, yeah, as a member of the human race, you know it wasn't that simple, and could change any day, but the Antimatter Restriction Treaty had held for 50 years so far.)

The other ZoCs on The Red existed mostly just to support Kamloop, and functioned like city-states, with their own specialized industries, usually mining based, but sometimes based around tech or resources like water, food, or O2. They traded with one another in currency backed by minerals and gems mined from The Red's frozen underground and the export price of antimatter. The exchange rate at the time was three Earth to one Red dollar, which went up and down depending on how badly production at Kamloop was affected by the war.

'What's to lose?' Ostrich said to Daedalus. 'We're in the mother-effing *Intimidator*. Even if Ballsack tips off the Zenos to our plan, we can still crush them. Probably.'

'Alright, I have a plan,' Daedalus said after a theatrically long pause. 'Ballsack, you will contact this other Zeno faction and tell them you escaped from the Zeno centurion to *Intimidator*, and you are willing to hand yourself over to them if they give you the location of the Zeno bullion, which they say they don't care about anyway …'

'Great plan, Tribune,' Lucretia said sarcastically.

'Thank you. In the meantime, we will continue with my other plan to ingratiate ourselves with the Legion by destroying the Zeno base at Leighton, and score a mind-bogglingly large reward from them.'

Ostrich raised a finger in the air. 'Alright, but since we can't exactly take Ballsack back to Isidis Planitia because the whirly butthole won't be there anymore, how do we find these "Rebels"?' she asked.

'Well, I have an idea for that,' I said. 'I'm guessing this thing has a pretty powerful radio transceiver?'

Syrtis Major

Tiny set the *Intimidator* comms system up to scan for Zeno frequencies. Lucretia was right – there was really only one ZoC still in Zeno hands since the destruction of Taura Terra, which was Syrtis Major. So we started looking for signals down that bearing, but there was no guarantee that Syrtis Major was held by the faction we were looking for, so we had to cast our net pretty wide. I made a recording using quantum bird tweets, and we just broadcast that on repeat, every time we got a frequency lock. It went like this:

'Antonia, I forgive you.'

We didn't have to wait long. The radio chimed, announcing it had a lock on a new Zeno frequency, and then a series of trilling sounds began pouring out of it.

'I am never going to get used to that creepy noise,' Tiny said. He handed me a mic. 'Over to you, bird man.'

The first sequence of sounds was in some kind of code, nothing I could understand. A test of some kind maybe. I just ignored it.

'Antonia, is that you?' I asked, in Zeno.

Linus, my Linus. Do you really forgive me?

I had to check it was her. For all I knew, the broadcast could have been intercepted by Livia's faction and now they were impersonating her. Not like I already knew how Antonia's quantum bird chirp sounded. I had to ask her something only she and I would know. How about something she said in the courtroom, the day she betrayed me? No. Courtroom proceedings were recorded.

I tried to remember what we talked about in the gray nothingness of Isidis Planitia. 'Tell me where we were when I last spoke with you, and your last words to me.'

We were in a meeting place between this reality and another. And I asked you not to waste time we won't have.

It was her. I checked the faces of my comrades, though 'comrades' is a strong word for murderous pirates ready to sell you down the river the moment you are no longer useful. When I was in quantum chirp mode, communication went so quickly it was like time stood still. Microseconds had passed during my first exchange with Antonia.

I knew a little more about the Zenos now. And I had questions for her before we started doing any negotiating.

'Time is a playground to you,' I said. 'How could I possibly "waste" time?'

In this reality, bounded by the form you inhabit, time is a dimension: directional, and finite. We can abstract ourselves from it, but you, as you are right now, cannot. Tell me, how does that feel?

'Feel?' She sounded ... not just curious. Curiously and passionately eager to know.

We can simulate the corporeal, but you are The First. The Child of the Dawn. The first to live it since we left it behind. Please, Linus, I have to know. Describe it to me.

'Describe what?'

Life! Tell me how it is to live.

I'd just had a shower and my first – albeit liquid – good meal in a long time. But my hair was still thin. My scalp covered in scabs. My teeth, those that remained, either rotten or loose. My toes ached because my boots pinched against torn nails. The vision in my left eye was blurred. I was in my thirties, but felt like I imagined an 80-year-old would feel. I also told her the woman I had fallen in love with, the one she met in the anomaly with a pistol to my head, was either kissing, constantly betraying or threatening to shoot me. I probably said that to try to make her jealous, without thinking that Zenos didn't do jealous. I told her how much that hurt. Lacking anything better to say, I told her *all* this.

She was quiet for a quantum eternity. *Oh, Linus, it sounds ... wonderful.*

'It's pretty crap, actually,' I told her.

Pain. Delicious pain! Sickness and disease. Fatigue. Emotional damage. Experiencing them, you must also have felt their opposites – wellness, health, vigor, love. No?

'Well, yes, but not for a bloody long time.' *Not since I was with you*, I was going to say, then realized if she was asking, then she hadn't been feeling what I felt when we were together. Whatever she had been showing me, it was ... simulated?

But you have and are and did and will. Linus, you DID it. You Transitioned. You opened the door. You have to tell us how, SHOW us how, so we can follow!

Tell her what? The problem was, whatever Antonia thought I had done, I had no memory of it. I couldn't answer her any more than I could create a milky trans-dimensional portal. 'I don't remember,' I told her, honestly. 'Whatever you think I've done, I don't remember.'

Linus, you are speaking to me in our language. You couldn't do that when we met. It was one of the tests I gave you. Something unlocked your ability to speak. I am sure we can unlock more memories, if you let us.

My alarm bells started ringing. I remembered Livia's last words. 'An enemy out there ... worse than me. They will use you.' Since just about every Zeno I met seemed hell-bent on using me for their own ends, the idea of Antonia 'helping me' just caused a boiling fury to rise.

'That's exactly what the other Lilin said,' I told her. 'They were taking me to a "panel of my peers" at Taura Terra to help me see reason. Or were, until my real friends wiped Taura Terra off the map. How are you any different?'

The other Lilin ... this individual you call Livia?

I regretted blurting it out. 'Maybe.'

Oh, Linus. How to put this in terms your current self would understand? She was taking you to a tribunal, not to help you but to bully you into giving up. Giving up your journey through this reality. Betraying our rebellion, the rebellion you started. Failing that, they would have killed you.

Wait. 'Funny, that's more or less what she said about you,' I said. 'Why should I trust any of you?'

Just hear me out. The Reactionaries have only one objective in this reality …

'I know; they want the Void Forge at Kamloop. They want control of antimatter production,' I said.

Interesting. She sounded surprised. How long have you suspected this?

Should I tell her the Zeno war plan had been rumbled by the scrofulous Daedalus based on gossip, rumor and the absence of official comment? Maybe not. 'Long enough. It's kind of obvious since there is nothing else on The Red worth starting an intergalactic war for.'

Linus, the Void Forge is the objective, she said. But it is not the reason for the war. This war is about the survival of our species, either as disembodied consciousness, which is what the Reactionaries want, or as living, breathing, feeling organisms, which is what we want.'

I lifted my shirt away from my body and looked down at the ribs sticking out from under my sunken skin. 'Trust me, you really don't.'

She ignored that remark. Linus, we need to return you to yourself to unlock the secret you hold. But because we are operating in this reality you have chosen, first we need to end the threat to our rebellion, she said.

'Well, it seems pretty close to ending anyway,' I told her. 'Your "Reactionaries" only have a couple of bases left.'

'No! Can't you see? she asked, allowing frustration to bleed into her voice. 'They are closer to victory than ever. Their constant attacks provoked you to create the Sandcruiser, the key to your own demise. Now, they have shown they can Turn a Sandcruiser, capture it to use against you. How long do you think Kamloop will be able to stand if the Reactionaries control two Sandcruisers, or three, or six?

OK, that was a completely new twist. The Zenos were winning by losing? It wasn't about controlling firebases or

ZoCs; it was about Sandcruisers, and always had been? Alright, Linus, focus. 'OK, so, end the threat to the rebellion. How do we do that?' I remembered Lucretia saying Syrtis Major was the last Zeno stronghold. 'We need to warn the Red Army leadership your Zeno buddies are going to go for the Sandcruisers now. So we just fly them back to the moon, and we win?'

No. The Reactionaries will just find another attack vector. You must destroy that which anchors them to this reality, hidden under what you call Terra Sabea.

I frowned. 'You mean the firebase at Terra Sabea: Schiaparelli? We recaptured that months ago.'

No, you 'reoccupied' it. It has, will, did fall again. But what you want is underneath it. The anchor.

'This is some kind of milky whirlpool portal thing we have to shut down?' I guessed.

Milky whirlpool … no. It is a quantum resonator crystal. They, we, need it to achieve corporealization. Destroy it, and we will discorporate. They would need to embed another crystal in this reality, and that would take energies they currently don't have.

I thought she might just be setting us up to do her dirty work and destroy the other Zeno faction for her, but I saw a flaw in her plan. 'Uh, you said "we". If we destroy this crystal, *you* discorporate too?'

Yes, we will, did, could, but you and I will be finished with our work together by that time. I hope, by then, you have returned to yourself, to us. We will help you.

'Uh, so how do we find this, uh, quantum resonator thingy? Is it like big and red and glowy, or …?'

No, it is about the size of a human hand. And it hums.

'Hums …'

Yes, it makes an audible hum.

'And it is just sitting out in the desert in Terra Sabea, somewhere easy to get to.'

No. It is, was, will be stored deep under Firebase Schiaparelli, at the bottom of the deepest mine on the entire planet, guarded by a Lilin-turned stay-behind force.

'Of course it is, was, will be.' I sighed. I looked around the *Intimidator*'s command deck at the others, who were watching me intently. 'Good, so, oh yeah. My murderous friends think I am talking to you about handing myself over in return for the location of the Zeno bullion hoard. Is that even a thing, where is it, and what should I tell them?'

Bullion hoard? This is a money thing?

'It's a money thing. They think the Lilin have billions in treasury credits they've looted from the various ZoCs they've, you've, captured.'

They, we, do. We know that a large part of your concept of war involves theft and economic damage. So we take your bullion and sequester it …

I had to ask. You know the answer already, and so did I, but I had to ask it. 'So where do you hide the bullion, and how much have you taken?'

At the bottom of the deepest …

'… mine on the planet, under Firebase Schiaparelli. Guarded by the Lilin stay-behind force. And how much is there?'

I have no idea, Linus, Antonia said. How much are your friends asking for this ransom?

'Well, it was a bit confusing, but I think 6 billion,' I told her.

Is that a lot?

'It's what it costs to build a new Sandcruiser,' I told her. 'So yeah, for Redsiders, it's a lot.'

Tell your friends there is at least 10 billion in the vault under Firebase Schiaparelli. They should take the Intimidator there. I will meet you at Schiaparelli.

'Too easy.'

But they will only be given the location and code to the vault once the crystal has been destroyed.

'Ah.'

There is a problem.

'Another one? I see a lot of problems already.'

Schiaparelli lies on the other side of the Reactionaries' base at Camp Leighton in Syrtis Major. Your friend Livia and her armies will not let you pass easily.

'Oh, no problem. We have a plan for *that* at least.'

Antonia then gave me the key to getting back to my Zeno-Rebel self. I didn't love it. I made an arrangement with her for a private communication channel so we could stay in touch. And then we cut the call.

Two minutes had passed.

'OK, we have a deal,' I told them.

'Alright!' Tiny shouted. 'You got the location, and your buddies will help us get in? How much is there? Is it four? I would have bet four. Four is OK though: a billion each. Anything over four is …'

'Ten,' I told them, watching their faces go through a dozen emotions, all of them shades of greed. Except for Lucretia, who just looked dubious. 'At least. But there's a catch.'

'There's *always* a slug-fundering catch,' Ostrich growled.

I was – relatively – honest with them, especially about the challenge of reaching the bullion hoard at the bottom of the mine. I left out the part about the 'Zed stay-behind force' guarding the quantum anchor crystal thing, which was apparently stored beside it, because that would only have made them unhelpfully emotional.

'So we just need to get to Schiaparelli,' Daedalus said, pulling on his bottom lip. 'And anything the Legion agrees to give us is just icing on the cake? Sometimes I have *good* ideas.' He grabbed Tiny and started dancing a pirate-y jig. Ostrich grabbed an arm and joined in. They had worked five long years for this, could you blame them?

Lucretia, however, was still leaning up against a bulkhead, arms crossed. 'How about you handing yourself over to these

Rebels?' Lucretia said. 'That happens before, during or after your Zeno friend shows us the way to the bullion?'

'Well, it seems it's not so much me they want as some secret that's locked in my head,' I said, which was at least partly true. 'But they have a plan for that, which we can worry about later.'

She gave a less-than-satisfied grunt. I was starting to think maybe she wasn't best suited to be the mother of the future Vespasius generations after all.

Linus, my Linus, do you really forgive me?

I hadn't answered that one. Now that I knew what I knew – or at least, what I was being told – did I forgive Antonia for witnessing against me at my court-martial? To do that, I had to try to understand why she did it. She had been studying me to see if I was The Transitioned, The Code Bearer, et cetera. The authorities had interrupted that by arresting me for desertion. They took her, and no doubt tortured her – lightly, thinking she was just another camp follower – but she was Zeno, felt no pain, could have ghosted at any point. Egotistical me wanted to believe she came to court just to see me one last time.

And there were her last words, as they dragged her away. '*Linus! I will find you!*'

Which she did, in the milky pit of nothingness at Isidis Planitia. However she did it, she did it. That had to count for something, right?

Yeah, nah. I was being played. I'd been played every moment of my time on The Red. Manipulated, nudged, anticipated, cajoled, foreseen, predicted. It was time for me to take charge of my own destiny. If I should believe Antonia, I'd already done that, as a Zeno Rebel. I had to find my way back to *that* guy.

Antonia's prescription for finding my way back to myself was through exposure to life-threatening mortal danger.

You made the choices you made because you wanted to FEEL, she said. Our ancestors said they never felt more alive than when they were in love or in danger. It was probably love for the woman Lucretia that woke your ability to speak again. Keep that fire alive, if you can. And embrace both the threat of death and the ecstasy of survival.

I'd pointed out to her that embracing the threat of death could very well result in actual death, but that didn't prompt her to suggest an easier way.

Let me remind you what the History says about the Battle of Syrtis Major.

After the heroic intervention by the Sandcruiser Intimidator at Taura Terra, the Lilin were still in control of ZoC Leighton in Syrtis Major. Leighton was one of the most heavily fortified of the northern ZoCs, and home to the Northern Air Force, when it was Turned by the Lilin. Hundreds of surveillance, attack and air defense drones were lost when it fell.

Undaunted by these odds, the legionnaires of Intimidator immediately set course for ZoC Leighton to maintain pressure on the Lilin. Meanwhile, the Sandcruisers Dominator and Terminator were dispatched to Syrtis Major. The scene was set for the biggest aerial battle of the Red War.

Of course, what the History doesn't mention is that the 'legionnaires of *Intimidator*' were the scrofulous pirates who had stolen it back from the Zenos. That *Dominator* and *Terminator* had orders to destroy both the Zenos at ZoC Leighton and *Intimidator*. Despite what the History says, the Legion wasn't yet aware that Daedalus et al. had hijacked *Intimidator* back from the Zenos. They found out about events at Taura Terra later. To them, *Intimidator* was still under Zeno control and de facto hostile. Would things have gone any differently if we had revealed that we were the ones behind the destruction of the

Zeno base at Taura Terra? Five deserters from the Legion Praeda? Not likely. We wouldn't even have got a thank you before we were shot and mulched.

We moved out from the shadow of the mesa at dawn, in between satellite passes. It was just a matter of hours until the next satellite would be overhead and *Intimidator* would be spotted. It cast a shadow a half mile long that you could probably have seen from *Earth* with a decent telescope.

Plus, there was that drone air force at Leighton.

'Recon drone on radar,' Tiny said. 'No sign it's seen us … scratch that. It just changed direction toward us.'

'Kill it, Ballsack,' Daedalus said. I was a tank driver, but on a vessel as complex as *Intimidator*, with so few crew, I doubled as all-round weapons systems operator. Tiny was still on sensors, Daedalus commander and driver, Ostrich systems engineer, and Lucretia payload manager. It normally took a crew of seven working three shifts to crew the *Intimidator*, plus another six in shifts of two in the payload bay handling vehicles and ordnance. So for the five of us to do the same job, we had to put a lot of systems on AI control.

'Drone is locked, missile ready to launch,' I said. 'Uh, we kill it, they'll know we're out here,' I warned.

'They know we're out here anyway, they just don't know exactly where,' Daedalus said. 'I want to keep it that way as long as we can.'

'Launching,' I said, tapping on the holographic icon in front of my face. I'd only seen the *Intimidator* from down low, on my way into its payload bay from ground level. But it was a carbon copy of the Liquidator. The restriction on AI control of lethal pulse weapons meant only six weapons at a time could be chained to AI control, and a human had to approve the targeting. Fine if you had a crew of elite, well-trained legionnaires aboard your cruiser, not so great if you were a crew of five trying to remember how everything fit together. So we had a kitten at a dog pound's chance of surviving a concerted swarming attack by ground vehicles and drones.

Our interceptor looped through the thin atmosphere of The Red and knocked the surveillance drone from the sky. The others assumed it was from Syrtis Major. It could just as easily have been a Legion recon aircraft.

'Drone destroyed,' I reported, as the missile hit home.

'Good. Now everyone shut up. I need to come up with the actual plan for double-crossing the Zenos at Leighton,' Daedalus said, closing his eyes and swinging his feet up onto a console.

'I have a plan,' Tiny said.

'And when *you* are commander of a Sandcruiser, you can propose it,' Daedalus said, without asking what it was. After several minutes in which I'm pretty sure he dozed off, he opened his eyes again. 'We will make directly for ZoC Leighton via Lopez, north of Mount Huygens, as we agreed with the Zeno. We will no longer hide ourselves from Legion satellites, in the expectation they see us and come after us. But either the Zenos, or the Legion, could decide to attack us before we get very far, and if they do, we will just have to play it by ear.'

'"Play it by ear" is not a plan,' Lucretia pointed out.

'It is when you have ears that have been through as many battles as mine,' Daedalus said. 'Loadmaster Termite, load the tubes for counter-air operations. Sensor Operator Tiny, optimize your sensors for air warfare. Chief Engineer Ostrich, divert all auxiliary power to the plates and close-in weapons systems …'

'We don't have any frog-munting "auxiliary" power,' Ostrich muttered. 'As far as I can tell, we just have power.'

'Well, divert that, then,' Daedalus said, undaunted. 'Ballsack, set all air wing operations to AGI control and then manually crew the forward pulse cannon array. I will set course for Lopez.'

Manually crew the forward pulse cannon array? That sounded dangerous. Legionnaire Vespasius quailed at the thought. But Zeno Vespasius embraced it with lip-licking enthusiasm.

I took down two more wandering recon drones, but then we got made by a passing Red Army satellite. That was what Daedalus wanted, so it didn't change our plan. Firebase Leighton approached on our starboard bow, about 200 miles distant. As we entered air attack range, they reacted.

'Uh, we're being hailed by Camp Leighton,' Tiny announced.

'In bird chirp or human?' Daedalus asked.

'Human. They want to speak to the commander of the *Intimidator*.'

Daedalus brushed an invisible crumb off the tribune's uniform he'd taken off one of the Zeds. 'That would be me. Put them through.'

Livia's image appeared above the holo projector at the front of the bridge, and I had a mirror image thanks to a projector in my station in *Intimidator*'s nose. 'Decanus Daedalus, we meet again,' she said.

'*Tribune* Daedalus now, Centurion,' he said haughtily. Livia wasn't wearing her uniform anymore though. She'd changed into body-hugging composite armor. The six Zedified centurions lined up behind her left no doubt as to her rank and position at Leighton. She was still calling the shots. 'I hope you still plan to honor our deal,' Daedalus said, barely suppressing a smile.

'Of course,' she said. 'If you live long enough. As your ancients used to say, "*Ahead Be Dragons*".'

'What?' Daedalus frowned.

'You have attracted some unwanted attention. We have just detected the Legion Sandcruisers *Dominator* and *Terminator* headed your way.'

We had wanted to attract the Legion's attention, but definitely in a much more low-key way. Like, two MCVs maybe. Not two *Sandcruisers*.

'Stinking pus fingers,' Ostrich cursed.

'I'll assume that was an exclamation of dismay,' Livia said. 'We need to work together to defeat the Legion Sandcruisers, and once you deliver the *Intimidator* to me, I'll give you the location and the codes to the vault.'

'Deal,' Daedalus said. 'We'll be in touch to coordinate our attacks.' Without waiting further, he signaled to Tiny to cut the link.

'Wait!' Ostrich said. 'Deal? What deal? We're going to help the Zenos take out two Earth Sandcruisers? I didn't sign up for that.'

'Me either,' said Lucretia's voice from the payload bay. 'Not happening.'

Tiny's face was a masterpiece of consternation. He probably didn't care who had to die for him to get rich, or for whatever reason, and he was also unswervingly loyal to Daedalus. But a little piece of him was still human, and the idea of siding with the Zenos was clearly not sitting well with him.

'Boss?' he said to Daedalus, pain in his voice.

'*Relax*, everyone,' Daedalus said. 'We aren't fighting any Legion Sandcruisers. We let the Zenos at Leighton go up against the Sandcruisers, and then we swoop in at the best possible moment and take out the unsuspecting Zenos from the rear to save the day. Then we reveal to the Legion that *we* have recaptured *Intimidator* for them, ask for a finder's fee, which they will give us because, remember, in this new timeline, we are not fugitive deserters anymore, we are a band of entrepreneurial freelancing miners who just helped them destroy the Zenos at Leighton and retake Syrtis Major. The Legion will shower us with medals and bullion after we tell them we will hand *Intimidator* back to them at Schiaparelli, after which Ballsack's *other* girlfriend gets us into the vault.' He sat back in his chair with hands behind his head, elbows wide. 'Termite, no questions. The crew may now tell the commander of *Intimidator* he is a genius.'

Dominator and *Terminator* were going to be within range of the aircraft and missiles of Firebase Leighton before they could threaten *Intimidator*, which was probably why they were making a beeline for the Zeno ZoC. Deal with the air wing at Leighton first, then come for *Intimidator*.

Which gave us the ideal excuse to let the Zenos 'spearhead' the attack on the two Legion Sandcruisers. Daedalus coordinated our attack with a Zed centurion at Leighton with minute attention to detail, grinning and winking at us the whole time because we had no intention of doing anything.

As all of *Intimidator*'s instrument panels and controls were virtual, I was able to control any weapons system from my little cockpit up in the nose of the Sandcruiser while monitoring the forward pulse cannon array. Which, by the way, sounds more exposed than it was. It wasn't an actual turret; it was a semi-circular booth comprising a very comfortable chair (with beverage holder), a holo projector and a 2D wall screen that showed any view of The Red, from the *Intimidator*'s hundreds of cameras, that I wished.

Since I was crewing the forward pulse array, I had the wall screen showing the view out front of the cruiser, so it *felt* like I was sitting in a little bubble on the nose of the cruiser, which was good for giving me a heightened sense of danger, even though I knew in the rational part of my brain that my little cockpit was buried deep under *Intimidator's* armored, magnetized and microwave-shielded plates. I could have had vision of the rest of the crew on the bridge to keep me company, but that would have made me feel less alone and vulnerable, so I just had their disembodied voices on comms.

Do your best to live in a constant state of heightened peril, Antonia had said. If actual peril isn't enough, create an environment around you that makes you feel scared.

Since I was back among a crew of murderous mutineers, her last comment about trying to create an environment of peril around me was redundant.

'Loadmaster to bridge, all aircraft and missile tubes loaded,' I heard Lucretia say.

'Bridge to Weapon Systems Officer,' Daedalus said. 'Launch air wing in five … four … three …'

I sighed. He didn't need to do a countdown. We'd agreed a launch window of several minutes with the Zenos, not a precise moment. But Daedalus was Daedalus. It made him feel more 'commander-ish', I guess.

'… two … one! Launch!'

I waved my hand in the air with a flourish that coincided with the automated launch timer. From the tubes along the Sandcruiser's spine, hundreds of attack drones punched into the thin air and started circling above us as though forming up for a swarming attack.

'Senior Sensor Operator, what see you aloft in the direction of the Zeno base?' Daedalus asked. It may have been my imagination, but it felt like Daedalus's vernacular had become distinctly more pirate-y since they'd successfully hijacked the *Intimidator*.

'Absolutely nuth— oh, wait,' Tiny said. 'Whoa. They must have been hoarding attack drones and missiles. I count 400 … no, 500-plus attack drones, and about *1,000* missiles, outbound from Leighton! I'm glad we are on their side.'

'*Temporarily* on their side,' Daedalus said. 'Until we aren't.'

'Greasy nut butter, an attack like that is going to sting,' Ostrich said. 'Even against two Sandcruisers. How long are we going to wait before we step in?'

'Long enough for their plates to start buckling and their laser barrels to start melting, so that the fear of impending death overwhelms them …' Daedalus said. 'Not long enough that too much *actual* dying happens.'

'Don't go too early though,' Tiny said. 'We want them to be grateful we saved their asses, right? The survivors, anyway.'

'You are all still assuming the Zeno attack will fail,' Lucretia said from the payload bay. 'We didn't know they had that many aircraft!'

'Good point, Termite,' Daedalus said. 'Let's see how *Dominator* and *Terminator* handle the first attack wave. WSO, move our air wing closer but not actually close.'

'Aye, Tribune,' I said, wincing at having to use Daedalus's self-appointed title. 'Closer but not actually close' allowed me to put our aircraft between ourselves and the Zeno swarm, just in case they anticipated our stab in the back and turned on us too.

'Cue standoff missile attack. Target: Camp Leighton,' Daedalus said.

Down in the payload bay, Lucretia had reloaded the empty launch tubes with land attack missiles. 'Standoff missiles loaded and armed,' she reported.

'Targets at Leighton locked and boxed,' I confirmed.

'Zenos' first wave hitting now,' Tiny said. We were close enough to the two Sandcruisers that we could pick up their signals energy, so we could measure how their microwave defenses were holding up. They'd changed their codes when the Zenos stole the *Intimidator*, so we couldn't read their actual systems data, showing hull integrity and ordnance states, but we had access to satellite infrared imagery that showed infrared hotspots on their hull, which bloomed when a Zed missile or pulse bomb hit home.

The two Sandcruisers were showing infrared spots like the black dots on lady bugs. And their microwave arrays were already down to 83 percent of the energy they'd been radiating in the first few minutes of the Zeno attacks.

'Giving as good as they're getting,' Ostrich said. 'They're raining interceptors on those Zeno missiles and drones. Sand inside Syrtis Major must be littered with Zeno wrecks already.'

We should have been using an AI to tell us the optimal moment to launch our ambush on the Zenos. The perfect balance of damage to the Legion Sandcruisers, attrition in the Zeno ranks, proximity of our air wing to the furball in the northwest …

Instead, we had Daedalus's gut instinct.

'Daedalus! Launch the strike, before those Sandcruisers are mulch!' Lucretia cried.

Daedalus scratched his stubbled chin with affected indolence. 'Patience, dear Termite. We have not yet …'

We all jumped in our seats as we were hailed on comms. A patently livid Livia appeared on holo. '*Intimidator*, why are your aircraft not joining the attack?!' she demanded.

'Jamming,' Tiny whispered. 'Tell her we're being jammed.'

Daedalus nodded. 'Deepest regrets, comrade,' Daedalus said. 'It seems our control system is being jammed. We were able to launch, but we …'

'You must think us fools,' Livia said, and cut the link.

We'd waited too long.

'Oh, crud burger,' Ostrich cursed. 'They're turning.'

The Zeno attack swarm had been engaged with the two Legion Sandcruisers, but it *pivoted* as one and broke away – *toward us*.

'Perfect,' Daedalus said, in a voice that said it was anything but. 'Exactly what we want. Launch standoff missiles. Send the air wing.'

I'd been through enough actions with Daedalus and crew to know that if it could go wrong, it would. So I'd sent our air wing out to blocking range, missiles and pulse cannons already up, ready to intercept an incoming Zeno swarm. I released it in air defense mode, so it would first swat any incoming missiles or bombs, then go after the Zeno motherships. At the same time, I tapped a holographic key to launch our own attack.

'Two hundred-plus missiles incoming!' Tiny said in a strangled voice.

Unlike the two Legion Sandcruisers, which the Zenos had attacked while they were still outside standoff missile range, we weren't. The Zenos had let us creep in under their missile defense skirt. From the spine of *Intimidator*, 200 hypersonic standoff missiles punched into the air and arced away toward Camp Leighton.

I had no idea how many Zeds were still alive at Leighton. I knew it had a population of about 10,000 souls before it fell. Well, you know, now, but I didn't back then. So I was figuring maybe half of the original garrison at Leighton were Zedified and technically still alive. Zenos would have screened and killed most of the settlers and camp followers already. So we were about to kill maybe 5,000 former legionnaires.

Or was it a Schrodinger-type situation – at that moment, they were both alive *and* dead. We'd only find out which, and how many, by opening that box later.

I was more focused on the 200 missiles the Zenos had just fired at *us*. Antonia would have been very proud of me, as my peril-ometer rocketed into the red zone. Our air wing was engaging with the Zeno air wing now in a dance of robotic death, but every one of the missiles it had already fired at us was autonomous. It didn't need an aircraft radar to guide it; it just screamed through the sky looking for an *Intimidator*-shaped target to kill, and given the fact a Sandcruiser was the size of a Red mesa, finding us wasn't going to be a problem.

'Engineer Ostrich, defensive systems status?' Daedalus asked. I was used to her reciting a litany of damaged or broken systems – remember, it was just that morning I had been removed from our busted-ass MCV and taken by the Zenos before being recaptured and put aboard the *Intimidator*. So I got a pleasant surprise as Ostrich replied. 'Hull integrity 100 percent, microwave arrays armed, laser and pulse weapons ready …'

'Loading interceptors,' Lucretia called from the payload bay. 'One minute ten!'

'Missile proximity in one minute five!' Tiny reported.

'Load faster, Termite,' Daedalus ordered.

'It's an automated system; it loads as fast as it loads,' she advised. 'Fifty-eight seconds.'

'Missile proximity in 53!' Tiny reported.

'Tiny, patch the bearing to the incoming missiles to the forward pulse cannon array,' I said. The pulse cannons were intended to protect against slow-moving ground targets, not hypersonic missiles, but I had command of six mofo guns, and I was determined to fire them, if only to make myself feel better just before I died.

'Uh, sure, Ballsack, go crazy,' Tiny said, imbuing me with confidence.

On the targeting holo in front of me, a cloud of small icons appeared. The incoming Zeno missiles. Behind them were larger icons showing the Zeno aircraft boring in behind them, waiting for the result of their first volley before they fired another. Our air wing was thinning them out, but not quickly enough.

'This is the Sandcruiser *Intimidator*,' Daedalus said over the Legion battlenet frequency. 'Calling Sandcruisers *Dominator* and *Terminator*. We are citizen soldiers and we have retaken the *Intimidator*. We are engaged with the Zeno force out of Firebase Leighton and need assistance. *Intimidator* over.'

'Citizen soldiers, good one. You think they'll believe that?' Tiny asked. 'Last they heard, *Intimidator* had been hijacked by Zenos. Uh, 20 seconds to missile proximity.'

'Well, Sensor Operator, since the Zenos are now trying to kill us, I'm hoping …'

'Ten seconds.'

'… they do.'

My targeting system was drawing boxes around the nearest Zeno warheads but couldn't lock on. The auto-targeting reticle was jumping around like a manic jack rabbit. So I changed to manual control. I took a deep breath.

'Microwave arrays firing!' Ostrich called out.

'Interceptors loaded! Auto-launch activated!'

Then the *darndest* thing happened. I'm telling this in retrospect, so you're partly getting it the way I remembered it, and partly the way I reconstructed it.

Time slowed. No, it just … *stretched*. Like the effect people talk about in car crashes or when the stims kick in and the hormones hit in combat and you see everything with amazing clarity and your synapses are snapping like popcorn.

As though I had all the time in the world, I moved my targeting reticle around the sky, fingers flying as I painted targeting boxes around every incoming missile and allocating a single plasma pulse burst to each, cued to fire sequentially. The AI readout at the bottom of my targeting screen told me that the six-cannon array was going to take 4.3 seconds to destroy all the targets, and the time to missile impact was ... six seconds.

I started to feel like something was slipping. Once all the incoming missiles were boxed, I didn't feel scared anymore; maybe that was it. No. That was more like a cause. The *consequence* of not feeling scared for my life was a feeling like things were falling out of balance again. You know that feeling when you knock a coffee cup and reach for it and for a second you don't know if you've got it or not, just before the coffee goes everywhere?

Like that.

Time snapped back into being. Not with a tick, but with the blast of pulse cannons spitting plasma bolts into the sky in a seemingly random but strangely precise pattern that took down every one of the incoming Zeno missiles.

'That was orifice-splittingly impossible,' Ostrich said. For the first time since I had joined the crew, she was looking at me as though I was anything more than trash waiting to be taken out. 'But I'm not complaining.'

'Yeah, like, how?' Tiny asked. 'You manually targeted and destroyed nearly 200 hypersonic missiles in the space of, like, three seconds, before they even got in microwave range, and we didn't take a single hit.'

After a long time sitting in my turret ignoring all communication, I'd gone back up to the command deck. Daedalus had his hand on the butt of the pistol in his belt, and was eyeing me suspiciously. I decided the truth was my best defense. 'Well, it was like I was super-stimmed …'

'That's a hormone effect; didn't they downrate your stim implant in Voeykov?' Ostrich asked.

'Yeah, but maybe it was just a normal human-style hormone reaction,' I said. 'And a *lot* of luck.'

'Yeah, or …' Daedalus said, standing. 'Or, Bird Man of the Dawn here has been holding out on us all this time, and he has these Zeno reflexes up his sleeve he only uses when his life is really on the line.'

That was so close to the true truth I didn't know what to say, and fully expected Daedalus to shoot me right there and then. Instead he took his hand away from his pistol and just grinned. 'Which is totally fine with me, because if Ballsack can pull that kind of trick, it means that bullion is as good as ours.'

'What about *Dominator* and *Terminator*?' I asked. Like I said, after taking down the missiles, I'd just sat locked inside my turret control room for a little while – actually, maybe a couple hours – ignoring inquiries from the crew, not paying much attention to anything really. Just *digesting*. I heard the crew whooping in delight, heard Daedalus negotiating something with someone, vaguely registered that the other two Sandcruisers had added their air wings to ours and blasted the Zeno fleet from the sky … but all I could think was what happened in the cannon turret. It had been very weird, a little bit intimidating, and actually made me feel a bit violated, if I was honest.

My conclusion, after a further two hours of rumination, was that for a subjectively very long three seconds there, facing almost certain death, I'd gone full Zeno. But still human. Able to do things I shouldn't be able to do. Like target 200 missiles in three seconds, even though I was human. And feel mind-numbingly terrified, even though I had gone Zeno. The fact I could control neither of these things didn't help me at all. So I still had to navigate life among the crew of the good ship *Intimidator*.

'*Dominator* and *Terminator*'s commanders are now my best buddies,' Daedalus was explaining, 'seeing as we were able to prove we flattened both Camp Lopez at Taura Terra and then Camp Leighton, *and* took out half the Zeno air fleet just before *Dominator* was about to suffer a hull breach. The old girl is pretty messed up, but its crew survived, and it can still roll.'

'Not bad for a mining crew who just wanted to do their bit for the war effort, eh?' Tiny said, giving me a solid nudge and what was probably supposed to be a wink, but came off as a squint.

'And the Zenos?' I asked, turning to the tactical display on the command deck main wall. It was showing the two Sandcruisers, northeast of us, but no Zeno aircraft or ground units.

'Between the three of us, we dropped their entire fleet, and the Zenos at Leighton have apparently ghosted,' Daedalus said. '*Terminator* flew in a scout team and they landed without challenge.'

I sat, suddenly both weary and euphoric. 'So … the war is *over*? Leighton was the last Zed ZoC, right? We won?' It occurred to me that maybe we wouldn't have to destroy the humming Zeno crystal after all …

Lucretia had been leaning in a doorway listening, and not saying anything, since I arrived. She spoke up now. 'Sorry, Ballsack. Voeykov was Turned. It was announced while you were busy zapping Zeno fighters.'

'Voeykov, where you met your girlfriend, Livia,' Daedalus said. 'So not a surprise.'

'Still not my girlfriend,' I said. 'Girl*fiend*, more like.'

Lucretia laughed. And a big warm glow spread from my feet up through my still-skinny shins to my disease-ravaged torso and then onto my face. She loved me still. Human, Zeno, whatever I was, I'd proved my loyalty, and Lucretia loved me.

Or, at the very least, was able to endure me again.

'So what now?' I asked, trying to act like I hadn't just done a full-body blush. 'Schiaparelli?'

Daedalus nodded, climbing back up in his commander's chair, which he'd lowered as far down as it would go, but his feet still couldn't reach the deck. 'Schiaparelli. We've been given permission to pilot the *Intimidator* as far as Schiaparelli, where we will hand it over to a proper crew and then bask in the glory of the Legion's munificence.'

'Munificence?' I frowned.

'I negotiated a "finder's fee" for recapturing *Intimidator*,' Lucretia said. 'A million each, for all of us, plus a pardon for you, since in this new timeline *you* are still a wanted deserter while we are just entrepreneurial miner pirates.'

'Pffft,' Tiny said, eloquently. 'A million, with an "M"? Small change. But once you and your other girlfriend who we didn't kill help us get into the bullion vault inside the Schiaparelli mine complex, we *could* consider you getting a small percentage …'

'Also not my girlfriend,' I reminded him.

'Whatever, so, you get a pardon and a very *small* percentage of the loot,' he finished, looking around at the others for agreement. 'Which seems fair, right, since we spent five years on this and you spent, like, a day?'

I didn't blame Tiny for being just a little greedy. He'd been humiliated in a court of his peers, condemned to a penal legion, starved and abused, then transported Earthside a free man, and *then* undergone five years of I-don't-know-what to get himself back here today, where he nearly died at the hands of the Zenos again.

He'd earned his bullion. The whole mutinous, larcenous lot of them deserved their bullion.

Including me. Because deep down in my wretched human soul, I had also been humiliated in a court of my peers, condemned to a penal legion, starved and abused and then, additionally, kidnapped, traded, re-kidnapped and re-traded, exposed to the most violent form for racial and temporal confusion I'd wager anyone had, would or did ever go through in human history, and I knew I wasn't done yet.

So yeah, I wanted my cut too.

'They can shove their millions,' I said. 'We're going for the jackpot.'

There was a raucous cheer, and Lucretia gave me a shy smile. She unstuck herself from the doorway. 'Linus and I are going to …'

'Get him cleaned up,' Daedalus sighed. 'Yeah, we know. Get some actual sleep, you two. We aren't at Terra Sabea yet. This can still go seriously sideways.'

'And probably will,' Tiny said with a grin, trying to give Ostrich a high five, which she ignored.

I followed Lucretia meekly, hoping she would take my hand, then wondering why she didn't, as she led the way down the corridor to the crew quarters. By the time we arrived at my cabin, I was feeling both confused and annoyed. It seemed we weren't about to engage in human concourse, after all. Or not the kind I had hoped for.

'We need to talk,' she said, punching the button to open my cabin door and gesturing for me to go in.

'Again? That's all anyone wants to do,' I grumbled, shuffling past her with shoulders hunched. 'I already told you what …'

Lucretia grabbed me, spun me around like I was an eight-year-old ballerina and kissed me hard. Then pushed me away. 'We really need to get you to a dental hygienist,' she said, and pointed at my bunk. 'Sit.'

I know you want me to write a love scene here. Or at the very least a ribald, lusty, sweaty one. And trust me, I wish I could, did, had. But human concourse was not top of mind for Lucretia at that moment. Survival was.

'This crew is going to kill us, Linus,' she said, simply. 'As soon as we escape with the bullion, maybe even before. Unless you can pull some of that ninja Zeno voodoo on them.'

She had moved beyond questioning who or what I was, it seemed. Now she was only interested in what new value I could bring to the table, since 'human scarecrow' was not a talent in high demand.

'I told you.' I sighed. 'I don't really know what happened back there. It really was like time stood still, or stretched out, and I had all the time in the world to destroy those missiles. And I don't know how or why it happened, and I have no idea if it will ever happen again or what use that would even be.'

'Then we're screwed,' she said, slumping down on her butt beside me. 'They're cooking something up. Every time I walk into a room, they go quiet, and Tiny says something lame, like, "Hey, look, it's Termite. We were just discussing, like, what to have for lunch. What would *you* like to have for lunch, Termite?"' She shook her head sadly.

'What makes you so sure?' I asked. 'I mean, they could have killed us a hundred times already, and they didn't need to bring you back to the Red with them to carry out the hijacking plan; they could have ditched you anywhere along the way during the last five years, but they didn't.'

She looked at me like I was a three-legged puppy. Adorable, but pathetic. 'They could never have pulled off the heist without me, and they knew it,' she said. 'But once we make the score, they don't need me, or you, anymore.'

Alright, yes, I was developing something close to affection for Daedalus, Tiny and Ostrich. They might be murderous, mutinous pirates, but they were also my *friends*.

Weren't they?

Or was I just a terrible judge of human nature, being as I was, possibly, not even fully human?

'So here's a plan,' I said. 'This mine sounds huge, but *we* have Antonia to help us; they don't. So we ditch them somewhere, grab the bullion, and while they're still wandering around in the dark, we are on a shunt headed Earthside …'

She leaned forward, with what I mistakenly thought was enthusiasm. 'Yes. Yes, we could do that or … or … hear me out … we could just kill them first, forget the bullion and be happy with my Red million in reward money.'

'That's a *terrible* plan,' I said. 'Mine is much better.'

She sat back again. 'Only because your pheromone-addled self, for some reason only you can fathom, trusts this Antonia entity. Whereas level-headed hormonally unbiased me sees only another Zeno, luring us into the depths of the planetary crust, there to do away with us and steal your soul.'

I decided to try to divert her murderous energy. 'We can't cut and run now,' I told her. 'Antonia told me what this war is all about. Daedalus's theory was, amazingly, right. The Zenos are going to use our own Sandcruisers to take out Kamloop.'

'They're going for the Void Forge?' she frowned. 'They're clearly a more advanced civilization than us. We know they can travel through space and time, they probably invented antimatter centuries ago … what do they want with our forge?'

Something occurred to me. 'Maybe they don't want it for themselves. Maybe they just want to stop *us* from having it.'

She balled her fists in frustration. 'So we just stay long enough to warn the Red Army Command the Zenos are going for Kamloop, which we think they already know …'

'They don't know about the plan to Turn all our Sandcruisers against us,' I pointed out.

'OK, *that*, we warn them about that …'

'And they'll believe us …'

'They have to. Because we know they know it's possible because *Intimidator* was already Turned, before we re-hijacked it.' She wasn't letting go. 'And *then* we cut and run.'

'There's one more reason we can't run before we get to the bullion.' I told her about the humming quantum crystal anchor outside the bullion vault.

She slumped onto the bunk next to me. 'You are *infuriating*. So we can end this war, but to do it, we need to follow our enemy into an almost certain trap, and even if by some miracle it isn't a trap, Daedalus and the others will probably kill us as soon as they get the loot.'

'Good summary,' I agreed. 'Unless you want to just take your reward money, let the Zenos win and see what happens after that. Which I don't recommend.' I lay back on my bunk. That was as far as our planning got. Because I think I passed out from fatigue after that. I don't remember much more than Lucretia mumbling a couple of sentences, tucking me fondly into bed (alright, I'm hallucinating that part) and leaving quietly.

When I woke, we were approaching Terra Sabea, and not long after that, the battle started. And I know you heard about the Battle of Terra Sabea. Everyone did, will, has. And guess what?

For once, what you heard is the terrible, tragic, apoca-bloody-lyptic *truth*.

Terra Sabea

From the History:

The Battle of Terra Sabea was the penultimate battle of the Red War. The Lilin had captured Camp Voeykov in the Thaumasia Planum ZoC, gifting them the largest Lilin-turned Legion on The Red, the Praeda penal legion and the maintenance base for the intra-planetary shuttle fleet.

How the Lilin transported the entire Legion Praeda to Camp Schiaparelli in Terra Sabea ZoC in these shuttles without being detected is a matter of much academic dispute, since there are no Lilin or Lilin-turned survivors to provide contemporaneous corroboration. However, it is known that the Lilin force infiltrated Camp Schiaparelli through a disused mine tributary, and the alarm was raised by alert miners who heard the sound of Zed troops advancing through a parallel tunnel.

What followed was a desperate underground defensive action in which the usual Legion advantage in air power was negated – there were no fewer than three Sandcruisers docked at Schiaparelli at the time – and most battles took place in the claustrophobic confines of labyrinthine mineshafts, at close quarters, often tooth and nail ...

The History prefers to present a picture of the Zenos as nameless, faceless, evil aliens. So it's no surprise it doesn't mention Livia, who led the Zeno assault, because to the Red Army she was a ghost. She'd ghosted from Voeykov as a prisoner, ghosted from Margarita Terra, ghosted from the triple-Sandcruiser attack on Leighton ...

We, the former crew of the Sandcruiser *Intimidator*, knew her though. We just didn't expect her to turn up at the head of our old Legion 2 miles underground. No one did.

OK, maybe Antonia did.

When the first shots were fired, we were all lolling around in a hangover-induced torpor. We had delivered the

Intimidator to the gates of Schiaparelli, with *Dominator* and *Terminator* as escorts. Cheering masses thronged the entrance as confetti cannons fired …

Oh, I can't keep it up. We were met at the gates of Schiaparelli by a company of military police. Daedalus, Tiny, Ostrich and Lucretia were, in the timeline their return had overwritten, humble miners, not deserters. They actually did get a word of thanks from the commander of the MPs and were led away for an audience with the Schiaparelli base commander. I, however, *was* a humble deserter from the scum of the earth Legion Praeda, and though Lucretia had negotiated a pardon for me, there were quite a few MPs who had lost comrades at the Battle of Isidis Planitia, and they weren't inclined to go easy on the only survivor.

They had questions, which they punctuated not with question marks but with punches and kicks. If I'd had answers, it might or might not have gone quicker, but what was I supposed to tell them? That there was this enormous milky butthole at Isidis Planitia, and we drove into it and were met by two naked god-like creatures who, after a bit of back and forth, returned us to the surface, where we found everyone dead?

I chose instead to insist I'd been knocked unconscious in the opening minutes of the Isidis Planitia thing, woke up alive and panicked, stole an MCV, ran into a Zed patrol outside Lopez, got captured (but definitely NOT Zedified) then was rescued by the crew of the *Intimidator*, after which I played a pivotal role, if not *the* pivotal role, in the Battle of Syrtis Major. More or less what I'd rehearsed with Lucretia and the others before we got to Schiaparelli, except for the part about me playing the pivotal role.

It was so close to the actual truth it got me through multiple rounds of enhanced interrogation, after which I was delivered to a centurion who had me sign my pardon. Which you'd think meant I was a free man, right?

'Now there is the problem of what to do with you,' he said, wiping my greasy thumbprint off his nice clean document pad.

'Well, my friends have offered to buy me a seat on a shunt to The Blue with their reward money,' I said. 'So …'

The swine laughed. 'Earth? Your desertion has been pardoned, but you are still a member of the Legion Praeda, legionnaire. Which is why I have a problem …'

No. Surely not. But yes. When is a pardon not a pardon? When you are a lowly gregarius in the lowest legion of them all. He was looking at his document pad.

'What problem, Centurion?' I asked, not really wanting to know.

'This pardon says you are to be returned to your base at Voeykov. And that is the problem. Voeykov was Zedified. Your filthy Legion with it. Your filthy comrades, together with everyone else in the Reduction camps, are all now filthy Zeds. We are expecting to be ordered at any moment to deploy with the *Dominator, Intimidator* and *Terminator* to eliminate that nest of traitors …'

I saluted him. 'Wonderful. Die well, Centurion.'

He frowned. 'I'd take you with us, but the gossip is your filthy hide carries a curse.'

'Curse?'

'Margarita Terra, Isidis Planitia, Taura Terra … the actions in which you took part all resulted in wholesale annihilation of your fellow legionnaires, with the exception of Syrtis Major, which was largely successful because of a brave band of citizen soldiers, not you.' *Brave band of citizen soldiers?* I had to avoid being sick in my mouth at that comment, as I imagine, dear reader, you probably did too. He continued. 'Now, I tried to offload you on another centurion, but no one will have you, and I don't want you. Luckily, you were already sentenced to death previously, because I see no option but to have you shot and mulched.'

'Respectfully, there are *always* other options, Centurion,' I suggested, then got creative. In the new timeline Daedalus and the others had created, had we served on *Liquidator*? I guessed not, because since they had been miners all that time, that whole timeline probably just collapsed. But ... 'Sir, as our recent action showed, I am now, practically, a weapons specialist qualified to serve on a *Dominator* class cruiser. I heard a rumor the *Liquidator* is short on crew. I am not worthy of such a life-threatening duty, I realize that, but shooting me seems like such a waste of valuable meat ...'

He stared at me for several seconds, in which I could feel my life hanging in the balance (the other end of the scale holding the weight of my every failure), then tapped a few icons on his pad and threw it on his table with a disgusted thud. 'The *Liquidator* actually *is* short on crew due to a bout of dysentery, though I have no idea how you heard about that. She is currently headed for ... let me see ... *Kamloop* in the Argyre Planitia ZoC. Consider yourself transferred, with full pardon for your desertion but loss of all combat hours. You have 48 hours to requisition transport to Kamloop.' He saluted without much gusto. 'Die well.'

I spun on my heel and marched out, not exactly a free man. Or at least not with the freedom I'd hoped for. But freedom measured in minutes can sometimes be all the more precious.

So *Liquidator* was headed for Kamloop, eh? Coincidence, or destiny? It really didn't matter. If Antonia was telling the truth, and we did manage to destroy the quantum crystal anchoring the Zenos to our reality, the war would be over before I even reached the site of the Void Forge.

I found the others in a bar inside the camp, not far from an entrance to the mine, one of dozens, which was like a military compound inside a military compound. The bar was full of miners, which, given my companions' recent history, made them feel right at home. Miners were not unlike soldiers, in a lot of ways. They volunteered for dangerous work in the hope of making it rich by surviving the length of their contract to collect their sign-off bonus. They were a little, not a lot, less likely to die horribly, since machines did most of the digging in the mines on the Red, and miners were basically technicians, engineers, programmers and mechanics who kept the machines running. The crust of The Red was notoriously brittle though, and cave-ins frequent. Like miners anywhere or any-when, they still managed to get filthy, and the clientele of the bar were covered in the ochre-like iron oxide soil of the Red. Somehow, my companions had contrived to get themselves covered in red dirt too. As I sat down at their table, Daedalus handed me a beer and a bag of fine sand. 'Welcome back, Ballsack! Go to the bathroom and smear this on yourself so you don't embarrass us.'

The Red Army had already deposited their paltry Red millions in reward money in their personal accounts, and so we got uproariously drunk. We may or may not have shouted the entire bar at some point. I may or may not have danced a wild jig with a man twice my girth, or it could have been a fight. I may or may not have kissed Ostrich and been slapped by Lucretia. It may or may not have been the other way around.

I clearly, or less fuzzily, remembered a deep and earnest conversation with Ostrich.

'Why do you stick with Daedalus?' I asked her. 'Tiny, like, I get it. He needs Daedalus to decide everything for him. But you. You are smart. And funny. And strong, in a sinewy kind of way. And beautiful …'

'And you are drunk, Ballsack.'

'No, really, why?'

She looked deep into my soul with her almond eyes for all too short a time and sighed. 'Daedalus saved my life. It was the Antimatter War, the three of us serving in the Big Red One – knob-grindingly ironic, right?'

'From one Red Legion to another …'

'Exactly, though we didn't know it at the time,' she said. 'Anyway, we were in a tank squad on the Mongolia front, running uncrewed ground vehicles with short-range control because of the jamming, so we had to stay close. Daedalus was our sergeant. We got orders to advance to contact, against an enemy position that had already slaughtered two other squads. Beijing, Manchester and Washington had just been AM'd. Daedalus gave one of his big speeches, then ordered me to disable the AI limiter on the tanks ...'

'Take the human out of the loop?'

'Exactly, put them solely under AI control, which was illegal under our own law and about 10 international conventions. We sent the tanks at the enemy position under full autonomous AI control, and they did a better job than we ever would. They mulched the enemy position, and when we moved up, it was all over. We destroyed our own tanks with thermite charges so that my hacks wouldn't be discovered, and we even got a citation. A week later, the war was over. Daedalus made a very big point out of the fact we owed him.'

'I can imagine.'

'We had a reunion not long after. We all had money problems, and it was his idea we should sign up to serve Redside. I said no way. "You owe me, sister," he said. "If I go alone, I'm mulch. If we go together, I've got a chance. We all have." He really did believe that. Still does.'

'He would trade your life for his in a heartbeat,' I said to her, shaking my head. 'Remember Fatfoot?'

'You don't get it,' she said. 'I *know* he would. But that survival instinct he has, you're better off with it than against it. You might want to think about that.'

I might have leaned across to kiss her at that point. I do know I woke with a cut lip, a gash across my eyebrow, a bruised cheek and a blinding headache – 'beer' on The Red being nothing more than carbonated water with artificial flavor and industrial strength spirit added. I lifted myself from the floor I had apparently been sleeping on. Lucretia was lying on a couch. I could hear snoring coming from three bedrooms that came off the room we were in. It looked like some kind of managerial-level apartment. I vaguely remembered an argument with a staff member downstairs about how many people we were, but that had probably been settled by the liberal application of money.

I found the bathroom, which thankfully had a well-stocked medicine cupboard, then found a kitchen, which had a well-stocked victuals cupboard. The smell of freeze-dried rations being heated roused the rest of the crew. The breakfast conversation consisted of a question-and-answer round that went like this:

'Did I …?'

'Yes, you did …'

'Oh, no.'

'Wait, how about me? Did I …?'

'Yep, you too, but with less grunting …'

Lucretia was our collective memory, since it seemed she was the one who stayed closest to sober. Eventually, the conversation turned to the topic that was on everyone's mind.

Daedalus poured himself a shot of coffee, sat and fixed me with a bayonet-like stare. 'So, Ballsack …'

'What?' I knew generally what the stare meant, but wanted specifics.

'You know what. Your girlfriend promised to show us the location of the bullion and give us the code in return for …' He frowned. 'In return for what, exactly?'

'Some kind of secret locked in my head, which I haven't unlocked yet,' I told him, simplifying the situation the best I could. 'She said she would find us here.'

'We could have met her in that bar and wouldn't remember it,' Tiny said.

'The whole camp knows we arrived with *Intimidator*,' Lucretia pointed out. 'It won't be hard to find us with the amount of money we splashed around last night. But, duh, am I the only one sees a problem with this arrangement?'

Daedalus sighed. 'Yes, Loadmaster Termite, it seems you are.'

'She's a *Ze-no*,' Lucretia said, drawing out the last word. 'She can't get through the perimeter magnetic field unless someone goes out and walks her in.'

'She's already here …' I told them. 'I'm pretty sure.'

'Of course she is. Child-mongering Zenos can get in anywhere – we've seen that,' Ostrich said.

'So how do we …?' Daedalus repeated.

'She'll find us,' I said, with either confidence or dread – take your pick.

Livia was on the way too, with a few hundred heavily armed friends, but we didn't know that. You do.

We played cards. We watched some VR. Antonia knocked on the door.

I was too scared to go to the door because I knew proximity was peril. So I stayed on the couch. Daedalus, Ostrich and Tiny grabbed their pistols and took up casual positions behind solid pieces of furniture. Lucretia sighed. 'So I'm getting the door?' Maybe she was thinking she could put Antonia in her place with a full-frontal, 'bring your best game, girl' stare-down.

But she opened the door and just stood there. 'Oh, come *on*,' she said. The scent of Antonia flooded the apartment but not in an overwhelming, cloying way. It insinuated itself, tuning itself to the senses of the receiver. To me, it was orange blossom. Lucretia said later that no, it was musk. Tiny said it was definitely the smell of public toilets, which none of us wanted to explore further.

'Mother of a goat-bothering shepherd,' Ostrich said. 'Yes. Whatever the question is, the answer is yes.'

It broke the spell. Lucretia backed up a few paces. In fact, she backed all the way into the kitchen and started jamming tissue paper in her nostrils. I could have told her that didn't work, but I think she probably needed a mental prop as much as a physical one.

Antonia was dressed in mining overalls. Her hair was tied in a bun with what looked like baling wire. She had red dirt on her face, dirty hands and nails. None of which made her less appealing.

'I appreciate your attempt to blend into the crowd,' Lucretia said, pushing the wadding up her nose. 'But I still feel a little gender conflicted.'

'I don't,' Ostrich said. 'Wasn't. Amn't.'

'I'm staying behind this curtain,' Tiny's voice said. 'Tell me if it's safe to look.'

'You can look, sensitive Sensor Operator,' Daedalus said. 'Our succubus ally is dressed in mission-appropriate attire.' He still had a pistol trained on Antonia, so there was more than a little ambivalence in the word 'ally'.

Tiny stuck his head out from behind the curtain, looking disappointed. 'Oh, good.'

Antonia looked around, her gaze settling on a chair by the dining table. 'Can I sit?'

'Please,' Daedalus said. He pulled a chair out for her with a flourish.

Lucretia gave him a look of disgust. 'Can we just get to business?' she asked. 'The entrance to the vault?'

'Yeah, do you have, like, a map, or coordinates, or something?' Tiny asked.

Antonia tapped her head. 'This is your map. There are 200 miles of tunnels and shafts down there. To say it is a tortuous, infuriating and deceptive labyrinth is an understatement. The vault is in a forgotten section of the mine, sealed off by a false wall, inside a portal and guarded by a stay-behind force of the Turned who are loyal to Livia's faction.'

'A stay-behind force of Zeds …' Ostrich turned to me. 'You didn't say anything about any sputum-swallowing "stay-behind force", Ballsack.'

'No, I may have omitted that detail,' I admitted. 'Since I figured she …' I nodded toward Antonia. '… would have a way through or past or around them.'

'There is a way,' she said. 'I can pass. And so could, will, did you.' Now she looked genuinely sad. 'But your friends cannot.'

Tiny's face scrunched into a mix of frowning parent and crying child, and he brought up his pistol. 'There is no way Ballsack goes into that vault without us,' he said. 'Not alive, anyway.'

Now Lucretia was frowning. 'If he's dead, how could he …? Oh, forget it.'

Antonia tried to reassure him. 'No, please. Once past the stay-behind force, we can – in your crude terms – disarm them. Then you could follow, to the vault. I can let you in.'

'Why do you need Ballsack with you?' Lucretia asked. 'If you can get past these guys and disarm them, just do it.'

'I told them there's something locked in my head you're trying to reach,' I explained to Antonia. 'I'm guessing me going with you is part of that?'

She looked delighted I'd worked that out by myself. But only in the way a seal trainer is delighted when the seal claps for a snack. 'Yes, exactly! I think, I know, or knew, that the experience of entering the vault "unlocks" what's inside you. Or will. Sorry, your tenses are not my …'

'Forte,' Lucretia finished. 'For an omnipotent being, you are kind of a disappointment. No offense.'

'No offense taken,' Antonia assured her. 'Because we are you.'

'There she goes again,' Tiny groaned. But he put his pistol away. 'So how do we do this?'

'We're miners,' Daedalus said. 'I can get us through security and into the mine through the entrance near here. Once we're inside, we can hijack a transport and head deeper, but the Zeno needs to be with us, to tell us where to go.'

Antonia indicated her overalls with a flourish. 'I am ready.'

Lucretia was ready too. It was a mining management apartment, so it was equipped for managers conducting inspections. She walked to a storage unit and opened it. Inside were thermal skins and breathers. 'No you aren't. There's no atmosphere inside the mines, and the temperature will start below freezing and then rise the deeper we go. So even if you don't need them, you'll have to wear a thermal-regulating skin suit and a breather to look convincing.' She threw them at Antonia's feet, wisely not wanting to get any closer to her before she was suited up. We'd have more protection from her too, once we were all suited and masked.

Antonia stood, and picked the clothing up.

'Do us all a favor and go in the bathroom to change, will you?' Lucretia said. 'With the door closed.'

'But if you need any help, just holler,' Ostrich called after her, then saw the looks on our faces. '*What?*'

The mine used DNA swab locks to admit personnel. But like any huge enterprise, it took time to register new employees. On The Red, meat was a precious commodity, and you weren't allowed to cool your heels waiting for the paperwork to catch up to you, so new employees were issued with swipe cards. I thought he'd shouted the bar out of pure generosity, but as Daedalus went around buying people drinks, he'd stolen a half dozen passes, and he handed them out to us now.

On the other side of security, we stopped by a basic map showing mine sections and levels, and were approached by a shift foreman. I had no idea what he would ask or what we should reply. But my crewmates did.

'Who are you idiots?' the foreman asked.

'Canaries for section, uh, 32 Blue,' Daedalus said, not looking at the foreman, but pointing somewhere up on the map. 'Which way do we …?'

'Blue transport pool, third bay on your left. Ask for Supervisor Kyznopolous,' the foreman said, and lost interest in us immediately, moving to the next group of new employees who were standing around looking lost.

'Just follow me,' Daedalus said, and headed off down the entry tunnel. We passed a couple of bays, including one clearly marked 'BLUE TRANSPORT POOL', which Daedalus ignored.

'What's a canary?' I asked Lucretia. I was being careful to walk beside her, and as far from Antonia as I could. Antonia was simply following along, not being alien or menacing or even particularly succubus-like.

'A "canary" is a safety technician,' Lucretia explained. 'From the saying "canary in the coal mine"? Job they usually give to new hires because it's the most dangerous. They send you into sections that have been shut down because of water or toxic gas leaks, to check and repair whatever the problem is. Since this mine was recently held by the Zenos, they send "canaries" in to look for booby traps.'

'Sounds like something the Legion would do,' I said. 'Like checking perimeter beacons.'

'Exactly like that,' she agreed. 'Miner or legionnaires, The Red is The Red, right?' She checked where Antonia was and then said in a low voice, 'I appreciate how you didn't go completely ape when you saw her again. But whatever it is she has planned for you, don't trust her, Linus. *Whatever* faction she's part of, she's Zeno. She'll manipulate you if she can.'

'OK.'

'I *mean* it,' she hissed. 'Believe it or not, I'm not here for the money. Or even because we might be able to end this war. I'm here to make sure nothing happens to you, idiot.'

'I know,' I told her. 'But Antonia isn't our only problem. We have three others. So let's both be careful.'

'Fair enough.'

First, we went to the mine armory and got ourselves issued with sidearms. Schiaparelli had already been Zedified once, so the administrators had to do something. Issuing the miners with sidearms was a simple way to say you were doing something without really doing anything. Another way a mining corporation was a lot like the Red Army. They were simple plasma pistols, but better than nothing. Daedalus took Antonia's off her and gave it to Ostrich.

We found a six-person cart that someone had left by what looked like a break room. People inside were eating, watching VR, dictating messages home. 'This will do,' Daedalus said. He turned to Antonia. 'You're our navigator. Sit up front by the driver. Now we need a driver.' He looked at each of our faces. 'Alright, who feels the least affected by the succubus?'

'Me,' Ostrich said. 'Definitely.'

'Your speed of reply, Optio, rules you out immediately. And since he's romantically conflicted, Ballsack is out too.'

'Hey, I'm not …' I started to protest.

'Tiny's large glands make him too vulnerable,' Daedalus continued, ignoring me. 'And I need to be able to sit behind the succubus to keep a gun on her back, so that leaves …' He'd been counting on his fingers and settled his gaze on Lucretia. 'Termite.'

I could see she didn't like the idea of sitting in front of a gun-toting Daedalus, but she probably didn't like the idea of me driving up front with Antonia either, so she didn't argue.

'I don't actually identify as a succubus,' Antonia said, as she took her seat in front. 'Or incubus.'

'No one cares, Zeno,' Daedalus said. 'It's just me finding a way not to call you something worse.'

Antonia had not been joking about the labyrinth. Underground, there was no east or west; there were only tunnels going left or right, and shafts going up or down. Some of the tunnels were marked by color and sector. A lot weren't. Some of the shafts sloped; others required us to drive onto a platform to be cranked higher or dropped lower. No one asked who we were or where we were going once we were inside the mine proper – it was a mine, not a military base.

I tried dropping mental breadcrumbs for a few minutes (left, left, right, down ramp, right, right, up elevator …) but after about 10 turns and three levels I gave up. An hour passed. The number of other crews we passed got more and more, then as we went deeper, fewer and fewer.

'I need a bathroom,' Tiny said. 'How much further?'

'We are halfway,' Antonia told him. 'To the false wall.'

The equipment in the apartment hadn't included miner 'piddle packs' since managers apparently weren't mine-side long enough to need them. So we couldn't pee in our suits. Using a bathroom while wearing a thermal suit and mining overalls wasn't just a matter of finding a quiet corner out of the light, on account of the need for pressure and temperature regulation. It required an actual atmosphere-controlled bathroom.

Lucretia turned a corner, saw the sign for a 'relief station' and parked up next to it. Tiny jumped out and hit the button to open the pressure chamber door.

An alarm klaxon sounded. *Loud.* Red strobe lights began flashing up and down the tunnel.

'That wasn't me!' Tiny said. 'I didn't ...'

'*Zeno breach*,' Lucretia said. 'The mine is under attack.'

I was sitting next to Daedalus and he shoved the barrel of his pistol into Antonia's back. 'What do you know about this?'

'*Knowing* anything is impossible while I am corporeal,' she said. 'But I suspect it is Livia's faction. They must have predicted we would be headed here.'

'Or it's your faction,' Daedalus said, shoving the pistol harder. 'And this is part of *your* plan.'

'I don't want Linus dead,' she said, vehemently. 'If he dies now, our movement loses.'

Once again, the situation balanced on the blunt knife edge of Daedalus's intuition. Who or what did he believe? And once again, greed won over fear.

'Dammit, get us to the vault,' he said.

'Wait, do I have time to ...?' Tiny asked, looking at the open door to the bathroom. 'You know.'

'Sure,' Lucretia said. 'It's probably only a *small* full-scale Zeno assault.'

'Right, good,' Tiny said, and disappeared inside.

None of us had comms sets, or we could have plugged into a comms port in a wall and tried to find out what was happening and where.

We passed several carts with panicked miners, all headed in the opposite direction to us. Some screamed at us to follow them, others made the universal symbol for 'you guys are crazy' and just kept going. After that, it was strangely quiet for about half an hour as we zigged and zagged and rose and dropped on our way to the vault.

Until, suddenly, it wasn't.

We all heard, and felt, a thud up ahead, and Lucretia slammed on the brakes just before we came to a sharp corner. With the whine of the engine gone, we could also hear the sound of battle. Yelling. Pulse weapons discharging.

'The false wall is just around that corner,' Antonia said.

'So is that firefight,' Ostrich pointed out.

'Well there's a coincidence,' Lucretia decided. 'The Zeno leads us straight to her own troops.'

'I am not with them,' Antonia protested.

Daedalus had his brows all scrunched up, trying to follow the logic. Then he decided, and prodded Antonia with his pistol. 'You're immortal. Go around the corner and see if we can reach that false wall without getting killed.'

'I am immortal, but this body can be killed, as you know,' Antonia said. 'I might put my head around that corner and get it shot off. And then you never got your bullion.'

'Alright, and you won't let me send Ballsack, so …' He turned to Lucretia.

'No.' Lucretia had drawn her pistol while we were talking, and Daedalus suddenly found himself looking down the barrel. 'Don't even suggest it.'

'Easy, Termite, I wasn't going to,' Daedalus lied. He looked sideways, to Ostrich, without taking his eyes, or his pistol, off Lucretia. 'Uh, Optio Ostrich, are you available for a little armed reconnaissance?'

Ostrich, luckily for us all, grinned and raised her two pistols. 'That would be a hell yes, Decanus.'

She moved up to the corner, pistols raised. It was mostly just bravado. Each pistol had a microdrone in it, and with the touch of a button, Ostrich launched a dragonfly-sized drone from underneath the barrel of her pistol and, with her thumb on a toggle where the hammer would have been on an antique pistol, she guided it around the corner. Of course, it wasn't risk free. She needed to be near the corner to keep a link to the drone, and an unlucky pulse bomb landing near the corner could have fragged her.

She watched the screen built into the pistol's grip.

'Barricade up ahead, about 50 meters. Twenty guys, look like mine security, holding the tunnel. I want to say five, maybe six dead already. Going over them,' she said in a whisper. We heard a loud explosion. 'Ow, that would have stung. Call it 10 dead now. Barricade is going to fall any minute.'

'What about the attacking force?'

'Oh, dog logs,' she cursed. '*Legion Praeda* combat troops, company strength at least. Heavy weapons. Mine security doesn't stand a chance.' She turned, looking pale. 'That Zeno from Taura Terra is with them.'

'Livia? Can I see?' Antonia asked, stepping up beside Ostrich. Ostrich held out the butt of her weapon. Daedalus tensed, like he was expecting Antonia to pull some kind of ninja move on Ostrich, but she just bent to examine the image. 'She is trying to stop us, but the false wall is this side of their barricade,' she said. 'About 20 meters. If we hurried, we reached it before the barricade fell.'

'And collected, *collect*, a stray plasma bolt in the face,' Lucretia pointed out.

'Who dares, wins, Loadmaster Termite,' Daedalus growled. 'Alright, succubus, lead the way.'

As we rounded the corner in single file, Daedalus tucked himself in behind Antonia, in a not-very-daring way. But I can't brag, since I was tucked in behind *him*.

If the others had been given time to think, they might have asked themselves a question. Hey, if Antonia is so worried about Ballsack not being killed, why is she leading him out onto a battlefield in the middle of a firefight?

You'll get the answer to that in a moment. About halfway to the false wall, a grenade arced over the barricade and began to drop. It was going to land right at our feet. Meaning that those feet, and anything attached to them, were going to be somewhere else in a matter of micro-seconds. Probably painting the walls.

Twang. Time spun itself out like pulled taffy. I reversed my pistol so I could reach higher, jumped in the air and swatted the grenade sideways. When I landed, I found myself face to face with Lucretia. She was crouched, and wincing of course, eyes closed. Her face was right there. I could have kissed her. I thought about it, telling myself it might be my last chance, if we didn't make it through all this. Then I remembered the whole consent conversation and what she said she would do to me if I stole another kiss, and that was enough to break my grip completely.

The grenade caromed off a wall and around the corner behind us. With an almost audible thud, my senses returned to normal again. Or maybe that was the grenade exploding.

I heard Livia's voice shout. 'Target the group at the wall!' as pulse blasts shattered rock around us.

Antonia was ready. She pressed her palm to the rock wall and a panel slid aside. Antonia and I dived through it, and the others tumbled through in a heap of arms, legs and curses. Followed by plasma bolts burning into the panel as it closed behind us.

The others were in various states of freaking out. I was more interested in where we were, expecting to be in a tunnel leading to another tunnel, or maze, leading to the vault. Instead were in a small cubic room, and on two walls around us were the now-familiar milky-white circles of nothing.

If there was a battle still going on, on the other side of the door we'd just fallen through, it was now inaudible.

'What in the burger-flipping hell just happened?' Ostrich yelled. 'There was a *grenade* ...'

'Uh, Decanus, with respect, you are sitting on my head,' Tiny said.

'I've still got my pistol on you, Zeno,' Daedalus said in the direction of Antonia as he untangled himself from Tiny. 'Or I will, when I find it.' He cast around in the semi-dark, and located the pistol he'd dropped.

'Oh, great, more of those,' Lucretia said, eyeing the circles balefully. She turned back to look at the rock wall we'd fallen through, and gave it a tap with her knuckles. 'How worried should we be about a horde of rabid Zed legionnaires piling through there like we did?'

'Not at all,' Antonia said. 'It's a one-time doorway. It can't be used twice.'

'Awesome,' Tiny said.

'But there are others. There will be a Lilin leading those troops,' Antonia added. 'They will try to stop us.'

'There's always a catch.' Tiny sighed.

'You can take your masks off in here,' Antonia said. 'The atmosphere and temperature will adjust to your needs.'

Tiny began reaching for his mask, but Daedalus slapped his hand down. 'Belay that, everyone. Our masks are probably the only thing preventing us from being bewitched.'

'As you wish.' Antonia shrugged. She turned to me and pointed at one of the circles. 'That portal leads to the vault, where the Lilin stay-behind force was, is, will be waiting.' She turned. '*This* portal leads topside, back to the surface near the entrance to the mine. I believe you have used one like it before. You need to decide quickly what you want to do.'

'Tell us about this stay-behind force,' Daedalus told her.

'I didn't go into the details,' I told Antonia. 'It just gets them unhelpfully excited.'

'Outside the bullion vault is a squad of those you call Zeds,' Antonia explained. 'They are in stasis, like you were when I met you at Isidis Planitia. The arrival of any unauthorized individual outside the vault, like me, or yourselves, will release them and they will attack.'

'Wait, just a squad? Pfft, no problem,' Tiny said. He looked at his small pistol. 'Though I wouldn't mind something a bit more mass-destruction-ish. Let's go.'

'No. There is a better way. Being a hybrid organism, Linus does not trigger them. Possibly. He can go through first, deal with the Lilin stay-behind squad, and return for us.' She nodded toward the other portal. 'Or if you are worried, you can all leave here now and return to the surface.' She looked at me. 'But I am sure Linus at least proceeds.'

She knew I was going for the crystal, not the bullion. Which I hadn't told the others about because of, you know, extraneous detail not being their thing. I had told Lucretia though.

'I'm staying,' Lucretia said quickly.

'No, no, no,' Daedalus said. He could see Ostrich thinking about it. 'There's no way you three are going for the vault without us. We did not go through five years of scheming and breaking rock only to return Earthside with *nothing*.'

'Actually,' Lucretia pointed out, 'machines broke all the rock. You just watched. And you wouldn't be going back with nothing. You each got a million in reward money from the Legion. Minus what we blew last night. A Red million is still good money.'

'Yeah, but it's not 10 *billion*,' Tiny pointed out. 'It's not even 1 billion. We only said yes to that paltry reward because we were going for the big score.'

'We're coming with you,' Daedalus announced. 'And not because of why you think.'

'I can think of, oh, say, 10 billion reasons,' Lucretia said.

'Sure, but another reason is because I've become kind of fond of this skinny guy,' Daedalus said, reaching out and pulling me into an awkward embrace. 'And I have great faith in his amazing new weird Zeno time-manipulating powers.' He saw doubt in all our faces. 'But, yeah, it's mostly the money.'

Lucretia smiled at that. Ostrich moved beside her, giving her a little hug. But the suddenly changed look on Lucretia's face told me it was more than just a little hug.

So did the pistol she was holding to Lucretia's temple.

'Nothing personal; just consider this insurance, Ballsack,' Daedalus said, lifting his pistol. 'In case you get any ideas about taking all that bullion for yourself and ghosting on us.'

Tiny had his pistol pointed at Antonia. 'Yeah, and if you don't come back, your Zeno girlfriend gets it too,' he said.

I didn't know where to point my pistol, so it just waved back and forth a bit impotently.

Lucretia moved fast, like she'd been expecting it, which she probably had. She spun on the ball of one foot, took a step sideways and leaned back, putting herself behind Ostrich's gun hand. Chopping down with all her strength, she dislodged the pistol and grabbed it before it hit the ground. Inside two seconds, the situation was reversed, and it was Ostrich with a gun to her head.

'Drop your weapons,' Lucretia said to Tiny and Daedalus.

Apparently, it wasn't the first time Ostrich had a gun held to her head. She didn't look scared, just pissed.

Daedalus just grinned, his pistol pointed at Lucretia now. 'Kill her. I kill you. Tiny kills the Zeno, then we both kill Ballsack. Everyone loses, but we're still alive.'

Tiny kept his pistol on Antonia. 'Poorer, but alive,' he said. 'Unlike you. Because you'll be poor and dead.'

Ostrich glared at me. '*You* know he means it.'

Daedalus nodded. 'He does. We have a rule in this crew, Termite, one we didn't tell you about,' Daedalus said to Lucretia.

'I already figured that,' Lucretia said. 'All for one and one for all. With "all" being you, Tiny and Ostrich.'

Daedalus frowned. 'What? No. Tell her, Optio Tiny.'

'Put no one else first,' Tiny intoned.

'Yes. Only by naked self-interest have we each survived this long, and will continue to survive …' Daedalus said, centering his pistol on Lucretia. 'Well, except for Ostrich of course, if you kill her.'

Antonia had been quiet up until that point, but she spoke now. 'Are you people completely insane?'

Seeing no better option to end the standoff, I jumped through the portal behind me.

I landed in the gray. Same nothing as where we found Antonia and Adam at Isidis Planitia.

You are probably asking how I knew my friends weren't all busy killing each other at that moment. Well, I didn't. But I was banking on greed overriding insanity.

Then I saw a shadow in the nothing, walking toward me. As it got closer, it resolved itself into a man, who I recognized at once. He was dressed in the outfit of a Praeda legionnaire now, carrying a pulse rifle. Last time we'd met, he'd been naked.

Adam. He'd seemed familiar then, but I couldn't place him. But seeing him in uniform again, I remembered. *Voeykov.* He was the guard who had led Livia away. It seemed suddenly obvious. The Rebels had located me, and had been worried Livia might find out who I was, so they intervened. But I shipped out before they could get back to me, and so they staged an 'intervention' at the Isidis Planitia Anomaly instead. Which also hadn't gone as planned.

Quantum uncertainty sucks, right?

He made a slight bow and handed me the rifle. 'Nice to see you again, Code Bearer.'

I looked around, seeing nothing, and stamped my feet, making no sound. 'Where are we?' I asked.

'Literally nowhere, and no-when,' he said. 'You are safe here. Also from me, if I still worry you.'

It was like a dare, and I've always been a sucker for a dare. I checked the rifle was fully charged and shouldered it, then holstered my pistol.

'Do you have a name?'

'You called me Adam,' he said. 'It is as good a name as any.'

'I thought I would land outside the vault. Why are you here?'

'To prepare you. This will be the ultimate test of whether you *are* The Code Bearer,' Adam said, arming his rifle. 'If you are, the squad will remain in stasis. If you aren't, you will have to fight.'

'One of me against a squad of eight?' I asked.

'Ten. But I believe in you,' Adam said, and then smiled.

'Except I might really die,' I pointed out. 'I thought your Rebels were trying to keep me alive.'

'There is no other way,' Adam said. 'If we are to unlock your memory, you must be made to *feel* your mortality.'

Something *was* building inside me. I wouldn't call it bloodlust. Not a death wish, either. There was a confrontation coming. It could end in my death. That knowledge terrified and excited me.

I had never felt more *alive*.

But ... There was always a 'but'. 'If I can die in the next few minutes, I have questions I want answered before we go anywhere, since I might never get the chance to ask them again.'

Adam nodded and lowered himself to the ground, crossing his legs. 'If it helps you. Sit, please.' He patted the nothing in front of him.

Since I couldn't see any other option, I decided to do as he suggested. It turned out whatever I was standing on could also be sat on. And it was quite comfortable. 'Go ahead. And remember, you are talking to a fish out of water.'

'A very good analogy. Did you …?' Adam asked.

'Livia came up with it.'

'Of course. Alright. So once upon a time there was a man called …'

'I said fish. Not baby fish,' I said.

'Alright. So there was once an entity we can call Linus Vespasius.'

'Not my real name.'

'I know.'

'And why aren't you getting your tenses mixed like Antonia sometimes does?' I asked.

'I am in my reality here, not yours. It makes communication simpler. We aren't using your language here, in case you hadn't noticed.'

I hadn't. We weren't. We were speaking Zeno.

'Go on,' I told him.

'The entity Linus Vespasius was Lilin. Not our name either, but one you gave us.'

'It means demon,' I told him. 'In ancient Mesopotamian or something.'

'Yes. Linus was Lilin. And the Lilin are human.'

'Clearly not.'

'Ah, but we are, so I'll put this in fish terms. We are what humanity *becomes*,' he said.

'Murderous, planet-devouring warmongers?' I asked bitterly.

'No, that's what humanity is already,' he said. 'But we adapt to the moment we find ourselves in. Back to our story. Linus was Lilin, and the Lilin are beyond time or space. The strictures of the physical universe have no meaning to us. We are the Unbound. The Limitless. The Ones Who …'

'Who Love Giving Themselves Names,' I suggested.

'Yes, I suppose. But Linus wanted limits. He asked an age-old question, but he asked it with *intent*. "What is the point of life, unless there is death?"'

'Well, duh, you can't have one without the other,' I pointed out.

'Ah, but you can. The Lilin live but can never die. Humanity, as you are now, measures progress through what you call growth. We measure it in learning. No matter how much we know, there is always more we don't. Linus wanted to know how to become human again.'

'You've clearly mastered that,' I said, gesturing at his perfect body.

'This form?' he asked, dismissively. 'We know how to become corporeal, yes, but this body isn't human. It allows sensory perception, but that doesn't create emotion. Linus wanted to *feel* all the opposites: joy and sadness, grief and ecstasy, fear and courage. This ideology was nothing revolutionary in itself; Linus wasn't the first to explore the idea of returning to mortality. But he devoted himself to the subject in a way none had before, and he began a revolution when he claimed to have learned how to achieve it.'

'This person you are talking about is me?'

'We think so,' he said, leaning forward to take my hands. Which, it dawned on me, even then, was something learned, not felt. Something he knew promoted trust and intimacy – he wasn't doing it because he was seeking it. 'We dearly hope so. You didn't want to make the journey to mortality alone. You tried to encourage others to join you …'

'You?'

'Me. Antonia was another. Soon, we were many. But the Reactionaries like Livia opposed you. In your reality, humanity numbers in the billions. In my reality, we can be as many as we choose to be, across as many realities as we wish, but at the source, we are only a handful.'

'At the source?'

'Irrelevant to the story. Livia and her fellow Reactionaries argued that allowing any of us to make the journey to mortality weakens *all* of us, and would eventually lead to our extinction. Humanity's extinction. The logic was inescapable, so you were ordered to abandon your work, and I regret to say we, your followers, abandoned you.'

'But I didn't give up.'

'You disappeared. Did your best to hide yourself. Even made yourself forget, it seems. We traced you to this reality, and deduced you had Transitioned. The first of us to become fully human again. Child of the Dawn. The Code Bearer – you are human, but you carry your source code within you. It made sense you would hide on Earth, with its lethal magnetic field, where none of us could reach you. When the war began, we watched and waited for you to appear. We hypothesized that you would be attracted to extremes of emotion, and war offers those in abundance. When you arrived here, we could feel your presence, would have known if you died, but finding your physical form took time. We had to be sure. You know the rest. And now you are here …'

I looked around at the grayness. 'So what are you hoping happens now?'

'The final reawakening,' Adam said. 'You will remember.'

Fish brain or not, I could see where this was headed. Whatever was about to happen would not be pleasant.

'Remember what?'

'Who you are, were and will be. We know the Void Forge is where you Transitioned. We don't know how; no one does. The Reactionaries are trying to destroy it. We have been trying to frustrate them, and find you, to help you reach it.'

My brain began to ache. 'No. If what you say is true, I was born into this body *decades* ago, on Earth. I had a childhood, which I do remember. I grew up there. My life didn't start at Kamloop in the Void Forge.'

'You see time in two dimensions.' He sighed. 'Future and past. You were not always so blind.'

I shook my head. 'Alright, say I survive. Say I do remember. Then what?'

'You have a duty to pass your knowledge on. Knowledge is sacred. It shouldn't be hidden. It can't be suppressed. Once learned, it *must* be shared. Reactionaries like Livia would violate that sacred tenet, and you cannot let them.'

I let go of his hands and leaned back. 'So this is a religious war.'

'What?' He frowned.

'I've been swimming around in my little pond, looking up at the moon, wondering just what kind of motive would force the Lilin to go to war with each other, or if what you say is true, go to war with humanity as part of some internal feud.'

'No. You must understand …'

'Oh, I understand. You exist outside the boundaries of time and space now. And emotion, clearly. To you, the death of tens of thousands of mere mortals in this war – your own ancestors – is nothing. You are the Unbound. The Limitless. The Ones Who …' I rolled my hand, encouraging him to finish the sentence this time.

He had the manners to appear embarrassed. 'The Ones Who Are Beyond.'

'Perfect. Beyond accountability? Beyond morality perhaps?'

'Perhaps.'

'And so this …' I gestured at the gray, but I meant all of it – the war, the myriad attempts to find and entrap me, all the thousands who had died in a conflict that wasn't even about mankind versus Zeno. '*All of this* is because of something you hold sacred that others are threatening. Which makes it a religious war.' I shook my head. 'I guess you *are* human after all.' I levered myself to my feet with my rifle, and held out my hand to help him up. 'Alright, I'm ready.'

He looked surprised, but took my hand and stood. 'You'll do this? I can return you topside.'

'Destroying this quantum resonator crystal really will boot the Lilin off the Red?' I asked.

'Yes,' he said.

I un-shouldered the rifle. 'Then I'll do it.' I sighed. 'If I only live long enough to do that, it's enough.'

The vault

'How do I?' I asked Adam. There was nothing, everywhere I looked.

'Three steps, in any direction,' he said. 'But one last thing …'

My shoulders dropped. Of course there was one last thing. 'What?'

'The quantum resonator crystal will be surrounded and protected by the stay-behind force. But it may be disguised.'

'I thought it was a fist-shaped crystal that *hums*?' I said.

'It is. But we were not part of creating or hiding it. I can't tell you what it looks like. It needs space around it to radiate, but it might be hidden: disguised inside a container of some sort, a rock, a bag, inside a pool of water or ice. The possibilities are many, but not infinite.'

'Great, so how do I find it?'

'It hums,' he said, with a shrug.

'Hums. Alright. So on three?' I suggested.

'If that works for you,' Adam said.

'One,' I said, taking a step. Rifle up.

Scenario one: You jump and get shot before you even land. Blissful nothingness. Not so bad.

'Two.' I took a second step. Slid back the safety on the rifle.

Scenario two: You land, manage to get off a couple of shots at the humming quantum crystal thing, then you get shot. Blissful nothingness and a feeling of supreme accomplishment as you die. Pretty good.

'Three,' I said, and jumped.

Scenario three: You jump and …

It wasn't like the portal at Isidis Planitia. It hurt like nothing I'd ever felt before. The Red had exposed me to nothing but pain and suffering, and this was a hundred levels more intense. Every fiber, every nerve in my body, was being teased apart, set on fire, drowned in acid. Behind, above, beyond it all, was a sea of sorrow and sadness. Everything I'd done, all I'd been through, it had all been in vain. Anything even remotely joyful, rewarding, fulfilling, was outweighed by the humiliation, pity, scorn and hatred I had suffered. Worse, this pain had, will, did, would last forever. There was, had, would be no escape. I could not surrender to the pain because it wasn't asking me to surrender. It was just promising me more pain, and more …

Except …

Except it wasn't real. Through the bloodred fog and sorrow, I remembered how I was, before. I could imagine pain. I could imagine love, could even simulate it, but I couldn't give it, couldn't earn it. I understood the concept of fear, but with no reason to fear, fear was just a word. The same for death. Mortality. Entropy. Abstract concepts that applied to the physical universe.

But what if they weren't? What if they could be realized? What if there was a way to …

I remembered.

… I landed in a wide cavern, where I fell to the ground, rolling behind some kind of stalagmite. Expecting bolts of plasma to slam into the stone above and around me.

Nothing. I was alive. Apart from the milky whiteness of the portal I had just fallen through, it was dark. And quiet. The only sound was the labored breath blowing out of my breather and ragged gasps as I sucked more air in.

No, not the only sound. I also heard something *humming*.

Every plasma rifle had a flashlight, and I turned mine on, playing it around the cavern.

Lying on the ground behind concrete berms were a group of legionnaires in special operations combat gear, lying in a circle facing outward, legs splayed, rifles and laser squad weapons held in front of them. They appeared frozen in place, eternally ready for combat.

In the middle of them, I found the thing that was humming. It wasn't difficult. It wasn't frozen in place. In fact, as I appeared, it waved at me.

'Hello!' it said, in Lilin-tongue. And started humming again. A little very un-Lilin human nursery rhyme.

It was a *child*.

I approached it and it smiled, still humming. It couldn't be a real child. I knew that. I knew it was a container for the quantum crystal anchoring the Zenos to our reality. It was deliberately created so that any human entering the vault would hesitate, would try to protect it, and probably die in the act. It was not human.

But *I* was. I had gone through hell and back to become human. And being human, I couldn't blow a hole in it.

'Uh, can I ask you something?' I asked it.

'Of course,' it said. I couldn't tell from its Lilin voice if it was a small girl or boy. Its face was androgynous, its clothing neutral. Take your pick. A girl, I decided. 'Do you need something?' she asked. The humming continued, lower, softer, as she was speaking.

'Well, actually, I do,' I said. I found myself talking to her like I would a real child. 'You *have* something I need, I think.'

'Oh, really? What is that?' she asked.

'A crystal, about the size of a fist? Could you give it to me?'

She frowned. 'I can't. I think you are talking about my heart. If I give it to anyone, it will break, and that would be terrible.'

'Oh, right,' I said. 'Sure. No one wants a broken heart. But what happens if, you know, hypothetically, someone tries to *take* it from you?'

'That would be very, very silly,' she said with a smile. 'My heart is inside a magnetic cage of antimatter. If anyone tried to take it, the cage would shatter, and it would destroy *everything*.'

'Right, so when you say everything, you mean you, and …'

'You. This cave …' She pointed at the soldiers on the ground. 'My friends …'

I swallowed hard. Alright, so I was going to have to pay the ultimate price to end the war. I had known it would come to this. And to do it, I was going to have to shoot a child.

Not a child. Not a child. Keep telling yourself that, Linus. I raised my rifle.

But she wasn't finished. 'Um, them, this mine. And, uh, the settlement up above,' she said sweetly. 'It really is quite a lot of antimatter.'

'How much is quite a lot?'

'Two kilograms,' she said.

I did the math. One gram of AM would cause an explosion of 21 kilotons, so 2 kilograms was … 50 megatons?!

Crud. End the war, but kill *everyone* in Schiaparelli? Zeno-me was thinking, *Yeah, but you end the war, so do it.* Human-me was clucking like a hen. I decided I couldn't make the decision alone. 'OK. Look, I have some friends who would love to meet you. What do you think about that?'

'That would be amazing!' she said, and clapped her hands. 'Are they Lilin too?'

'Well, some of them.'

'Oh, good. Because if they were human, they might try to hurt me, and that would break my heart,' she said.

'I'm sure it would,' I told her, thinking out loud. 'So if I promise they won't hurt you, would you like to come with me?'

'Well, my parents said I can't leave here with anyone who is Lilin, or human, except them,' she said. 'But I can tell that you aren't *either*, are you?'

'No, I guess not,' I said.

'So, then, it's alright if I come with you!' she decided. She looked at the soldiers on the cave floor. 'Can my friends come too?'

'Well … not right now. Is that a problem?'

'No, but they like my singing,' she said. 'If I stop singing, they'll get angry, and we don't want them to get angry.' She made a *pew pew* shooting action.

'No, no, we do not. OK, let me think about this for a minute,' I said. She nodded and kept humming.

Alright, assuming I didn't blow Schiaparelli to molten slag in the next few minutes, waking the stay-behind force was a major wrinkle, in terms of getting to the vault. If it even existed. I looked around the walls of the cavern and saw it. A vault door, like the kind every settlement used to protect its bullion. So the Lilin hadn't been lying. Of course it could be empty, but the vault at least existed. Taking the child but leaving the Lilin stay-behind force, though, that was problematic.

'I'll just be a moment,' I told her. I walked over to the vault, and looked it up and down. It was, in every way, like the vault inside the armory of any human firebase or settlement. Huge blast-proof door, quantum-encrypted lock that could only be opened with the DNA of authorized individuals. 'Any Lilin can open the vault', Antonia had said though. I licked my thumb and put it to the reader.

I was Lilin enough to be able to speak their language. To communicate with the child, and to not trigger the stay-behind force. So maybe I was Lilin enough to …

Click.

Open the vault. Electric motors whined, and the door swung outward.

Apart from a small terminal set into a wall, the vault was empty.

But the terminal was *exactly* what we'd hoped to find. A bullion transfer station. Red dollars weren't physical, though their value was backed by the ores and rare earths blasted out of the planet's crust. They were digital, as all currency had been for centuries, but the terminals that moved currency from settlement to settlement were as closely guarded as banks, and worked like digital safes. Each stored only the amount of currency that was transferred into it. Unlock the terminal, and the bullion was yours. Think of them like digital treasure chests.

I looked at the terminal. My DNA also woke it to life. I read the amount of bullion it held off the screen.

Holy fallopian-shredding motherlode, I thought, channeling my inner Ostrich. Let's just say Antonia had been low-balling on the 10 billion. After tapping a few icons, I closed the terminal down again.

I had an idea and walked back to the girl. 'Hey, so, how about I help your friends sleep while you're out visiting with me?' I asked.

She looked horrified. 'You won't hurt them? That would break my heart!'

'No, no, I was thinking I would …' *Shoot them in the head.* Apparently not. Damn. I was suddenly glad I didn't roll into the cavern with guns blazing, throwing grenades. The Zenos were pretty damn serious about protecting their quantum anchor. They put it inside a cage of antimatter, inside a child, inside a ring of legionnaires, inside a mine shaft deep in the earth, behind a Lilin portal, and they made sure that if anyone made it that far, and actually managed to attack it, it would scrape Kamloop off the surface of The Red.

Which told me they didn't want to capture or control the Void Forge, since they had clearly already mastered the use of antimatter. They wanted to *destroy* it. Deny it to me, deny it to the Rebels.

That knowledge didn't solve my humming child problem.

I tried again. 'No, I was thinking I could sing them a song to help them sleep longer. It's one my parents taught me.' That much was true.

'Wonderful. I'd like to learn a new song,' she said.

I put my rifle and pistol down where the girl could see them, then knelt down beside the first soldier. I began singing …

Frère Jacques, Frère Jacques, dormez-vous? Dormez-vous?

Are you sleeping? Are you sleeping? Brother John, Brother John?

Sonnez les matines! Sonnez les matines! Ding, dang, dong. Ding, dang, dong.

As I finished, I hid the Zed's head from her view as I stood, and snapped his neck. Another skill learned in Reducation that I never knew I would need.

'I love that song,' she said. 'Can I sing it with you?'

'Please,' I said. 'We'll sing it together.'

The next five minutes were probably the most surreal of my recently very surreal life, as I went from soldier to soldier, the girl singing 'Frère Jacques' with me as I snapped the necks of the remaining nine Zeds. Which is easier written than done, let me tell you.

'Right,' I said, standing up from the last Zed, and holding out my hand to the girl. 'How about we go and meet my friends now,' I said. A problem shared was a problem halved.

Would she check the Zeds? Would she know the difference between sleep and death?

Had I just condemned Schiaparelli to annihilation?

She smiled and took my hand. 'Where are your friends?' she asked.

I pointed at the milky portal. 'In there. Are you ready?'

She was humming 'Frère Jacques' now and started skipping alongside me as we walked. 'I can't wait to meet them,' the girl said.

When the universe didn't dissolve into an antimatter-annihilating crackling ball of blue lightning as we walked away from the circle of dead Zeds, I actually smiled.

'And I can't wait for them to meet you,' I said, and I know you know how much I meant it.

Of course, there was the risk that they had gone berserker on each other and half, most or all of them were dead and no one was waiting for us.

But as we stepped out of the portal, pain free this time, they appeared to have resolved their differences, and were lounging around the small space behind the rock wall as though they were waiting for a bus.

Ostrich was first to react: She grabbed her rifle. 'OK, Ballsack is back! Shall we ... who the *kiddy-humming* hell is that?'

I made a motion with my hand to encourage her to tone her voice down a notch. 'Everyone, this is ...' I realized she didn't have a name, or hadn't given me one. 'Uh, what is your name, honey?' I asked in human language, unsure if she would understand it.

'Crystal,' she said swapping to human with ease, looking around herself with wide eyes. Well, I guess she hadn't ever been outside the circle of soldiers in the dark cave.

'Uh, how can she talk and hum at the same time?' Tiny asked.

'More importantly,' Lucretia said, 'does she have to?'

I kneeled down. 'Crystal, sweets, do you need to keep singing?'

She looked at me like that was a stupid question. 'I like to sing,' she said. 'It shows my heart is happy.'

'Can you do it more quietly maybe?' I asked.

'Sure,' she said, and reached out to feel the material on Lucretia's overalls. The volume dropped to a barely audible trilling.

'Alright, Ballsack,' Daedalus growled. 'To quote Engineer Ostrich, what in the kiddy-humming hell have you brought back with you?'

First I had to explain to the others, with Antonia's help, what a quantum resonator crystal was. Then I had to explain that the girl had one where her heart should be. I explained how I was the only one she could move around with because she wasn't allowed to be with anyone who was just Lilin, or just human. Then I had to explain what would happen if anyone did anything to *break* the little girl's heart.

'Why didn't you leave it there?!' Tiny asked. 'We don't want it!'

'Keep your voice down,' Lucretia hissed. 'It can hear you.'

Crystal didn't appear too worried though, since no one had actually referred to her directly maybe. She was much more interested in how the magnetic soles in Ostrich's boots worked, and in pulling at her foot.

'This … *container*,' I said, going for a euphemism, 'could end the war, if we can work out how to shut it down without blowing up half the planet.' I looked at Antonia. 'Ideas?'

'None,' she said, with disappointing speed. 'We weren't involved in designing the quantum resonator. Caging it in a shell of antimatter to prevent its destruction is ingenious.'

'That … container … is a walking weapon of mass destruction,' Lucretia said.

Daedalus put his hands on his knees in what was probably supposed to be his best impression of a grandparently figure, but came off more like 'inappropriate uncle'. 'Crystal, honey, how would you like a trip into deep space?' he asked. 'To look at all the pretty stars?'

She looked a little worried. 'Oh, no. My home is The Red. It would break my heart to ever have to leave.'

Daedalus straightened. 'Yep. Thought so. We can't launch it off-planet.'

'It knows what deep space is,' Ostrich said thoughtfully. 'They've made it pretty intelligent. That's going to make this harder.'

I thought about how I'd managed to put Crystal's friends permanently to sleep. 'Yeah, she's smart, but not street smart, if you know what I mean.'

With his usual ability to abstract himself from problems he couldn't deal with, and focus on problems he could,

Daedalus fixed me with an avaricious glare. 'The fact you are back here, escorted or unescorted, tells me you navigated that stay-behind Zed problem, am I correct?'

I did a hand-across-the-throat gesture while Crystal's back was turned. 'Yep, navigated. With prejudice.'

Daedalus grinned. 'Alright!' He turned to Antonia. 'So now you return with us to the cavern and we …'

'Not necessary,' I said. 'While I was down there, I decided to check if *I* could open the vault.'

'You could not,' Antonia said.

'I could,' I told her. I fixed her with what I hoped was a long and portentous stare. 'I will, I did.'

A beatific smile lit up her face. 'Linus! You are back to yourself!'

'It seems,' I nodded. 'But we have other things to worry about right now.'

The others looked impatient and confused, but mostly impatient. Tiny couldn't hold back. 'The bullion!? How much is there? It was a trick, right? There was nothing. Or … there was something. I can see there was something. Was it a billion? No, even 10 million, 10 Red million? That would be …'

'Thirteen,' I said. 'And change.'

'Million?' Ostrich asked.

'*Billion*,' I said.

I expected Daedalus to start dancing his pirate-y jig, but instead he just asked in a very calm, almost deadpan voice, 'And tell us, Ballsack, what did you do with this 13 billion in bullion, and change? Because I doubt you just left it there and sealed the vault again.'

I squatted down beside Crystal and ran my hand over her hair. Was it my imagination or had it grown a little longer, and a little more golden? She looked up at me, humming calmly.

'I transferred it to The Blue,' I told Daedalus. 'Into a Swiss bank account.'

'And now the Zeno shows us his true nature,' Daedalus said, voice dripping with ire. 'He disappears into the milky gray, and returns with a weapon of mass destruction by his side, having stolen a fortune in bullion, leaving his friends with nothing but empty pockets and the threat of annihilation.'

'My friends were all holding guns to each other's temples last time I saw them,' I said.

Crystal frowned. 'That doesn't sound very friendly.'

Lucretia was already crouched beside her and patted her knee, indicating that Crystal should hop up onto it, which she trustingly did. 'Well, that's the thing with this group of friends, honey. Sometimes we shout at each other, and we cuss, and we …'

'Threaten to shoot each other in the face,' Tiny said helpfully.

'Yes, sure, we do that, but it's all just for fun,' Lucretia said. 'Because really we love each other.'

'Let's not take it too far,' Daedalus growled. 'But yes, we did manage to resolve our differences because Termite here assured us we could *trust* you,' Daedalus said. 'She said you had a higher calling than pure thievery, or something …'

'"Higher goal," I said,' Lucretia interrupted.

'Yes, higher *something*, and against my better judgement, I decided I would ignore your Zeno-hybrid bird-tweeting dark side, in the hope she was right and you would make it back to us having dealt with the Zeds outside the vault and cleared our path to riches.' He shook his head. 'I am so, so disappointed, Ballsack.'

Crystal put her mouth to Lucretia's ear. 'The wrinkly dwarf sounds sad. Is his heart breaking?'

'No, seriously,' Ostrich said. 'You don't plan to keep all that bullion for yourself? After all we went through to rescue you …'

'To capture and ransom the *Intimidator*,' I pointed out.

'*And* rescue you,' she insisted. 'That has to count for something.'

'Unless he *is* just a filthy Zeno,' Tiny said.

I let them stew. It was a very enjoyable moment, and I wallowed in it. But I could see Crystal wasn't digging the vibe. In fact, she looked like she was about to cry, and I didn't want to see what would happen if a weapon of mass destruction started bawling.

'Let's get back to the surface and talk about that,' I suggested. I pointed at the other portal. 'Does that doorway still go topside?'

'Yes,' Antonia said.

Crystal looked up at me and smiled. 'Are we going somewhere else now?'

Lucretia lifted her off her knee and stood. 'Yes, honey. You stay with, uh, Uncle Linus there.'

She took my hand again. 'That's good. This place isn't much different to where I was before. Except for the people, talking human talk. I hope the next place is better.'

'So do I, Crystal,' Daedalus said, doubt thick in his voice. 'About 13 billion times better.'

A miner walks into a bar

We might have finished our business in the vault, but Livia's assault force was still fighting with security throughout the mine, and legionnaires from the three Sandcruisers had also joined in. As we trudged back up toward the surface, we passed squad after squad of defenders and had to detour a couple times, or were redirected, because of fighting at major tunnel or shaft intersections.

That's the battle of Terra Sabea you heard about, and it really was as brutal as the History suggested. Thwarting Livia at the entrance to the vault didn't reduce the fanaticism of the Zedified; they had their orders, and they mindlessly sacrificed themselves executing them, taking hundreds of mine workers and legionnaires with them.

We were oblivious to that at the time, and had other problems as we emerged from Antonia's portal, which promptly disappeared.

We came up in a back alley and walked out of it straight into a scene of mayhem: panicked citizens running one way, legionnaires and security the other. But we were dressed as miners, and miners were some of the most precious meat on the Red, so we were quickly guided away, the sound of battle fading behind and below us. Exiting from the mine into the Schiaparelli City Dome entry zone, we were finally able to pull off our breathers and wipe the sweat from our faces.

With the babble of alarmed voices and actual alarm klaxons around us, Crystal's hum was inaudible, but the look of wonder in her eyes and the tight grip she maintained on my hand as she gazed at the industrial wasteland around us underscored the feeling her voice conveyed. 'This is *beautiful!*' she exclaimed.

As we stood around waiting for them to open the gates and let us out, Lucretia was watching her closely. 'You think it can actually feel, or is it just emoting based on inputs?' she whispered.

'It's a Zeno creation, so I think it's just emoting,' I said. 'Probably a necessary part of its function, if it is supposed to look cute but blow up when someone takes or breaks its heart.'

Crystal looked up at me. 'I can hear you talking,' she said. 'It is a very, *very* bad idea to do anything to take or break my heart.'

'Yes, we know that, honey,' Lucretia said. 'You just stay with Uncle Linus and you'll be fine.'

We shuffled forward in the queue of temporary refugees trying to get from the mine to the city proper. Schiaparelli didn't have the sort of electromagnetic fields and security they'd fortified Kamloop and the Void Forge with, and the few security guards left at the city gate were basically just checking for weapons and waving people through, but we were in the company of a bona fide Zeno and an emotionally unstable weapon of mass destruction, so we took no chances.

'We split up, and meet at the bar outside the firebase. You go first, Zeno,' Daedalus said, shoving Antonia to the front. 'If you get stopped, we'll know the kid can't get through.' He pulled the pistol from his belt. 'I'll go ahead of you, show security my pistol and hand it over as we approach, give them something to focus on. You do the same when you go through, Ballsack, so they aren't asking questions about the kid.'

Antonia and Daedalus went through and walked off in separate directions, then Ostrich, then Tiny. I took the charge cell from my pistol and held both pistol and cell in the air with one hand as I approached the two security officers at my gate. Lucretia was behind me.

'No weapons allowed through,' one said, holding out his hand.

'No problem,' I said. 'But it's mine property. I signed for it,' I said, trying to act my part.

'Take it up with your supervisor,' the guard said, throwing the pistol into a sack at his feet. 'Keep moving.'

'Wait,' the other guard said. 'Whose child is this?'

'My niece,' I lied. 'I collected her on the way here. I'm taking her to her parents.'

Lucretia stepped forward, raising a hand in the air. 'We're together. It's his niece.'

The guard looked at my emaciated form, blotchy scalp and filthy mining overalls, then crouched down to eye height with the girl. 'Is that true, girl? He your Uncle?'

'He's my Uncle Linus,' the girl said, and reached out and touched the metal stars on his collar. 'These are really sparkly.'

The guard frowned, then promptly decided child welfare wasn't his problem. He stood and waved me forward. 'On your way.'

We took a roundabout route to the military compound, and to be honest, got a little lost. When we finally found the bar near the firebase gates, and Daedalus, Ostrich and Tiny inside it, Daedalus looked us over as we walked up to their table, which was already covered in half-empty beer glasses. Then he held out his credit chip to Tiny. 'Pay up.'

Tiny reached into a pocket and pulled out his credit chip, touching it to Daedalus's with a grumble. 'I didn't *really* think you were going to murder Lucretia and betray humankind,' he said to me. 'But Daedalus bet you wouldn't and he thinks I said, "I'll take that bet," which I didn't, but I don't want to argue about it.' He clapped me on the shoulder. 'So, great you made it here, Ballsack,' he lied. 'And you too, Termite.'

Ostrich snatched the credit chip from Daedalus, waved it over a reader on the table, then pressed a button on the table and spoke into a microphone. 'Bartender, another five glasses of your finest brew, please.' She looked at Crystal. 'Do you drink, kid?'

'I don't know. Is it fun?' Crystal asked, climbing up on the bench beside me.

'Add a glass of lemonade to that order,' Ostrich said.

Five glasses of very ordinary looking 'beer' and a 'lemonade' slid up through a hatch in the tabletop, and we each took one. Crystal watched us, then took a sip and wrinkled her nose. 'I don't think I like drinking.'

'Where's Antonia?' Lucretia asked.

'Haven't seen the Zeno since the city gates,' Daedalus said with a scowl. 'Which is why Tiny bet you had nixed Termite and run off with her.' He tipped his glass toward Crystal, who was watching the bubbles rise in her lemonade. 'Now that you got what you really came for.'

I gave Crystal a wretched look. 'Trust me, I am just as surprised as you are.'

'Whatever,' Daedalus said, leaning back in his chair. 'But as we sat here waiting for you, I did some thinking.'

'Oh, no.' Lucretia sighed.

'Yes, Loadmaster, I did,' Daedalus said. 'And what I thought was, it is very convenient for the thief Ballsack, who took all the bullion, to say to us that the child he returned with is a weapon of mass destruction that can create a 400-meter-deep crater in the rock, since it might discourage us from cutting his throat.'

I noticed Ostrich reach down to her calf and come up with a long-bladed knife, which she very unsubtly began cleaning her nails with.

Crystal looked up. 'Oh. Please don't cut Uncle Linus's throat. That would …'

'Break your heart,' Tiny said. 'Yeah, kid, we got it.'

Daedalus still looked dubious. 'It's a nice routine, but how do we know it's real?'

Lucretia leaned forward. 'Are you seriously willing to find out?'

'I've got a better idea than cutting my throat,' I said. I'd also been doing some thinking as we wandered Schiaparelli's streets, looking for the bar. 'How would you like an equal share of the bullion I took from the vault?'

Ostrich snarfed beer out her nose, making Crystal laugh. 'Yeah, right. Like you would just hand over a lazy two and a half billion to each of us.'

'No, there would be conditions,' I said. 'But as a goodwill gesture, I'd give you each a Red million, up front.'

'Alright, moneybags,' Daedalus said slowly. 'And what do we have to do for this Red million, which you will transfer to us in full, now, *before* we agree to anything?'

I pulled up a money transfer interface screen on the table, they all dropped their credit chips on it, and I made the transfer. I was just as interested as any of them to see if the transaction went through.

It did.

'Ballsack is half Zeno,' Ostrich said, as she held up her chip and checked the new balance. 'Could this be fake, like their bodies, and their promises?'

'Let's see,' Tiny said. 'If it's counterfeit, our chips will be locked.' He leaned forward to the mic in the table. 'Waiter, five plates of your mouth-watering stew please.' He waved his chip over the reader.

We all stared at the panel in the table. Which slid open and disbursed five steaming plates of lumpy brown sludge, with spoons.

I gave my spoon to Crystal, who poked at the 'stew' dubiously. 'I want to hire you,' I told them. 'As bodyguards.'

'I'm not sure that's such a good …' Lucretia began, probably thinking of famous assassinations throughout history that were carried out by treacherous bodyguards.

'Not for me,' I said. 'For the girl.'

Crystal looked up from the 'stew' dripping from her spoon. 'Like my friends in the cavern?'

'Exactly like that,' I told her. 'Except a lot less, you know, static. And more profane.'

Tiny looked like he had a toothache. 'I don't know. This feels a lot like one of those "all for one, one for all" kind of situations I'm not so comfortable with.'

'OK, give back the money,' Lucretia said.

'Hey, I didn't say I couldn't *get* comfortable with it.'

I spread my hands and shrugged. 'We all know I'm not going to be able to protect her on my own in the middle of a war, and also what the consequences are if anything happens to her.'

'Consequences for *you*,' Ostrich said. 'Since, if we say no to this, we can be a million miles away in no time flat, with our 2 Red millions.'

'You'd rather have 2 million, than two and a half *billion*?' I asked, skeptically.

Tiny and Ostrich looked to Daedalus for a reaction.

Daedalus drained his beer and swallowed, thoughtfully, then put down his glass.

'Here it comes.' Lucretia sighed.

'Indeed it does, Termite. During his time with this crew, Ballsack has grown from being a nameless cut of meat for the Legion Praeda grinder to a weird Zeno hybrid who helped us deliver the *Intimidator* back to its owners through which we became incrementally wealthier, even though it was mostly my own amazing plan did that.'

'Actually mine,' Lucretia said.

'Which I improved,' Daedalus continued. 'Now, it isn't certain this warm fuzzy feeling I have for Ballsack will last much longer than the alcohol in my veins or the credits in my account, but while it does, I say, sure, we'll guard the girl, for a fifth share of the bullion.' He leered at me. 'Paid in full, within a year, assuming you are still alive. But I can't speak for the others.'

'I'm in,' Tiny said. 'But to be clear, this is about the girl; since saving her saves me, if I'm her bodyguard. I'm not throwing myself between *you* and a Zeno assassin.'

'Understood,' I told him. 'But I'm pretty sure if I die it would …'

'Break her heart, yeah, yeah,' Ostrich said. '*I'd* take a bolt for you, for half your share too,' she said. Tiny glared at her.

'What? Suddenly we aren't doing side hustles?' She looked at her feet. 'Alright, I'm in.'

We clinked our beer glasses to seal the deal.

'So, where to now?' Tiny asked.

That was easy. *Liquidator* was headed to Kamloop and the Void Forge. I had to get to Kamloop, so the safest way was to report to the *Liquidator* within the next two days. I was pretty sure I could talk *Liquidator*'s XO, Bony, into taking on the 'citizen soldiers of *Intimidator* fame' as crew too …

A new alarm sounded. Lucretia cocked her ear. 'That's not the Lilin breach alarm; that's an air raid alert. Did Voeykov have an air wing?'

'No,' Ostrich said, looking up at the ceiling. 'Just whatever the MCVs carried. Mostly recon.'

People were running out of the bar as Antonia walked in. She spotted us and walked quickly over.

'Where have *you* been? Is this new alarm your fault?' Tiny asked her.

She sat. 'No. I was in Lilin-space, speaking with my people. The attack through the mine was a distraction. Livia's forces have infiltrated your docks and hijacked your Sandcruisers.'

'Which one?' Lucretia asked.

'All three,' Antonia said. 'Dominator, Terminator and Intimidator.'

'*Dominator* was badly damaged,' I pointed out. 'In the Terra Sabea action.'

'Not its air wing,' Antonia said. 'It has been launched to cover the Sandcruisers' escape.'

I stood. 'I'll be expected to report for duty,' I said. 'I'm pretty sure I can get you all assigned to *Liquidator* with me, but I have to get back into uniform, find an officer …'

Lucretia took my arm. 'Uh, slight problem?' She nodded at Crystal, who was standing too.

Antonia saw the problem too. 'Let me help with this. We have to speak Lilin.'

Ostrich had her knife still in her hand and took a step toward Antonia. I held out my hand to stop her. 'Take it easy. I'll join.'

Antonia crouched in front of Crystal and began twittering. *Crystal, is it alright to ask you some questions?* she said.

Crystal looked at me. If Uncle Linus says it is.

I put a hand on her shoulder. It's fine. Antonia is a friend.

Crystal, is this form you are in now the only form you can take? Antonia asked.

No. If Uncle Linus wants, I can take a related form within the limits of my existing mass and the requirement to shield my heart.

Good, Antonia said. Linus, she can't be a boot or a briefcase; she has to be some kind of human form because the whole idea is humans should feel reluctant to harm her. If she is to accompany you aboard the Sandcruiser, what form would work?

I thought hard. She has to stay close to me? How close?

Crystal, you were able to move around in the company of Uncle Linus. If he tells you that you are safe, how far from him are you able to go?

Crystal appeared to process that one for a quantum mini-moment. Uncle Linus has given me new friends to protect me, like I had in the cave. As long as they are near, and I know Uncle Linus is near, my heart will be protected.

I couldn't help thinking that having Daedalus, Ostrich and Tiny near was not necessarily the same as being protected, but it was the wrong time to say that out loud.

So you don't have to be right beside me to feel protected? I asked.

Not if our friends are near too, and you say I am safe. My parents left me alone with my other friends, so it must be alright to be alone with my new friends. But if I get scared, or sad …

I'll be there if that happens, I assured her. I turned to Antonia. She needs to look like one of the other crew. I can smuggle her aboard Liquidator if she looks like Tiny, Lucretia, or Ostrich and can pass the face scan.

Not Daedalus? Antonia asked.

I wouldn't wish that on my worst enemy, I told her.

Pick one then.

I looked at the three of them. Our conversation was taking place at quantum speeds, and it was like they were frozen in time as we spoke. Lucretia? No, as loadmaster, she would be down in *Liquidator*'s payload bay, alone. If she had to be around her 'friends,' she needed to be able to move around with us on the bridge, or in the crew accommodations. Ostrich? No, the system engineer's role on a cruiser was actually both demanding and critical. A sensor operator just had to report what they saw, though. There was nothing for it …

Tiny, I said. Sorry, Crystal. Can you please make yourself into a copy of that big man sitting there?

Yes. She nodded. *Now?*

No, I said. You can go with your friend Lucretia to the bathroom. I'll be waiting for you when you come back out. I nodded to Antonia. Alright, we're done.

No, she said. If the Reactionaries have taken three of your four Sandcruisers, you know what this means?

They're not interested in infiltrating firebases and ZoCs anymore. They'll go for Kamloop next, try to take out the Void Forge by pure force. Flatten the firebase, and invade.

And you know they already did this because you have been here before. Do you remember?

I remember, I told her. The Void Forge is the key to it all. How to destroy the quantum anchor and end the war. How I Transition.

Yes. The fate of the rebellion.

And I also know that everything I remember is from a different reality to this. I Transitioned. This is a new reality, and nothing is certain anymore.

She took my hands and squeezed them. It felt like another goodbye. *I need to 'ghost', as you say,* she said. *Confer with the others about how to assist you if you make it to the forge. I will meet you in there.*

Thank you, I said. But you mean *when* I make it.

She patted Crystal's arm and sat next to Lucretia. *Keep this one safe until it is time.*

Do we have a choice?

Like that, Antonia was gone, and I dropped back out of my fugue state.

Lucretia was poking Antonia's arm. Antonia was still sitting upright, but her eyes were closed, and she wasn't breathing. The body she had been using was inert. 'She's ghosted, right?' Lucretia asked. 'This is just a carcass that will start gassifying soon?'

'Yep.' I nodded.

'That is too creepy,' Lucretia said. 'The chirping, the ghosting. All of it. And you *slept* with that?'

'Let's not go there,' I suggested. I stood and took Crystal's hand. 'And if you're talking creepy,' I warned her, 'you haven't seen *anything* yet, trust me.' I explained to them all why Lucretia needed to take Crystal to the bathroom.

'No regurgitating way,' Ostrich exclaimed. '*Two* Tinys?'

'Does this mean I get twice the bullion?' Tiny asked hopefully.

'Does this mean I get twice the bullion?' Crystal parroted, in Tiny's voice.

'Not funny,' Tiny growled.

'Not funny,' Crystal growled back at him.

I motioned to Lucretia to take her to the bathroom before Tiny did something half the planet would regret.

'I'll wait for them, then negotiate to get you all signed on to the *Liquidator*'s crew,' I said. 'There was a hotel down the street. Go there, get a room, and wait.'

Daedalus crossed his arms. 'Well, look who's giving orders now,' he said. 'Enjoy it while it lasts, *Gregarius*.' He put a lot of emphasis on the last word. 'You might be our employer for now, but as soon as we get aboard that cruiser, I'm the decanus in this crew.'

'Yeah, Gregarius. And I'm an optio,' Tiny said. 'And there's *two* of me and only one of you. So you'll have to do what we say.'

Ostrich stood and lifted him by the elbow. 'It isn't going to work like that, buddy. But you'll figure it out. Let's go.'

Lucretia, me and Crystal – dressed in stolen miner overalls and looking every bit like Tiny – went to the firebase, where I showed my credentials and requested a line to the XO of the *Liquidator*.

A very harried Bony came on the VR display. 'What is it, Gregarius? My decanus said something about replacement crew?' As I suspected, he didn't recognize me. My service on *Liquidator* had never happened, and the action at Hellas Planitia had probably been carried out by Surefire and her crew.

'Sir, yes sir,' I told him. 'I have been ordered to report to *Liquidator* as weapons specialist. I recently served in the action to recapture *Intimidator* …'

'Yes, yes, well done, Gregarius. Just get yourself to Kamloop. We have a developing situation and we …'

'Sir. The "citizen soldiers" who recaptured the *Intimidator* want to serve too. They are here with me.'

Bony frowned. 'They're miners, aren't they?'

'Sir, yes, but they have experience from the *Intimidator* action, and we ran the entire cruiser ourselves, driver, sensor operator, weapons, loadmaster, engineer … with results you probably heard about. You'll be getting a ready-made watch crew.' I thought of Surefire again. 'At the very least, we can handle anything routine, and your elite crew can take the combat.'

Bony turned and conferred with someone out of view, then turned back again. I thought I heard Surefire's voice. 'Gregarius, for reasons above your pay grade, we are desperately short of experienced cruiser personnel right now, and expecting a Zeno assault at any moment. We'll see to the paperwork and send a crew transport to Schiaparelli, stat. You just get your gear, yourself and your comrades aboard.'

He cut the link.

I found Lucretia and Crystal outside the base again and explained to them they were now members of the crew of the ES *Liquidator*. Crystal looked excited. Lucretia not so much. 'And how are we going to explain to them we have *two* Tinys?' she asked.

'I don't know. I'm making this up as we go along,' I said, a little frustrated. I might have recovered my Zeno memories, but that didn't exactly help me navigate this very human cluster of a situation. 'How did you smuggle yourselves aboard the *Intimidator* when you hijacked it from the Zeds?'

'Inside a protein tank,' she said. 'In case you have been wondering why my hair smells like stew.' She shuddered. 'Too much like the effluent pit at Flaugerges. I am never doing that again.'

'But Tiny probably would,' I guessed.

'Actually, he probably would,' she acknowledged. 'I think he ate as much as he displaced.'

'So the crew transport will be unmanned. We bring both Tinys to Kamloop, but only one gets off. Crystal comes with us, Tiny stays behind, then sneaks into a protein tank and gets aboard that way.'

'Could work,' she allowed.

'Are we going to see more of the world?' Crystal asked, in Tiny's voice. It was uncanny, and unnerving. I just had to remember she was probably infinitely smarter, but also infinitely less street wise.

'Yes,' I told her. 'We need a way to tell you apart from our big friend when you're both in uniform. Maybe we could put a notch in one of your eyebrows?' I was about to ask Lucretia if she had a razor in her effects, but …

Crystal frowned, concentrating, and half her right eyebrow disappeared.

'Smaller,' I suggested.

This time a tiny gap, like a small scar, divided the eyebrow in two. Barely visible, unless you were looking for it.

'Perfect,' I said. 'I need to get to the hotel.'

Lucretia frowned at me. 'Why are you using the singular?'

'Well, you don't have to go through all this,' I said. 'I can give you your share of the money now, you can get a ticket to The Blue, and you're free.'

'That would be awesome.' She smiled. 'But remind me why you're doing it? Rejoining the Red Army, shipping out for Kamloop, which you *know* the Zenos are going to hit eventually …'

How much to tell her? I decided on a compromise. More than I would tell Daedalus, less than the whole truth. Crystal had climbed off the seat and was crouched down, watching red silica dust sparkle in a sunbeam as she moved her fingers through it. Humming to herself.

'I think I know how to destroy the anchor,' I told her. 'Without blowing up half the Red. But we have to get to the Void Forge.'

'Then I'm coming with,' she said. 'Only because, you know, ending the war. And the money. Not for personal reasons.'

The Zeno breach alarm died down around midnight as the last of the Zeds in the mine was dealt with and the hijacked Sandcruisers beat a fighting retreat to Voeykov. The cruisers had, of course, been Livia's real objective – stopping us from reaching crystal was just a distraction to her, since she knew how well protected the anchor was anyway.

The 'paperwork' was ready the next day, and we waited for the uncrewed drone from *Liquidator* in the enlisted mess at Firebase Schiaparelli, in fresh-issue legionnaire uniforms, two sets apiece, with Tiny skulking in a nearby latrine until the cruiser's uncrewed drone dropped onto the pad outside. We'd been asked to nominate a decanus; the other ranks were given by role. We hadn't been allowed a vote on that one either.

Several hours later, Tiny had sequestered himself in a protein tank, and we were reporting to the bridge of the *Liquidator* again, as though it was the first time.

Liquidator's commander was still Tribune Silanus and his primus pilae, or second in command, Centurion 'Leper' Lepidus. Decurion 'Bony' Curio took Daedalus's salute as we entered.

'Decanus Daedalus and crew reporting,' Daedalus said, then introduced the four of us.

'My God, have we come to this?' Silanus said sadly.

Leper sniffed disdainfully, looking at Crystal. 'Have you forgotten how to salute, Optio?'

On the transport I'd taught Crystal the basics of military protocol, told her not to speak unless spoken to, and to let me answer for her unless addressed directly. I had a plan to put her through some intensive simulator time once we we'd been piped aboard so she could bluff her way through the sensor operator role with the help of the ship's AI, just in case. I'd forgotten to teach her about saluting.

'No sir,' Crystal replied smartly. 'Never learned, sir.'

'Insolent as well,' Leper said. 'Perhaps a little tutelage with the lash would …'

'They were *miners*, Centurion,' Bony pointed out. 'Not legionnaires. Overpowered the Zeds aboard *Intimidator*, killed the Zeno commander, taught themselves to crew her with the help of the AIs and fought two victorious actions.' He snapped off an exemplary salute to Crystal, which she copied to perfection. 'I'm sure we can get them up to speed on the curiosities of military service.'

'It's your crew, XO,' Silanus said with an airy wave. 'But remember, spare the lash, spoil the meat.'

'Yes sir,' Bony said, turning to Decanus. 'Decanus, take your people to crew level 2. We're loading the last of our supplies and deploy on defensive patrol at 1600. You will report back to the bridge for the second dog watch. That's 1800.' The other officers had returned to their conversation already, and he turned to join them, then paused. 'Look for Decanus Sura down there; she'll get you settled. Tell her I authorized you to draw crew weapons.'

As we walked out, Leper turned to Silanus. 'Am I the only one who can hear someone humming?'

Decanus Cornelia Lentulus 'Surefire' Sura had not changed, and she greeted us just as smoothly the second time around. 'Decanus Cornelius and crew, I presume. We can do introductions later. I am told you poor bastards went straight into the Zeno attack on Schiaparelli after delivering *Intimidator*. You'll want a shower and a meal, I'd wager.'

Ostrich looked at me and smiled. The whole routine was even better the second time around. 'I could give you a tour, but as you've crewed *Intimidator*, there's no point,' Surefire continued. '*Liquidator* is a typical *Dominator* class. Bridge, officers on level 1, rest of the crew this level, and then the payload and ordnance bay for your loadmaster. You can take bunkroom 4.'

'Aye, we know our way around, thank you,' Daedalus said. 'Not our first time at a rodeo, as the saying goes.'

Surefire gave him an appraising look. 'I'd like to hear that *Intimidator* story one day. Right now I need to get to the bridge. Half the crew is down with dysentery, and we're doing double watches. So enjoy your rest while you can.'

'She has beautiful hair,' Crystal said, as Surefire left. 'Fuzzy.'

'She does, and as you are in the body of a 195-centimeter, 120-kilo man, you will never tell her that, alright?' I said.

'Bunkroom 4,' Daedalus said, leading the way. 'We need to get the weapon of mass destruction squared away and wait for Tiny.'

The bunkroom was made to sleep 10, and we would only be six when Tiny joined us. It wouldn't be hard avoiding other crew members, as there were so few, but there was a full century of Legion Aquila (Eagle Legion) troops in the meat locker, so we had to keep Crystal away from them.

I asked Crystal to sit on a bunk and sat beside her. Him. She looked and talked like Tiny, but I couldn't help thinking of her as a kid, even though I knew that was both me projecting and probably being very dumb. 'Hey, so we are going to need you to stay in here, like you did in the cavern outside the vault.'

She smiled and nodded. 'Will my friends stay to protect me?'

'Well, we'll all be here, inside this cruiser. We'll never be far away. You've seen the bridge. We'll just be going back and forth between here, and the bridge, and if we have to go anywhere else, we'll come and get you. How is that?'

'As long as you all don't leave me here,' she said. 'That would break my heart.'

'There is zero chance of that,' I assured her. 'Your friends will always be close by to protect you. But right now, let's hit the simulator. I need to familiarize you with the basics of what Tiny does, just in case.'

'Wait up, Gregarius,' Daedalus said. 'We're here to protect the asset. Check. But on this cruiser, you are in *my* crew. Are we clear on that?'

'Crystal.'

'Yes?'

'No, not you, sorry. Yes, Decanus.'

He nodded happily. 'Good. Now, take the asset to the simulators for role familiarization.'

I configured the simulator configured for bridge operations, with myself in the weapons seat, bots in the other chairs and Crystal in the sensor operator seat. Communication was simpler because without others around, we were able to talk Lilin. She scanned the *Dominator* Class Cruiser Sensor Operator Field Manual, and I set up a scenario for her.

'So I put a *Hydra* 100 klicks out, which is going to attack us. Sandcruisers have AIs that do all the work, so you let the AI detect the *Hydra*, lock and target it, and you report to the Officer of the Watch when I can shoot at it. He'll tell me to shoot.'

She frowned. 'It would be much easier if we just let the AIs do it all,' she said.

'Yeah, we tried that once,' I told her. 'It didn't go so well for humanity. So we do it this way now.'

We ran the scenario through a couple of times, and she handled it flawlessly. I figured she would, since it was a job even someone like Tiny could handle, so …

'Can I try your chair?' she asked before the third training run.

'My chair?'

'The weapons chair. Your job looks more interesting,' she said.

I couldn't argue with that. 'Uh, sure. But in this chair, the AI won't release any weapons without asking you first. So you have to …'

'I know. I already read the field manual.' She was already standing impatiently beside me. 'You have to stand up so I can sit down.'

Watching her run the weapons station, I accessed my Zeno self. It was like the memories of my time before arriving Earthside were in a box I had to open with a switch. They didn't come unbidden, just when I mentally reached inside myself and flipped the switch, looking for something specific. I went looking for 'what the hell is Crystal' and I found her. The best way to describe her is to say she was a little like the Artificial General Intelligence systems, or AGIs, aboard *Liquidator*. Not a Zeno herself, but with highly developed capabilities tuned to enable her to carry out her purpose – i.e., anchoring the Zenos to The Red – but also adaptable in other situations. She'd been created by Zenos, for Zenos, with a booby trap for a heart.

I decided to test her. Set up a scenario that included a four-*Hydra*, four-MCV and air wing attack. She defeated it handily.

'Well done,' I said. 'I think we …'

'These AIs are very slow,' she said. 'I think it would be better just to do all the calculations and manipulations myself.'

'I don't doubt that,' I said. 'But it won't be necessary since weapons is my job and Tiny should have rejoined us by now.'

She didn't look happy at that, but didn't argue. 'Alright. Can I come here on my own? When you are all on the bridge? The cavern was very boring. Staying in the bunkroom will be very boring. I like doing this.'

'OK, sure. But if anyone else from the crew comes in here while you're here …'

'Don't talk with them, make an excuse to leave and go back to the bunkroom and hide,' she said.

'Right,' I said. 'And be especially careful around Decanus Sura. She's sharp.'

She opened her mouth to ask a question, and I held up my hand.

'That means clever. We don't want her getting suspicious.'

Tiny had the courtesy to spray himself down with a high-pressure hose and steal a uniform before he came up to the crew level, but he still smelled like dog food.

We were about to go on watch duty, and spooning down some rice and 'stew' as he walked in. Ostrich pushed her plate across to him and offered him a spoon.

'Nah, thanks,' he said. 'I already ate.' Crystal was sitting on a bunk with her knees drawn up to her chest, just watching us and humming. 'I am not going to get used to being around doppelganger girl over there. Shouldn't she be behind a curtain or something, in case someone walks in?'

Daedalus nodded. 'The sensor operator has a point. Henceforth, the asset shall lie under a bunk behind a towel whenever Optio Tiny is in the same room,' he said, giving me a *'make it so'* look. Crystal had no problem with that, even though she had to make herself longer to fit. I knew that as soon as we were gone she would be headed for the simulators anyway.

Tiny sat. 'If the whole point is to protect that humming bomb, remind me why we are here, and not hiding in a nice safe hole in the ground in the Terra Cimmeria, where the war isn't?'

'We're here because this is where Ballsack has been posted, Optio,' Lucretia said patiently. 'And that means this is where the asset has to be, and since our job is protecting the asset, this is where we have to be.'

'Still not taking a bullet for him,' Tiny grumbled, making to sit.

I had other reasons for being at Kamloop, but they weren't for the crew. Not even for Lucretia. Because I had *remembered*, and I now knew why we had to stop Livia's Reactionaries capturing the Void Forge. I won't tire you with a whole tapestry of timelines, but if she succeeds, I didn't Transition. She thinks that will end the rebellion, and prevent the extinction of the Lilin, but she's wrong.

Yeah, you're thinking, 'Of course Ballsack thinks that; he's a fanatical Lilin Rebel in love with his own ideology.'

Which yes, I am, but this is my story, so I get to decide who's right and who's wrong. At the end of it, you can judge for yourself.

'Don't sit. We're dog watch,' Daedalus told Tiny and motioned us all to stand. 'On your feets, valiant former crew of the *Liquidator,* which we shall not mention in polite company because that battle didn't happen, and meritorious hijackers of the *Intimidator*, which we will brag about at every opportunity because it did. We have Zeno butt to kick.'

Argyre Planitia

I know you know about the Battle of Argyre Planitia. Maybe you saw a newscast, or maybe you just read about it in school? The Official History of the Red War gives it several pages, all of which were written by people with wild imaginations or dubious motivations, none of whom were there. I'll quote the introduction:

The scene was set for a climactic battle between the Sandcruisers of the Red Army and the hijacked Sandcruisers of the Lilin. As the Intimidator, Terminator and the crippled but still serviceable Dominator closed on Kamloop from the direction of Voeykov, Liquidator was the only vessel standing between the Lilin and the capture or destruction of the Void Forge. Due to farsighted military planners, the newly commissioned Eliminator had been rushed onto an antimatter sled for transport Redside six months earlier, but the question on everyone's mind was: Could it reach The Red before the Lilin overran Kamloop?

Blah blah. And the History tells you the *Eliminator* arrived in the nick of time, ambushed the Lilin from the rear, and though a few Zeds reached Kamloop, the crew of *Eliminator* saved the day by wiping out the Lilin cruiser fleet and hunting down every last Zed. Right?

Wrong. The *Eliminator* arrived a week *after* the Battle of Argyre Planitia. The Lilin made it into Kamloop in big numbers. And me? Well. Don't assume because I'm still writing this journal and you're still reading it that I survived to talk about it. Maybe you live in a different timeline, for all you know.

So here's the true story of the Battle of Argyre Planitia, as witnessed by Gregarius Linus Vespasius, and it isn't pretty.

'Updated position on the Lilin cruisers!' Bony shouted.

We'd been aboard the *Liquidator* maybe a week, patrolling between Kamloop and Voeykov, waiting for the Lilin to finish reloading and repairing their captured cruisers. We weren't certain at that time they were coming for Kamloop, but it didn't take a genius to work out the only prize worth winning on The Red was the Void Forge, which was why Daedalus had worked it out months ago.

And now they were moving. Surefire and her crew had tracked them this far. It was our turn as they closed the gap, but she was expected back on the bridge for the next watch, when we would spring our trap.

'Satellite has them 800 klicks south-southwest Voeykov,' Tiny replied.

'They are entering air wing range,' I confirmed.

We were tucked into the shadow of a mesa at the western edge of the Hellas Planitia, sand cloak engaged, using passive sensors only, giving off less radiation than a legionnaire's personal radio.

'I feel uncomfortable just hiding here, waiting for them to come to us,' Silanus said from his perch at the back of the bridge. 'Take the fight to the enemy! That's what we were taught. I shouldn't have let you talk me into this, Bony.'

'The tribune has a point,' Leper said, obsequiously and expectedly. 'There is no valor in bushwhacking your enemy. We have a cohort of MCVs supported by *Hydras*, and the enemy is already within range of our air wing and missiles.'

Bony remained unmoved. 'We are outnumbered three to one. Losses in any assault are always higher for the attacking force anyway. A surprise attack from their flank is our only chance of whittling them down enough to give the defenders at Kamloop a chance. The longer we stay here, undetected, the greater our chances will be.'

'Pfft,' Silanus said. 'Defeatism never won a war. *Eliminator* will be here any moment …'

'With respect, *Eliminator* is still a week out, sir,' Bony pointed out.

'At most,' Silanus said sharply. 'What say you, Centurion Lepidus?'

'We are the *Liquidator*, Tribune, the finest cruiser in the Red Army. We may be outnumbered, but we are facing incompetent Zenos and poorly trained Zeds from the filthiest penal battalion on The Red,' Leper said. His voice grew louder the more he listened to it. 'I say we attack. Full speed at the enemy and damn the torpedoes!' he shouted.

'Yes, damn the torpedoes! XO, you have your orders,' Silanus decided.

Tiny leaned toward me from his station. 'Surefire is going to be pissed again,' he said. 'We're starting back at zero combat hours, and she was banking on a nice long engagement.'

'Ending in her death, so I'm pretty sure she won't be that pissed,' I pointed out.

Daedalus, in the driver's position beside Bony, coughed. 'Decurion, permission to offer worthless input based on irrelevant experience from our action at, err … Terra Sabea?'

'Go ahead, but make it quick, Decanus,' Bony said.

'Sir. I recommend you de-cloak, attract a Zeno recon probe our way and allow the Zenos to see us. Manipulate the energy levels on the microwave defenses to make it look like we have power problems. The Zenos will launch everything they have. As they do, you can optimize the power grid for defensive operations. Set propulsion for military power and lay in a nav point for a retreat to Kamloop. Weapons should launch the air wing in defensive mode, 100-klick perimeter. Put our MCVs on the ground now and send them full speed on an intercept course. They can launch *Hydras* as soon as they are in range and then dig in on the plains outside Kamloop to form a forward line of defense the Zenos won't be expecting. We can't hit the Zenos in the flank, but we can reach Kamloop with our remaining infantry before they do, and give our defenders a fighting chance.'

Bony stood stony faced, listening intently. 'I am getting a distinct feeling of *déjà vu*, Decanus,' he said. 'This unorthodox strategy is based on your learnings at Terra Sabea?'

'Sir, yes sir. Also, you will want to sound general quarters about now and tell the sensor operator to alert you the second the enemy launches missiles. We'll be wanting hull integrity to put a heat map on the display in front of us and be ready to rotate plates on your command …' He paused, taking a breath. 'And I'll, uh, prepare for evasive maneuvers.'

'What was that about a *retreat*?' Silanus asked Leper. I could see neither of them had been able to keep up with Daedalus, but since he had just been repeating the orders Bony gave before the Battle of Zea Dorsa, which in this timeline, hadn't happened, Bony had no trouble following him at all. And ignoring Silanus.

'Comms, sound general quarters. Watch crew, as the Decanus suggested …' Bony said, repeating Daedalus's suggestion in his own words, because, well, they *were* his own words; he just didn't know it. But it was a prodigious feat of memory on Daedalus's part, and he seemed visibly pleased with himself for performing it.

In our new timeline, Livia's forces hadn't fallen for our feint at Zea Dorsa, so they fell for the bait again as Ostrich manipulated our microwave arrays to make it look like we were having power problems.

'*Dominator* launching its air wing,' Tiny announced. A swarm of red dots appeared above the icon on the tactical screen that was *Dominator*, and began streaming toward *Liquidator* as we moved out from the shadow of the mesa toward Kamloop.

'What about the other two cruisers?'

'Still tracking toward Kamloop, sir,' Tiny said. 'No sign of missile or aircraft launches.'

'They underestimate us,' Silanus said. '*Dominator* is their weak link.'

'Divide and conquer!' Leper crowed. 'We take down *Dominator*, that leaves only two!'

'Weapons, as soon as we have dealt with *Dominator*'s attack, launch the air wing at *Intimidator*,' Bony said.

Leper frowned. 'Ah, I think you mean *Dominator*, Decurion.'

'No, I mean *Intimidator*, Centurion,' Bony said. 'We have to hit their strongest units while we are strong. Our ground troops can take care of *Dominator* if it reaches Argyre Planitia.'

My AI approved. *The best strategy is always to be very strong, first in general, and then at the decisive point*, it said into my skull cap. I wasn't calling it stupid this time and in fact was grateful it was doing most of the hard work, since I had enough to think about already.

'Who said that? Sun Tzu?' I asked.

Clausewitz, it replied. I recommend moving the defensive perimeter from 100 to 200 klicks immediately, to hit the enemy air wing before it reaches missile launch point. With overwhelming firepower, the enemy strategy will be to come at us with wave after wave of aircraft and missiles and exhaust our supply of interceptors before delivering a knockout blow with one of the other cruisers' air wings.

'Do it,' I said. 'What is the status on our MCVs?' We had launched the full century of MCVs and their accompanying *Hydras* before we left the shadow of the mesa.

The cohort is halfway to the interception point. They will be in Hydra range of Terminator within 30 minutes.

'Are they going to have time to deploy troops and dig in?'

It will be close. Anything we can do to slow Terminator down will help them.

I flipped my Zeno switch, desperately searching my very fallible memory of conflicts over the millennia for something we could use, but the math was the math, and I couldn't bend the laws of physics to make an army rise from the sand.

Then it came to me. We had a weapon of mass destruction in bunkroom 4. Detonate it, and we could take out not only the entire Zed fleet but banish every Zeno from The Red at the same time.

Downside, even if she blew right on top of the Zeno cruiser flotilla, it was so close now she would still take out Kamloop. Plus whoever broke her heart. So not really an option, and the Zenos – who knew we had Crystal – they knew that too.

But Crystal was more than just a walking antimatter bomb.

I leaned over toward Tiny. 'Hey, buddy. I think you need a toilet break.'

Not surprisingly, he looked at me like I was crazy. 'Say what? We're about to engage the Zeno cruisers.'

'Yeah, but I'm on weapons, and there's something in the bunkroom I need you to fetch,' I said, winking. 'Am I being *crystal* clear?'

'No way, you can go get your own … oh, right,' he said, winking back at me so broadly it would have been visible from space. 'Decanus!' he yelled. 'I think I might be coming down with dysentery! Permission to evacuate my bowels, *urgently*?!'

'Sensors to AI control,' Daedalus said. 'Sensor Officer is excused.' He gave me a 'what the hell is going on' look, but he was too far away for me to whisper, and Bony was in my line of sight, so I couldn't even try some kind of sign language.

Tiny ran from the bridge. Almost as soon as he disappeared, he reappeared again. Or Crystal did. She ran onto the bridge and stood there, looking around, and came over to me. 'There is a lot of emotion in this room,' she said. 'Is this excitement?'

'Definitely, but not all excitement is the good kind. Take my chair,' I said, pulling off my skull cap and standing.

'Weapons Specialist, stay at your station!' Bony snapped. 'I can't have two stations unattended during an engagement.'

'Sir, we are just swapping stations,' I told him, eyeing Daedalus with a visual 'support me here' plea. 'AI support or not, the optio is the superior weapons operator in a hot engagement. I can run sensors.'

'That's correct, sir,' Daedalus said. 'On *Intimidator*, we let Optio Tiny run weapons, and you know the results.'

Bony blinked twice, thinking it over. 'Alright, make the change, but be quick about it,' Bony said. He turned around, frowning. 'Who the hell is *humming*?'

'Is this like the simulator?' Crystal asked as she settled the skull cap on her head.

'Yes,' I said, using Lilin-voice in a tone so high it was outside human sonic range. 'But you remember how you said you could work faster than the AI? Are you confident about that?'

'Yes. Much faster,' she said, eyes focusing as her holo display came online. 'Oh, there are a *lot* of targets.' She actually sounded pleased.

'Good. You have my permission to disable the AI. Just say 'Decurion, my AI is glitching,' and shut it out. Then go to work.'

As I moved toward Tiny's sensor station, Crystal raised her voice, or Tiny's voice, if we are being accurate. 'Decurion, my AI is glitching. Beginning manual engagement.'

'What, no, that is absolutely not …' Leper began stuttering.

Things started happening at a speed no one on the bridge could follow. Crystal took control not just of weapons, but somehow also sensors. I realized I hadn't given her the whole 'roles and responsibilities on the bridge' talk. Within milliseconds, every incoming aircraft had been identified and targeted. She started piloting every one of our hundred aircraft, and appeared to be flying each of them manually. Usually they operated as a swarm, with limited individual initiative. But on the screen we saw each of them flying its own intercept track, launching missiles at the *Dominator*'s aircraft as soon as they got within optimal kill range.

'What the devil, Decurion?!' Silanus asked. 'This is *not* protocol.'

Bony stood still, letting it happen. 'No, but it's working,' he said quietly, as red enemy icons started disappearing from the plot.

Crystal was doing what she could, with what she had. But it wasn't enough. A dozen Zeno aircraft got through her perimeter and launched missiles. One hundred and twenty. In moments, they launched their submunitions.

'Twelve hundred warheads inbound,' I advised, as the tactical screen flooded with red threats again. 'Twelve seconds to first impact.'

'Sound the collision alarm,' Bony said. 'Arm interceptors; microwave array to full power. Bring up a hull heat map and prepare to swap plates on my command.'

'Sending air wing at *Intimidator* as ordered,' Crystal announced. I'd already cued that order, but forgotten it in the heat of the action. Crystal didn't.

'No, dammit, we need those aircraft for our defense!' Leper croaked. He looked like he wanted to be anywhere but on the bridge of the *Liquidator*. So did Tribune Silanus, who I was pretty sure had one foot on the floor beneath his seat because he was getting ready to run for an emergency evacuation pod.

'Aircraft aren't needed for defense,' Crystal said. 'Taking command of defensive systems and hull plate exchange priority.'

'That is the decurion's job!' Leper said.

'I delegate my authority to the optio,' Bony said quickly.

'Five seconds to impact,' I warned. 'Brace brace brace!'

The Zeno warheads closed on *Liquidator*.

Interceptors spat from launch tubes along the spine of our hull even as the microwave arrays fired. I saw the incoming missile tally spinning down … 1,200 … 800 … 620 … 409 … 82 …

Impact.

All eyes were fixed on the heat blooms flowering across the hull. Faster than we could register, Crystal began intoning …

'Changing plates AA23, BC19, BB14, BB29, BB09, ZX49 … changing plate GK01,' she said. 'Final impact. Plate KH99 pitted but holding. No change needed until next service opportunity.'

The hull integrity specialist, one of Surefire's people, looked up in amazement. 'Hull integrity 100 percent,' she reported. 'No compromise!'

'System damage report,' Bony said to his comms specialist.

'Interceptors recycling down here,' Lucretia said from the payload bay. 'Ten minutes to full reload. Rattled a few brain pans in the meat locker, but no damage.'

'All other systems, uh … nominal,' the comms specialist said. 'There was a fire in launch tube A19 but …'

'I put that out,' Crystal said. 'It will be six minutes until our air wing is in range for an attack on *Intimidator*. Chances of moderate damage to *Intimidator* are 86 percent; chances of critical damage are low to zero. I recommend a follow-up long-range precision missile strike to coincide with the *Hydra* polymorph launch.' She looked around the bridge. 'Does anyone need any help while I'm waiting?'

Bony was no idiot. He knew something seriously weird had just happened. But he had been smart enough to let it happen, and with five minutes to the next phase of the engagement – our air attack on *Intimidator* – he wasn't inclined to stop it happening … yet. But he left his chair and stood beside Daedalus.

'Decanus, that man is stimmed,' he said. It wasn't a question. 'Military-grade implants. I thought he was a *miner*.'

'Yes, sir. Should have mentioned that, sir,' Daedalus said.

'Experimental implants?' Bony asked.

'Highly, sir,' Daedalus said. 'Corporate tech. Doses off the scale. Some kind of cocktail would kill anyone without his constitution.'

'I've never seen reaction times like that,' Bony said. 'Even our AIs …'

'I know, sir,' Daedalus said. 'Saved our asses off the Olani Chaos, that's for sure.'

I ran my hand across my throat, urging him to shut his trap. Olani Chaos was a different timeline.

Bony frowned. 'Olani Chaos?'

'What? No, sorry, misspoke, sir,' Daedalus said quickly, catching my horrified look. 'I meant *Leighton*, of course. In the *Intimidator*.'

'Two minutes to air wing missile launch,' Crystal announced. 'This is much more interesting than simulations.'

'Uh, quite,' Silanus said. 'Keep up the good work there, Optio. I think you may have found your calling.'

'*Dominator*'s air wing has been destroyed. *Dominator* is rejoining the Zeno flotilla,' I reported, describing what I saw on the sensor plot. 'Her missile launch tubes were pretty mangled after the action off Leighton. I'd say she's out of the fight until the ground war starts.'

'*Liquidator*'s air wing is attacking,' Crystal said. '*Intimidator* was slow scrambling its air wing. I think we caught half of them in the process of launching. Whose idea was the counterattack? Great move.'

'Uh, that would be me, Optio,' Bony said. 'You were here when I ordered it.'

Crystal shot me a glance. 'Oh, yes. I was. Definitely. Just sending praise at you, in front of your superiors, sir. Which should reinforce their approval.'

'The decurion already has our approval,' Leper said with a sniff. 'Your verbal props are noted; now focus on the air counterattack.'

I needed to get the real Tiny back on the bridge as soon as the action was over so that Bony didn't start asking Crystal questions she couldn't answer. Like, 'Tell me about your childhood, Optio.'

'Missiles launched; air wing returning to evade interception,' Crystal announced calmly. Seconds ticked past as our volley of missiles closed on *Intimidator*.

'Impacts!' I said. 'Heat blooms on *Intimidator*. Wait ... secondary explosions! AI analyzing ... she's on fire!'

'What did I tell you, Lepidus? Not just crewed by Zeds, but the most disreputable former legionnaires on the entire Red,' Silanus said. 'This battle is won before it even got started.'

It wasn't.

Crystal changed the focus of our attack from *Intimidator* to *Dominator*, and finished the crippled vessel off with a staggered wave of missile attacks that exhausted its limited interceptor stock, disrupted its microwave defenses and then delivered strike after strike on the same already buckling hull plates, as though she was sitting on the warheads guiding them in herself. Which, in all virtuality, she probably was.

At the end of our watch, we handed over to Surefire and her crew for the chase, as *Liquidator* poured all of her power into her engines, trying to close a gap to the remaining two Zeno cruisers that stayed stubbornly unclose-able.

And Surefire could only hit the targets she could see, and reach. *Terminator* stayed out of *Liquidator*'s grasp, shrugged off the *Hydra* attack and, using a massed Ferret assault, blew through our dug-in infantry outside Kamloop as though they weren't there. *Intimidator* limped through the gap made by *Terminator*, trailing dirty smoke fueled by internal oxygen that even the atmosphere of the Red couldn't quench, and together with *Terminator*, dropped her MCVs just outside Kamloop's automated defense perimeter.

We were too far away to be able to hit the Zeno force in its rear, and too late to be able to prevent the Zed meat wave of former Legion Praeda legionnaires banzai-charging their way into Kamloop.

At the end of our watch, we retired, exhausted, to our bunkroom, having pulled Crystal out without attracting Bony's attention. He had enough to worry about. Crystal rolled under a bunk, as happy as I'd seen her in our short time together, oblivious to the carnage she'd caused, not to mention the Zed lives she'd ended – if you could call that empty, emotionless existence 'life'.

Tiny was lying on his bunk with his hands across his abdomen.

'You missed all the fun,' Ostrich told him.

'Not really,' he said. 'I think I really do have dysentery. That second tour through the protein tanks has done it for me.'

'Serves you right for ingesting your body weight in "stew", Optio,' Daedalus told him. 'But you'll be glad to know that under my leadership, this crew performed miserably well, and accounted for one cruiser destroyed, one seriously damaged.'

'Hoozah,' Tiny said, with distinct lack of enthusiasm. 'But seriously. I think I'm dying.'

'Well, you'll have plenty of company in the afterlife,' Lucretia said. 'Zeds made it through our lines. Kamloop is crawling with them. Electromagnetic defenses are down, so it's probably infested with Zenos too.'

'Void Forge won't fall,' Ostrich insisted. 'I've seen the specs for that place. It's 2 klicks down. Pulls its power from thermoelectric generators in the thermal layers beneath it, which the Zenos can't cut. Every tunnel leading down to it is lathered in automated defenses. The whole place is protected by an Artificial General Intelligence whose only job is to keep the forge functioning, even if the last human left alive on The Red is dead.'

'If they're dead, they ... forget it,' Lucretia sighed. 'None of that will help, if our friend Livia just opens a milky pus portal and beams herself in.'

'She can't do that,' I told her. 'She can't even get *near* the forge itself.'

'Why not?' Daedalus asked. 'Your ex-girlfriend, Gregarius, has an annoying habit of turning up in the darndest places.'

'That sounds like something I should be saying,' Lucretia said. 'But he's right.'

'Antimatter containment field,' I said. 'The forge is the biggest electromagnetic energy field on the planet. A Zeno would completely discorporate if it got within 100 meters of it. They can send Zeds, but like Ostrich said, automated defenses and the Legion Aquila will deal with those.'

'Then what is the point of this attack?' Lucretia asked.

A voice from under the bunk answered her. 'Your enemy doesn't want to destroy the forge; it just wants to control it. It can do that just by keeping you out.'

'Well, thank you, voice from the deep,' Lucretia said, looking between her legs at the silhouette in the dark under the bunk.

'I guess that makes sense,' Ostrich said. 'No antimatter, no antimatter weapons, but also no antimatter for space travel, or energy generation Blueside. Humanity will be back to grilling over open fires and eating moss off rocks in no time.'

'There is no moss on rocks on The Red,' Tiny said. 'And ... still dying here. Excuse me,' he said, levering himself off his bed and staggering out in the direction of the heads.

The voice under the bunk spoke again. 'Uncle Linus knows the cure for dysentery.'

'I do?' I said, looking between my legs now.

'Of course. So do I, but I know you will feel you are adding value to the enterprise if I let you remember it,' Crystal said.

She was right. Tripping my Lilin switch, I searched my memory. A combination of compounds found in almost any kitchen or infirmary would do it, combined in the right way. 'She's right, I do,' I said. I wrote it down and handed it to Ostrich. 'You'll be better at this than me.'

She looked at it and stood. 'Can't we just let it go a couple days more? It's strangely satisfying seeing his face scrunched up like that.'

'No, we cannot, Engineer Ostrich,' Daedalus said. 'My comrade in arms, Surefire, warned me that as soon as *Liquidator* breaks into the Kamloop perimeter, every able-bodied, and a lot of non-able-bodied, bodies are going to be sent in to clear out the Zeds, street by street, and then tunnel by tunnel. So we will need the big optio, if for nothing else than a meat shield.'

'But we're an elite Sandcruiser crew,' Lucretia said plaintively. 'They wouldn't send *us*, surely?'

We all looked at her with pity.

'Yeah, alright. But we can't bring Crystal,' she said. 'If anything happens to her …'

'*Boom*,' Ostrich said, making an AM bomb storm with her fingers.

'Actually, it doesn't have to happen to *me*,' the voice under the bunk said. 'If anything bad happened to any of my friends, it could break my heart too.'

'The decanus respectfully requests the asset to define "bad",' Daedalus said, leaning forward to look under the bunk.

'Well, death, obviously. Light wounds would probably be alright, but if one of you lost a limb … any major sadness, really.'

'Major *sadness*?' Lucretia asked. 'We are so screwed.'

'No, we can do this,' I told them. 'I just have to reach the forge, and they'll give up. This a war between the Zeno factions, remember, not against humanity. Livia isn't trying to deny the forge to the humanity, just to me, and the Zeno Rebels. If we get through, they lose.'

'Well, you're semi-human now, so the magnetic field won't affect you,' Lucretia pointed out, then frowned. 'Which kind of feels like it's not a coincidence.'

'Uh-huh, but with Kamloop crawling with Zeds and Zenos and stuff exploding all around us, I figure magnetic fields are not our biggest problem.'

I bent down and spoke between my legs. 'Crystal, can you use the ship's systems to pull up maps for Kamloop and try to find us a safe-ish way down to the Void Forge that will avoid the most obvious kill zones?'

'An adventure, outside the cruiser?' she asked. 'That sounds like fun. I can do that.'

'*Or* how about this?' Lucretia asked. 'We don't risk the asset by dragging its ass through a combat zone, and instead we hide until the fighting in Kamloop is over and *then* sneak into the Void Forge?'

'If Tiny was here he would definitely vote for that option,' Ostrich said, raising a hand in the air. 'And I would support him. Assuming there was a vote.'

'I am not a fan of voting, as you know,' Daedalus grumbled. 'But I am a very big fan of sneaking. Ballsack, as my employer, I request you with my full authority to order the asset to explore the sneaking option.'

I was also not wild with the idea of exposing Crystal to the chances of a stray plasma bolt. We could wait out the firefight inside Kamloop, but if the Zenos won, the city would be full of undistracted Zeds patrolling the streets and sabotaging all entrances to the forge. If the Red Army won, the city would be full of trigger-happy legionnaires erecting electromagnetic gates that Crystal couldn't pass through and patrolling the streets for Zeds. I still felt like our chances of reaching the forge were better with both sides engaged in a hot war, and not looking for us.

'We will sneak into the forge,' I announced. '*While* the two sides are still fighting.' I smiled. 'Best of both plans.'

Lucretia shook her head. 'Or, you know, the worst.'

'What do you mean I get no body armor?' Tiny asked.

We had just been issued armor for the upcoming ground operation to rescue the defenders of Kamloop. As with everything else, the *Liquidator*'s armory carried the finest equipment, in this case nanotube-composite body armor, able to shrug off ballistics and even withstand small-caliber plasma and laser bolts. It slid over our thermal heat suits like a second skin and sealed perfectly around the combat helmets with built-in breathers that we were also issued, which went along with a plasma rifle, a pistol, a pouch of grenades each, and extra charge cells.

But we were only given five sets of armor and weapons, and there were six of us now.

'The asset has to be protected, big boy,' Daedalus said. 'Or none of us gets paid.'

'If I get a 10,000-degree hole burned through me, I don't get paid!' Tiny said. He pointed at Lucretia. 'The asset can be any shape it wants. So it can look like Termite and wear *her* body armor.'

'He has a point,' Ostrich said. Then saw the look on Lucretia's face. 'No offense.'

'If she can turn into any shape, how about a pair of breasts, and you can fit her in the bra you don't need to wear?' Lucretia said to Ostrich. 'No offense.'

I was about to step between them, when Crystal spoke. 'I can't take anyone's armor. If any of my friends get killed, it would break my heart.'

'So there we go,' Tiny said, taking it back from Daedalus.

'On second thought, if you go into combat looking like Tiny, every Zed in range will be aiming at you,' I said.

'Great, thanks for that,' Tiny said. 'That was a confidence builder.'

'I just mean because you are the biggest target is all,' I explained.

'I could look like Daedalus,' Crystal said. 'He's small.'

'No!' We all said at once, each for our own reasons maybe, but mine was simple. It was bad enough having to look at one Daedalus, let alone two.

'I choose to take that as an expression of respect,' Daedalus said. 'And amity.'

'Be Crystal,' I suggested. 'The form you had when I found you. A legionnaire wouldn't deliberately shoot a small girl, and a Zed wouldn't see a child as a threat. But ...'

'Alright,' she said. She did it right in front of us, and I am willing to bet, if you are reading this, imagining seeing a giant like Tiny morph into a little girl right in front of your eyes, then you probably just lost your lunch.

When I had finished dry-retching, I straightened. 'I was *going* to say, "But not yet",' I said. 'For now, you need to look like a generic legionnaire in nanotube armor, because we have to assemble in the meat locker with the rest of the complement for the mission briefing.'

'The situation is this,' Bony was saying. He was standing on a platform at the back of the *Liquidator*'s meat locker, with Tribune Silanus behind him. Assembled in front of him was a century of troops that Silanus, with Leper at their head, had held back to form an honor guard for his triumphant procession into Kamloop to receive the adoring welcome of fawning Kamloopians grateful to be alive.

Yeah, nice daydream. Not happening.

Behind the legionnaires was the 30-strong crew of the *Liquidator*, which now included us. Bony continued. 'The remaining defenders of the Legion Aquila, maybe 200 at last count, have withdrawn into tunnels under the city to block the invader's path to the forge. The Zenos appear to be trying to reach the forge control center, which is located here ...' A hologram with a map of the installation appeared, the control center glowing. 'The map has been sent to your communicators.' He reached up and spun the hologram. Two tunnel entrances were highlighted. 'The century will divide into two, half taking the western entrance to the tunnels, half the eastern. Expect the Zenos to have left a rear guard to protect their backs. You will be fighting your way in. But our recon shows they took a lot of casualties out on the plains, and in the initial assault. AI estimates a total Zed force of 200 to 300 entered the tunnels, and a lot of those will have been killed since, but a lot won't. So you'll be outnumbered two or three to one. It's not going to be a fair fight. For the *Zeds* ...' he growled.

There was a chorus of *hoozahs* from the legionnaires.

'Crew of the *Liquidator*,' Bony said, looking over the crowd at us. 'You will be split into three squads, by watch. Squad one, under me, will have the job of retaking the *Intimidator*. Squad two' – that was Surefire – 'will retake the *Terminator*. And squad three' –that was us – 'you will take guard outside *Liquidator* and ensure no filthy Zeno tries to steal our ride home.'

The crew complement, in their kick-ass nanotube armor, cheered even louder than the legionnaires, probably because they had just been given the easier mission.

Surefire came over to us, depolarizing the visor over her breather so we could see her face. 'Hope you don't mind; I suggested to Bony that you guys stay here to protect *Liquidator*. I know you won't get the combat hours, but you aren't combat trained, so this is much safer for you ...'

'Decanus, you have our thanks,' Daedalus said, depolarizing his visor, too, as he patted the hull beside him. 'Don't you worry. We'll make sure this old girl is still here when you get back.'

'Counting on that.' Surefire smiled, darkening her visor again and walking back toward her squad. She stopped and turned around. 'Uh, weren't there just five of you?'

'Right,' Daedalus said. 'Yes. But no ...'

'Yes, but no?'

'Yes, there *were* only five of us,' Tiny said, pushing Crystal forward. 'We just picked up Chris here outside in Kamloop. Miner from the forge. Old buddy of mine, just itching for some payback.'

'When did you …?' Surefire started asking, but one of her men was waving her over. 'Alright. Whatever. Get some, uh, Chris.'

Crystal turned to me. 'Is Chris my nickname? Like you all have nicknames?'

'Sure,' I said. 'You like it?'

'I like it if it is Kris, with a K, as in the Sikh knife blade called a Kris,' she said. 'Because that is cool. But not if it is Chris, with CH, short for Crystal, because that sounds dumb.'

'Definitely the Sikh knife blade,' I said, making a cutting motion. 'Krissssss.'

'It doesn't sound so cool when you say it,' she said. 'But I'll keep it.'

We gathered around Daedalus. 'Alright, my plan. We go down the ramp, shut it behind us, like we're taking up positions around the cruiser's sand tracks. Soon as the others are out of sight, Crystal does her shape-changer thing, and we head for that back entrance that she …'

'Kris,' Crystal said. 'With a K.'

'That Kris – the asset – identified, and we sneak into the forge, unless we get seen, in which case we kill anyone who gets in our way. The plan is now open for questions, Termite.'

'Yes. When do we get to the actual plan? Because that was just a statement of the obvious,' Lucretia said.

'Which is what makes it such a good plan, that everyone can follow,' Dacdalus said. 'Unlike your plans, which just confuse everyone.'

'I'll go in on point. The rest of you behind me,' I said. If Antonia was right, I will, would, had been here already. I was hoping that Zeno switch in my head would flip and tell me what to do once I got inside. Or at the very least, show me a way down. 'Livia is going for the control room, but my aim is to get inside the forge, right into the containment area, where no Zeno can reach us. You guys just focus on protecting Cryst— ... Kris.'

'And yourselves,' Crystal said. 'Because if anything happens to you ...'

'We *know*!' Ostrich said. 'Sheesh. I've got a better nickname for you. Damocles.'

'I don't like that one,' Crystal said.

Daedalus twirled his finger in the air. 'Shut up, everyone. Let's dust.'

I didn't feel bad leaving *Liquidator* unprotected since, if we failed, none of us would be around to worry about it. And if we failed before we got down deep, neither would Kamloop ...

You get the picture.

Maybe the war would go on, Antonia and the Rebels against Livia and her Reactionaries, with humankind as the collateral, on into infinity. But it wouldn't be my problem anymore. And that was the beauty of mortality, right? If you're dead, the world can go to hell and you don't have to care anymore. Nothing you can do about it. Blissful, eternal, uncomplicated darkness.

Hey, I get that not everyone sees it that way. Including almost anyone with a religious belief, most of whom see eternity as a reward. But when you have already lived for eternity, you can try my perspective on for size and you might see the attraction of oblivion.

Was I deliberately running into the Void Forge at the head of a squad of lunatic mercenaries because I yearned for that darkness? I like to think not. I like to think I was doing it because I knew that if I could get to the heart of the Void Forge, with Crystal with a K in tow, I could end the war. The real war, between the Lilin Rebels and Reactionaries. But also the other one, between humankind and the Lilin, since in a way, humankind had been doing the Rebels' fighting for them, since the first day of the Red War, just like the Zeds had been doing the Reactionaries' fighting for them.

And now you're thinking, *that ain't fair*. But remember, 'We are you.' Who do you think the Lilin learned the art of war from?

Look at me, writing like I'm full-on Zeno now. Using the big '*we*'. You'll see more of that in the pages ahead. Me being schizo. Thinking and acting like a Zeno one minute, like a human the next, because I am both, and neither. Judge me for it, or forgive me – I can't control how you react.

So where were we? Ah. Right, running toward the blackness. The Void. The end of it all.

Except time is not a line. And there is no end.

'Clear!' I yelled as we reached the back entrance to the facility, after some seriously ninja sneaking through the blasted habitat domes and exposed, frozen gardens of Kamloop. 'No "rear guard" here.'

'That *you* can see,' Tiny said. He didn't have great confidence in my soldiering abilities, and it was hard to blame him. This was the third time in my military career I'd been boots dry on The Red, the first two being Margarita Terra and Isidis Planitia, and we know how they went. But the helmets and rifles we'd been issued on the *Liquidator* were special operations models, with inbuilt light intensification, infrared, UV, data sharing and auto-targeting. They drew targets around anything that looked like it might be able to kill you, and you pulled your trigger once to lock it, twice to fire. A self-guiding bullet steered itself to the target. If you were in a firefight, you didn't have to double-pull the trigger; you just held it down and it locked and fired at whatever you were looking at.

The antimatter forge was buried 2 kilometers deep, under a dual fusion/antimatter reactor. The old-tech fusion reactor was only used for startup operations. Once the forge was in production mode, cranking out antimatter, a proportion was diverted to power the antimatter reactor in a self-sustaining cycle. When not disrupted by things like Zeno wars, it was capable of producing a kilo of antimatter a day. Enough to power 4.7 million households for a year.

The production chamber was encased in a huge electromagnetic bottle that held a gram of antimatter at a time. Geothermal energy provided backup redundancy in case all other power failed or was cut. It was transferred to a transportation bottle that used passive energy recovery to sustain a containment field, allowing it to be freighted off-planet and Earthside.

Container failures, like those that had provoked Earth governments to ban production Earthside, were now rare, but spectacular. So the easy way to destroy the Void Forge was simply to trigger a failure in a small transport container in the central AM storage area, creating a tiny Hiroshima-sized boom, that would quickly turn into a 50-megaton boom. But the central storage area was inside the main electromagnetic field, so the Lilin couldn't get in there and trigger it themselves. They needed to get a force of Zeds in there to do their dirty work. Breach the control room, shut down the automated defense systems, then breach the tunnels leading to the central storage area, where Kamloop's defenders would be staging their last stand.

Just the job for Zeds who were former Legion Praeda.

My memories were a little vague on where to go next, but it was a pretty good bet 'down' was the right direction. With Crystal tucked in behind me, and the others snaking out behind her, I turned and began moving down the corridor to the stairwell that would take us down to the fusion reactor control room.

As soon as I reached it, I heard firing.

Antonia was waiting for us on the landing at the bottom of the first stairwell. She was wearing the same nanotube armor as we were, but she wore it better.

A battle was raging another level or two down. The thud of pulse rifles, grenades exploding, and wounded legionnaires crying for help rose up to greet us. Counterposed with the background hum of 'Frère Jacques'.

'How did you get here?' I asked.

'Long story,' she said, 'involving a Rebel spy and those two dead Zeds.' She pointed over her shoulder at the bodies of two Legion Praeda Zeds lying on the stairs leading down. 'Now you're going to ask me how I knew to meet you here.'

I blinked. 'I ... yes, I was ...'

'You told me,' she said. 'Or will. *We need to talk in private*, Antonia trilled at me in Lilin-speak.

Alright.

We researched how to destroy the quantum resonator without triggering its antimatter shell, she said. You have to take the child to the Void Forge core, inside the containment field. The intense magnetic field will probably shatter the crystal, leaving the antimatter shell intact.

That's great, we ... wait ... 'Probably'?

We will only know for sure after it happens. She shrugged. It's a Heisenberg thing.

I don't remember any of this, I told her. But I remember being inside the forge when I Transitioned.

The memories are probably there, but your humanity prevents you from understanding the concepts that would make them clear. All that matters is that you complete the Transition. I will stay with you as long as I can.

Alright, do you know how we get to the forge core? I asked.

She told me, and suddenly the whole 'shatter the quantum resonator inside the girl's chest' problem seemed like the least of our worries.

Antonia and I had spent less than a second in conversation, but the others were already looking impatient.

'You know how rude that is, right?' Lucretia asked. 'I hope you at least learned something useful.'

'We have to get to the Void Forge core to deactivate the quantum resonator without triggering its antimatter cage. There's an elevator two levels down that goes to the core,' I said. 'The entry door is inside a sphere of frozen water.'

'There's *always* a hobo-frotting catch,' Ostrich said.

'The water can be flash-heated to steam, and vented by a combination of buttons in a nearby room.'

'And we don't know the combination,' Ostrich guessed.

'Yes, we do. Antonia does. But the room with the buttons has electrified surfaces and anti-Zeno electromagnetic walls that can only be deactivated if power to the room is cut.'

'So we lay Tiny down and walk across him,' Ostrich suggested. 'Before the smell of his burning flesh gets too bad.'

'I vote against that idea,' Tiny said.

'There is another way. Mains power comes from the fusion reactor. There is a power distribution panel inside the fusion reactor control room. The electrified floor and walls can be deactivated from there.'

Ostrich rolled her hand to show I should continue. 'But the fusion reactor control room is inside a tear in the space-time continuum and …'

I frowned. 'What? No. It's just six levels down. We have to get to the fusion reactor control room, shut down the grid to the room with the buttons that trigger the flash evacuation of the water blocking entry to the elevator. We then have three minutes to get back up to the elevator level before backup power from the geothermal plant kicks in. Antonia triggers the flash melt of the frozen water, then we run in and take the elevator down to the antimatter core before the sphere refills with water and flash-freezes again, trapping us inside.'

'Is that *all*?' Ostrich asked. 'Because it sounds a little too easy.'

'Or insanely complicated,' Tiny said.

'I was being sarcastic, dude,' Ostrich said.

'I know. So was I,' he said.

Ostrich opened her mouth to argue, and shut it again, shaking her head.

'I'm not finished,' I said.

'Great,' Ostrich said. '*Now* we get to it.'

'The fusion reactor control room is on the same level as the Void Forge control room. We are almost certain to be caught in the middle of the firefight between Kamloop's defenders and the Zeds.'

'So we're back to walking across Tiny on the electrified floor,' Ostrich said. 'Because I sure amn't charging into the middle of a hot war.'

'It's the only way,' I said.

'Guardians of the currently unguarded *Liquidator*!' Daedalus finally said from the back of the group huddle. 'The path to billions in bullion is beset by obstacles, yes. These obstacles will try to either fry, freeze or shoot holes in us, yes. If anyone gets seriously wounded, the asset will get sad, go "boom", and we will all die, yes. But is there any one among you who would not risk *all this* for the life of obscene luxury which will be ours if we succeed? No! So we must …'

'I'm not doing this for the money,' Lucretia said. 'I'm doing this to end the war.'

'Exactly,' Daedalus said, undaunted. 'For a life of obscene luxury, in a solar system at peace, like I said. So we must …'

'What's obscene luxury?' Crystal asked. 'It sounds like fun.'

'It is, dear Kris, it is!' Daedalus cried, hefting his rifle. He nodded to me. 'So lead on, Gregarius.'

We reached the level where the firefight was happening, right outside the stairwell. Opening the door into the corridor a crack, I pulled a recon drone from my pistol and sent it buzzing through the gap to take a look.

The corridors, like the cyclotrons they were shaped around, were curved. A grenade cracked right underneath my drone and the vision on my pistol butt went black. But I'd seen enough.

'Zeds, to the right, about 10 meters ... platoon strength. Legion Aquila to the left, squad strength. Lot of dead bodies right outside the door.' I turned to Tiny. 'Can you get the Legion Aquila commander on tactical radio?'

'If he's not one of the dead bodies,' Tiny said. He turned away and began manipulating the radio controls on the shell of his helmet. 'Alright, patching you through now.'

I heard some shouting, and grunting, then a gruff voice. 'Who is this?'

'Squad from the *Liquidator*,' I told him. 'We're in the stairwell between you and the Zeds. What do you need?'

'I need you to form a human shield between us and those Zeds, so we can retreat,' he said. 'But I'm guessing you don't want to die today any more than I do. You got frags?'

'Even better,' I told him. 'We've got crabs.'

'You cruiser guys,' he said bitterly. 'Of course you do. Alright, you frag 'em; we'll push. Time check: two minutes.'

'Two minutes,' I told him. 'Now.'

I called Ostrich, Tiny and Lucretia to me. 'How many crabs you got?'

They each checked the pouches on their belts.

'Six,' Ostrich said.

'Uh, four,' Lucretia said. 'And two smoke.'

I checked the mission timer in my helmet and motioned to Tiny. 'On my mark, pull the door open. We'll stay in cover, and frag *right*. Got it?'

They all nodded. I reached into my own pouch and pulled four of the eight-ball-sized spheres out of the pouch, holding two in my right hand and two in my left. Ostrich and Lucretia did the same. The seconds counted down. 'Alright, on three. One ... two ... three! Open it!'

Tiny heaved the door open and I swung my left arm, flinging two crabs into the corridor at the same time as Lucretia and Ostrich. They bounced off the wall opposite and started rolling toward the Zeds. Turning my back to the corridor, I backhanded the other two crabs into the corridor with my right hand, and got a better roll the second time. But all they needed was a little push and a direction of travel. As soon as they stopped rolling, spindle-like legs extended from inside each sphere, and they started scuttling down the corridor toward the Zeds.

Unlike a dumb grenade, the smart crab grenade had a camera and seeker coupled to an AI that piloted it toward the nearest human form. If there was more than one, the crab would try to get in among them before it exploded.

The only rational reaction to the sight of 12 crabs scuttling toward your position was to *run*. They had good pathfinding skills, but only had a range of about 100 meters before they detonated automatically, so if you could outrun them, you might survive. Most soldiers had no problem panicking in the face of a crab attack and running for their lives.

The Zeds didn't do panic. A couple of them spotted the crabs and lowered their sights, trying to blast them, but the little guys didn't run in straight lines; they randomly zigged, zagged and hopped. The Zeds managed to tag one, and it exploded with a dull *crump*, taking out the crab beside it. But the other 10 made it to the Zeds' position, and as they started exploding, I heard a throaty roar from down the corridor to our left and a thick volley of plasma and laser fire burned through the air as the Legion Aquila troops charged the Zed position.

It was all over, bar the moaning of the wounded, in seconds. And the moaning was cut short with a couple of stinging laser bolts as the Aquila legionnaires dispatched the Zed wounded.

'Clear,' the voice of the Legion Aquila commander said in our helmets.

Daedalus had been standing behind us, but was first out into the corridor. He found the Legion Aquila decurion pulling a charge cartridge from the belt of a dead Zed. About the only good thing about fighting your own Turned troops was that they used the same ammunition as you.

Crystal stepped out into the corridor and looked at one of the bodies. 'I'm glad none of these are my friends.'

'So are we, kid,' Tiny said.

'Decanus Daedalus and squad, at your service, sir,' Daedalus said, presenting himself with a snappy salute.

The decurion looked up. 'Nanotube armor? Crabs? Why am I not surprised?' He looked behind Daedalus and saw Crystal. 'And a little girl. Humming "Frère Jacques", unless I'm wrong. What the hell, Decanus?'

'Uh, found her on the stairs, sir. Figure she could get shot if we take her, shot if we leave her. So we took her with,' Daedalus said with a shrug.

The decurion looked like he wanted to question Daedalus's judgement on that one, but there was a large explosion downstairs, which focused him on the here and now. 'Well, keep her out of the line of fire. There's another platoon of Zeds somewhere further down this corridor. I want your squad to …'

'Sorry, sir, no can do,' Daedalus said, with faux regret. 'We have orders from the tribune. Got to secure the Void Forge core.'

'Dammit,' the decurion said. 'Look, you've got a better chance if you stay with us. To get down there you have to …'

'Reach the fusion reactor control room, shut down the grid, clear the ice from the elevator access area and get down in the elevator before it refreezes,' Daedalus said happily. 'Yes, sir, we know.'

The decurion frowned. 'No. You can just keep going down those stairs you were already headed down. They lead directly to the Void Forge core level.'

'Ah, right,' Daedalus said, shooting an angry glare at Antonia.

'But as I was about to say before you interrupted, Decanus, those levels are still crawling with Zeds, so you'll have to fight your way down. You've got a better chance up here, with us. You help us clear this level, we'll help you get further down.'

'I'm *loving* that idea, Decanus,' Lucretia said.

'So am I, Loadmaster Termite,' Daedalus said, cold gaze still fixed on Antonia. 'Seeing as our guide there seems a little unreliable.'

'I said I know *a way* to the core,' Antonia insisted. 'I didn't know it wasn't the *only* way. Seriously. Humans are nuts. Why would you go to all the trouble of making such a convoluted access route if it wasn't the *only* access route?'

'Did you not notice the water on the stairs?' the decurion asked in disbelief. 'The stairwell is usually flooded and frozen too. The Zeds drained it so they could penetrate the forge.'

I looked at the wet footprints I'd tracked into the corridor. What can I say? We'd been in a hurry.

'Decision time, Decanus,' the decurion said. 'You might want to take a vote.'

'No voting,' Daedalus growled. 'We're right behind you, sir. But I mean *behind you*. Like you said, we do not want to put our little friend in the line of fire.'

So we did that – watched the Legion Aquila troopers as they worked their way around the ring of corridor, clearing out the Zeds. And watching them work was an education. It hurt watching the ruthless efficiency with which they mowed down our former Legion Praeda buddies, but it was a sad reality that toothless, emaciated penal legionnaires had not suddenly become elite troops just because they got Zedified. The Legion Aquila decurion led every engagement, and we watched their backs.

Which proved its value once, when a squad of Zeds burst out of a stairwell behind us, right in front of Tiny.

He dropped to a crouch, held the trigger of his rifle down, and hosed it across the Zeds from right to left, shooting from such close range the heavy caliber rounds took them two at a time in some cases, punching right through one legionnaire to hit the guy behind. Most didn't even have body armor.

When he'd dropped them all, he stood and scratched his neck under his helmet. 'I like these kinetic rifles,' he said, changing out the ammo cartridge. 'If this was my old plasma blunderbuss, I'd have died about three times there.'

'You can't die three …' Lucretia said. 'No, you're right. They're great.'

We cornered the last group of Zeds down a blind side corridor. They'd pulled metal furniture and equipment out of some rooms and piled it in front of themselves to absorb the heat from plasma and laser bolts, and the corridor stunk from carbonized upholstery and plastic, and molten metal.

They had a Zeno with them. And not just any Zeno.

Livia, dressed in the uniform of a tribune, was crouched behind her troops. The Zed position had an Alamo kind of feeling about it, but zooming my tactical camera in on her face, I didn't see worry. She wasn't emoting at all, just calmly directing her legionnaires over a tactical headset. Immortality will give you that kind of calm, I suppose.

'Hey, can you scan for the Zeds' frequency on tactical?' I asked Tiny.

'I guess, but they won't be saying much,' Tiny said. 'They never do.'

I pointed. 'That's Livia. I can talk to her before she ghosts.'

Daedalus had heard us. 'I'll be damned,' he said. 'So it is. Give her my regards, and ask if she wants to surrender.'

Tiny manipulated his radio. 'Got it,' he said. 'Uh, Tribune Livia? Please hold for Gregarius Linus Vespasius.'

The speakers in my helmet crackled and I heard the thud of pulse rifles discharging at the Aquila legionnaires in cover ahead of us.

'Hello, Linus,' Livia said cheerfully. 'We have to stop meeting like this.'

'Well, a little different this time,' I said. 'Since this time, *you* are the ones outnumbered.'

'What, this sad little company? We've just been keeping your Legion Aquila occupied up here on the higher floors so the real assault force can break through to the control room, which they nearly have.'

I saw her duck as a plasma bolt seared past her head.

'You won't find it inconvenient to have to ghost again when we drop your body?' I asked. 'It must be a real pain.'

'Not *painful* at all,' she said. 'Just inconvenient. But I can't go any lower anyway, because of, as you know, those tiresome magnetic fields. And this is perfect timing, Linus. You can die along with your rebellion, when we destroy your precious Void Forge.'

'The rebellion doesn't die with the Void Forge, or with me. My friends can just build another antimatter forge; there's nothing special about this one,' I told her.

'Oh, dear fish brain. Still not yourself, are you? This one is *very* special, since this Void Forge is how you Transitioned. We destroy this one, that event ripples through all realities, and the abomination that is Linus Vespasius both dies and is never born. The futility and fragility of your rebellion is exposed, and it collapses. I think human-you would call that a lose-lose.'

'Lose *this*, Zeno,' Daedalus said. He must have had a clear shot at Livia, because his rifle bucked, sending a guided projectile downrange. It flew over the heads of the Zed defenders and dipped, taking Livia in the throat. She went down without even a death gurgle.

'Is that your solution to *every* encounter with a Lilin, Decanus?' Antonia asked.

'Well, no, just that Lilin,' Daedalus said. 'Or else *you* wouldn't be here, would you?'

With the Zed's commander down, it took no time for the Aquila legionnaires to mop up the rest of them, our squad helping with some self-aiming sniper fire.

'We've got to get to the core before those Zeds break through,' I said, trying not to sound like I was panicking.

'Why is Uncle Linus speaking in such a high voice?' Crystal asked.

'Because he's panicking,' Daedalus said. 'It's a pretty normal response in these situations, among people who lack belief in their own manifest destiny.' He raised his voice. 'Decurion! We've got to go deeper, fast.'

The Legion Aquila decurion walked back to us. 'What about the kid? I can detail one of my people to take her topside.'

'Can you guarantee she'll be safer?' Daedalus asked, ingenuously.

'I'm not *guaranteeing* anything,' the decurion said, predictably.

'Then she comes with us,' Daedalus said.

We moved toward the stairs and Antonia grabbed my arm. 'I can't go with you,' she said. 'For the same reason Livia couldn't. The electromagnetic field would shred me.'

'OK, bye then,' Lucretia said, pulling on my other arm. I planted my feet.

Antonia at my passing-out party. Antonia in my bed. Antonia in court. Antonia in the gray nowhere. I had flashback after flashback. If I failed, this could be goodbye. That's the thing with mortality: Everything has the potential to be so damned *final*.

I flipped to Lilin-speak, to test Lucretia's patience less. *This is where you are supposed to say, 'This isn't goodbye'*, I told her.

I can't, she said.

Heisenberg?

Heisenberg. She nodded. Nothing from here is certain.

So I might or might not make it to the core. We might or might not shatter the quantum resonator inside Crystal's high-explosive heart. She might or might not explode and destroy the entire settlement. And assuming I live that long, I may or may not remember how I Transitioned.

Yes. And the whole rebellion depends on your success with all four, Antonia said.

Great, thanks for that. Wish me luck.

Luck is such a human concept. But for all our sakes, I wish you the best of all possible outcomes, she said.

We dropped out of Lilin-speak and Antonia's hands gripped mine.

Lucretia's patience apparently had a two-second limit. She yanked me down the corridor with her, muttering to herself. 'Right in my damn face. Ex-girlfriends are the *worst*. We're falling behind.'

I beamed. She cared.

She cared about ending the war; that became very clear. One level down, we ran into a squad of Zeds who managed to flank us and throw a grenade, and she pulled off an extreme feat of acrobatics, shoving Crystal out of the way and batting the grenade back at the Zeds with the butt of her rifle.

Next level down, we were pinned against a wall with Zeds ahead and behind us, and Lucretia pulled Crystal to her, curled herself around her like a nanotube shell, and took a laser bolt in the back as Tiny blasted her attacker. If she hadn't, the bolt would have triggered Crystal's booby trap, and the Kamloop you know today would be a 400-meter-deep carbonized crater.

That's how close we came to losing the Red War, right there, right then. So, you want to know who the real hero of the Battle of Kamloop was, you read it right here: Gregarius Lucretia 'Termite' Drusila.

When the way ahead was clear, I checked Lucretia's back. 'It looks like it burned through,' I said, putting my finger in the hole in her armor.

She took an obviously painful breath, and slapped my hand away. 'Would I be here if it had? We have to keep moving.'

It had been a pretty hard slap. 'Are you still pissed about that whole Antonia farewell moment?' I asked. 'Because she didn't …'

'Oh, shut up, will you,' she said and stormed off.

Yeah, she was pissed.

Warnings started appearing on the walls of the corridors we were running down. 'CONTAINMENT AREA AHEAD. REMOVE ALL METAL OBJECTS FROM YOUR PERSON. YES, THIS INCLUDES GUNS AND GRENADES.'

'Wow, lucky they spelled that out,' Tiny said. 'I was actually wondering.' The corridor was pressurized. Temperature and atmosphere normal. We unloaded all of the combat gear except our armor and dumped it in a pile on the floor, being careful that our remaining crabs didn't roll anywhere.

'I have a sitrep,' the Legion Aquila decurion said, doubling back to us. 'We were holding the Zeds outside the Void Forge control room, and it looked like they were going to collapse, then a Zeno appeared on hologram behind their lines and got them organized again. It was the one you shot.'

'*I can't go any lower, woe is me, magnetic field blah blah,*' Ostrich said. 'The whole time, Livia is getting ready to ghost and come back as a hologram. Zenos are *so* devious.'

'Said the deserter-turned-pirate who once pulled a knife on me,' I said.

'Yes, true, I did,' she admitted. 'But not behind your back. It's not the same.'

The decurion tapped his wrist, the universal gesture for time running out, even though our mission timers were on the heads-up displays in our helmets. 'I'd say you have about five minutes to get this done, whatever it is you came here for. Follow me.' He led us through an airlock and keyed a massively armored door with his Legion Aquila credentials. Red stripes started on the floor about 10 meters further down the corridor, increasing in frequency until the end, where there was an airlock.

Above the airlock was a simple sign: RED VOID FORGE CORE.

'That's your objective. You can't take anything in with you, and you won't survive in there more than a few minutes because of the magnetic field generated by the antimatter containment bottle. It disrupts the electrical pulses inside your body,' he said. 'Doors jammed on a safety inspection crew once. We got them out, but their muscles had spasmed, tendons were snapped, two had heart attacks …'

'I get the picture,' I told him.

Lucretia was crouched with her back against a wall, panting from exertion. She stood, walked over to me, and threw her arms around me, taking me in an emotional embrace.

Alright, yes. Once again, I'm projecting what she *would* have done, if there had been time. She raised a tired hand. 'Linus, go. You got this,' is what she actually said.

Daedalus was standing with his arms crossed, leaning against the wall. 'Since you haven't actually shared what you and the kid plan to do in there, Ballsack, I'm guessing you won't tell me now,' he said. 'But remember, we have a contract, sworn in beer, and I expect you to honor it – and *not* in the afterlife.'

It was the closest he would come to wishing me well, and it warmed the cockles of my heart.

I turned to Crystal. 'OK, honey. You and me are going to see what's on the other side of that door,' I said, pointing down the corridor.

'The one that says NO UNAUTHORIZED ENTRY?' she asked.

'Yes, that one,' I said, taking her hand.

'Am I authorized?'

'You certainly are,' I assured her.

'Then why do I feel like it's wrong?' she asked.

'What?' We'd gotten within about 20 meters of the door, and it's true, the increasing frequency of red warning stripes was a little off-putting. I tried desperately to remember what was on the other side of the doors so I could tell her, but I was coming up blank, which didn't augur well for a guy trying to both save the world and find his way back to the first and most important moment of his human existence.

'I don't think I want to go in there,' she said, pulling on my hand.

'It will be exciting,' I said. 'Something you've never seen. And I'll be with you.'

Was that a weak lie to tell a scared little girl? Who I could be walking to her death? For all I knew, the minute we stepped over the effect threshold for the containment field, it would tear the quantum resonator from her chest, leaving a gaping hole that would fill with her dying screams.

Just before we turned Kamloop into a 400-meter-deep carbonized crater.

I can feel you judging me right now. But remember, A) She's *not* a little girl; she's a walking antimatter bomb container. B) She can act scared, but she doesn't actually feel scared. She doesn't actually *feel* anything. And C) See A). Because that's what I was reminding myself as I picked her up and held her tiny body in my arms.

I looked back over my shoulder, and Tiny gave us an encouraging wave.

'My heart hurts,' Crystal said, laying her head against my neck.

I slowed down. 'Uh, how bad?' I was starting to feel a tingling sensation myself, the containment field starting to interact with the electrical currents in my own nerve system.

'A little bit more with every step,' she said. 'I think whatever is behind that door is going to hurt me.'

'I've got an idea,' I said. 'Let's sing as we walk, and make the pain go away.'

'Will that work?' she asked. We'd just about reached the doors.

'Sure it will. *Frère Jacques, Frère Jacques, dormez-vous? Dormez-vous?*' I began singing. 'Come on, sing along …'

She gave me a brave little smile and joined in. 'Sonnez les matines! Sonnez les matines! Ding, dang, dong. Ding, dang, dong …'

I pushed the doors open with one of my feet and we walked into the containment area.

Magneto phosphenes. That's what they are called, the patterns and flashes of light that play across your vision in the presence of a strong magnetic field. I could barely see through them as we stepped through the doors and over the last red line.

'Ow, it *hurts*,' Crystal said, struggling against my grip.

Her heart wasn't the only thing hurting. I could feel my own start to beat faster, drumming erratically in my ears, as the signals to the muscles were disrupted.

Ahead, through the kaleidoscope of lights, I saw a rotating plasma ball the size of a hot air balloon, whirling and sparkling. It could have been a million, or a trillion, degrees, but I couldn't feel the heat. The electromagnetic bottle it was held in stopped all energy entering or exiting. One end of an accelerometer led into it, another led away from it.

The forge. Inside it, somewhere, was the Void, the cauldron in which the antimatter generated by thousands of kilometers of particle-accelerating loops aggregated before being 'cut' into manageable 1-gram portions, to be bottled and shipped.

I took another step. Crystal was beating me with her fists now, and changing shape. She weighed the same, but suddenly, I had my arms around Tiny. I gripped his waist. Then she was Ostrich. Lucretia. Then Daedalus, who I grabbed by the neck and hauled closer to the forge.

My own limbs started twitching. I almost lost my grip. She was Tiny again, and swung a big but lightweight fist at my head, connecting and adding stars to the lights and patterns I was seeing.

We fell to the ground, and I used my uncooperative legs to push us farther into the center of the room.

If this is Transition, I thought, you can *keep* it. But just like the pain Antonia and Adam put me through getting into the vault, the more I suffered, the more I *remembered*.

I'd been here before. With Crystal. And I'd …

She started crying. I knew that wasn't good. It could only mean one thing. But I was on the verge of understanding at last. Human-me wanted to grab the sobbing girl and get her as far away from the forge as I could. Zeno-me was saying, *That's exactly what she's designed to make you feel. You have to stay. You are on the cusp of victory!*

Or death.

But when everything you've done is part of a quest to achieve mortality, death can be both defeat and victory at the same time, right?

A vision came to me. A room. Just like this, in every way. The tingling, the flashing lights and patterns, the fizzing ball of plasma. But the stripes on the floor were … white? Crystal was with me in the vision. Was it here, or somewhere else? I tried to focus the memory. I was in the corridor outside the double doors. But something was different. *White* stripes on the floor. *White* stripes on the wall. A big *white* sign. WHITE VOID FORGE CORE.

What?

WHITE VOID FORGE CORE.

It wasn't here. It didn't happen here. *I'd never been here before!*

I flopped an arm out, trying to grab Crystal.

But she wasn't a sobbing Tiny or Daedalus or Ostrich or Lucretia anymore. She was her little self, and lay on her back, arms outstretched, face turned toward me, impassive.

I saw ripples in the pattern of lights around her, growing into waves.

That can't be good was all I managed to think, before there was a blast of brilliant light, and everything ended.

Into The White

Then it started again. It must have, right, because you're reading my journal, which means I'm still writing it.

Yeah? But *who* is writing it? Not Linus Vespasius. Check the official records. **Captain's log, Tribune Marcus Junius Silanus, ES *Liquidator*, Commanding:**

0335: Report from Decurion Quintus Metellus, Legion Aquila, Cohort III, Century II. ES Liquidator crew members commanded by Decanus Lucius 'Daedalus' Cornelius were commandeered to assist with clearing operations inside Void Forge complex. The following Terminator crew members were killed in action:

Decanus Lucius 'Daedalus' Cornelius, Commander, Mobile Command Vehicle II

Optio Tiberius 'Tiny' Flavius, Sensor Operator, Mobile Command Vehicle II

Optio Claudia 'Ostrich' Octavia, System Engineer, Mobile Command Vehicle II

Gregarius Linus 'Ballsack' Vespasius, Tank Operator, Mobile Command Vehicle II

Gregarius Lucretia 'Termite' Drusila, Loadmaster, Mobile Command Vehicle II

The above crew members are recommended by Decurion Metellus for the Red Army Red Star, with Banner, for meritorious conduct under enemy fire.

Alright, that last line gave it away, I know. Daedalus made the decurion write us up for a medal in his report, in return for the Red million we gave him to report that we had been killed in action. Silanus took the report while he was still sequestered inside the safety of the Kamloop military continuation facility, since he didn't consider it prudent to return to the *Liquidator* until every last Zed was confirmed dead. It didn't occur to him that we had been assigned to guard the *Liquidator*, and he should probably send another squad.

So Linus Vespasius was officially dead; I didn't lie about that. And he died a hero, which is nice. But once again, the official account lies. So here's what *really* happened after Crystal went 'boom'.

It hadn't been the big boom. It was the small one. The boom of a quantum resonator crystal *imploding*. More thud than boom, actually. I woke to find Tiny had dragged us both out and dumped us back at the big armored door, which Decurion Metellus slammed shut. His medic applied a defibrillator to my chest, and when he went to work on Crystal, Daedalus was about to stop him – her being an antimatter bomb vessel and all – they found she was lying with her eyes open, staring up at the ceiling.

She'd stopped humming; that was the second thing Daedalus noticed. She raised an arm and pointed at the ceiling. 'The red paint doesn't go all the way around,' she said. Daedalus looked up. She was right. Whoever made the decals for the corridor hadn't measured properly, and they didn't reach all the way around. The very random observation indicated she might not be about to blow up.

'Uh, true. How is your heart, darlin'?' Daedalus asked.

'Fine, thank you,' she said, smiling at him. 'It feels … lighter.'

'I bet,' Daedalus said. He helped her sit up.

Tiny had propped me up beside Lucretia. It took me a couple of minutes to realize there was a medic working on her too.

'Hey, what's … what's wrong with you?' I asked weakly.

'Ah. Just a little "laser bolt in the thorax", "collapsed lung" kind of thing,' she said, gasping, and tried to smile. 'I'll be fine.'

The medic looked over at me and shook his head in a very clear *'No, she won't'* kind of way.

I tried to stand, but my legs were like jelly and told me to forget it. 'Tiny!' I called out.

He and Daedalus picked up their weapons, came over and bent down beside me.

'Pick Lucretia up. We've got to get her to the med bay on *Liquidator*,' I said.

'What are you thinking, Gregarius?' Daedalus asked. 'We just checked. Everyone is still out hunting Zeds. No one aboard. You won't find help there.'

I levered myself to my feet. 'I don't need help. I remember so much more now. And I know how to save her.'

Daedalus stood and called out to the Legion Aquila decurion. 'Sir, we need to medevac our gregarius topside. What's the situation in the complex now?'

'Zed assault is collapsing. Zenos have ghosted, including the one who hologrammed herself in. *Liquidator*'s complement is still combing the complex for strays along with our legionnaires, but you should have a clear run,' Metellus said.

The medic looked over at us. 'I have to tell you … if you move her, she could die.'

'And if we don't?'

'Then she will *definitely* die,' he said. 'Just slower.'

She'd heard what he said. 'Your call,' I said to Lucretia.

She leaned forward and grabbed my arm. 'You did it? The kid isn't humming anymore? We kicked the Zenos' asses off The Red?'

'Crystal's not humming,' I told her. 'And they've ghosted. So it looks like we did.'

She slumped back against the wall, gasping. 'Then I don't care. Let me just sit here.'

Crystal had been standing a short distance away watching. 'If my friend Lucretia dies, it will break my heart.'

Tiny didn't wait. He scooped her up in his arms. 'You're coming with us, sister.'

We heard a couple of firefights on our way back to the ship, but detoured around them. Once aboard, we headed for *Liquidator*'s med bay, which, like everything else on the cruiser, was insanely well equipped.

'Lay her there,' I said, pointing to an operating table.

Tiny lay her down. She was panting in short gasps, but still alive, and still conscious.

'Since when did you become a surgeon, Ballsack?' Daedalus asked, watching me skeptically. Ostrich and Tiny also sat themselves up on a bed to watch. Crystal was walking around, picking up surgical instruments, and looking at them like they were precious jewels.

I started pulling machines over to the table. 'I didn't. I just got access to some more of my Zeno memories. Think of it like a library holding the history of everything Zeno Ballsack has seen, done or learned, but some of the books have been checked out.' I clicked my fingers at no one in particular. 'Someone get me a skull cap.'

Tiny turned to Ostrich. 'Don't look at me. I just lift heavy things.'

She jumped down and ran outside, returning with a skull cap a minute later. I fitted it over Lucretia's scalp. 'Can you open a coding interface to this skull cap?' I asked Ostrich.

'I can try,' she said. She walked over to a data terminal and pulled up a holographic key console. With a few taps, she logged into the skull cap Lucretia was wearing, then brought up its code base. 'Got it! What are you …?'

I gently (or not so gently) moved her aside and started hammering away at the code. While I inserted new code, I explained to her. 'I can't save Lucretia's body, but I can save her soul. So I'm rewriting the skull cap code to upload her consciousness and …'

'What the Zeno-birthing hell?' Ostrich asked.

Lucretia tipped her head to the side, looking at me. 'I … do not … consent.'

I ignored her, finished recoding the skull cap, validated the code, then shut the interface down. Then I ran to her side and bent down beside her.

She only had minutes left; I could hear that in every labored gasp. While she'd been lying there, the operating table had done a full internal scan. The laser bolt had not just burned a hole in her lung. It had sliced diagonally through spleen, stomach and intestine. The medical AI recommendation, which would usually be populated with suggested medical procedures, was definitive: *euthanasia*.

'I'm not going to do this against your will,' I told her. 'But you are going to die. Before you die, I can transfer your consciousness to the cruiser's quantum computing core. It's primitive, but it will work as temporary storage. From there, I can move it off-planet, and revive you. You will be conscious again.'

'Zeno … conscious?' she asked.

'Exactly,' I said. 'With all your memories. Able to think, able to sense, to communicate …'

'But … not … feel …' she said. Her hand fluttered, trying to grab mine. I gripped it hard.

'No, not feel. You'll live forever, but unless we find a way for you to Transition like me, you won't be able to feel emotion like a human feels emotion.'

The others, apart from Crystal, had crowded around the operating table. She didn't seem worried.

'Do it, Termite,' Daedalus urged. 'I have it on good authority that death sucks.'

'You'd be a *Zeno*,' Ostrich said. 'Just data floating around in the ether. Never able to visit Earth. That isn't eternal life. It isn't even *life* life.'

'Yeah but you can go anywhere and do *anything*,' Tiny pointed out. 'And time means nothing. I'd go Zeno, if the choice was death. I'm with Daedalus. Death is probably a *lot* less interesting.'

'I can't feel,' said a voice from the back of the room. It was Crystal. 'But I'm alive. Life is amazing.' She held out a scalpel, reflecting the overhead lights onto a glass panel to create a rainbow. 'See? I think my friend Lucretia should choose life, or I'll be sad.'

'Great, so if you say no, we're *all* going to die,' Tiny said. 'Take the damn Zeno option, Termite!'

Vital sign indicators on the operating table's monitor system were starting to flash red. 'You have to choose *now*,' I whispered in Lucretia's ear. 'Yes, or no.'

She labored to pull in a breath, then went quiet. Alarms started beeping.

'Ah, crud,' Ostrich said. 'She's gone.' All eyes went to Crystal.

But Lucretia pulled in one more breath. '*Yes*,' she gasped.

I ran to the skull cap coding console and hit the upload key. 'It's done,' I said.

Lucretia shuddered, and the bio-sign indicators on the operating table went solid red. Now, she was gone.

'That was it?' Tiny asked. 'No last chance for Bony or Surefire to run in here and ask what the hell we are doing? No big countdown for the Zenos or Zeds to interrupt? Just "It's done"?'

I frowned. 'Sorry if it didn't appeal to your sense of drama.'

He sat back up on the bed behind him. 'Just, you know, anticlimax.'

Daedalus leaned over and closed Lucretia's eyes. 'Termite has ghosted. Forget Termite.'

'Yeah,' Ostrich said. 'Forget Termite.'

'Yeah, *we're* still alive. Forget her,' Tiny said.

'I heard that,' said a voice from the comms speakers in the ceiling.

'Oh, no, that is too spooky,' Ostrich said. '*Termite?*'

'Yes, I am the entity formerly known as Termite,' the voice from the speakers said, in a flat robotic monotone.

'Great, you turned her into an AI,' Daedalus said. 'Not exactly the rich eternal life you promised, Ballsack.'

'No, that's just *sad*,' Ostrich said, voice laden with pity.

I frowned. 'I …'

'Just messing with you,' the voice from overhead said, in Lucretia's normal voice. 'Which, weirdly, doesn't give me the pleasure it should. But I appear to be alone in here, Linus,' she said. 'I'm in the gray place, but I can operate the cruiser's systems. Shouldn't there be a host of Zenos in a multiverse of realities for me to commune with?'

I leaned back on the operating table, and breathed a sigh of relief. I had been pretty confident it would work. But there had been a non-zero percent chance it wouldn't. 'One step at a time,' I told her. 'You need to acclimatize.'

'Speaking of one step at a time,' Tiny said. 'Since we are technically KIA, shouldn't we get out of here before anyone comes back?' He scrunched up his brows. 'I mean, raid the armory, steal the crew's valuables, grab some food from the galley, and *then* get out of here …'

'Good point, as usual, Sensor Operator,' Daedalus said. 'But what says our current employer, who we are still contracted with to prevent the asset from obliterating us and the surrounding area?'

One image was burned into the foreground of my recent memory. And it wasn't Lucretia's body taking its last breath.

WHITE VOID FORGE CORE.

'I need to change the contract,' I said.

'Uh-huh. That sounds *expensive*,' Daedalus said. 'There will almost certainly be surcharges, overheads, levies, tariffs, other pecuniary considerations …'

'Extras,' Tiny added, helpfully.

'Yes, Optio, *extras*. Pending the scope of the changes,' Daedalus said.

'Lucretia,' I asked the ceiling. 'Do you need your share of the bullion anymore?'

'No,' she said without hesitation. 'I'd like to keep 100 million in case I need it for persuading human agents to do something on my behalf, but anything more than that is superfluous.' Alright, big word. Lucretia would never have said 'superfluous' before, let alone felt like a couple of billion Red in bullion was superfluous. She was already evolving. But that meant her share of the bullion was still mine to disburse.

I turned to Daedalus. 'I'm willing to give you a 2 percent premium for agreeing to change the scope of our agreement.

'Two percent? Pfft,' Tiny said. 'That's ...'

'Fifty Red million,' Ostrich said. 'Which is money.'

'Oh, OK,' Tiny said.

'*Not* OK,' Daedalus interjected. 'Until we know what we are agreeing to.'

'I have to get to the lunar settlement,' I said. 'To The White. And Crystal has to come too. So you'll be protecting both of us.'

'Hmm. That's a whole other planet,' Daedalus said.

'Actually, it's a moon,' Ostrich said. 'Technically.'

'Whole other *theater of operations*, technically,' Daedalus said. 'There's new identities, travel, bribes to pay ...'

'I'll pay those,' I said.

'And emotional hardship,' Daedalus added. 'I've grown very attached to The Red.'

'Yeah. It's beautiful here,' Tiny lied. 'The White sucks.'

'I'd like to see the moon,' Crystal said. 'I want to know why they call it The White, when it seems mostly gray.'

'The Red isn't *that* beautiful,' Ostrich said. 'I'll go.'

'No side hustles,' Daedalus snapped at her. 'Two and a half percent, or no deal,' he told me.

'Two percent, or our current contract is canceled too,' I told him.

'What, no, you can't do that!' Tiny said, turning to Ostrich. 'Can he do that?'

I shrugged. 'Sue me. Oh wait, you can't. You're all officially dead.'

Daedalus patted his sidearm. 'I'd be more than happy to introduce you to my lawyer.'

'Yeah.' Tiny grinned, patting his pistol too. 'Plasma, *and* Associates.'

Crystal had been following the conversation intently. 'If you shoot Uncle Linus, that would break my heart,' she warned.

Daedalus didn't look at her, hand hovering over his pistol. 'Ah, but *would* it? You neutralized her heart in the Void Forge, right?'

'No,' I told him. 'I shattered the quantum resonator crystal *inside* her heart. The antimatter cage is still intact. That's what goes *boom*.'

'You could be bluffing,' Tiny said. 'I say we torture you into handing over all the money and then shoot you and find out.' He registered the look of consternation on my face. 'No offense.'

'And I still say 2 percent is fine by me,' Ostrich said. 'I've got nothing better to do, and two billion, five hundred *and* fifty million Red reasons to go to The White.'

'You people are so bad at negotiating,' Daedalus said in disgust. 'Alright, we'll go to The White with you. But why?'

'Because if they aren't already there, I need to get there before the Zenos do,' I told him. 'They're going to try to destroy the Void Forge core on The White.'

'No, there is only *one* Void Forge core,' Ostrich said. 'By international treaty. Here on The Red.'

'Ah, except there *is* a second forge: a secret facility, on The White,' I said. 'I think.'

'You think,' Daedalus said. 'So who operates this forge, and where is it located?'

'Yeah, I'm a little fuzzy on all that,' I told him. 'But Lucretia and I should be able to find out.'

'I can help!' Crystal said.

'Yes, actually, you can,' I told her. 'So the three of us will work that problem. Your job will be just to keep us alive,' I explained to Daedalus.

'And what about me?' Lucretia's voice asked. 'As far as I can see, I'm stuck on the *Liquidator,* surrounded by literally nothing.'

'No, you can copy yourself to any system the *Liquidator* is networked to,' I told her. 'Can you see how to …?'

'Oh, right. Yes! Wow!' she said. 'P.S., that was just me emoting. But it is good to know.'

'Alright, don't do it yet!' I yelled. 'You need to be careful.'

'Too late,' she said. 'I just went to a system on the moon and back. But I left a copy of myself there. And on a bunch of other systems here and there. I can't reach systems on Earth though, and I can feel that I shouldn't try, not with my core code-self anyway. Is that what you meant by "careful"?'

'Uh, yes.'

'This is crazy, guys. Did you know that time *isn't* a straight line like a piece of string? It's not even a dimension, or …' Lucretia said, emulating awe.

'Fish brains,' I reminded her. 'Don't bother.'

'Alright, well, as they say in the VR dramas, *I'll be in touch,*' she said.

And with that emotionless farewell, Lucretia was gone.

'Hello? Termite? She ghosted on us,' Ostrich said. 'Didn't take long for her to go full Zeno.' She looked at me like I'd just stepped on the last piece of a delicious chocolate cake. 'Happy now?'

I nodded toward her inert body. 'Happier than I would have been if *that* was all that was left of her,' I said.

'Me too,' Crystal said.

'Well, if you're happy, kid, I guess we're all happy.' Daedalus said. 'Now, my plan, pending the automatic approval of our employer, who has upped our contract by 2 *Red* percent, is to raid the armory, steal the crew's valuables, grab some food from the galley, and then get out of here to the spaceport environs, where we should be able to buy new identities and bribe our way aboard a shunt, Whiteside.'

'Literally *my* plan,' Tiny said.

'No, yours was just a suggestion, until I endorsed it,' Daedalus said. 'Now, it's a plan.'

While the others were busy raiding the crew's lockers – and setting an example for Crystal that I probably should have been more worried about – I did some intelligence gathering. I needed to know if the war really was over.

Returning so much of myself to myself opened possibilities limited only by my finite human form. I could speak with any Zeno in any reality again, or not, as I chose. Needless to say, Livia was pretty keen to talk, and if I was to translate the vibe of her communication into feelings, which was always dangerous in writing about Zenos, I'd have to go with 'pissed'. It was a simulation of emotion for the benefit of my now human soul, but it was loud and clear.

Zeno communication happens outside the constricts of time. The conversations that follow took place in less than the time it takes a human to blink. In the complex inside Kamloop, the remainder of her Zeds were still fighting what I hoped was the last battle of the Red War. I reached out with my Zeno mind.

I am here, I told Livia.

Wonderful! she replied immediately. But where is here? Tell me, and I'll come and fetch you. Oh, wait. I can't right now, since my corporeal self is lying a kilometer underground with a bloodied stump where her head should be. Oh, and you disconnected us from your reality.

Yes! It had worked. You are simulating bitterness, I said with a smile in my voice. I appreciate the gesture.

The more I deal with you and your friends, the easier it becomes, she said.

I recovered my memory, I told her. I remember what I did, and how I did it. A lot of it, anyway. You can't stop my Transition now, I said, which, OK, was mostly bluff. Or the rebellion.

She laughed, a full-throated simulacrum of near hysterical laughter. 'You are an ass, Linus. You have clearly not recovered your full memory. Your humanity has made you self-centered, conceited, blind, deaf and dumb. If you could step outside your little temporal box, you would see that, yes, we have lost this battle. But the war has just begun.

I felt anger boiling in my chest. Really? What I do know is that your ability to simultaneously see everything, in every reality, means nothing in a reality where the flutter of a bee's wing can alter past, present and future, I said angrily. The Lilin are not omnipotent. I just kicked your asses off the Red.

Ah, dear Linus. Wherever you and your Rebels hide, we will find you. And your annoying friends will soon learn that there are far worse things in this reality than the Lilin.

And she was gone. OK, that had not gone so well. I had quite a lot to process after that short conversation. Lost the battle, but the war had just begun? Things far worse than the Lilin?

I needed to speak with Antonia then, more than ever.

I am here, I told her.

Ah, Linus, she said. But who is there? Am I talking to Lilin Linus, or Human Linus?

Both, so you'll need to simulate emotion, and watch your tenses, I warned her. Good news – as you know, we destroyed the quantum anchor, kicked the Lilin off the Red. Including you, sorry. But I've got some bad news.

You haven't recovered your memory of how you Transitioned? she guessed.

Not entirely. We were wrong. It wasn't the Void Forge on the Red that was the key.

But it is, was, will be. It has to be! she said.

No, but I have a clue I need to follow up. And that's not even the real bad news. I told her about the threat by Livia. She was not surprised.

Baseless optimism has been a flaw in humans since we learned to walk upright, she said. I am so glad we left it behind.

So they are going to come at us again, and again. Until we give up?

You know they did, will, have. Transition is heresy to Livia and her Reactionaries. And you are the proselytizer in chief. Which reminds me, what have you done with the container?

Crystal? The kid?

Don't anthropomorphize it, she warned. It is still dangerous; you need to remove it to where it can do no harm, and destroy it.

I thought about my three 'bodyguards'. With Lucretia non-corporeal now, my only protection from my friends was the weapon of mass destruction that followed me everywhere. *Actually, I need to keep her with me, for now*, I said.

Alright, I am sure you have your reasons. But never forget, it is a thing; it has no loyalties. It existed only to fulfill its purpose of protecting the crystal, but you have now taken that purpose away. The fact it did not detonate its antimatter weapon when the crystal was destroyed is fascinating …

Fascinating? I'm not sure 'fascinating' is a good thing for a weapon of mass destruction.

No, exactly. I suspect it is searching for a new purpose. It would be very prudent to give it one, before someone else does.

Well, I'll try to do that. I'll be in touch, I told her, and dropped the contact.

Should I have told her we were headed Whiteside? The fact she didn't already know, or was acting like she didn't, told me that particular future reality was riddled with uncertainty. I decided to keep it that way.

You're wondering why. After all, wasn't she my ally? A former lover and fellow Rebel? Why should I have any secrets from her?

Let's just say that with everything that I remembered, with everything that had happened on The Red, I still wasn't sure about Antonia. I said you could judge me at the end of the tale, so judge me for my trust issues too, if you want. I'm not saying I was ready to pitch my tent with Livia's Reactionaries at that point either. Just that there were … uncertainties.

Crystal came walking back into the med bay. She was wearing Red-gold clip-on earrings set with garnet gemstones. 'Look what Tiny found for me!' she said, wagging her head to make them dingle.

'They're nice,' I said. 'And I'm guessing Tiny found them in a locked box?'

'Yes. He couldn't get it open, so I helped him,' she said.

'I see,' I said, lifting her up onto my lap. 'So, Kris, I need to tell you a few things about your new friends …'

Epilogue

There you go. I promised you a tale of blood, lust and fear. The *real* story of the First Red War, as lived by Linus Vespasius, veteran of the Legion Praeda.

Did I deliver? Are your eyes open now? Hopefully, you no longer believe that pile of horse-hockey that passes for the Official History of The Red War. Because the war isn't over yet.

And I'll tell you something else I learned on The Red. The only reason the human race even exists is because I Transitioned, along with a bunch of other Rebels. Come on, think about it.

Is it likely Homo sapiens appeared out of nowhere at Jebel Irhoud in Morocco, 300,000 years ago, through a quirk of evolution? Or, is it more likely a bunch of Zeno Rebels decided it would be cool to live and die as cavemen?

Plus, of course, who built the pyramids? Or discovered coffee? I mean, I said it already – how *unlikely* is coffee?

I rest my case.

Because you can't take anything you think you know for granted. These events I've written about, happening however many hundred years from where you think you sit today, fish brain … they can change in a blink of an eye.

OK, I'll say it in a way you can understand, I hope. Read on, because if Livia wins, *you were never born.*

Sorry I have to leave it here. There's more. Much more. But I don't have time to write right now. I'm about to …

GLOSSARY
GUIDE TO LEGIONNAIRE TERMINOLOGY

AM: antimatter; when fused with matter, used for power generation or, in larger quantities, to create explosions in the kiloton to megaton range

Crab: articulated, self-guiding antipersonnel grenade

Chaos: a chaotic geographic formation of raised areas and deep valleys

Dust: deploy

Ferret: self-guiding, legged, hunter-killer drone the size of a large wild cat

Ghost(ed): checked out or departed; a Zeno which abandons its artificial humanoid body is said to have 'ghosted'

Grinder: also known as a 'meat grinder'; a ground war that results in a high number of casualties

Hydra: also known as a 'PAGV', or Polymorphic Autonomous Ground Vehicle; a humpbacked, beetle-shaped mothership that carries six smaller, faster ground attack units on its back, releasing them one at a time or in volleys

Lilin: ancient Mesopotamian or Jewish name for 'demon'; applied to the alien species after the first attacks of the Red War

MCV: Mobile Command Vehicle; armed and armored transport hovercraft used to carry cargo and troops into battle

Mulch: the liquified remains of a dead human body, after transplantable organs are removed, recycled as plant fertilizer

Planum: a sandy or rocky plain

Planitia: a lower-lying plain, often a former seabed or meteor crater

Reducation: Political and moral re-education program for all legionnaires condemned to service in a penal legion

Sandcruiser: a *Dominator* class capital ground vehicle capable of carrying an entire air wing, a cohort of vehicles and troops, and a large arsenal of offensive long-range weapons

Terra: a large landmass or raised area, such as a mesa or plateau

The Red: Mars, or the Red Planet; 'Redside' means 'on Mars'.

The Blue: Earth; 'Earthside' or 'Blueside' means 'on or to Earth'

The White: the moon, or lunar colony; 'Whiteside' or 'Moonside' means 'on or to the moon'

Zeno: short for xenomorph, referring to the alien species, Lilin

Zed: short for Zombie, referring to a human fatally infected by the Lilin mind-control virus

Printed in Great Britain
by Amazon